DAKOTA
Hearts

LISA
MONDELLO

Dakota Hearts Boxed Set
Copyright © 2014 by Lisa Mondello

Contents

HER DAKOTA MAN
Dakota Hearts Series Book One

Chapter One

One look on Logan McKinnon's face told Poppy that his foul mood had very little to do with the devastating destruction all around the Badlands of South Dakota … and everything to do with her showing up in town after nearly ten years.

She didn't have to be standing next to him to feel his anger simmering just below the surface of his composure. Sitting in her rental sedan was close enough. What the hell was she thinking coming back home? *Why had she made that ridiculous promise to Kelly?*

She parked the car next to his truck and took a deep breath, mumbling under her breath as she pulled the door handle, "This may just turn out to be the stupidest thing you have ever done, girl."

Truth was, even as pissed off as Logan looked, he was still an amazing sight to see. Part of her had hoped that she was wrong. That she'd gotten over him a long time ago. That she'd take one look at him, make sure he and Keith were okay, and be able to get back in her car and drive right to the airport in Rapids City.

He turned to her, standing tall and proud. His thick dark hair blew in the March wind, fluttering around his face and making him all the more strikingly handsome.

Yep. *Stupid.*

He was taller than she'd remembered, and he'd long since lost that too-lean teenage body that had driven her crazy in her youth. He worked hard on his ranch, and it showed in how much his arms and chest had filled with muscles.

Despite the cold, he'd taken off his jacket while he worked in the yard, and Poppy had a clear view of just how much his male body had filled out in places she'd dreamed of touching.

Lord, help her. She was in trouble. And she hadn't even stepped out of the car yet. She pushed the door open and stepped outside to get it over with. It was either going to be the shortest visit on record … or the life changing experience she'd been dreaming of ever since she was a teenager.

"Hi, Logan."

Logan stared at her for a long, agonizing moment. She read the emotional tug of war playing on his face as the sudden chill from the South Dakota winds bit into her exposed skin like a whipping.

Then his expression turned hard. "What are you doing here?"

He must have heard the car drive up. But Logan's four-year-old son, Keith, remained so focused on the mud puddle he was poking a stick into to even notice anyone was around. That was good. The next few minutes would go easier for both of them if Keith weren't aware of the tension.

Logan stared at her as if he'd been startled. Or maybe too focused on making sure his son was safely playing nearby to notice her car had driven up.

Or perhaps he'd been too pre-occupied with assessing the damage the recent angry South Dakota weather had done to his property. Poppy had seen just how Mother Nature had shown no mercy to her childhood town as she drove from the airport to the ranch. She couldn't exactly blame Logan for being in a foul mood because of that.

Seeing her was just the icing on the cake.

"What the hell are you doing here, Poppy?" he repeated.

She took in a deep breath, smelled the muddy earth and decay all around her, and said, "I came to help."

He took one long look at her, from her high-heeled boots, up the length of her legs, pausing at her hips. She could almost feel his eyes as if he were staring at the flesh beneath her fresh pair of blue jeans. When his gaze finally reached her face again, she slid her sunglasses to the tip of her nose and stared right back at him in challenge. A slow smile played on her lips. She could never last as long at this as Logan before caving into laughter. But she knew Logan was in no laughing mood.

"*Poppy Ericksen.* Rudolph was practically washed off the map from all that rain we had. After all this time, what makes you think I need anything from you?"

Even though his voice was even, she could tell he was still pissed. But he'd never show it. Keith was still poking at the mud and puddles on the driveway just a little ways away, completely unaware of present company.

"What's the matter, Logan? You don't look happy to see me," Poppy said, pulling her sunglasses off her face with a wary smile.

A big splash had them both quickly looking over at Keith, who'd apparently gotten sick of the noise the stick in water was making and had graduated to a rock in favor of something more dramatic. Even though Logan had outfitted his boy in a heavy jacket and rubber boots, Keith still managed to find every puddle in the yard. What was left of it. *Yeah, this kid was a McKinnon through and through.*

Turning back to Logan, she caught a fleeting smile aimed at his son before he brought his attention back to her.

As if just noticing a car had driven into the driveway, Keith paused just before testing another puddle and called over to his father, "Who's that, Daddy?"

Poppy's face brightened with Keith's attention. "Hey, little big man! Remember me? Auntie Poppy?"

Keith gave a quick glance to Logan and then ran over to him, offering up his dirt-covered arms. Logan picked up his son without hesitation.

Logan's jaw tightened as he glared at Poppy. "What did you expect? He doesn't even know you."

Poppy's smile faltered. "Well, of course he doesn't know me to see me. But we talk on the phone all the time."

Logan's brow knit tight. "You talk ... When?"

"Just about every day when he's at your Mom's house. Don't we, Keith? I'm mommy's friend from New York."

Keith smiled with sudden recognition. "Auntie Poppy," he said sweetly.

"That's right."

Irritation replaced the angry look. Apparently Kate McKinnon never told her son that Keith had a phone friend. Why, she didn't know. But Kate McKinnon always had a reason for what she did.

"Mom didn't say anything about it."

Poppy shrugged. "It wasn't a secret. I'm sure it just slipped her mind."

"Every week?"

Their gazes locked for a brief moment, but the connection was cut short as Keith wiggled in Logan's arms, a signal he wanted to get down.

"Hey, little man," Logan said, gently putting Keith back on the ground. "I need a big job done. Can you help me out?"

"I can give you big help," Keith said, jumping up and down.

"I know you can. You're the best." Logan pointed to a small pile of twigs a few yards down the driveway. "We're going to do some burning a little later, and I'm going to need those little twigs put in that wheelbarrow over there. Can you do that big job for me?"

"I can pick up the big sticks." Keith stretched his little arms wide and lifted on his toes for added emphasis.

Logan laughed. "I know you can. But I don't need the big ones. Just the little twigs. Can you do that big job for me while I talk for a bit?"

"Okay, Daddy." Keith ran off and quickly moved into task as Logan turned his attention back to Poppy.

"He's doing good," Poppy said quietly. "Getting big."

"We're managing. You didn't answer my question."

Her lips twitched. "I didn't think I needed an invitation to come home."

"This isn't your home. Not anymore."

His words hurt her more than he knew. Or maybe he did, and that was why he said it. Regardless, Poppy refused to let her emotions show on her face and quickly added, "I, ah, didn't mean this house. I meant back to Rudolph. I know this house isn't my home anymore." She glanced quickly at Keith and shifted her weight to one leg as she crossed her arms. A move she always did when she was nervous. "After all the damage the storm did around here, I thought you could use some help."

"We had a bad few weeks, I'll give you that."

"It was all over the news."

"New York City news?"

"National news. But you forget I have connections here in South Dakota, Logan. I don't need the news to have me riveted to what's going on back home."

"You could have fooled me," he said under his breath.

"What's that?"

He didn't answer. Instead, he looked around at the devastation that had once been her home as a child. In some ways, it was unrecognizable. Trees that had been standing in the pasture for over a hundred years were toppled over, their roots pulled from the ground by the softening soil from the rising water.

Poppy took a moment to take it all in, holding back emotion.

"The house was spared," he said.

She nodded. "Thankfully."

The rest of the place was a disaster. There was debris and run off from all the water that wind and icy rain had dumped on the Badlands over the past two weeks.

Yet, as upsetting as it was to see, they'd been blessed. Poppy knew from Logan's mom that Logan and Keith had been at the house during the worst of it. They'd survived. Everything else could be replaced.

"Lot of folks close to the river lost everything."

"I heard."

Kelly and Logan had been married for nearly eight years before she'd died last year. It had been over ten years since she'd stepped foot on this ranch. Kelly had convinced Logan to buy the property when it came on the market again the year Kelly had been pregnant with Keith. "The house always had good memories," Kelly had told her. And yet standing there in front of Logan, the years between them melted away and Poppy felt as if she were still the young girl who'd dreamed of one day loving this man as passionately has she had in her teenage dreams.

They'd stood across from each other on summer nights hundreds of times. They'd been inseparable back then. Sometimes the three of them. Many times just her and Logan. Yet Kelly had been the one to love Logan the way that Poppy had dreamed. How it happened no longer mattered. Especially since Logan was glaring at Poppy as if she'd let Kelly down in the cruelest and most unforgivable way, not knowing it was actually the other way around.

She was a stupid woman! What had convinced her he'd care about the truth now?

For a fleeting second, Poppy wanted to climb back into her rental car and drive as fast as she could until she reached Rapid City. She didn't belong here. To hell with the promise she'd made to Kelly. But she'd be damned if she spent her entire life wondering if things would have been different if Logan had only learned the truth. If she left, she'd never know.

"How's this, Daddy?"

Logan's attention turned to Keith, who was quite pleased with the pile of sticks he'd made in the middle of the driveway. Walking over to him, he said. "Little buddy, that's a fine pile you just started. I'm so proud of you. But we can't have the fire in the middle of the driveway. Do you think you can move these sticks over to big pile over there?"

"Okay!" Unaffected by Logan pointing out his error, Keith quickly went on his way of picking away at the pile a stick at a time and running over to drop it in another pile off the driveway. Poppy was grateful for the slight reprieve of talking with Logan.

Glancing back at Poppy, Logan sighed. He didn't want her there. That much was evident. Her determination renewed, she lifted her chin and decided she was digging in if she had to dig a hole to do it. Logan was going to have to deal with her at some point, like it or not, so they might as well get it over with now.

As if he'd come to the same conclusion, he took a few long strides toward her. "Look, I can appreciate you wanting to come out and check on your family home and all. You lived here your whole life, so that's understandable. But as you can see, the house is still standing."

"You can appreciate? Well, that's very dignified of you to say it that way."

"In case you hadn't noticed, I'm not feeling very dignified right now. So you can just get in your car and head back to New York if you don't like it. I don't need you here."

"You say that. But I know different, Logan McKinnon. You need me now more than ever."

Logan watched Poppy's expression collapse, saw the hurt on her face that he didn't want to acknowledge he'd caused with his words. There was a time when his sole purpose in a day was to make Poppy Ericksen smile. To hear her musical laugh. Not today. But despite his anger, hurting her didn't make him feel any better.

In the distance, echoes of chainsaws and other equipment resonated from all the surrounding houses and across the fields. Now that the rain had stopped, everybody was outside trying to do their best with whatever resources they had at their disposal to try to get life back to normal.

The small town he'd grown up in wasn't a stranger to floods or other natural disasters. Harsh Dakota weather was a way of life for the people in these parts. But they'd never seen anything like the floods that had swept through his town this past week. Ice, rain and the drought from last year had made the ground prime to nearly wipe some parts of South Dakota clean off the map. There had been little warning and scarcely any time to prepare for it.

Did he need help? Sure. Every single landowner around here was sorely lacking in resources despite the fact people were traveling from out of state to help. He'd be stupid to pass up help from anyone willing to pitch in and get dirty. But Poppy wasn't talking about the flood.

"Why now? You weren't here when Kelly got sick. You didn't come back to see her when she'd spent those last months in the hospital dying. What makes you think anything you do now will make a difference?"

She looked at him directly. And damned he'd always admired the woman for that. Poppy had never been one to sink back from an argument. She'd always met it head on. And if she got caught in a wrong, she quickly owned up to it. *Damn her.* Logan didn't want to admire Poppy Ericksen for anything.

"Because Kelly asked me to."

It was like he'd just been sucker punched in the gut. *Kelly had asked her?*

He chuckled sarcastically. "Those words are pretty easy coming from your mouth with Kelly not here to dispute them."

"Say what you want about me, Logan. But when have I ever lied to you?" Poppy asked.

He was angry. He'd even go as far as saying he was disappointed in Poppy given the history the three of them had together. But a liar? No, she'd never been that.

He looked at her designer boots standing in the mud. Her blue jeans must have cost a small fortune, and the tailored coat she was wearing probably cost as much as his mortgage payment. This wasn't the Poppy he remembered,

11

the young girl who always turned his eye with the unexpected. That girl didn't need designer threads.

"What makes you think I'd welcome any help you offered?"

Before he could even process the cruelty of that statement, she said, "Because right now there isn't a person in this county who doesn't already have too much work to do on their own property who is standing here offering help. So you're hardly in a position to turn me away."

Logan couldn't argue that point. The magnitude of the cleanup work that lay ahead of him was overwhelming. When he and Keith had emerged from the house yesterday, and he saw just how bad the world outside around him was, it nearly leveled him. And he hadn't even had the chance to survey the entire property.

Her chest rose and fell on a heavy sigh, then she walked to the back of the car and opened her trunk, pulling out a large designer suitcase. She kept the trunk open.

"Unless of course, you'd prefer I stay somewhere else."

"There is no place else in this county that has space available," he said quickly. "Hotels are all full up with people who lost their homes or workers from out of town who are here for the cleanup."

"I was talking about your mother's house."

"My ... my mother?"

She chuckled, shaking her head. "Don't look so shocked. I always got along with your family just fine. I've known Kate McKinnon since I was able to walk across the floor of her restaurant. When I stopped in town at the diner earlier today, she offered to put me up if you turned me away."

"You talked to my mother about staying here?"

She laughed and looked up at the sky. "Men. Am I speaking a foreign language? I don't know what you're having such a hard time with, Logan. It's not like we haven't slept under the same roof before. Your mom thought maybe you could use some help with Keith while you cleaned up since she's going to be too busy feeding people doing cleanup to keep an eye on him."

His mom had told Logan as much earlier in the day. Keith loved spending time with his mom at the diner, but too many other people were in need right now for him to monopolize her time or any of his relations. His brothers would be coming to help when they had spare time, but in truth, Hawk was too busy at the clinic, dealing with injuries and Ethan, his twin brother, was working down at the police station coordinating search and rescue efforts. His military training was too much of an asset to those in need for Logan to expect him to rush over here. Word had it Sam was on his way home from Colorado at some point, but he wasn't sure when. And Wade ... After four years missing, the notion of his older brother showing up in Rudolph was just a wish, not a likely reality.

And Keith was his responsibility alone. Truth be known, Logan didn't want Keith anywhere but with him after hearing stories of flash flooding that swept people right out of the arms of loved ones. It had been scary enough worrying about Keith with all that water coming in around them during that long night of heavy rains and river swells. The fact that the house was still standing the next morning was enough to put his brothers' minds at ease for the time being.

And yet, here was Poppy. She'd come all the way here from New York City like she'd appeared out of a dream. *Damn her.* He didn't want to think about Poppy as a dream at all. He'd let that go years ago.

Poppy reached up and slammed the trunk closed.

"So what's it going to be? Am I moving into your old bed at your mom's house or my old room here?"

"You can't."

Poppy's shoulders sagged as she nodded slowly.

"Keith has that room now. I moved him in there after Kelly died so he'd be closer to my bedroom. You can take the room down the end of the hall. It's bigger anyway."

She picked up her bag and walked slowly toward him, a crooked smile playing on her lips, one that made him feel like smooth velvet rubbing against his skin.

"You afraid of what your mom would have said if you turned me away?" she said, quietly goading him. "Or are you afraid of people talking."

People were talking already if Poppy Ericksen rolled into town and stopped by the diner. Rudolph was a small town, and everyone knew everyone.

He rolled his eyes, then glanced down at her. She was incredibly close. And she smelled damned good. She always had, he remembered. She'd never been one to wear heavy perfume or makeup. And today wasn't any different. It was just *Poppy*. He hated that he was reminded of that. He didn't want those memories, so he pushed them back where they belonged. In the past. He was only allowing Poppy to stay for one reason.

"As you pointed out, I could use help with Keith while I do some cleanup here. If you could do that for me … it'd be good."

She smiled then, and her eyes lit up. He'd forgotten just how much they twinkled when she smiled. Something deep in his gut tightened.

"Good." She started walking away, then turned back. "I'll just bring these upstairs and get changed. Be back in a minute."

Logan took a moment to steady himself while checking on Keith's progress. The little guy had managed to transfer all the wood, one stick at a time, to a pile about ten yards away from the one he'd made in the driveway. Logan smiled at his son's tenacity. "Great job, little man!"

Keith beamed with pride. Logan heard the screen door creak and saw Poppy standing on the porch holding the door open, one foot on the threshold and the other on the porch. Her wide smile was genuine as she gazed over at Keith. The look she gave him was one of pure affection and admiration.

"Awesome job, Keith," she called out before walking inside.

He wanted to stay angry at Poppy. Deep down it was easier that way than dealing with the feelings stirring inside of him from seeing her again.

Chapter Two

A symphony played so loudly in Poppy's chest that she thought her heart would burst. She placed her hand on her chest to steady herself. All she'd done was walk into the house, and it felt as if she'd just run a marathon.

Logan hadn't turned her away. Maybe everything Kelly had said was true.

Poppy had questioned her best friend's confession on her deathbed over a year ago. Surely Kelly was delirious. She couldn't know what she was saying. But it had been important to Kelly that Poppy listen to her final words and so she did. Every one of them. She'd sat next to her best friend and held her hand, wanting to do so much more for her in the little time they had left together.

That was a year ago, and it had taken all this time for Poppy to muster up the courage to make due on the one promise she'd made to Kelly that day.

She picked up her suitcase and made her way to the stairs like she had so many times in her childhood. The house smelled the same. Poppy had always loved the smell of the air blowing through the windows on a hot summer day or a cool autumn night. Or the scent of burning wood from the wood stove in the basement. Logan had the stove burning, and she could smell smoldering wood. It was early spring, and the windows were closed tight against the Dakota cold. The house hadn't been lived in by her family in years. But there was still a hint of *something* that brought Poppy's memories back to her childhood as she climbed the narrow staircase to the second floor.

She didn't peek into the first bedroom at the top of the stairs, or her old room, which as Logan pointed out was now Keith's room. Instead, she walked straight down the hall to the front bedroom that used to be her grandmother's before she'd died. The door was open. Poppy walked inside and dropped her suitcase on the floor at the foot of the bed, then turned around to look at everything.

It all looked the same. The chenille bedspread had been changed out for a fresh country quilt, something Kelly had always loved. But the style of eyelet curtains was the same as Poppy remembered. Touching the fabric, she was instantly transformed back to her childhood.

She gazed out the bedroom window to the front yard where Logan and Keith were now building a fire surround with rocks. Logan was carrying over large stones, and Keith took small pebbles and dropped them in the ring that Logan had started.

"What the hell am I doing here?" She sighed.

Pulling herself away from the window, Poppy quickly stripped out of the clothes she'd traveled in and slipped into something more comfortable and practical for running around with a four-year- old on a muddy ranch.

She skipped down the stairs and then paused at the front door, staying inside so Logan wouldn't see her. He was exactly the man she remembered from when they were kids. He'd been a young man then. Tragedy and hard work had changed him some over the years, but he was still the same Logan. As angry as she knew he was with her, she still noticed how the light in his eyes blazed when he looked her. Oh, he'd tried to hide it. But it was there. It gave her hope.

Poppy had known all these years she'd been in New York that her childhood best friend had loved Logan McKinnon. And there was no denying Logan had loved Kelly. Probably still did. Maybe he always would. But their love had always been a quiet love, something that had built over time.

She recalled the tear-filled confession Kelly had made in the hospital. Would all their lives be different if Poppy had known the truth? If Logan had known? Would that little boy laughing out in the yard be her son instead of Kelly's? There was no way to know that now. No way to undo what had been done. And as much as her heart twisted with the words of truth that Kelly had spoken, it was still heavy with the burden of uncertainty Kelly had carried all these years because of it.

Nerves raced inside her as she reached for the doorknob. It had taken a while for Kelly's words to sink in. Poppy had spent a year revisiting that conversation in the hospital, running the gamut of emotions that came with knowing the truth. But would Logan believe her when he learned the truth? Would he hate her for even bringing it up? Would he even care?

"Oh, Kel. I'm here, just like you wanted. Now what?" Poppy mumbled as she pushed through the door.

♥ ♥ ♥

Logan turned as Poppy stepped out onto the porch. His body and mind fought an internal battle just looking at her standing there like she had the day he'd pulled up in his dad's pickup truck and found out her parents were selling the ranch and moving to New York. *Taking Poppy away from him.*

She'd been crying that day, and she'd run to him just as broken as a little bird with wings that had been bruised. Poppy wasn't crying now. Instead, she looked around at all the damage, smiling as if she didn't even see the destruction that had Logan's heart heavy with distress.

Now that she'd changed into a simple pair of jeans and boots, she looked as if she'd never left South Dakota. Her auburn hair glowed in the bright sunshine, just as it had when she was a young girl. It amazed him how 10 years just melted away like they'd never happened. But they had, and Logan fought hard to remember all that had transpired since that last day he'd seen her on the porch, just to keep himself grounded in the here and now, and not sink back into memories that he'd let go of long ago.

Guilt ate at him just a bit, recalling how he'd treated her earlier and how she'd walked into the house, shoulders sagging with defeat from his ungraciousness. His mother would have been plenty irate about his lack of manners in not offering to help her with that heavy suitcase. Never mind that he was a grown man. But it wasn't until Poppy had closed the door behind her that Logan had let out a slow sigh of relief.

What the hell was he going to do with Poppy Ericksen here? Poppy had always had a way of frazzling him. Today was no different. Logan had only just gotten to the point with Keith where their lives were moving at a steady pace again after Kelly's death. Now with Poppy here, it was a reminder of everything they'd lost, bringing unsettling heartache back to the surface.

The sight of Poppy navigating all the debris in the driveway, maneuvering around sticks, mud puddles and such proved to be more enjoyable than Logan wanted to admit. Which only got under his skin further. She did it without stumbling or even complaining once. Every step she made was one of determination.

She glanced up at him only once and then turned her eyes to the path ahead. He almost expected her to be mumbling under her breath about what a colossal jerk he'd been earlier. But Poppy wouldn't say a word or give him the satisfaction of showing he'd ticked her off.

Same old Poppy. And if he weren't so irritated by his body's immediate reaction to seeing her, he'd be admiring her for it.

Keith ran up to Logan as Poppy approached.

"This is your … Auntie Poppy. You remember talking on the phone with her when you're at Grandma's?"

Keith shyly nodded, clutching Logan's denim clad thigh.

"She's here to help us clean up the big mess around the house today. Would you like to help her?"

Poppy crouched down in front of Keith. "How are you doing, little man? That pile you started over there is pretty cool. Can I help you work on it?"

Keith nodded and smiled, obviously proud all his hard work had been noticed.

"We've got a lot of work to do so let's get to it, okay?"

Poppy glanced up at Logan with wide green eyes that were filled with moisture as she took Keith by the hand. "He's in good hands, you know."

Logan nodded without a word, then turned away toward the bigger problems he had to deal with. Somehow those were easier than looking into Poppy's eyes.

After everything Keith had been through over the past year, and then the past few weeks, Logan had been guarded about each step he took. Keith had been through enough. But his son took Poppy's hand without hesitation and skipped alongside her as they made their way to the pile of sticks he'd already collected as if Keith had known her all his young life. He paused just briefly to bend down and pick up a small stick along the way to add to the pile.

The way Keith was so open to Poppy had Logan wondering just why Poppy had been calling his mom all this time. *And why his mother never bothered to tell him that Keith had a phone friend in Poppy.* That was a conversation he'd have with her later.

A dull ache formed in the pit of his stomach as he turned away and headed in the opposite direction toward the barn in order to assess the damage. How the hell could he explain Poppy to Keith?

He didn't want her here. He couldn't exactly throw her out though. At least not tonight. The last thing he wanted was to lie in bed and think about Poppy Ericksen at his mom's while he was out here. She'd chosen to turn her back on what was important a long time ago, and they'd all lived with her decision. Surely there'd be a flight to New York leaving tomorrow some time from Rapid City. She could stay the night, and then he'd just tell her in the morning she had to be on one of them.

He kicked the ground and a chunk of mud lifted from the driveway and flew in the direction of the barn, leaving an angry hole he'd have to fill along with all the other ruts and holes in the driveway.

The sound of tires spitting up wet dirt and gravel on his driveway pulled Logan out of his thoughts. He glanced up and saw his brother Hawk's Jeep easing down the driveway. Hawk waved to Keith and Poppy as he drove by, but being too deep into their stick pile project, neither of them noticed. He then parked next to Poppy's rental car before climbing out of the Jeep and walking over to him.

"It doesn't look like a total loss," Hawk said, pointing to the barn.

"The water receded fast."

"Honestly, I'd expected worse. We can probably just replace those boards on that one side of the barn and then dry out the floor if the damage inside isn't too bad."

"It isn't. It's already drying. I'm just grateful we don't have heat right now to create mold or all that hay in the loft would have to go. The rest should be an easy fix, but an extra hand will go a long way toward getting it done faster. "

"Looks like you already have extra help," Hawk said, glancing in the direction of where Poppy and Keith were hard at work, talking up a storm to each other.

Logan stared at Poppy with a little fingernail of jealousy scraping the back of his neck that his son was having such a good time without him. *With Poppy.* He suddenly longed to know what stories they were trading back and forth that was causing all that laughter floating back to him. She'd come running back here from New York City just to check on a house that wasn't even her home anymore. A place she'd abandoned years ago along with the people in her life.

Logan dragged his gaze away, looking instead at the house that Kelly had insisted they'd find a way to buy when it came on the market. She always said the house was a home they'd both loved as kids, so when the house came up on the market eight years after Poppy's parents sold it, Kelly was adamant they had to have it. She wanted to raise a family there.

"I'm just glad the house was spared. Kelly loved this house."

"Poppy, too. I remember her crying her heart out in mom's arms down at the restaurant when her parents sold it. She moved away that year after high school."

Logan didn't respond. "All things considered we got lucky. I heard John and Beth Talbert's property is still under water."

Hawk nodded with the stark reality of the truth. "I saw what I could of it earlier today. Beth came into the clinic with the boys. I've got them staying at my house until the water recedes and they can get a trailer put on their place."

"That's kind of you," Logan said, a sense of pride at his brother's generosity reminding him he needed to be more grateful for the people in his life. It only punctuated the fact that there was really nowhere for Poppy to go but here. He could hardly turn her away, at least for tonight.

"Where else could they go? The house is too big for one," Hawk said with a shrug. "It doesn't seem right to have empty bedrooms when people are in need."

"What made you come out?" he finally asked. "I thought you were strung out at the clinic."

Lisa Mondello

"We had some doctors come in from out of town. Mom is helping with meals at the shelter in town, but she thought you might need a hand with Keith. I know the area so I thought I'd go out with Ethan to check down the river on some of the folks who haven't check in yet. Honestly, I'm afraid of what we're going to find."

Their younger brother, Ethan, a retired Navy Seal, was now in law enforcement in Rudolph.

"Uncle Keith!" Keith squealed when he finally caught a glimpse of Hawk standing with Logan. There was a special bond between Hawk and Keith that went beyond sharing the same name. No one in the family, except for little Keith and his mom, called Hawk by his given name.

"Hey, buddy!" Hawk opened his arms, and Keith ran to him, launching himself the last few feet. Hawk scooped him up into his arms and lifted him high, planting a big kiss on his cheek. "Who's that pretty girl you're with over there?" he said as Poppy walked over, smiling. "Are you gonna introduce me?"

"That's Auntie Poppy! We're making a campfire!"

Hawk placed Keith on the ground. "I can see that."

"Hi, Hawk," Poppy said, running over to him. Hawk opened his arms and Poppy slipped right into them, giving Hawk a big hug.

"It's been too long, Lady. Good to see you."

"Same here," she said.

Logan's gut tightened, and he had to look away. The sudden pang of jealously that grabbed him was like a vice

26

he couldn't ease. Hawk and Poppy had always been friendly as kids because Poppy and Kelly were always with Logan. Hawk had no reason for ill feelings toward Poppy, so it was only right he'd be happy to see her. But seeing Poppy in Hawk's arms grated on Logan more than he wanted to admit.

"Are we going to stand around hugging all day, or get some work done?" Logan said.

Hawk released Poppy, but she kept her arm draped around his shoulder.

"Keith and I have a pretty good pile going over there. When did you want to start burning?" she asked.

Her smile, which had been radiant when Hawk had accepted her so openly, only faded slightly when she finally looked at Logan.

"A little later when Keith goes down to bed. He'll be tired from all this fresh air."

"Well, okay, then I guess we'll keep gathering as much wood as we can."

Logan nodded and watched Poppy walk back over to the pile of sticks. Keith lifted his hand to Poppy, and she easily took it into hers as they walked.

"Poppy Ericksen," Hawk said with a smile.

"Yeah?"

"She looks good."

"I hadn't noticed."

Hawk laughed. "Yeah, right."

"What'd you come out here for anyway?"

"Since when do I need a reason?"

"I just thought you were busy."

"Mom said she'd take Keith tonight if you want. She's having Skylar over for dinner after they close the restaurant and thought Keith might want to play with Alex."

Logan hesitated. Keith loved playing with kids his own age, and he loved playing with Alex, a little boy in town who was about the same age as Keith. They got along so well and his mom often called them the Irish twins because they were only a few months apart and looked so much alike with their Irish freckles and rich black hair that they could easily be mistaken as brothers. His mom often said they reminded her of Sam and Wade when they were kids.

"You seeing Skylar tonight?"

"Jeez, Logan. Her divorce was only just finalized."

"That hasn't stopped you from taking her out to dinner."

"As a friend. Let's leave it at that. It's bad enough I have to listen to Mom talk about 'the lonely doctor.' I don't need it from you, too."

At the sound of laughter, Logan glanced over at Keith and Poppy.

"Keith could probably use some playtime," he finally said.

Hawk laughed. "He looks like he's having a good time with Poppy."

The look he shot Hawk was sharper than he'd intended. But it didn't faze Hawk.

"You'd probably have a good time with Poppy, too. If you let yourself," Hawk added.

"What the hell is that supposed to mean?"

"You two were once pretty tight friends. It might be nice to catch up without having to run after Keith."

"She said she's here to help with the cleanup."

Hawk chuckled softly. "Are you worried you're going to have to explain having a woman stay in your house? You've known Poppy since you were in grade school. She was Kelly's best friend. It's not like you're doing anything wrong."

Logan sighed.

"Aah," Hawk interrupted. "You're worried about wanting to do something. Hey, she's a beautiful woman. Always was."

"Back off, Hawk. You're not helping," Logan said.

His brother looked at him sympathetically. "Kelly has been gone for a long time now. You don't have to act like a married man anymore."

When Logan shot him another look, this one more lethal than the first, Hawk put up his hands as a sign of retreat.

"All I'm saying is life goes on. Just remember that."

"You don't get it, Hawk."

"Maybe not. Just think about it, 'kay?"

29

Logan fisted his hand in his pocket as he looked over at Keith and Poppy doing an Indian dance around the pile of sticks they'd created. Keith was singing a made up Indian chant as they danced.

He was having fun. And he didn't want his son to have fun with Poppy, selfish as it was for Logan to feel that way. But Keith was just a kid. He missed his mother. There was no doubt there. As time went on, Logan found it was easier to distract Keith from missing Kelly. Now that the danger of more bad weather had passed, there was no reason he couldn't have a play date with his best friend in town. It would keep Logan from having to see just how much of a good time he was having with Poppy.

"Hey, buddy!" he called out. "Want to play with Alex this afternoon?"

Keith stopped chanting and dancing. His eyes lit up. "Are we going to Alex's house?"

"No, it's just you and me, Keith," Hawk said. "Your dad is going to stay back here with Aunt Poppy."

Keith ran over, and Logan bent down and gave his son a kiss and hug. Within a few minutes, Keith was loaded into Hawk's Jeep, and they were headed to town, leaving Logan alone. Well, not alone.

"I guess it's just you and me," Poppy said.

He looked at Poppy and wanted to hold tight to the anger that had sustained him for so long. But she was smiling up at him with that same innocence she had when she was seventeen. He couldn't resist that smile then. He was having a hell of time doing it now.

He couldn't remember the last time they'd stood so close. Oh, he'd seen Poppy over the years a few times. But she'd always been dressed sharp in her city clothes, looking polished like new silver. The visit was always quick, and Poppy always had a pressing reason to run back to New York, back to her life.

Now she was standing there as if she'd never left Rudolph at all. Her boots were already full of mud, but she didn't seem to mind. Her jeans had dirt smudges where she'd wiped her fingers clean or from Keith getting too close to her with a filthy stick while they'd made their pile. But she didn't seem as though she even knew that dirt was there. It didn't jive with the Poppy he'd convinced himself she'd become. It was every bit the young woman he'd once known.

Logan paused, trying to catch his breath. Poppy had always been a beautiful woman whether she was dressed to the nines or dressed casually. She wore an old sweatshirt and torn jeans as naturally as those designer clothes she'd arrived in. And today she looked simply breathtaking. Damn her. Her auburn hair was pulled up in a high ponytail, and she had a sparkle in her green eyes, almost as a challenge that she was ready to do whatever she had to in order to help.

"How long were you planning on staying?" Logan asked.

His question seemed to take her off guard. "Ah, I'm not sure yet. We'll have to see what happens," Poppy replied. "Are you trying to kick me out the door already?"

"As if I could do that …" He quickly recovered. "You're wearing half that mud pile on your jeans."

She looked down at herself as if to confirm it. "So I am."

"There's some mud and debris clogging up the pipe that drains the runoff. It's over by …"

"I know where it is. I used to live here." She smiled, pleased with herself. "That drain has always been a problem. Remember the year the beavers decided to dam it all up, and we ended up with what looked like a lake out in that far pasture?"

He did remember. He also remembered snakes and rodents crawling and floating since they'd been flooded out of their holes. He glanced down at her boots, impressed she'd remembered to wear something so practical for the job at hand.

"Since you're in a helping mood, you'll need some gloves. I know how much you love spiders and snakes."

"Oh, you had to mention those."

She made a face of disgust that had him laughing despite not wanting to. "We may see a whole nest of them before we're done unclogging that drain pipe. As soon as it's unclogged the rest of the pasture should drain, and the ground should dry up."

"I didn't bring a pair of gloves."

"Kelly kept a pair in the kitchen under the sink. I'm sure those will fit you."

Poppy nodded. "Be right back then."

She walked away toward the house, and God help him, he turned his head to watch the gentle sway of her hips and the lightness of her step. They'd been friends. More than good friends. But there had always been something special about Poppy. Since Kelly's illness, he'd been able to forget that part of their history. Poppy turned back once, smiling at him, and that smile touched some place deep in his chest, making it hard to hang onto the reasons why he'd been so angry at Poppy in the first place. And it was harder to remember the reasons he didn't want her back in Rudolph at all.

Chapter Three

Despite the cold March weather, sweat poured down the center of Poppy's chest, soaking the skin between her breasts beneath her jacket as she hauled away more branches that had been swept onto the ranch by the flood. Both she and Logan had worked alongside each other tirelessly for hours. They'd spoken barely a word other than to give each other direction.

Just when she thought he might stop and take a break, giving them much needed time to reconnect, he pushed on with the next task as if she was no more than a hired hand. If she didn't know better, she'd think Logan was purposely pushing her to see just how far she'd go before quitting.

Or maybe he was trying to tire himself out so badly he'd fall asleep at the kitchen table and avoid dinner conversation later. Either way, Poppy's back was screaming at her to rest. But she'd be damned if she'd give Logan McKinnon the satisfaction of besting her.

"How's the kitchen stocked?" she asked when the sun started sinking low in the afternoon sky.

Logan stopped midway through tossing wood in the pile. He used the back of his hand to wipe sweat off his forehead, leaving a streak of dirt in its place. Memories invaded Poppy's mind once again, as they always did when she was with Logan. He wasn't that hot, sexy teenager she'd spent just about every waking minute with as a kid. He was a handsome grown man who worked hard and his chiseled muscles beneath his shirt showed just how much.

She'd never been able to erase the memory of what it felt like to be in Logan McKinnon's arms. She knew just how strong his arms were when they were wrapped around her. Not as a lover. She'd never had that privilege although she'd gone there many times in her adolescent dreams. But there were memories that she held dear, and she revisited when the pain of them wasn't too hard to bear.

She pulled herself from her memories, and wild childish dreams, and swallowed hard.

"I just thought you might be getting hungry."

"You cook?"

She made a face. "Not really. But I can figure out how to make a hamburger if you have some beef. I'm sure we can make a meal without your mother giving instruction. Unless your culinary skills have evolved beyond macaroni and cheese."

Logan cocked his head to one side, looking completely impish and adorable. "Keith and I actually eat over at my mom's a few times a week. She's busy at the shelter tonight. But...I can make macaroni and cheese ... and spaghetti with bottled sauce." He chuckled, showing the deep dimple that always marked his left cheek. She longed to brush her finger over the mark.

"Good. Then we won't starve," she said, laughing. "Thank God for your mother."

Logan thought a minute and shrugged. "I haven't been to the store. I don't think we have much in the cupboards. We might have animal crackers and cereal. I don't even have cheese for grilled cheeses."

"I can run to the grocery store and see if there is anything still left on the shelves that hasn't been picked over. There was a ton of people in town earlier after the delivery truck arrived so there may not be much left."

"We may do better seeing if my mother has any leftovers from the meals she's preparing down at the shelter for all the displaced folks."

"I'm game if you are."

He eyed her as if he was teasing. "It won't be up to New York City restaurant standards. You'll probably be eating off a paper plate."

Poppy let his comment slide despite feeling slighted. It would do no good to allow Logan to get under her skin more than he already had. "If your mom cooked it, I'll love it. Always have."

His lips lifted to one side in a slow smile that had her knees weakening beneath the weight of her.

He glanced back toward the house. "We can clean up now or later. Your call."

A hot bath was definitely in order to ease out the aches and tightness from all the lifting today. Her skin had scratches she couldn't see, but felt with every movement.

Her hands had calluses that were about to break open. But all the fresh air and work had made her starving.

"I have a feeling we won't be any dirtier than anyone else who's been outside all day. I've worked up an appetite. I have a feeling if I take a bath now all I'll want to do is crawl into bed and sleep."

Their eyes locked for a good long moment. She wondered what it was that she'd said to cause the flare of light in Logan's eyes.

When he said nothing, she added, "We can pick up Keith while we're at it so Hawk doesn't have to make another trip out here.

Logan nodded. "We'll take my truck."

As they drove into town, Poppy once again took in the devastation that hit Rudolph so badly over the last few weeks, glad that it was now dark and she could only see the damage under glaring lights from generators as people continued to work into the night. Riding through town a second time didn't make it any easier than it had this morning when she'd arrived. No matter how long she'd lived in New York, Rudolph had been home, and it pained her to see the people she knew and cared about suffering so badly.

She was relieved to get to the shelter at the elementary school. She was starving, but more than that, she wanted to make sure the people she knew were as okay as they could be after losing so much. Logan had taken off quickly, so Poppy milled around the open gymnasium, talking with old friends that had settled into cots with what little provision they'd managed to grab before the water got too high. She looked around and didn't see Logan and decided he must be in the cafeteria where meals were being served.

"Hey, guys. I knew I'd find you where the food was," Poppy said when she found Logan and Keith sitting at a table with his brother Ethan. Ethan … now there was one surprise. Once the hellion of the McKinnon brothers, he'd straightened himself out after the death of his best friend in a four-wheeling accident by joining the military and becoming a Navy Seal. Today he was dressed in police blues.

He smiled and stood up when he saw her coming around to his side of the table. "Now this is a surprise," she said, giving him a quick hug.

"Which part," Ethan asked. "Me being home after all this time or me wearing a badge?"

Laughing, she said, "Both. It's good to see you."

"Same here."

Ethan stood as tall as Logan and shared the same dark hair and blue eyes, but that was where the fraternal twins' resemblance ended. Logan and Ethan were the youngest of the McKinnon boys, not that it mattered much since Kate McKinnon had given birth to five strapping Irish boys in six years.

Keith giggled and pointed to her.

"Did I miss something?" she asked.

"Your face is all dirty," he said, still laughing.

Ethan bent down, took a napkin from the table and dabbed it in his cup of water. "I'm surprised my idiot brother didn't tell you about the mud streak along the side of your face."

"What?" she gasped, taking the wet napkin and scrubbing it against her skin. She looked at Logan and saw how he was fighting to keep from smiling. "Thanks a lot! I've been all around that gymnasium talking to people. Why didn't you say something?"

"You said you were hungry and would clean up later," he gave her an impish grin that made her knees turn to butter.

"And I'm supposed to be thankful for your consideration?" She threw the napkin at him, and he moved to keep it from hitting his face. It bounced off his shoulder and then landed on the table.

"Please tell me you at least saved me a plate of food."

"Mom has it warming in the kitchen," Logan said.

"I'll get it for you Auntie Poppy!"

Keith was quick to jump down from the bench in his excitement.

"We'll both get it, little man. I have to tell Grammie I'm heading out again." Ethan turned to Poppy and gave her a quick peck of a kiss on her newly cleaned cheek. "Don't be a stranger, okay?"

"I won't."

She sat in the seat next to Logan and propped her elbows on the table.

"Tired?" he asked.

"Yeah. But I'll bet your mom is a thousand times more tired than me. She had to have been cooking all day."

"She was. But she's taking the morning off. Skylar is taking care of everything at the restaurant so she'll be able to sleep in. Not that my mother ever does. But you know what I mean."

"Yeah, I do."

"Did you get to visit with everyone?"

"Some. I can't believe Dan and Sherry Boden's house lifted right off the foundation and floated down the river!"

Logan grimaced, worry and fatigue both pulling at his handsome features. "Yeah, thank God they made it out of the house and to higher ground before that happened."

"Were you home when the water came in?"

"Me and Keith were in the bedroom upstairs. I tried to keep him distracted and away from the window. I kept checking outside, but it was too hard to see in the rain and then in the dark. I'd kicked myself a thousand times that night that I didn't leave earlier and bring Keith over to Mom's for the night."

"These floods happen so fast. I mean, I don't ever remember it being as bad as it is this year. But once when I was small, I remember my parents getting real nervous about the rains and my dad saying he had the boat ready just in case the water came."

Ethan and Keith appeared at the doorway to the kitchen. Ethan was crouched over, steadying Keith's hand with a plate. It looked like he was giving him serious instruction that Keith was paying very close attention to. When he straightened up, he watched Keith walk over to the table slowly with a smile of pride.

"Dinner has arrived," Logan said, beaming with the same pride Ethan had and Poppy felt deep in her chest.

Ethan gave a quick wave when Keith made it halfway to the table and then turned toward the door, propping his police cap on his head.

"Is this for me?" Poppy said when Keith made it to the table. She took the plate, and Keith's face instantly showed relief that he hadn't spilled anything.

"It's for you, Auntie Poppy."

"Thank you so much. Oh, it looks so good."

"Grammie said you have to eat all of it because you're too skinny."

"Too skinny!" Poppy said. "My pants are going to burst if I eat all this food. Look at this plate!"

"And she said Dad can't steal any of the food from your plate, too."

"Did she," Logan said, laughing and showing that deep dimple on his cheek. "Then I guess I won't be having seconds."

It felt incredibly good to laugh with Logan after all this time. As she took a fork full of food and savored the taste of it in her mouth, she was transformed back to a time when anger wasn't part of their relationship. When lies hadn't stood between them.

♥ ♥ ♥

"Is he asleep?" Logan asked, taking a quick glance off the road to look at Keith, who was in his booster seat, sleeping with his face pressed up against Poppy's arm.

She glanced down at Keith and smiled. "Out like a light. Good luck giving him a bath."

"It'll probably rouse him enough to be awake the whole night."

"Then skip it."

"What? Skip a bath?"

"Sure. Just put him to bed in his clothes. He can always have a bath in the morning."

"Did you see how hard he played in the mud today?"

"Yeah, I noticed. I was right in the thick of it with him, remember? No one was rushing to get me to wash my dirty face. What's it going to hurt? So his sheets get a little soiled. We'll wash them in the morning, too. This way he'll sleep."

Logan shrugged. "I guess it can't hurt to wait for a bath in the morning."

"But not for me," she said with a quiet chuckle. "There is no way I can sleep with all this mud on me. And just for the record, you're none too clean yourself right now."

"Then it's settled. You can have the bathroom first while I put Keith to bed."

Logan parked the truck and then carefully unbuckled Keith from his booster seat. Keith woke up enough to wrap his arms around Logan as he carried him up the stairs to his bedroom. Poppy watched it with awe. Logan was a good father. She'd always known he would be, but this was a different Logan than the man she'd always known. And she liked it a lot.

Fifteen minutes later, Poppy stood just outside Keith's bedroom door listening to father and son chatter on about their day as she towel-dried her hair.

"Alex has a new video game," Keith said. "It's really cool. Can we get one?"

"Why not get a different one that Alex doesn't have. That way the video game will be special when you play it over his house, and your video game will be special to him when he comes to visit."

Silence. Poppy could almost picture Keith pursing his little lips, thinking about the prospect. His next words caught her off guard.

"Is Auntie Poppy going to play with me again tomorrow?"

43

"Uh … Auntie Poppy?" Logan seemed to stumble on his answer. "I … don't really know if she's going to be here tomorrow, Keith. You know, she lives far away and may have to go home."

All the joy of the being at dinner with Logan and Keith faded in that one statement. He was already ready for her to leave.

"She's funny," Keith said in a small giggle that hinted of the smile she imagined he'd have on his face. They'd had fun today, and she was glad she wasn't the only one who felt that way.

"Yes, I suppose she is," Logan said quietly.

"She laughs a lot," Keith continued. "It makes me laugh."

"Don't I make you laugh?" Logan asked.

"You never play pirates."

The silence that dragged on was probably only just a few seconds, but it still hit Poppy right in the chest. She knew Logan well, despite distance and time between them. Those four little words probably hurt Logan more than he'd ever admit. She recalled how hard it was for her dad to stop working and play with them when she was a kid. Ranching was hard work and long hours.

She was genuinely surprised when Kelly told her that they'd purchased the spread. Logan had had other dreams of wanting to travel like his brother Wade had done in the Peace Corp before he'd gone missing in a tsunami in Asia a few years ago. Perhaps losing Wade had been the catalyst for Logan deciding to settle permanently in Rudolph. There was no day off here on the ranch. Kelly had told her that plenty of times when she'd come out to visit Poppy in New York, alone that Logan worked from sun up to sun down.

Stepping into the room, she greeted father and son with a smile, hoping her presence wasn't as intrusive as it felt to her.

"Well, maybe we should ask Daddy to play pirates with us tomorrow. What do you think?" she said, standing on the other side of the bed from where Logan was sitting.

Logan offered up a weak smile, confirming exactly what she'd suspected. He probably had little extra time to play when there was so much to do.

"That'd be fun," he said, eyeing her with skepticism.

Keith's blue eyes grew large and expressive, showing enthusiasm at the prospect.

"Daddy you can be the captain and I'll capture your ship. Arg!"

Logan mimicked Keith and then said, "Why don't you get some sleep and we'll talk about it at breakfast tomorrow."

"Okay." He reached his arms up to his father for a hug and said, "Love you, Daddy."

"Love you, too, little man."

Then Keith turned to Poppy and to her surprise, he lifted his arms to her. With tired eyes and a sweet smile, he said, "Love you, Auntie Poppy."

She eased down on the bed next to Keith and wrapped him in her arms. "I love you, too, sweetie." Keith put his head down on the pillow, and Poppy reached up and pushed his silky hair away from his face. She felt more than saw Logan staring at her and decided to leave the two alone for the final nightly ritual.

As she made her way to the door, Logan said, "Goodnight."

She turned back. "I'll just be a few more minutes in the bathroom and then it's yours."

Logan nodded.

Poppy had to catch her breath as she walked those few steps toward the bathroom. She'd thought Logan was in her past. Kelly had insisted otherwise. Now Poppy wasn't sure if she'd ever stopped loving him.

The realization hit Poppy hard in the chest as moisture filled her tired eyes. She couldn't wait any longer to tell Logan the truth. But she'd have to find the right time, a time when Keith was at Kate's or on a play-date with Alex. The longer she waited to tell him, the harder it was going to be to leave if it all went bad.

Logan turned off the light next to Keith's bed and sat in the dark watching his son until he fell into a deep sleep. He knew it wouldn't take long. It had been a long day. Playing hard in the fresh air was all the drug a little boy needed to fall into deep slumber. It gave him a moment to get his bearings.

No bath. It was such a small thing. But Kelly never would have done it. Slow, steady and predictable. That was Kelly. Logan could almost hear her yelling at him about more sheets to wash and dirty feet on the floor.

Easing himself up off the bed so as not to disturb Keith, Logan brushed his hand over his tired eyes. Already things were changing, and Poppy had only been here one day. He thought about the hug his son so willingly offered Poppy. His boy missed having a mother. Try as he may, he couldn't be both. He wasn't starved for maternal love. Kate McKinnon gave her grandson love in spades, no matter how busy she was at the restaurant. But it was different, and he hadn't really seen what Keith was missing until his son gravitated so strongly to Poppy that afternoon.

It was clear that Poppy not only had a hold on him, but on his son as well.

When he closed the door to Keith's room, he was surprised to see Poppy standing in the hallway as if she'd been waiting for him.

"That didn't take long," she said.

"He'll probably sleep until …"

"Six?"

Logan chuckled. "Probably not much longer than that." He paused a moment, weighing his words while he took in the beauty of her smile and the sparkle of light in her eyes under the overhead hallway lamp. He'd pushed them from his mind a long time ago but now that she was standing in front of him, it was hard to keep those memories at bay. Or the way his body had always reacted to her. Was still reacting …

"Thank you for today," Logan said. "We got a lot further than I thought I … that I know I would have gotten alone. Especially with Keith running around."

"He's a great little boy."

Logan cleared his throat and averted his gaze for just a moment before looking at Poppy again. "You're probably heading home tomorrow?"

Her smile faltered. "I don't know. I have no definite plans."

Logan looked at her and let out a slow breath. "I don't want you to take this wrong. I really do appreciate everything you did today."

"But you don't want me here."

Direct and to the point. That had always been Poppy's way. When she'd left for New York, she'd told him directly. She didn't wait for him to find out any other way.

"It's been tough on Keith since Kelly died. Routine is very important for him, and I don't think …"

"Don't stop there. What?"

"I don't want him to be confused."

She nodded stiffly. "One night not taking a bedtime bath too much for him?"

"Kelly had everything—"

She shook her head. "You don't have to tell me about Kelly. I knew what she was like. She was as regular as the day was long. She knew from the moment she woke up in the morning exactly what she was going to do for the day, and she did it. That was just Kelly. She was happy that way."

"You sound like you had a problem with that."

"If I did, she wouldn't have been my best friend, Logan."

"That's something you seemed to have forgotten."

"No, Logan. My loyalty to Kelly was real."

"What's that supposed to mean?"

She sighed and looked away. Then turned back to him.

"Look, if it's too difficult for you to have me here, I'll leave right now."

"You don't have to do that."

"Why not? Your mother already offered me a bed. It's not like I'm going to have to sleep in my car."

"No one is sleeping in the car. Not tonight or any other night."

"Then what do you want, Logan?"

"I saw the way Keith was with you today. He misses his mother. I don't want him to get attached and then be heartbroken when you leave."

Realization showed on her face. "Are you sure it's Keith you're worried about?"

He cleared his throat. "Of course. He's always first in my mind."

"If it's too difficult for you both, then I'll leave in the morning."

He looked at her directly, fighting a war of emotions inside himself that he couldn't define.

"I don't want you to leave."

Pure emotion flared in her beautiful green eyes. "You don't?"

He stumbled on his words, not finding any that made sense to him. "You said you came here to help...so I guess...if you can care for Keith, I can get started cleaning up the barn tomorrow."

She nodded. "And then?"

"Let's not make this what it isn't, Poppy."

"And what's that?"

He didn't utter a word, but his face said it all. He believed all the lies. Well, that shouldn't surprise her. She'd believed them too. Poppy was standing right in front of Logan and yet she felt as far away at that moment as she'd been when she was in New York.

♥ ♥ ♥

He should have slept like a log, but as Logan pulled himself out of bed due to the sound of cartoons on the TV downstairs in the living room, he felt like road kill. Cartoons. Early Mornings. That was normal. *Having*

Poppy Ericksen sleeping in the bedroom down the hall, most likely naked, was not. He hated that he remembered such details about the woman.

At least he'd have a few minutes to collect himself with a cup of coffee before Poppy got up, and he had to face the day with her again.

He quickly dressed and quietly walked downstairs. From the center hallway, he peeked into the living room and saw Keith sitting in a child-size plastic chair in front of the television, watching his favorite Saturday morning cartoon. He quietly walked by the doorway to the kitchen, hoping he could catch a few minutes alone before starting their morning breakfast ritual. He stopped short as he walked into the kitchen.

Poppy stood in front of the stove with a grimace on her face reading the side of a box of pancake mix. On the counter, he saw an empty bowl, a measuring cup and a full cup of hot coffee.

Her gaze lifted to him when she noticed him standing there. "Do you know this pancake mix doesn't call for adding any eggs?"

"Good thing. We don't have any."

She chuckled. "Yeah, I guess you're right." She put the box down on the counter and picked up the cup of coffee, handing it to him. "I figured you could use this first thing. I just poured it, so it's really hot."

He looked at the coffee cup, a little taken aback that she'd set the tone of the day this way. "Aren't you having some?"

"I've already had two. I'm still on East Coast time. This is from a fresh pot."

"Oh." He took the cup in his hand and sipped it. Strong coffee, something he was not used to. Kelly had always made it weak and liked it light. He'd gotten used to it that way. But this tasted good. "How did you know I was awake?"

"It doesn't take a Ph.D. I knew you wouldn't let Keith stay up by himself that long. And I heard you coming down the steps."

Recollection dawned on him. "The creaky step?"

"Bagged me every time," she said with a smile. She waved the box. "Want some no-egg pancakes?"

"We have no maple syrup."

"I saw some strawberry jam in the fridge. That'll do."

"Oh, okay, sure. But you don't have to make us breakfast."

"I can do pancakes with, or in this case, without eggs. Why don't you give Keith his bath and I'll fix breakfast for all of us? It'll be done when you are."

He nodded his thanks. "Call out if you can't find anything in the kitchen."

Once the warm bath was filled, and Keith was playfully splashing in the water, Logan allowed himself to think about how normal it all seemed. He'd missed the scent of hot coffee brewing this morning, but now it was unmistakable. The smell of food cooking was coming upstairs and invading his senses. He hadn't had anything like this since before Kelly died, and suddenly it reminded him just how alone he'd been this past year without her.

Keith giggling pulled him from his thoughts.

Logan picked up a pile of soapsuds with his fingers and dotted Keith's nose. "What's so funny?"

"Auntie Poppy's singing."

Logan listened for a minute. Indeed she was. It brought back memories from their childhood, and he realized Poppy always had. He'd forgotten how he used to hear her coming down the hall at school long before she walked into the classroom because she'd been singing whatever popular song was on the radio. It was almost as if she was unaware she was even doing it.

Keith splashed some water that hit him in the face, and he realized in that moment he'd been smiling with the memory. He quickly pushed thoughts of the past away. Poppy hadn't even been here twenty-four hours, and the normal cadence of their lives had been shattered.

Routine had been important to Kelly, especially when she'd gotten so sick. Logan diligently followed that pattern, especially after Kelly passed away. He reasoned it was best for Keith to stay in their normal routine, something he could count on.

But he hadn't woken that morning thinking of the normal routine that had sustained him. He'd thought about

Poppy. She'd been the last thing on his mind last night and the first thing he'd thought of when he'd opened his eyes. He'd been angry with her for so long that it was hard to imagine that the woman who'd greeted him this morning was the woman who'd walked out on her best friend in her time of need. And every time he thought about that, his anger swelled again until Logan thought it would choke him. It had been hard enough to keep that anger in check yesterday.

Truth be told, Logan could hardly be angry with Poppy for leaving South Dakota all those years ago. She hadn't wanted to leave. That had been forced on her by her parents' decision to sell this very house.

No, Logan's anger grew as the years went on because, despite her promise on the day she'd left, Poppy hadn't come back. Not even for Kelly. It had always been Kelly who'd felt compelled to visit Poppy in New York.

Anger surged through him with the memory of Kelly's tears those months when she was sick every time she'd talked about Poppy. Why hadn't Poppy come back then? None of it made sense. Least of all, Poppy showing up on his door yesterday. Why now after all this time? He just didn't understand it.

As Keith splashed in the tub, Logan thought of how he'd tossed in his bed last night, knowing Poppy was just a few feet down the hall in bed. He knew she always slept naked because he'd walked in on her once while in high school, sending his teenage hormones through the roof in one fell swoop. He'd never been able to get the image of her lying in bed; auburn hair splayed out on her pillow, her creamy white breasts looking full and every bit a young man's dream.

A splash of suds hit his face, pulling him from the thoughts. The way his body immediately reacted to the memory only fueled his anger toward Poppy, but he pushed it aside as he pulled the plug on the tub and grabbed a towel. He wasn't a teenage boy lusting after a beautiful girl. He was a father and a rancher.

"Okay, little man, I think you're wrinkled enough. I smell pancakes downstairs."

Within a few minutes, they both made their way downstairs, the creaky stair tread announcing their approach. Keith ran to the kitchen and climbed on a kitchen chair in front of a place setting with a tall empty glass in front of it. Without a word, Poppy reached over and swapped the empty glass with a cup of milk in a plastic cup. Keith grabbed the cup and took a quick sip.

Logan looked at the table, set with a tablecloth he'd forgotten they'd had. He could smell the warmed strawberry jam now sitting in a gravy boat on the table. He looked at everything Poppy had put together and then glanced at the smile on her face. Even still tired, with her face scrubbed of the makeup she'd worn yesterday, she was an incredibly beautiful woman. The years hadn't changed that.

He cleared his throat and searched for something appropriate to say.

She tilted an eyebrow at him. "You hungry?"

"Yeah," he finally said. "This is … this is nice. Thank you."

"You haven't tasted it yet."

"Can I have a pancake?" Keith asked.

"Please," Logan reminded him.

"Can I have a pancake, please?" Keith repeated with his best manners.

"Sure can."

"I don't ever remember you being this chipper first thing in the morning," he said as he sat down.

Poppy took in the surprised look on his face. "I'm used to New York time. To me it seems much later than it is right now."

"Oh," Logan said.

"Sit next to me, Auntie Poppy!" Either way, Poppy would be sitting next to Keith at the table. But the sweetness of his request startled Logan, making it clear to him that his little guy missed having a mother, or at least a woman around the house, more than he thought.

♥ ♥ ♥

Poppy washed the dishes as she'd done hundreds of times at that very sink. She hadn't wanted to admit how stiff she was from the days' worth of work and playing in the yard with Keith. Her only reprieve had been when Keith had gone down for a very brief nap.

But more than the work of watching a young boy in his quest to explore endless puddles in the yard, Poppy was emotionally drained. March was always a cold month, but the chill she'd been getting from Logan all day had gotten the best of her. As the water drained from the sink, she felt the tears that she refused to let fall. How had the man who'd once been her best friend become this stranger? How could she have let it happen? Even if she'd known about what Kelly had done at the time, would things between her and Logan have been different? She had to believe they would be. Otherwise, why had she bothered to come?

When the last of the dishes from their dinner of grilled cheese and tomato soup were dried and put away, Logan came into the kitchen.

"You don't seem as peppy as you were yesterday," he said.

"I'm fine."

"Keith can really run you in circles. It can be a lot when you're not used to it."

She wiped her hands with the dishtowel and dropped it on the counter. "You still trying to get rid of me, Logan?"

"I'm trying...to say thank you."

The sincerity in his voice managed to squeeze out the rest of the irritation Poppy had felt all day by Logan's cold shoulder toward her.

"Keith has always been fascinated by the heavier equipment, and I couldn't have managed to get as much done as I did if you weren't here to keep him at a safe distance."

"He told me about a hundred times how much he loves to ride the Bobcat with you."

"Yeah, he does. But today wasn't the day for that. You were a … help."

She drew in a deep breath and smiled, hoping the tears she'd been on the verge of shedding all day would go away completely.

"Careful, Logan. You may just remember you actually like me." When he didn't reply, she added, "You're welcome." She motioned to the living room where Keith was playing with some monster trucks on the floor. "He played hard out in that mud today. He needs another bath."

Logan gave her a half smile. "Of course he does. He's a McKinnon."

Poppy used the time while Logan was giving Keith a bath to unpack the clothes that had been in her suitcase since the day she'd arrived. She hadn't been sure how long Logan would tolerate her being there and didn't see the point in unpacking. Until now.

There'd been a shift. Something she didn't think was possible. Small as it was, the look Logan had given her in the kitchen was void of the anger she'd seen and felt since she'd arrived. They were still light years away from where she wanted to be, and they'd have to confront the truth before there'd be any real change, but this was a start.

As she hung the last shirt in the closet, Poppy's eyes fixed on the big decoupage hatbox that Kelly had always used as a little girl to put notes and mementoes in. It was sitting on the top shelf of the spare room almost like it was cast away. Kelly had always kept it by her bed, but that was when they'd been teenagers. They'd lie on the bed and look at the little notes they'd passed to each other in class and talk about boys and their future.

She couldn't take her eyes off the box for fear of what was in there now. Were there love letters from Logan? Had Kelly kept the angry letters that Poppy had sent her after she'd learned the truth? She reached up, put her hands on the box, and then paused.

Regrets were a hard thing to live with. Kelly had died with regrets. Poppy only hoped that during their last meeting, when Kelly was too sick to even pick up a pencil, that Poppy had been able to ease some of her friend's regrets with forgiveness.

She pulled her hands away from the box. It wasn't her place to rummage through Kelly's past without first talking with Logan about her true reason for coming back to Rudolph. As she closed the closet door, she played that conversation, as she had done many times, over again in her mind. *Maybe unpacking hadn't been such a good idea.*

Twenty minutes later, both Keith and Logan were emerging from the bathroom, and Poppy was still sitting on the bed mulling over how to muster up the courage to start the conversation she knew she had to have with Logan.

"Where are you going? You know it's time for bed," she heard Logan say. Keith came barreling through the bedroom in his motorcycle pajamas and launched himself onto the bed.

"I want Auntie Poppy to put me to bed."

Logan stopped short at the door.

"But we always read a story and say prayers together. Just you and me."

"No, Auntie Poppy do it tonight!"

Poppy's heart squeezed as she gazed on Logan's hurt expression. He glared at her, and she knew any ground she'd covered today was now lost.

Chapter Four

"Okay, I'll come in and give you a kiss when you're all tucked in," he said. Logan had never felt like an outsider with Keith since the day he was born, but tonight he had. And he didn't like it one bit.

He wasn't used to his son being so openly eager to spend time with someone outside the family. But then, Logan reasoned, like father like son. There had always been something about Poppy that had a hold on him. Despite the anger that had sustained him all this time since Kelly's death, it was still true, and it was a bitter pill to swallow.

He'd forgotten just what it had been like all those years ago. The memories of his quiet life with Kelly had forced those memories of laughter and wild teenage antics aside. He wasn't that man anymore and Poppy wasn't that woman. But at some point today, it sure began to feel like it, and the realization of that rattled him to the core.

There were times when they'd been kids that he'd felt the odd man out when he'd been with Poppy and Kelly. They had a sixth sense with each other, exchanging looks he couldn't decipher. Back then, things had been different. Back then, he'd secretly been in love with Poppy. He'd never told her, of course. He'd never told anyone. Not even Kelly.

Especially not Kelly.

But Hawk knew. He had always ribbed him about Poppy, just like he had yesterday when Poppy had arrived. He could keep the truth from everyone else. But he couldn't keep it from himself, and it suddenly dawned on him that he was angry at Poppy as much for not being there for Kelly as he was for not being there for him when Kelly had gotten sick. If nothing else, he and Poppy had been best friends, something he'd mourned when she'd left. His whole world had once been wrapped up entirely in his feelings for Poppy.

He walked into the back den and sat behind his desk, deciding it was better to put his mind to work in the present than let it roam in the past. But the memories he hadn't dared think about in years continued to flood his mind, just as they had since Poppy arrived.

But despite his own internal war, Logan couldn't help but marvel at how comfortable Keith was around Poppy. It was if they'd known each other his whole life. And he was beginning to wonder if perhaps, he'd been the odd man out there as well. Poppy said she'd been talking with Keith on the phone, something his mother finally confirmed to him last night at the shelter. Logan knew Kelly had taken Keith out to New York for visits, but Keith had been so young then. None of it added up to the type of warm and easy relationship that seemed to be building between Poppy and Keith now.

The light knock on the door startled him. Poppy was leaning against the door with a slight smile on her face.

"Book is read, and prayers for everyone in Rudolph have been made."

"That fast?" Logan asked.

It was if Poppy was having a hard time holding back her smile as she nodded. In the end, it broke free. "He's a speed demon, that little one. He wants you to give him a kiss."

Logan's heart melted. "Tell him I'll be right up."

He stayed with Keith until he'd fallen asleep. On any other night, he probably would have left his son's bed sooner. But Poppy was still awake. He could hear her moving around downstairs as if she were rearranging the kitchen pantry.

But when he finally left Keith's side, he took the stairs and found her in the living room. Photo albums that had been tucked away were spread out on the coffee table. And the anger that had slipped away during the day came surging back.

"What are you doing?"

Poppy glanced up at him quickly and then just as quickly she turned away. But not before he saw the tears staining her cheeks. She wiped her face with one swipe of her palm and sniffed. "Reminiscing."

"Don't." The harshness of his demand had her hands stiffening on the photo album. She stared up at him with confusion.

"I was just looking at pictures of us from—"

"Don't," he said, this time quieter.

He knew the photo album well. He'd stared at it many times since Poppy had left Rudolph and then again when Kelly had gotten sick. This photo album was filled with a life he used to live before things had become just he and Kelly. And then just him. It was of a time when he'd had wild dreams of a young woman he didn't marry. It was a reminder of what would never be again.

Looking at Poppy's determined expression now, it was easy for Logan to see how he could have forgotten those times and the man he used to be. He'd been different then. Different with Poppy.

Kelly had always been the predictable one who was very dedicated to a quiet and humble life. She was slow and steady, something he could always count on until cancer had blindsided them.

Despite being such close friends, Poppy was the polar opposite of Kelly. Everything about her was full of passion. Full of life and adventure. It didn't matter if the adventure was a grand dream or a quick little jaunt to the pond for a quick swim.

In those few seconds that passed between them, the memory was so clear in Logan's mind that it was if it had happened yesterday. He could still hear the splashing of water as he ran through the trees toward the sun-filled pond where they always swam. Even now, his body still reacted with the memory of finding Poppy's naked body, wet and glistening in the sunlight as she unabashedly floated on her back.

When she'd finally caught him standing there staring, his body hard and aching so strong with arousal that it didn't even embarrass him that she knew, she'd just smiled and asked him if he wanted to join her.

Poppy was all about living life to the fullest and had never held back on adventure, whatever the type. And she never held back what was on her mind. Logan had a feeling he was about to get a piece of it right now.

"Is remembering the way we used to be such a bad thing?"

"I don't want to talk about this."

"That kind of avoidance only worked with Kelly. Not with me."

"Don't you dare bring her into this."

"I think it's about time we should. After all, she is the reason we are where we are today."

"What the hell is that supposed to mean?"

"You tell me. You were the one who was here when I was hundreds of miles away waiting for any kind of word from you. When the only word I got was through her."

He drew in a deep breath and held it, trying to reign in the confusion he felt.

"I don't know what you're talking about."

"Don't be a coward about this. Not now. Kelly isn't standing here to facilitate our words anymore."

"That's right. Kelly's not here at all."

"I know. And in spite of everything, I miss her so much."

"In spite … What are you talking about?"

She proceeded as if she were walking on eggshells.

"Haven't you ever wondered what happened to us, Logan? Did you ever wonder how our friendship fell apart? I don't mean Kelly and me. Not the three of us. You and me."

He stared at her for a long moment. He had wondered. The woman who'd left Rudolph as a teenager, crying in his arms that she would do everything in her power to come back, him promising her the same, was staring up at her now. It amazed him how the years melted away in an instant. He wondered if he'd ever see this side of Poppy again. And now he wasn't sure he wanted to.

"Just leave it in the past, Poppy. It doesn't matter now."

"Are you sure?"

"I don't want to talk about this. And no amount of looking at that photo album is going to change a thing."

"That's just it, Logan. We don't talk at all. We haven't in years. Think back. We let Kelly do all our talking for us. I still don't know exactly how that happened. And now that she's gone, when you have the chance to actually say something to me, yell at me, curse me, to finally talk for ourselves, you just avoid me."

"We've just spent the last two days together."

"Talking about the flood and work and Keith needing a bath or breakfast. Anything but what we need to talk about. I could have been anyone lugging those branches yesterday or cooking in your kitchen today. You avoided talking *to* me. *With* me. You just talk at me as if I were some stranger."

He started to protest, but she broke in before he could utter a word. "Think about what's gone on here. We haven't seen each other in years, and all you have to say is 'we have no food in the kitchen' or 'would you mind watching Keith.' We *need* to talk, Logan."

"No, we don't."

He started to turn away, but she stopped him.

"Is that what it was like with you and Kelly? Did you ever get angry or argue about anything? Or did you just take everything she said at face value?" She shook her head, knowing the truth without his answer. They both knew Kelly too well. In the end, she answered for him. "Of course, you didn't. I know I did. Why would I have any reason to believe otherwise?

"Kelly was as steady as the day was long. She never rocked the boat. That was Kelly's way. But it was never your way, Logan. We argued plenty, and we laughed and talked. All of that made us closer. That's what made us such good friends."

He sighed and turned to her. In his eyes Poppy saw truth and a war waging that Logan didn't want to fight. And she could hardly blame him after the tragedy he'd gone through in the last year.

"Kelly wasn't like you, Poppy," he said, his whole body showing defeat.

"Why do you think I came back here, Logan?"

"I don't know."

"Sure you do. You knew the moment I pulled into the driveway. There's some unfinished business between us, something that was brewing long before I left South Dakota all those years ago. Things we should have said, but didn't because we were too young and naïve. You knew it and so did Kelly. That's what frightened her so much."

In the dark room, Logan's expression should have scared her. But it didn't. In his eyes, she saw need, something she'd felt herself for a long time. It wasn't just that she was standing mere inches away from a man she'd loved virtually her whole life. It was that they were so close to either finally coming together as she'd always wanted or totally self-combusting when all the secrets that had pulled them apart years ago came to light.

"Now is not the time for this," Logan said in warning.

"Really? And just when will the right time be? When we're all old or dead, and no one cares anymore?"

"You're a fine one to talk about caring. Where the hell were you when Kelly needed you?"

He picked up the photo album and shoved it back in place on the bookshelf.

"You're the one who left."

Poppy knew she wasn't going to gain any ground with Logan. She had left. The fact she had no choice didn't matter anymore.

"A long time ago, long before Kelly died, you let everything about you die. And since Kelly's been gone, it's like you're content to stay there. Don't deny it. Even your family ..."

"Since when are you so close to my family? You spend a year talking with my son on the telephone, and I don't even know about it. You talk to my mother. I was your friend. Kelly was your friend. Where the hell were you?"

"Exactly where Kelly wanted me to be. Far away."

She moved in closer, trying to keep herself from going overboard as she feared so many times she might. "I talked to your friends last night, Logan. Or the people who used to be your friends. Some of them haven't seen you in years. You never go out for a beer with your brothers or hang out with any of the people you used to see."

"What do you know about it?"

"They told me. Kelly did, too."

Irritation turned his face red with anger. "You keep saying that as if you were even around. What do you even know about what Kelly and my life were like?"

"Just because I wasn't physically here doesn't mean that Kelly and I weren't close. She was the best friend I've ever had aside from you. I would have done anything for her. That's why I'm here now."

He laughed wryly. "Because she asked you."

"I know you don't believe me, but she did."

"I've had enough of this."

He turned to walk toward the stairs, but she stopped him with her words. "I kept her letters. Not all of them. Some of them were destroyed when one of my old apartments in Greenwich Village got flooded after one of the pipes burst. She said she kept mine. You…had to have found them after she died."

Logan's whole body sagged as if she'd just kicked him in the gut.

"Didn't you even look? You had to have seen my letters in the mail. Weren't you even curious about me?"

She laughed cynically. When he didn't answer, her shoulders sagged under the weight of just how deep the separation had become.

"She never told you I wrote to her, did she? She never told you we talked on the phone just about every week?"

He said quietly, "There was a lot she didn't tell me."

With that, Logan abruptly walked to the stairs. Halfway up there was a creak in the wood, the same creak that had gotten her into trouble when she'd try to sneak out of the house to meet Logan when they were teens. In all the time they'd lived here, Logan hadn't bothered to fix it.

It was just one more reminder of the relationship she and Logan had before she'd gone away, and Kelly had claimed him.

Regret chipped away at her resolve. She'd pushed him too far, wanting to know just how much he knew, how much Kelly had confessed to him, if at all. And now it was clear the only confession Kelly had made was to Poppy. She'd lived these last ten years as an invisible friend; someone Kelly never shared with anyone, especially Logan. And because she'd pushed to unveil the truth, Logan had retreated battered and confused about a woman he'd married and shared his life with instead of her. Of course he didn't want Poppy here.

Everything inside Poppy wanted to reach out and tell Logan she'd leave if it stopped the hurting. The last thing she wanted to do was cause Logan more pain. But after talking to people in town, having a quick chat again with Hawk down at the shelter, Poppy was convinced more than ever that she had to stay if only to help Logan emerge from this well he'd allowed himself to hide inside long before Kelly died. Where was that spirited man she used to know? He was still there. She was sure of it.

Grabbing her mud-stained jacket, she opened the kitchen door and stepped out onto the porch. The light was on upstairs in Logan's bedroom. She could see the shadow of light stretching long across the dirt driveway.

Their lives had taken a dramatic turn years ago when her parents had decided to sell this ranch and move states away. Poppy had thought she'd die the day they'd told her. Tonight she realized she truly had.

The chill of the air made her shiver, and she turned to go back inside. Logan was standing in the doorway looking out at her. Without his jacket, he stepped out onto the porch and shut the door. He was still the same Logan. She pushed him to his limit, and he always came back for more. Well, *not always*, she thought with regret. There was one time she'd waited, and he'd never come.

"What do you want from me, Poppy? I have never been able to figure that out. Kelly always knew where she stood with you. But me…"

"Don't give me that. You always knew. You were just too scared or young or…" She laughed at the absurdity of going back all those years. "I've always loved you, Logan. Deep down you had to know that. That's why I can't understand why you didn't come to see me like you promised. I was so heartbroken when I left here, and you promised just as soon as you had enough money saved you were going to leave South Dakota to be with me."

He sighed. "That was a long time ago."

"Why didn't you come, Logan? I waited for you."

"I don't know."

Poppy balled her fists. "Please don't back away from this. Not now when you knew I wanted you…"

"You'd moved on."

She shook her head, fighting back tears. *Lies.* She could see how far back they'd gone by the expression on Logan's face.

"You think you knew Kelly," she said, trying to keep the regret she felt inside from being heard. "But you didn't know everything, Logan. I didn't either."

She walked past him to the door, her emotions dragging her down with every step.

As her hand connected with the cold metal of the screen door handle, he said, "She didn't tell me she was sick until months after she'd found out. She let me believe she was okay until..."

"It was too late," she said, finishing what Logan couldn't. "That was Kelly's way."

"The doctor said the cancer might have started after the fertility treatments. I didn't know she was even going until I found a bill in the mail from the treatment center."

"Her aunt died of ovarian cancer very young, too."

"If I'd have known she was going... She was desperate to have a baby. She thought it would...make things better."

Poppy closed her eyes, and for a split second, she weighed whether her coming here at all was a good idea. Everything he believed about his life would change instantly as it had for her.

"I think it's time you read the letters in that hatbox in the spare bedroom upstairs."

Lisa Mondello

He glared at her accusingly. "You went through Kelly's things?"

She rolled her eyes. "I didn't have to. She'd been storing little letters and mementoes in that hatbox since she was a teenager. When I saw it on the top shelf of the closet, I figured you'd put it there and forgotten about it."

"Letters won't make a difference."

Frustrated, she yanked the screen door open. "Fine. Don't read them. Stay in your dream world. But I won't let you blame me forever for what you think I did if you won't at least try to learn the truth."

Poppy turned to step inside the kitchen, but Logan caught her by the arm and swung her to face him. Anger was what she'd expected to be greeted with. She'd surely driven him to the brink. But instead, Poppy was met with raw emotion that was sharp and strong flowing from every move Logan made, and it only heated an already burning flame inside her. She should have been scared, but the flame in Logan's eyes brought her back to a time when she would have given anything to be this close to him. For him to wrap her in his arms and press his mouth against hers. She'd been hungry for that long forgotten kiss they'd shared years ago for too long. She wasn't about to back down now.

"What's going to make a difference for you, Logan? What's going to bring you back?" she said softly.

He dragged her into his arms and crushed her against his chest. There she felt at home, complete joy and elation

74

filled her. The memory of being in his arms had faded long ago, but it instantly rekindled. His body had changed and so had hers. They were no longer teenagers. His hard chest muscles pressed firmly against her breast as he wrapped his arms around her, pulling her ever closer.

Poppy lifted her face to him in invitation, which he immediately accepted by claiming her mouth with his. And it was more than she'd dreamed of, filling an emptiness she thought would forever ache inside her. Every bit of her was on fire and shaken to the core. After all these years, Logan still had that effect on her, a hold that no other man she'd ever been with could claim.

Wrapping her arms around his shoulders, she deepened the kiss and was rewarded with his low moan, and then a sharp intake of breath as she leaned her hips into his, feeling his arousal.

Logan abruptly pulled away. On his face she saw confusion mixed with raw passion. He pulled his arms away and took a wide step back, leaving Poppy empty again. She fought back the tears burning her eyes.

"What was that kiss for, Logan? To prove me wrong? I think you know it did the opposite."

Without another word, she stepped into the house and left him out on the cold porch.

She had wanted to blurt it all out to him tonight. *I'm not the one who betrayed you. I didn't forget about you.* He deserved the truth after all these years. And even now she feared his reaction to how he would take the news.

Logan couldn't have spent eight years as Kelly's husband if he hadn't loved her at least a little. And here she was trying to undo what couldn't be undone.

Poppy still couldn't get Kelly's words out of her mind. *I'm a terrible friend. I deserve to have terrible things happen to me.*

Of course, Poppy had tried to convince her that she'd been a wonderful friend, the best Poppy had ever had. And then Kelly confessed the truth, and all Poppy wanted to do was run away. She couldn't cry. She couldn't scream. She couldn't breathe. The whole course of her life had been changed that day, in that single moment.

Things would've been different for all of them. Maybe they wouldn't have been the way Poppy had dreamed, but they would've been different for both her and Logan. Most of all, it would have been different for Kelly. And the fear of that was what had driven her friend to do what she'd done.

It had been Kelly and her relentless letters to Poppy that had finally convinced her to come back to South Dakota. Poppy had forgiven Kelly because she knew Kelly needed to be forgiven as much as Poppy needed to forgive her before Kelly died. She would forever be grateful that she had made it to the hospital while Kelly was still lucid enough to know that Poppy was there. They'd talked while Kelly was awake. They cried. They even managed to laugh a little. She couldn't remember a time when she and Kelly had been that honest about everything. She died a few days later. And Logan had never known she was there.

It had taken Poppy a year to build up the courage to come back home to face Logan. She had to give him the same courtesy by allowing him time to feel whatever he was going to feel when he learned the truth.

Logan waited until he'd heard Poppy's bedroom door close. And then he waited a little longer, just to make sure she was asleep. He'd stayed on the cold porch, letting the South Dakota winds bite into his skin just so he could feel something other than Poppy's body pressed against his.

What the hell was he doing? Poppy was right about one thing. Kissing her hadn't proved he'd moved on from the feelings he used to have. It only showed him how much of an effect she still had on him, even after all these years.

As he walked up the stairs, he paid special attention to the creaky step, avoiding it so as not to make a sound. With each step, his legs and arms felt heavy, much like they had the day Kelly died.

Poppy wanted to talk about truths. But those were hard for all of them. Logan knew all too well the course of their lives would have been so different had Kelly not gotten pregnant that first time. It was only right that he marry her. It had gutted her to lose the baby so soon after the wedding, and Logan had fought the guilt he'd felt about wishing they'd waited. If only... their new marriage had taken the strain of Kelly wanting so badly to get pregnant again.

Logan stopped at Keith's bedroom door and listened. His little boy was asleep and probably would be until morning. It had taken Kelly four years to get pregnant with Keith. After that, Logan vowed to leave all the what-ifs that played in his mind in the past and devote everything to his family. Despite not wanting to be surrounded by memories, he'd even agreed to buy this house after Kelly got pregnant, for fear she'd lose another baby.

Logan turned to go down the hall toward his room when the hatbox on the floor outside of Poppy's room caught his eye and caused him to stop. On top of the hatbox was a stack of letters tied with a red ribbon. He moved closer, picking the stack up in his hand and pushing the satin bow aside to see the writing. His stomach fell. The envelopes were in Kelly's handwriting. The top letter was postmarked just a few weeks before she died.

He dropped the stack on top of the hatbox and shut himself inside his bedroom for the night, knowing that sleep was the last thing he'd be getting.

♥ ♥ ♥

"Hawk called while you were still asleep. He said Skylar was hoping to take Keith for an overnight to help keep Alex company while she helps your mother."

Logan nodded without looking at Poppy. He couldn't. Not because he was angry with her for anything that happened last night. He'd turned his anger on himself. He'd spent the better part of the night trying to figure out how he'd managed to be married to one woman for eight years and still feel the way he did about Poppy after all these years. And he did. That was the conclusion he'd come to as the dark sky had turned his room light in the early hours. Only then had he been able to finally fall asleep.

"He hasn't had his breakfast yet," she said quietly as she filled the coffee filter with coffee grounds. "But he's all dressed. He's just playing with his trucks in the—"

"He can have breakfast at the diner. I'll drive him," Logan said. "Could you feed the horses while I'm gone? That would be helpful."

He finally looked at her then. She was searching for answers. He gave her none.

"Sure," she said with a weak smile.

Fifteen minutes later, he was pulling into a full parking lot at his mom's restaurant. It didn't matter if there were no seats left in the diner. There was a family table out back in the kitchen where he and Keith had taken a meal on plenty of mornings. He parked the truck in the back next to Hawk's Jeep.

After giving his mother a quick kiss on the cheek he sat in his favorite chair by the window. Hawk was just finishing up his breakfast. Keith wasted no time climbing into the seat next to his favorite uncle.

"Hey, little man!"

"We're going to have good pancakes. Not like Auntie Poppy's."

Hawk laughed. "Auntie Poppy doesn't make good pancakes?"

Keith made a face and shook his head.

"It's a good thing Grammie does. Did you hear that, Ma?" Hawk called out. "Two helpings of pancakes."

"And chocolate milk!" Keith added.

"Heaven forbid I forget the chocolate milk," Kate said from the other side of the kitchen.

"Don't forget your manners," Logan said, eyeing Keith.

"Please!" Keith added.

"That's my boy," Kate said with a smile.

Logan grabbed a container of orange juice and a glass, and filled it before he sat down opposite Keith and Hawk.

As if Kate had been expecting them, she appeared at the table with two plates filled with pancakes. One had a stack of pancakes and a side of bacon and fried potatoes. She dropped that plate in front of Logan. The other plate had one pancake and one slice of bacon. With the plate still in her hand, she grabbed the container of maple syrup from the table and proceeded to make a smiley face on her grandson's pancake stack, much to Keith's delight before she placed the plate in front of him.

"Make sure you eat all of it. Alex is going to be here pretty soon, and you can't play until you've had your breakfast."

"I will, Grammie."

Kate paused at the table. "How are things going at home?"

Logan looked at her, knowing exactly what she was referring to.

"Fine."

She raised her eyebrows. "Good." Then she went back to her tasks in the kitchen.

Hawk laughed.

"Cut it out," Logan warned.

"I didn't say anything."

"I expected Poppy to come by with you."

"Since when are you so interested in Poppy?"

"Since you seem to be acting like a—"

"Uh, uh." Kate dropped a cup of chocolate milk in front of Keith and bent her head toward her grandson giving a strong look at her sons. "Little ears."

"My ears aren't little," Keith said.

She bent down and kissed him on the cheek as he ate. "And getting bigger and smarter every day."

As she turned to walk away, she paused and angled back to Hawk, mouthing, "Watch it."

Hawk shrugged his apology to his mother.

Logan chuckled. He quickly ate his pancakes and then helped finish up the rest of Keith's pancake while Hawk sat back and drank his coffee. When they heard Skylar come in through the back, it was all Keith needed to declare he was done with breakfast.

"Can I go play in the back room with Alex?"

"Finish your milk first." Keith drank enough to satisfy Logan, and then he wiped his face clean with his napkin before climbing down from the chair.

Logan waved hello to the babysitter, Donna, who usually watched the boys for a few hours while his mother and Skylar were working out front. Keith ran toward her.

"You know the rules here," Kate said to Keith, catching him halfway. "No running in my kitchen."

"I guess I need to be getting back," Logan said.

"Alright, fine. Don't tell me anything."

Logan drained his glass of orange juice. "There's nothing to tell."

Hawk's expression fell, and his brows drew inward. "Logan, you can lie to me all you want, but don't lie to yourself. You'll waste years of your life chasing a ghost that isn't there. Hasn't that gone on long enough?"

"I don't know what you're talking about."

Hawk shook his head. His older brother had always been an open book, direct and honest. You never wondered where you stood with Hawk. It was something he'd always admired about his brother. Right now, he had a feeling it was just going to piss him off.

"Now's not the time for this," Logan said, rubbing his jawline of the itch caused by facial hair that had grown too long.

"You're getting it anyway. You and Poppy always seemed like you were cut from the same cloth. Poppy was all about laughter and adventure, and she brought that out in you. When you got together with Kelly, that all changed. You hold yourself back. Sometimes I wonder what's driving you to stay there."

"I grew up."

"That's a lousy excuse and you know it."

Irritation coiled in him. "I have a family and responsibilities."

"Yeah, but you also have a life. You can enjoy it once in a while and still be responsible. Let's face it, you stopped living long before Kelly died, bro."

"What's that supposed to mean?"

Hawk hesitated and seemed to look around the corner to see if their mother was watching, just like he'd done a hundred times when they were kids and getting ready for a prank. Except this time there was no prank, just straight talk.

"Everybody, including me, was shocked as hell when you came home and said you were marrying Kelly. Don't get me wrong. I loved Kelly like she was my sister. But after the miscarriage ... well, I half expected the two of you to split before the year was over."

He threw his napkin on the table. "We didn't. We had Keith."

"I know. After three years of fertility treatments. But from where I was sitting Keith was pretty much the only thing you two had in common."

"Keith is the best thing in my life."

"He's the only life I've seen in you in years. Truth be known, I hadn't thought much about it for a long time until I saw you with Poppy the other night. Since then, I've been wondering if you and Kelly would have gotten together at all if Poppy hadn't left Rudolph."

Logan's jaw tightened. "Poppy made her choice not to come back."

Hawk nodded. "Would it have made a difference if she had?"

He was silent for a moment. He should have been shocked by Hawk's direct question, but he wasn't. Truth was Logan had mulled over that very question many times himself.

"It doesn't matter. It's not what happened. I married Kelly."

Hawk leaned forward in his seat, pushing his empty coffee cup to the center of the table. "Kelly was the real deal. She was a good person, a good mother, and a great friend. Thing is, Logan, Kelly is gone. All I'm saying is maybe you settled for something because you couldn't have the one you really wanted. And that person is here now." When Logan started to protest, Hawk stopped him.

"I know you loved Kelly. And you don't have to answer this if you don't want to, but ... were you really happy with her? Were you really *in* love with her?"

"Of course."

"Are you sure? I've known you all my life, and you're one of the most honorable men I know. But there was something always missing, and I haven't seen it in you since Poppy left." He hesitated a minute. "And as ticked off as you say you are that Poppy is here, I saw it again that day at the ranch when I saw you looking at her."

Chapter Five

The drive back home was filled with haunting memories Logan hadn't wanted to remember for years. He'd made mistakes for sure. But had it really been as Hawk said? He had loved Kelly, come to love her, but their love had never been a passionate kind of love he imagined people could have. It was comfortable. Steady. But was he happy?

That was a hard question to answer, and he fought to find closure with it as he pulled into the driveway and parked the truck next to Poppy's rental car.

He couldn't face her. There were too many demons in him that he was afraid of what he'd say. Kissing her last night on the porch had been as intense as it had been all those years ago. He could still taste her, feel her softness against him. And he suddenly couldn't remember the last time he'd kissed Kelly that way, if he ever had at all.

The thought of what he'd deprived his wife of made Logan sick to his stomach. How could he have been that kind of man to saddle Kelly with a husband who didn't love her wholly, the way she should have been loved?

He climbed out of the truck and decided to walk to the pond on the far side of the property, letting the cold March wind whip at his face and bite into his exposed skin. He needed it to feel something other than the emptiness of knowing that Hawk had been right. He'd traded happiness for duty. He hadn't been fair to either one of them.

He kept walking until he reached the trail through the woods that led to the large boulder jutting out into the pond. As kids, they used to jump off the boulder into deep water as the rock formation gave them a height of about fifteen feet to jump.

He stood there for a moment overlooking the water and remembered Poppy swimming the day she'd found out her parents had sold the house. She'd just come from his mother's restaurant and had been crying. He'd tried to console her, but she'd run away. Only when he'd gone to her house and her parents told him Poppy hadn't come home yet, he knew she'd come here.

The March winds whipped at him, but still he looked at the sun shining on the water, feeling the heat of that day as if it were real. He'd come upon her quietly and had ignored the clothes haphazardly dropped on the boulder. It was only after he'd seen her naked, wet skin glistening in the sun that he'd realized Poppy was skinny-dipping.

His initial relief that she was smiling, not crying, had immediately changed to blazing desire.

"It's a rite of passage to go skinny-dipping in a creek here in Rudolph and now's my chance," she'd said. "Are you going to just watch me swim or are you going to join me?"

The heat in her eyes that day still made his body react now the way it had as a young man. She'd wanted him. Under her watchful and unashamed eyes, he'd stripped down and jumped into the water. They didn't come together at first. But he knew they would. His fingers itched to touch Poppy in delicate places he'd only dreamed of in the darkness. And there she was, naked and wanting him like he'd wanted her.

She swam around completely unfazed that anyone might come upon them. She revealed her beautiful body without any shyness and swam around him as if it was a dance, seducing him and taking pleasure in teasing him with her untamed spirit.

So many times since that day, Logan had imagined the two of them making love in the water or right there on the shore. He felt himself grow hard just thinking about it again. But that had never happened. Kelly had come charging through the woods and discovered the two of them there. He'd been so angry with her for bad timing that day and the fact that she'd stayed there with her hands crossed over her chest telling them they were about to get busted by Poppy's parents if they didn't get dressed quick.

But none of that had any effect on Poppy. She'd just laughed, gave Logan a wink, and climbed out of the water in front of him naked as the day she was born as if she didn't have a care in the world. And despite her crying fit earlier, she didn't. That was Poppy. She'd done something to him that day that had stayed with him for ten years.

Funny how he and Kelly had never come here together in all the years they'd lived here. It was only now that Poppy was spinning his head in circles that he was back to where he was as a teen, all knotted up inside and aching with need for her.

Logan looked at the creek, and despite the flood, its water level was much lower than it had been a week ago. The watermark on the boulder was a telltale sign of just how high the water had gotten. Debris was pushed up along the banks, clogging the water's path. He grabbed a long branch that seemed to have wedged itself in a thick pile and pulled it free. That one small move was enough to allow the force of the creek to pull a chunk of more branches and leaves free, sending it downstream to where it belonged.

One small move. That's all it took to change the course of life. If not for his one small move in a fit of drunkenness, he would have driven all the way to Long Island to convince Poppy how much they belonged together, how much he loved her.

With a deep sigh, he pulled his cell phone from his pocket and checked for messages. There was none. His son was having the time of his life with his best buddy. Everyone in town was busy working on cleaning. And he was reminiscing about a woman a few hundred yards away from him instead of tending to a long list of things that needed to be done on his ranch.

The sound of an engine growing louder drew his attention to the path back to the house. He turned and saw Poppy out in the back pasture blazing around on the four-wheeler, driving all willy-nilly and at full throttle. The back wheels were spitting up mud all around her, but she didn't let off the throttle. She did some figure eights and then pulled onto the trail toward him stopping just short of the embankment to the creek.

She pulled off her helmet and let her auburn hair fall to her shoulders.

"I see you found my toys," he said.

Her smile was wide and full of expression and excitement. It took his breath away.

"Toy. There was only one! What gives?"

Logan shrugged. "I take Keith on it with me sometimes. He loves it. But I haven't done anything like you just did in the back pasture."

She laughed. "Yeah, I was eating dirt back there. I can't believe you haven't gotten Keith his own four-wheeler yet."

Logan sputtered. "He's four."

"Almost five. I'd say we need to put this on the top of his birthday wish list."

Logan shrugged, thinking about how much fun it would be to go riding with Keith. "He's all McKinnon. I have a feeling he'd tear up that pasture worse than you just did."

She smiled sweetly. "Sorry about that. I figured it was already muddy. I couldn't hurt it any more than the flood did."

"No problem. I'll be plowing it under soon anyway."

She took in a deep breath and looked around. "When I saw your truck and couldn't find you in the barn, I figured you must have come back here. I had a hard time getting this thing started though. You don't use it much?"

"There was always so much work to be done around here. Never had the time."

She eyed him speculatively. "Uh, huh. That's Kelly talking. She never did like this sort of thing."

A week ago that remark would have had him vehemently defending Kelly. But Poppy knew Kelly's quiet personality so well, and there was no malice in what she said that Logan couldn't argue with the truth.

He recovered quickly, and if Poppy noticed, she didn't let on. "Not exactly something you'd do in Manhattan."

She laughed. "No. Wish I could. It definitely beats breathing in the exhaust in the city. I'd forgotten how much fun this was. Is Keith going to be gone all day?"

"Until tomorrow. Keith is staying over Skylar's."

"I'll bet you didn't have to ask him twice."

He shook his head. "No."

Her smile widened. "Well, I guess that leaves just you and me. Hop on board."

He hesitated, which earned him a quick tilt of Poppy's eyebrow in challenge. "You are *not* going to tell me you have too much work to do, Logan McKinnon. The sun is shining. There is always going to be work to do around here, flood or no flood, so just give yourself the afternoon off to play."

He offered a half grin. "Is that an order?"

"Damn straight it is. If we do enough runs across the field, you might not even have to plow! Come on. We'll do double duty tomorrow. Unless you're too chicken to ride on the back of an ATV with a pro dare-devil."

He sputtered. "What makes you such a pro?"

"I've mastered riding in a New York City cab. If that doesn't make me a pro dare-devil, nothing will."

He laughed. "That bad?"

"Let's say I walk and take the subway more than I should. Get on." She handed Logan the extra helmet.

Logan eased himself onto the back of the ATV and wrapped his arms around Poppy's slender waist. It was amazingly intimate to feel that close to her body and incredibly distracting, so he grabbed the handles on the sides of the seat instead.

Poppy glanced over her shoulder before putting on her helmet and said, "Chicken." Then she laughed and revved up the engine, taking off full speed ahead toward the connecting trails that made their way through the grounds around the creek and the farms, slowing only when she saw debris on the trail or a low-lying branch.

He didn't know when it had happened during the ride, but he found himself laughing. The pleasure of the day seeped deep into his soul as they rode around the farm, passed the horses grazing in the drier pasture on high ground, to the lower fields where he'd plant his spring crops as soon as the earth dried. For now, it was their playground. Poppy remained fearless no matter how fast she was going. Logan finally had to wrap his arms around her waist to keep himself firmly in the seat.

Snug up against her body, feeling her auburn hair whip around him and breathing in her sweet scent with the fresh air was pure heaven. Hearing Poppy's musical laugh as she drove through the fields, spitting up mud all around them, it was hard to feel anything but happiness. It suddenly dawned on Logan what Hawk had been trying to say to him earlier. He'd been numb inside for a long time, long before Kelly had gotten sick.

All of the best things eventually have to come to an end, and Logan was disappointed as the ATV started sputtering. The four-wheeler died in the middle of the muddy field.

"I think we're out of gas," Poppy said. "We're going to have to walk through all this mud to get to the barn. Do you have any gas left in the gas can?"

"No, I used it for the generator." He climbed off the ATV and extended a hand to Poppy as she stumbled climbing off. "It'll be fine here. I'll get some gas in town later."

She looked at him for a long time, the corners of her moist lips tilted up to a slight smile, her eyes sparkling in the sunshine. Beautiful didn't even cover it in his mind. Then her expression turned devilish, catching him off guard. But not before he noticed the pile of mud in her hand.

"Don't you dare," he warned.

"What difference is it going to make? You're already a mess," she said as she hurled the mud at him.

He ducked to get out of the way, but still got hit on the arm. He laughed as he looked at the mess it made.

"Don't go pouting on me," she said, backing up quickly. "You're already covered with mud from head to toe."

It was true. Mud was in Poppy's hair, on her face and her clothes. The only part of her face that was still clean was the part where the helmet shielded her from spraying mud. Her boots sank into the mud on the ground as she moved away from him, laughing as she did.

Bending over he scooped up a handful of mud and quickly threw it at her. She screamed with laughter as she clumsily ran toward the house. He followed quickly, but trying to run on slippery ground thwarted his efforts. Still he kept right on her heels until they both spilled through the kitchen door, laughing hard and looking a mess.

They stood there staring at each other, and with each breath Logan took, he knew something had shifted. Things had changed.

It had been hard to see the woman he'd been so taken by in his youth, the friend that had been everything to him until life had put a wedge between them. Now he no longer remembered the details of what happened. Or maybe he just didn't give a damn anymore. Life had changed them all. And right now he was standing in front of a woman who was covered in mud, who took his breath away because her smile lit up his heart.

"Are you hungry?" she asked.

He shook his head.

"I am. But to be honest, I'm not really interested in food."

Neither was he.

She touched her cheek and looked at the mud on her fingers. "I feel like Kristy Dorning must have felt when Tommy Gillis released those homing pigeons during homecoming dance and Kristy got christened with bird poop."

He laughed with the memory. "Kristy's face was priceless. All things considered, I prefer mud to poop."

She laughed and suddenly he was light-headed just listening to the sound of her. He'd missed it.

Tendrils of hair stuck to her cheek, along with the spray of mud, and made her look irresistible. Without consciously thinking about it, Logan reached up and wiped the smudge off her face.

He chuckled softly. "I made it worse." And still he didn't move his hand from her cheek as she gazed up into his eyes. Every bit of his body came alive with that one touch. He wanted to kiss her, take her in his arms and melt with her, as much as he wanted and needed his next breath.

Her sweet lips parted and turned into a slight grin. "I think the only hope for us is to clean off in the shower."

Poppy turned on her heels and pulled off her jacket as she made her way through the kitchen, leaving him cold and frazzled in the seconds that passed. She draped the mud-splattered jacket over the back of the kitchen chair and turned back, looking at him over her shoulder.

"I'm going to leave the bathroom door unlocked, Logan." She gave him a half grin and then left him alone in the kitchen. He heard the creak of the stair tread as she made her way up to the bathroom. A few seconds later, he heard the water running, and he realized he was still standing in the kitchen like a lovesick teen, hard and aching with need for a woman that left him dying. Except Logan couldn't imagine ever wanting Poppy Ericksen like he did right at that moment.

It was ridiculous. He was a man. Poppy was a beautiful woman. And facts were facts no matter how much they hurt. He was no longer married. And he wanted Poppy. More than he ever had. The thought of her naked body slipping into the tub, getting soapy and wet, was driving him crazy. His groin hardened just thinking about it. And he'd be damned if he was going to stand there and just think.

♥ ♥ ♥

Poppy's heart pounded as she climbed the steps to the bathroom. If Logan didn't get her meaning, then the man was an idiot. And one thing she knew was Logan was no idiot!

It had been years since her heart felt as full and happy as it did today. Racing around the grounds on the ATV with Logan pressed up against her back, laughing and having fun, brought back such wonderful memories that she had to swallow the lump in her throat.

Pausing at the door, she listened ... and heard nothing. Logan wasn't behind her. Disappointment wrapped around her and left her cold. When would they jump that hurdle? Finding Kelly's letters undisturbed on top of the hatbox that morning had her convinced Kelly had been wrong. It was as simple as that. There was no reason to stay and prolong the misery she knew would eventually come.

She'd been prepared to tell Logan she would leave in the morning when she'd watched him get out of his truck after dropping Keith off for a play date. Instead of coming inside, he'd walked through the field. She knew he was going to the pond on the far end of the property; the one where they'd skinny-dipped and were interrupted by Kelly when she'd discovered them there. She was sure she and Logan would have made love that day ... if not for Kelly showing up when she did.

Instead of hiding from her, Logan had spent a glorious afternoon laughing and playing with her. It was exactly what she'd needed to give it one more try, and much more than she'd hoped for when the day had started.

Maybe those secrets didn't have to be told. Maybe all the lies of their past could just stay there … in the past. They could start brand new today.

She wouldn't bring up the letters again. Her and Logan had taken a giant leap today, and Poppy was determined to keep moving forward.

With renewed hope, she quickly stripped herself of her muddy clothes and left them in a heap on the floor. She turned the shower faucet on and waited a few seconds to feel the temperature of the water with her hand before she stepped in the tub and closed the curtain.

Just as she put her head under the spray, she heard, "Is there room in there for me?"

She closed her eyes and felt the tears behind her eyes. Tears of joy that she hadn't dared to feel in many years. *Logan was here with her.* Truly with her.

Taking in a slow breath, she pushed the shower curtain aside and revealed herself to him, body and soul, just as she had the day they'd gone skinny-dipping in the back pond. The look on his face told her that he was back there as if all these years in between had never happened.

Poppy waited for Logan to peel off each layer of his clothes until he, too, was standing there splendidly naked. She stepped aside to make room for him. With one touch, her whole body burned for him as he wrapped his arms around her, gazing into her eyes as if waiting for her to stop him.

"This may be a bad idea," he said.

"You know what a bad idea really is?" she asked.

He shook his head.

"Glorious fun." She smiled and waited for the uncertainty in Logan's expression to melt away before pressing herself against his hot, naked skin. Then she kissed him, forgetting about the past and just relishing in the here and now.

Logan's hand made a hot, slow trail from her shoulder, down her back and to her buttocks. He pulled her ever closer to him and groaned as they connected flesh to flesh, creating an immediate burst of fire inside her. Still, he didn't kiss her. He just watched her face and seemed to revel in her changing expression with each move of his hand across her body.

The spraying water over her face and head made it difficult to see. She strained to open her eyes so she could play this game. She ran her fingers lightly over his shoulders and down his back with one hand as she reached up on her toes to kiss his mouth. He pulled back just a little, a smile playing on the corner of his lips telling her he enjoyed not letting her have her way. With both hands, she cradled his face and pulled him toward her, giving her what she wanted. She breathed in his breath, his soul and all the love that he'd held back for so long. And she gave it right back to him in a kiss so powerful she thought she'd melt right there in his arms.

Cupping her bottom, he lifted her, and in one swift move, pressed her back against the cold shower wall, crushing her in place. The feel of cold tile against her back and hot skin against her chest was amazing. All her senses were alive and wanting to feel. Feel nothing but Logan and everything he was giving to her.

She lifted her face to him, and his mouth came down over hers, tasting her, devouring every bit of her, claiming her. And still she wanted more. She dug her fingers into his wet hair and pulled him ever closer, breathing in the scent of him, loving the feel of his tongue against hers.

He kissed her neck, her shoulders and then made a trail of kisses down to her chest. Cupping her breast in his hand, he pulled her nipple into his mouth and sucked gently, then used his tongue to ease the fury growing inside her until he went back for more. Tension built up inside her until she couldn't take it anymore. She pulled his head up to hers and kissed him again as his hand made a journey down her stomach and between her legs to the place where she was most on fire. The fire exploded into an inferno with his delicate ministrations.

Just when she thought she couldn't take any more, he cupped her bottom with both hands and lifted her. She wrapped her arms around him as he held her against the cold shower wall, both submerged in the hot spray of water.

And when Logan finally entered her with a hard thrust, Poppy cried out in pure delight. He filled her completely in every way, making her whole after what seemed a lifetime of being empty. With each thrust of his hips he took her higher, ever higher until Poppy thought she would self-combust. And then she did as her orgasm ripped through her, leaving her fighting to breathe. Seconds later, Logan held her tighter, and breathing faster, he joined her in bliss.

Chapter Six

Poppy couldn't remember the last time she'd felt happiness so deeply. Surely she'd been happy as an adult, but most all of her deeply held moments of happiness had happened right here in Rudolph. The sudden realization of that should have made her sad. Instead, she just stood at the kitchen sink and looked out the window up at the night sky, allowing herself to fully feel contentment.

"What's so interesting out there?" Logan asked, coming up behind her.

"The sky."

He leaned forward, looking over her shoulder. She reached both hands behind her to hold him in place. If she lived a hundred years she'd never forget the feel of Logan being as close to her as they'd been today.

Chuckling he said, "You can't see a thing from in here. Come on."

He grabbed their jackets from the hooks and handed hers to her. Since her boots were covered in caked on mud that she hadn't had the chance to clean yet due to an afternoon of lovemaking, she stepped out onto the porch in her woolen socks and held the door, waiting for Logan to follow.

"Now that the sun is gone, it's freezing outside," Logan said, slipping into his jacket.

"I think it might snow. No stars," she said, pouting. "Not like the time we climbed on top of the porch roof to watch the meteor shower that summer night."

"That was pretty spectacular. But we'll have to stay off the porch roof until I have a chance to check it for ice damage. Not that there would be much to see anyway. We haven't had many cloudless nights lately with all the rain."

"I miss looking up at the dark sky and seeing that massive array of stars. I used to sit at my bedroom window when I was little and couldn't sleep just looking at them all night. We certainly don't get stars in Manhattan like here in South Dakota," she said, looking up at the dark sky.

"I couldn't live there," he said.

She glanced at him, but his face was dark and unreadable. His voice said it all. "I know," she said. "I honestly didn't know how long I'd last there myself."

"I thought you loved New York. Kelly said that you ..."

She cut him off before he could finish. "I went to the city because I was offered a good job."

"You must really love your job then ... I mean to stay there so long."

"You can get a good job anywhere. It's just a job."

She hugged her middle, not wanting to talk about what he knew through Kelly. Poppy wanted Logan to hear her life, her desires from her.

"Long Island is nice though. We didn't live on the water, but it was always nice to be close to the ocean. It's nothing like swimming out here in the ponds in Rudolph."

"Not as private though."

She chuckled. "No, definitely not that. Some of the beaches barely have enough room to spread out a towel in the summer. But the ocean was a different experience. Kelly and I took Keith to the beach a few summers ago while she was visiting. She was still healthy then."

Logan became quiet, turning away. "She didn't mention it. I've never been to the ocean."

"Then I have a reason to drag you and Keith out to Long Island. Or New York City. Keith's a bit young still, but there are a lot of things he might enjoy."

"I really can't imagine you there."

"Really?"

"I didn't mean it the way it sounded." He laughed and scratched the back of his neck. "You just seem to fit so much more here. I guess I can't imagine it any other way."

"I don't think I fit very well at first. But like everything else, you get used to it. You adapt. You find something about it to love and make it your home. Home is where the people you love are, and that's where my parents live now."

"You have people who love you here," he said quietly. "You always did."

"That's nice to hear."

"I was ... really surprised you didn't come back to South Dakota." He paused a moment. "Why didn't you?"

Poppy played their conversation about her reasons for staying in New York and the letters from Kelly over in her mind. "That's for some other time," she finally said, not wanting to spoil the mood.

"Was there someone who kept you there? Or is that for some other time, too."

"There has never been anyone in my life special enough to keep me from coming back to Rudolph," she said.

He didn't look away, and she wished the porch light was on so she could read his expression so she would know Logan understood her meaning.

"All these years. There had to have been someone in your life."

She sighed. "Why are you pushing this? Not everyone is as lucky to find love. You and Kelly were ..."

"We were good partners."

Poppy sputtered. "Well, hell, that was real romantic."

He shrugged. "I'm not a fancy talker. You know that. But Kel and I were good friends. We worked well together. I know too many couples who don't even like each other."

"True."

"But enough about that. Didn't you ever get lonely?"

"You just don't let up, do you? Logan, it's a city with over eight million people in it. The sidewalks were crawling with people day and night. If I wanted to share a meal, all I had to do was go to one of the local neighborhood restaurants. I always knew someone there. Actually, it's really not unlike going to your mom's diner where you know people you grew up with your whole life. Just not as long a wait for a table."

"You're comparing my mother's restaurant with Manhattan?"

"It's not as homey. I'll give you that."

"You're avoiding my question."

"Am not."

He grabbed the railing with both hands and looked out into the darkness. "Kelly told me you were engaged a while back. Whatever happened to that?"

Poppy reached up and touched Logan's arm. He turned and looked at her face, and she hoped he could see her fully. It was all lies. She knew that, but Logan didn't.

"I was never engaged. Ever. I've never even gotten close."

"Never?"

Truths. Did they all really need to come out now? When she came here to Rudolph, she believed it was important in order for both of them to move on. But the shocked look on Logan's face told her he didn't know what to believe. Would he believe her? Did she even stand a chance at getting him to understand the truth without dividing him from the love he'd felt for the mother of his child? After today, she wasn't sure it mattered anymore.

Visibly uncomfortable, he moved on. "The few times we saw each other over the years, you never came back with a friend. Is our small town life so embarrassing that you'd prefer to keep your city friends away?"

Her stomach fell. "Is that what you thought all this time? Honestly, I don't know what you think of me when you talk like that. I talk about South Dakota to my friends all the time. But most of the people I know back East love the city, the theater and the museums. I love that, too. I've come to love it. Unless you've grown up in a place like this, you don't have a true appreciation for the beauty of it all. To some of them, it might as well be a foreign planet."

He sighed. "It's been looking like it these last couple of weeks. Every time I drive into town it feels like I'm in some crazy science fiction world with destruction everywhere. It's like nature put a huge scar on what used to be Rudolph. I wonder if it will ever be the same."

"Give it time. Time heals." Her eyes widened as she looked out into the yard. "It's snowing!"

She jumped off the porch in her stocking feet and started spinning with her face turned up to the sky. Yes, time heals all and washes away the stains of the past.

Would anything be left behind? Poppy didn't want to think about it anymore. She just wanted to laugh and to feel.

♥ ♥ ♥

"Woman, you are crazy!" Logan said, laughing. He watched Poppy dancing around in the yard in her socks. With her arms stretched open wide, she spun and laughed as she caught snowflakes on her tongue.

She was every bit as beautiful as she'd been as a teen, and it took his breath away just watching her. Earlier, when she was warm and naked in his arms, when he pressed himself against her and then entered her, he thought he'd died and gone to heaven. He'd wanted her so bad, had dreamed about it for so long, and he still wanted her.

Nothing had changed. All these years he'd been a fool to think he could forget about Poppy and happily live his life as if she'd never been a part of it. And he had to some extent, especially after Keith had been born. But there had been a part of him that had been dead inside. Until now. He didn't want to think about her leaving and going back to New York. He didn't want to think about anything but how to get Poppy naked and in his arms again.

She stopped her spinning and looked up at him. The moisture from melting snowflakes against her warm skin glistened from the light streaming out from the kitchen window. "What are you waiting for? Get out here with me!"

Logan couldn't help himself. He jumped off the porch and scooped her up in his arms, his heart feeling so full he thought it might actually burst. He spun Poppy around, laughing hard, feeling the fresh air in his lungs and breathing in the very essence of this woman who had haunted his dreams for years.

And later, he'd brought her upstairs and made love to her all over again. At first, his passion for her overtook his control, and they loved each other hard and with wild abandon. All the sweet passion he'd always seen in Poppy came alive in their lovemaking. And then he loved her again, this time slow. He wanted to know every inch of her as if he were imprinting himself on her, ruining her for no other man.

As he lay next to her in the dark, listening to her breathing as she slept, he thought of the letters on the hatbox, and for the first time, what was written in them mattered. *I was never engaged. I've never even gotten close.*

How could that be? So many of his decisions over the years had been made because Logan had believed Poppy had moved on and left him behind.

He recalled Kelly's confession years ago. He'd packed his bags and was determined to go after Poppy.

"I probably should tell you this," Kelly had said. "But I just don't want you to drive all the way out to New York and get your heart stomped on. Poppy is crazy in love with this guy she met at college. His name is Gary. They're together all the time. They're practically engaged."

And yet, when he hadn't believed Kelly and called Poppy's house later that night, Poppy's mother said she was out with Gary *again* and she didn't know when Poppy would be home.

He'd spent the whole summer that year saving his money working odd jobs so he could buy a car and have enough left over to get an apartment. The cost of living in the New York suburb where Kelly's parents had moved to was much higher than South Dakota. He figured he'd get a job doing something, anything, when he got out there. Young and stubborn, he'd wanted to prove to Poppy that he could make his own way.

He'd never made it out of the driveway. He couldn't understand why Poppy had never mentioned this other man to him. They'd talked on the phone. She'd always talked about coming home. And when she hadn't, he'd decided to go after her. Until …

She's practically engaged.

Logan couldn't stand the thought of another man touching Poppy. He'd been shipwrecked that night, body and soul, and ended up getting drunker than he'd ever been down by the creek. He couldn't remember much about that night, but he knew that Kelly had stayed with him, listening to him. It was the night he'd kissed her for the first time. That much he remembered, but nothing more. So many times he'd wished he could remember more. He needed to remember.

The next day everything about him reeked of alcohol and pity. And he couldn't remember a damned thing that had happened. *Even when Kelly had told him.* He could see how happy Kelly had been about what had taken place the night before, but Logan just felt sick. He had wondered just what kind of bastard he was that he'd take pleasure with a sweet friend just to get over his misery about losing Poppy. No one was more surprised than he was when Kelly told him weeks later that she was pregnant. They were married a month later. A week after that, she'd had a miscarriage.

He rubbed his face in the dark as if it would wipe his sins clean. It all seemed like a blur now. And every move he'd made since then hinged on that one night when ... *That's for another time*, Poppy had said. *I've never been engaged.*

What the hell was that all about? Poppy had urged him to read the letters last night, and he'd refused. Part of him didn't want to know the deep secrets shared between these two friends.

You didn't know everything, Logan. I didn't either.

Did he want to know now? Did it even matter after all this time?

Easing himself off the bed, he slowly made his way across the room. He paused by the closet to pick up the hatbox and the stack of letters Poppy had left on top. He didn't bother getting dressed, not wanting to disturb Poppy as she slept. Naked, he picked up the hatbox and letters and crept out of the bedroom and down the hall. He quickly pulled on a pair of gray sweatpants and a sweatshirt and carefully walked downstairs to the living room.

As he dropped to the sofa, with the hatbox and letters on the coffee table in front of him, he wondered for a brief moment if he should wake Poppy. These letters were important to her. And for some reason, they'd been important to Kelly, otherwise she wouldn't have kept them. But what could possibly be in these letters that Poppy would need to explain?

He pulled the lid off the hatbox and his heart stopped. The box held a sweatshirt, a stack of pictures, and an envelope in Kelly's handwriting … addressed to him.

♥ ♥ ♥

It was surprisingly cold when Poppy woke up. Reaching her hand across the bed, she found she was alone, and her heart stopped. *Logan was gone.*

If she lived to be a hundred years old, she'd never forget the way Logan had made love to her tonight. Logan had asked her about the men in her life, and over the years, there'd been a few. But no one special. None of them ever touched her heart the way Logan had. No one had ever loved her or made her feel his love the way Logan had tonight.

She ran her hand over her swollen breast, almost feeling the imprint of his hands caressing them as he had earlier or the way his mouth had loved them exquisitely.

She wanted him back in her bed, loving her again. No matter how much he'd given her, no matter how much her body ached from his lovemaking, she wanted more.

In the quiet night, she listened for sounds of him in the house. When she couldn't hear anything, she decided to go look for him. Poppy quickly got out of bed. Naked, she made her way to the closet to retrieve her bathrobe, but stopped short. Something was missing. In the dark, she couldn't tell. Reaching into the closet, she flicked on the light and turned around. The bed was unmade. Her clothes and Logan's were still scattered on the floor.

And then it hit her. Pushing the blanket off her, she bolted out of bed and ran to the closet, her heart in her throat. She searched the top shelf and found an empty space. She looked around the floor. Nothing. She didn't know where Logan was, but she knew what he was doing. The hatbox and all the letters were gone.

The creak in the stair tread told him Poppy was awake. He sat in the living room; pages of a long letter that was written long ago were spread out on the floor in front of him. No matter how he tried to piece it all together and make sense of it, Logan just couldn't.

When he looked up, Poppy was standing in the doorway. The robe she'd put on was wrapped tight around her as if to protect her from what was to come.

"You knew about this?" he asked.

"It's not exactly bestseller material, huh?"

Her attempt at a joke fell flat. All he felt was emptiness.

"When did you know?"

She took a deep breath. "Which part?"

"Part? All of it. All the lies."

"Kelly told me after she was diagnosed with cancer."

"You were ... never engaged. You were never going to marry some guy you met in college."

"Gary?" She rolled her eyes. "No, I couldn't stand the guy."

"Who was he?"

"Does it matter?"

He swallowed hard. "Yes. She said you talked about him all the time."

"I did. I was saddled with him on a project for my chemistry class. I was never so happy as I was when that semester was over."

"What about New York City? Why didn't you come back to Rudolph like you said you were going to? I waited for you."

She shook her head, her brows drawn together with a look of confusion. "It's all there, Logan. Didn't you read my letters?"

"There are no letters here from you. Only Kelly's letter to me."

Her mouth dropped open. "Of course there are letters. Kelly told me she saved my letters. She said they'd explain it all. They have to be in the hatbox."

He lifted the box to show her the contents.

"I wrote to her all the ... I kept her letters." Poppy took a deep breath. "She left you a letter?"

"I was on my way to New York City to see you. I was all ready to live there and see if we could ..."

"I know."

He looked at her hard. "When did you know?"

"After. When Kelly got sick."

"Why didn't you tell me?" His voice was accusing, and he knew deep down Poppy didn't deserve that.

"Logan, Kelly was dying! What good would it have done to tell you the truth then? I could barely understand everything that happened."

"Is that why you didn't come to her funeral?"

"I couldn't ... face you. I couldn't know what I knew and be near you. I was so torn apart by Kelly's betrayal and then her death that I just ... I just couldn't, Logan."

"I wanted you to be there. I needed you at the very least as my friend. If anything, I thought we at least had that."

"I know. But what was I supposed to do? Tell you at the funeral? You were grieving for your wife, Logan. Did you really think that telling you that your life was a lie then was going to matter? You wouldn't have believed me. You would have hated me."

"I did hate you. Because I thought you didn't give a damn. She was never pregnant. Did she tell you that?"

"Yes."

He picked up the letter from Kelly that he'd read with horror. "She'd made up the whole thing to keep me from going to New York. Did she tell you that, too?"

"Not at first. She knew you wouldn't run out on your responsibilities, Logan. She knew you'd never leave Rudolph or her if she was carrying your child. And she was right."

Logan bolted from the sofa and started to pace. "I didn't remember that night. I was so drunk I could barely move. I was shocked when she told me we'd made love and …" He looked at Poppy and saw the pain on her face. He'd been married to Kelly. He had a child with her. They'd built a life together. But looking back on that day, he'd always felt as if he'd betrayed Poppy, not Kelly. "I didn't sleep with her until after we were married. "

Poppy looked away. "She told me."

"What else did she tell you?" Tears filled her eyes, but he pushed her harder. "What are you not telling me?"

"That first summer when I was supposed to come back to Rudolph and stay with Kelly …"

"What?"

"She told me not to come. By the end of the summer she said the two of you were dating."

He looked at her in disbelief. "And you believed her?"

"She sent me a picture of her sitting on your lap. Logan, she was here, and I was in New York. I wasn't here to see what was really happening. And I had no reason not to believe her."

He closed his eyes. "That picture was taken before you left Rudolph. Ethan took that picture, and then Denny picked her up off my lap and tossed her into the pond. You came down to the pond right after that, don't you remember?"

She nodded. "That was before Denny had that accident and Ethan left for the military. She was so pissed off with Ethan and Denny that she didn't talk to either one of them for a month."

"Not until Ethan gave her the picture." Poppy shook her head with the memory. "I'd forgotten all about that picture."

"We weren't dating." Logan thought back to their entire relationship with sadness. "Kelly and I never dated. We just got married. How crazy is that?"

"Every time I called your house you weren't home."

"I was working like a dog, trying to save every penny so I could …"

"Why didn't you ever tell me?"

He thought back with regret and sank back onto the sofa. "I wanted to surprise you. To prove myself to you. I sure proved myself, huh?"

Poppy sat down next to him on the sofa.

"I was crushed, Logan. I wanted to be happy for Kelly. But when she told me the two of you were getting married … I was inconsolable. I avoided her for a while. I … didn't want to think about the two of you being happy together. I know that sounds awful. But then when she told me about the miscarriage …"

"That night she told me you were engaged changed everything."

A sheen of moisture filled Poppy's eyes. "She lied to both of us, Logan. I never realized how much she was in love with you or the lengths she was willing to go to keep you in Rudolph. I only knew that I loved you. What else was I supposed to believe? I trusted Kelly."

He had too. "I was on my way to you that night. Did she tell you that? I can barely remember that night other than her stopping me in the driveway as I was about to drive off, and telling me you were in love with someone else. I couldn't stand the thought of another man's hands on you. I was so tired from working and … my truck was all packed, and I would have driven all night. But then she stopped me."

"She thought she was going to lose you."

"She didn't have me then."

"You married her."

"She was pregnant." He picked up the letters he'd spread in front of him on the floor and fisted them in his hands. "But that was a lie. My whole life with her was a lie." He looked up at the ceiling and yelled, "Why Kelly?"

Poppy looked at him. "You had to have come to love her or you wouldn't have stayed married to her."

He had loved Kelly. There had been so many times during their marriage where it would have been easy for him to jump ship, tell Kelly it had all been a mistake. He'd certainly felt that way many times, and to this day the guilt of it ate him up inside knowing he hadn't given her enough of what she'd deserved.

Kelly never complained. And in the end he stayed. There were reasons that always made sense at the time. Kelly was depressed over the miscarriage. He couldn't leave her then. Then she couldn't get pregnant, and he felt he owed her to at least try. Then she'd gotten pregnant with Keith.

He didn't have Poppy, and he'd convinced himself if he only tried a little harder, he could make his marriage to Kelly work and be the husband she deserved. Things had gotten better once Keith was born. But was he truly happy?

"Why did she do this? Kelly wasn't a mean person."

And yet it was all there in Kelly's handwriting. They'd been husband and wife. The marriage may not have been perfect, but they'd been friends, and he always believed that was something. Now he knew he never knew Kelly at all.

Poppy picked up the letters Kelly had sent her. They were still wrapped in ribbon and tied in a bow.

She looked up at him, confusion on her face. "Either you got really good at gift wrapping or you didn't read these letters."

"I can't read those. Those were Kelly's letters to you."

"I want you to. I don't know exactly what she said to you in her letter to you, but maybe these will explain more about what drove Kelly to do what she did."

She sighed. "Even after all this time, even after hearing it from Kelly, it's still hard to believe. When I look back, I regret a lot of things, Logan. I should have questioned her. I should have tried harder to reach you to get the truth from you. I was angry with her for a long time after she told me. But she was my best friend. I took her word on blind faith. Why wouldn't I? Even when I went to see her in the hospital at the end, I still didn't want to believe it was true."

"You went … to the hospital? You saw her when she was sick?"

"Of course, I did. I had to at least try to make this right. I don't think I could have lived with myself if I hadn't. Did you really think I'd just let Kelly die without having the chance to say goodbye?"

"I don't know anything anymore. Whatever I thought before I read that letter …"

"It took me a long time to forgive her, Logan. I don't even think I truly did while she was still alive. But I did eventually and …"

"What?"

"I promised her I'd come back. On her deathbed, she begged me, and I made that promise to her. So here I am."

"Because Kelly asked you to."

She nodded. "I didn't want to at first. I couldn't face you. I was angry with her. Angry with you. Angry with myself. It was killing me. Everything I'd believed, every decision I'd made ..." Poppy sighed and shook her head as if she was somewhere else other than in that room. "Logan, she'd begged me. I thought that I'd gotten over you long ago after the initial pain of hearing that you and Kelly had gotten married wore off. She always told me you two were so much in love."

He turned away.

"Don't," she said. "Tonight is the night for the truth. I think there have been enough lies and secrets over the years, don't you? If we can't be honest now, what's left?"

He couldn't argue with that, so he simply nodded.

"She told me you both were happy," she said.

"She was happy. At least I thought she was." Logan got up and paced the floor. "I ..."

"What?"

"I wasn't ... I grew to love Kelly," he said, watching Poppy's expression.

But only when he'd pushed his feelings for Poppy out of his mind. The thought of how he'd still thought of Poppy while being married to Kelly had eaten him up inside for years.

Poppy nodded and smiled; a reaction Logan wasn't expecting. Somehow he'd expected her to be jealous, maybe as disgusted with him as he'd been with himself for so long. He'd certainly been jealous enough over the years listening to stories about the men in Poppy's life. Although after reading this letter, Logan wondered just how many of those stories were fiction, much like the novels that Kelly always read.

"I'm glad. I'd hate to think she did all this for nothing."

Anger simmered inside him, making him want to lash out at someone or something. Except the person he needed to confront wasn't there. "She manipulated me into marrying her under false pretenses."

The emotional mess he was caught in was just as devastating as the mess from the flood. Everything was spinning out of control. Everything he believed, everything he'd been able to count on for the past eight years evaporated. Numbness overtook the shock he felt, and Logan wished he could dial back to another time where life was real.

He'd loved Poppy tonight in a way he'd never loved any woman. Not even Kelly. And at that moment, he wished Poppy had never come to Rudolph again. How was he ever going to get his equilibrium back and go on with a life that had kept him putting one foot in front of the other for over a year?

Poppy didn't know when it happened exactly. But somewhere between the journey downstairs and now, she'd lost Logan. He wasn't angry with her the way he'd been when she'd first arrived a few days ago. Instead, he'd retreated somewhere and shut her out with his sudden silence.

Poppy extended her hand to him. "Come back to bed. Keith will be back bright and early. We don't have to figure everything out tonight."

Emotional fatigue dragged him down. "Not just yet. You go."

Poppy looked at Logan and knew the connection that had fused them all afternoon had been broken.

"Logan you're exhausted," she said, desperate to hold on to what they had a short time ago.

"I just need some time."

Without her. Poppy nodded. "Don't be long, okay? It'll be light soon."

"Keith is coming home early."

She stood before Logan and bent over to kiss his mouth, but he turned away. And she wanted to die.

"How long are you staying?" he asked, looking up at her with eyes filled with emotion she couldn't decipher.

"I don't know. That all depends."

"On what?"

She took a deep breath. "On you, I guess."

He bent his head and looked at his hands.

"Goodnight, Poppy."

With each step she took upstairs, her feet dragged behind letting the happiness she'd felt all day slip away. And her world had shattered all over again.

Chapter Seven

She'd lay in bed alone the rest of the night as she knew she would. She'd tossed in bed, hearing movement downstairs and then the door slam before light started to illuminate the room. She hadn't slept but for those few short hours after she and Logan had made love and then she'd awoken alone.

Dragging herself out of bed, she quickly dressed into a fresh pair of jeans, pulled on an oversized sweater, slipped into her sneakers, sans socks, and made her way downstairs. The living room looked much as it did last night. The long letter from Kelly that Logan was reading when she'd found him was spread out on the floor again. The paper was wrinkled and looked as if it had been smoothed out again. The letters Kelly had written to her were still wrapped in the ribbon she'd tied together with a neat bow.

Walking the length of the hallway to the kitchen, she'd hoped to find Logan sitting at the kitchen table, but was disappointed to find it empty. She pushed the curtains to the window over the sink back so she could get a better view of the barn. The red barn doors were open.

Keith was going to be home soon, and Poppy desperately needed to talk to Logan before they both had to pretend everything was normal in front of family and friends. Without the bother of her jacket, she stepped out onto the porch and quickly made her way out to the barn, hugging her middle to ward off the bitter chill of the South Dakota morning.

"Logan?" she called out as she stepped through the door. It took a second for her eyes to adjust to the difference in light, but then she saw him. His jacket was hung on a hook on a beam, and he was mopping the floor of a stall with such force that beads of sweat were pouring down the sides of his face. His shirt was soaked.

Poppy slowly walked toward him. He didn't stop working until she was standing just in front of him. He slammed the mop into the bucket and dragged it over to the next stall, pausing for a second before acknowledging she was even there.

"Talk to me, Logan."

"I'm no good right now, Poppy," he said. Such pain. In every move he made, she could see it, feel it.

"I understand how you feel."

He looked at her as if she were crazy. "How could you? I've spent the entire time I was married to Kelly beating myself up because I thought I'd saddled her with a loveless marriage. I couldn't be the husband she wanted. She was so good and so determined, and she loved me. She told me all the time. And every time she did it made me want to work harder to give her what she deserved. And I beat myself up because I knew I could never give her what she truly wanted. And now I find … You just don't understand, Poppy. She lied to both of us, but for me it was different."

"I understand more than you know, Logan. I've had a year to come to grips with all that happened. You've only just found out the life you lived was a lie."

"That's just it, it wasn't. Not all of it."

Shocked, she had to steady herself against the wooden rail to keep from falling.

"Kelly and I might have gotten together for all the wrong reasons. But we stayed together for the right reason. Keith. I could have left her before that. Neither one of us was happy. But after Keith was born, it was like we had a purpose. And we were both okay with that. It wasn't just Kelly's fault. Hawk was right. I became numb to what I wanted, to being that man full of passion and adventure that I was when I was younger. Now I'm thinking that man only existed when I was with you."

"What are you saying?"

"I wasn't in love with Kelly when I married her. That much was true. That hurts me probably as much as it hurt her. But not everything was bad. We were good together. And if she hadn't gotten sick, if you hadn't come back, we probably could have lived our whole lives content with that."

"Is that all you want in life? To be *content*? What happened to the man I knew? You were there with me yesterday. Listen to yourself, please!"

"I did. Last night after you went back to bed I came out here and yelled at Kelly. Yelled at the sky. And then yelled at myself more. We started out a lie. The friendship, the trust I thought was there was a lie. It was bad for a long time, but in the end we became a family."

His words were like a cold dagger to her heart. *We became a family.* And that family didn't include her. It never did.

She cleared her throat and fought to hold back her tears. "So what was yesterday all about?"

His expression warmed, and she waited to hear the words she so desperately needed to hear. That Logan was in love with her and had always been. That he would love her forever and that they would have many years of making love and playing in the sun as they had yesterday. He was so transparent with her, naked with emotion that it was hard to breathe.

"Yesterday was wonderful. It was a dream."

Her mouth dropped open. "A dream? That's it?"

"Do you ever wonder why we didn't let ourselves take that next step while you were still here? Why didn't we? You left, and it became clear to me that I wanted you. And believe me, I wanted you with ever fiber of my being. Why didn't we ever act on that?"

She didn't have the answer to that, and it's one she'd struggled with herself. "We were young, still figuring things out. Our friendship was everything, and it grew. Just because we didn't act on how we felt back then doesn't mean what we felt wasn't real. Everything about us, everything we did was full of passion."

"Maybe what we had back then was all it was meant to be."

She couldn't breathe. What was he saying to her? "So was making love to me yesterday your way of finally getting me out of your system? Unfulfilled passion finally realized."

The corner of his lips lifted to a bittersweet smile. "Passion. We always had that," he said softly.

"That's not all we had. Before Kelly—"

"What Kelly did was wrong, but it's always going to be there, Poppy. I can't wish it away without erasing everything that's good in my life now."

"Keith," she said."

"Lie or no lie, Keith is my life. Kelly will always be a part of my life because of him. Where do we go from here? How do you make something like that right without erasing the past? I can't do that.

"Regret is a tough thing to live with. I should know. I've lived with it for a long time. I thought I'd gotten past it. Maybe I will again. But to die with it is even worse. You said you forgave Kelly. She never even gave me the chance. Don't you see? You didn't come back for me, Poppy. You came back because Kelly asked you to."

She swallowed hard, trying to keep her emotion down. "Even now that Kelly is gone, she's still standing between us."

To his credit, Logan didn't turn away.

"She's still the one who is calling the shots, and she's not even here anymore. And I don't know how I feel about any of it."

Poppy cleared her throat before she dared to speak. "I guess that settles it. I've fulfilled my promise to Kelly. I came back like she wanted me to. Now you know the truth. I guess there's nothing left to say. I'll see about getting a flight out of Rapid City as soon as possible."

She turned and walked out of the barn. Rounding the corner, she placed a hand on the barn door and listened, waiting. She drew in a slow breath of cold March air. Nothing. Logan hadn't said another word. And he didn't come after her. *Again.* It was more than clear to Poppy now that Kelly had been wrong all along.

♥ ♥ ♥

Logan so desperately wanted to run to Poppy. And yet, he wished to God she'd never come back to Rudolph. Having her leave this time hurt worse than it did all those years ago. At least then he'd had hope.

He couldn't reconcile his feelings about what Kelly had done. He only knew that deep down, his feelings for Poppy had never changed. He knew that now. And worst of all, Kelly knew it.

I never had a miscarriage after we were married because I was never pregnant in the first place. I lied to you because I loved you so much, and I thought I was going to lose you forever.

The anger Logan felt inside was consuming. Anger for what Kelly did and anger with himself for not seeing it.

I thought if I could just get pregnant, we'd be a family and you'd stay. I thought I loved enough for both of us. I was wrong. It wasn't fair to you. I knew you weren't happy and that only made it harder for me to tell you the truth. I'm so sorry. I hope in time you won't hate me.

He didn't hate Kelly. He had loved her, but she was right. He'd never truly been *in love* with Kelly. Not the way he should have been. He'd worked so hard to make her happy, thinking that would be enough. But now he knew for sure he'd failed only because he'd known for the first time what true happiness was yesterday when he'd been with Poppy. And Kelly had known all along.

Even now, all I have to do is mention Poppy's name and I can see it in your eyes. You love her. You've always loved her. And a big part of you wished you'd married her instead of me.

Guilt ate at him to the very core. Kelly had settled for less than she deserved. And he'd settled too. He couldn't be angry with her about that either any more than he could wish Kelly hadn't done what she'd done. He wouldn't have his son otherwise.

Where did that leave Poppy? Kelly had betrayed her, too. And every single day Keith would be a reminder of Kelly and how she'd betrayed her best friend. How could he saddle Poppy with that? How could they ever get past that betrayal and have a future? He couldn't wrap his mind around it even knowing he wouldn't change a thing if it meant he wouldn't have Keith.

Yesterday had been amazing, a gift from God. Logan had dreamed of loving Poppy for more years than he wanted to admit. That was something he'd hold onto for the rest of his life. And now she was leaving.

The sound of the truck horn beeping as it came up the driveway startled him. It was only then that he realized he'd been crying. He wiped his face and took a few deep breaths to collect himself before walking out of the barn. The cold air hit him hard, and he welcomed it. At least he wasn't numb. He didn't want Poppy to leave. But the little guy who was smiling at him from the truck was the only thing that was going to ground him right now and he needed that in order to move ahead.

"Hi, Daddy!" he heard Keith say with excitement from the back seat of his mom's truck.

Kate McKinnon's concerned look gave him pause until he turned to see Poppy dragging her suitcase through the doorway while trying to keep the screen door from closing back on her. Kate rolled down the window as the truck stopped. "Now what did you do?"

"What makes you think I did something?" he said, opening the back door and undoing Keith's booster seat.

"There's no way Poppy Ericksen would be carrying that suitcase out the door otherwise."

Logan pulled Keith into his arms and gave him a squeeze before placing him down on the ground. Keith immediately saw Poppy and ran over to her.

"I'm going to need Donna to come out and watch Keith while I do some work. I need to finish disinfecting the barn floor and let it dry out before I can put the horses back inside. Can you spare her tomorrow?"

"We're pretty busy at the diner. More people coming into town means more people to feed. Maybe Donna can watch Keith and Alex together again. They'd played good yesterday."

"Yeah, sure," he said, grabbing Keith's backpack of clothes and toys, then slamming the door shut.

"What's going on?" Kate asked.

"Nothing."

"Don't *nothing* me. You and Ethan always thought you were getting something over on me, and I always knew when you were up to no good."

"She's going back to New York."

With a raised eyebrow, Kate said, "That's all?"

"Yeah."

"Then why is she crying?"

Logan turned quickly just as Keith launched himself into Poppy's open arms. He didn't have to be close to see it was true. Or to know that he'd been the one to cause her tears this time, not Kelly.

"Auntie Poppy, do you have a hurt?" Keith asked, his face serious as he hugged her.

Poppy reached down to give Keith a hug that warmed her heart. This little guy was so open hearted and so sensitive. The last thing she wanted to do was burden him with worry.

"A little one, but it's all better now with this nice big hug."

Keith smiled. "Grammie got me a new movie."

"We'll have to watch it together later," Logan said, walking up to them. He looked at the suitcase, then at Poppy. "Say, Keith, why don't you go into the house with Grammie and see if she can get that movie started on the TV."

"Yeah! Come on, Grammie!" Keith called out as he quickly climbed up the stairs.

"I'm right behind you, sweetie." His mother took Keith's backpack from Logan's hand and smiled at Poppy. "Why don't you forget that bag and come on in the house. I'll make you both some breakfast."

Poppy didn't say anything. Her jaw was tight as if she were holding back her emotion. To her credit, Kate didn't press the issue. She left the decision up to Poppy. Instead, she walked into the house jabbering to Keith about how he was getting big enough to help her unpack his clothes and toys from the backpack and put them away.

"When you said you were leaving, I didn't think you meant right this second. What's your hurry?" Logan said.

"I didn't think prolonging this ... whatever it is, was going to make things any easier. So why not just leave now. There's got to be a flight leaving out of Rapid City this afternoon."

"And if there isn't?"

She lifted her chin. "I'm used to doing things myself, Logan. I didn't have a *partner* to help me."

"What do you want to do, hang around the airport all day and all night until there's a flight?"

"If I have to."

"That's ridiculous. If you insist on leaving, at least make sure you have a flight before you take off. I mean, my mother is making pancakes and you know she's not going to let you leave until you eat."

"Logan."

"I don't want you to leave. Not like this." His admission surprised even him. The internal tug of war he'd been feeling all morning had him working hard just to break him somehow. And he didn't even know why.

Poppy glanced back at the house and then at him. "I'll have breakfast," she conceded. "I need to say good-bye to Keith anyway. I don't want him to think I'm just running off. He won't understand. Let me just get the bag in my trunk."

"I have it," he said, grabbing the handle of her suitcase. His hand connected with hers and immediately felt like an electric shock running through him. She lifted her gaze to him, and he knew in an instant that she felt it too. But then, just as she had on the day she arrived, she lifted her chin to him in challenge.

"I've got it," she said, pulling at the suitcase as she turned to walk in the other direction. Not wanting to let go of the tiny connection he had with her, Logan hesitated before letting go. But as he did, Poppy pulled in the other direction harder than she needed to and lost her footing when he released the bag. She went crashing down to the ground, toppling over the suitcase as she tried to right herself.

With his heart in his throat, he ran to her side to help her up. "Are you alright?"

"I'm fine," she said, slightly winded from the fall. Logan took both hands to help her to her feet. But as she put her weight down on her foot, it gave out and she slid to the ground again, wincing in pain.

"Where does it hurt?"

She closed her eyes. "My ankle. I stepped on this dried rut in the ground, and my foot just turned."

He heard the sound of the screen door opening and little feet jumping onto the porch. Logan turned and saw Kate standing on the porch with Keith, a worried look on her face.

"Is she okay?" Kate asked.

"Call Hawk," he said.

"No, it's fine," Poppy said. "I'll be fine."

"Sure you will. And Hawk will confirm that when he gets here. We'll put some ice on your ankle to keep the swelling down and just keep you off your feet."

Bending over, he picked Poppy up in his arms and held her tight. "Put your arms around my neck."

She did as she was told. Her face was incredibly close to his. He could feel her breath on his cheek, warming his skin against the cold wind.

"I didn't do this on purpose, Logan."

"It was an accident."

"I can still leave."

He climbed the porch and walked through the door as his mom held it open.

Keith looked up at Poppy with the same worried face Logan had seen many times before Kelly had died and Logan would have to carry her to bed.

"Auntie Poppy's going to be fine, little man. She just needs to rest. Everything is going to be fine."

And if he said it enough to himself, maybe he could will it to be true.

Keith snuggled up next to Poppy on the bed and looked at the stack of photos she'd brought with her to share with him. Hawk had come and gone and confirmed that Poppy's ankle was a sprain and as long as she didn't go dancing, there was no reason she couldn't take a plane home to New York tomorrow. She had one more night in the old house, and then she'd be gone. Logan had spent the day working outside, so she chose to spend her last night there sharing memories of Kelly with Keith.

"That's Mommy," he said, quietly pointing to a picture of Kelly and Poppy when they were in high school.

"That's right," she said. "And that is me."

It was one of the few pictures she had of just her and Kelly. Most all of the pictures she had were of her and Logan, or the three of them.

"Your mommy and daddy and me were always together back then." Poppy pulled out another picture from the pile and handed it to Keith. "See? I think this was a picture your Uncle Ethan took of us when we went to a carnival a couple of towns away."

Keith giggled. "Daddy's wearing a funny hat!"

"It's a sombrero. He won it playing a carnival game. He does look a little goofy in it, doesn't he?" They both laughed. She handed him another picture.

"Who's this with Daddy and Uncle Ethan?" Keith said, pulling a picture out of the pile.

Poppy looked at the picture and smiled bittersweet. "That was your Uncle Wade."

Keith frowned. "Did I meet him?"

"No, he … died before you were even born. He was your dad's oldest brother."

"Oh." Keith already moved on to another picture of a water balloon fight they'd had in the parking lot of Kate's diner. "Uncle Keith is all wet."

"That's because your dad soaked him with a big balloon filled with water."

Keith giggled. "Daddy is wet, too."

"We all were. See, here is another one." She handed Keith another picture of the bunch of them; the McKinnon boys, Poppy, Kelly, Denny and his younger sister Maddie. They'd laughed a lot that day. Even though Kate had taken the picture of all of them, she was mad as hell about the spent balloons all over the parking lot and made them clean it all up.

Poppy's heart squeezed with the memory. These days were true. She could look back on these memories and hold them dear without pain. She'd have to remember that when she returned to New York.

Logan stood outside the door listening to the chatter between Keith and Poppy until all he could hear was music from the TV, signaling Keith's movie had ended. When he looked inside the room, he saw that Keith was asleep, snuggled up against Poppy, and she was stroking his head, looking at him with love.

"I didn't think he'd last the whole movie," Logan said, slowly walking into the room. He sat on the bed next to Keith and just looked at his son.

"He looks a little like Kelly," she said.

"You think so? I think he's McKinnon down to the bone."

Poppy smiled at him. "No, there's Kelly there."

Logan was quiet a moment, struggling to find the words and knowing there was no better way to ask it. "Do you hate her for what she did?"

Shocked, Poppy stopped stroking Keith's head and stared at Logan. "No. I was angry. Crazy angry, in fact. But I never hated her. Especially after she told me why she did it. Kelly was and will always be my best friend. What she did was wrong. But I forgave her. And I'll always love her."

Logan nodded slowly, amazed that Poppy's unconditional love for Kelly had remained through it all.

"I should probably get him into his own bed, huh?"

Poppy smiled down at Keith. "He's fine. I don't mind him sleeping here. If he wakes up in the middle of the night, I can bring him back to his room."

"What about your ankle?"

She cocked her head to one side and gave him a half smile. "Do you really think I needed to be bedridden all day? I can hobble down the hall with no trouble. Even Hawk said I should be fine enough to walk as long as I don't push it."

He nodded and was about to leave her for the night, but something stopped him. He wasn't sure what. Maybe it was the familiarity of the room. Perhaps nostalgia, or maybe that Logan knew Poppy was leaving, and he wouldn't have another chance.

"I didn't want to buy this ranch. Kelly insisted. I wasn't … we weren't in a good place then, before this little guy was born. Everything about this place reminded me of you."

"That's why Kelly wanted it."

Confused, he said, "Why?"

"She knew I couldn't come here and watch the two of you live a life I'd dreamed of for us. That was her insurance."

"I don't understand."

Poppy stretched over to the nightstand where the stack of letters wrapped in a ribbon were sitting as if they'd been placed there for just this moment. Poppy handed the letters to Logan.

"This was never Kelly's dream. It was mine. I've always loved you, Logan. Kelly knew it. I just never knew that Kelly loved you, too, until it was too late."

Moisture filled her eyes, but still, she offered him a bittersweet smile. Looking down at the letters in his hand, he pulled the ribbon and sifted through the envelopes. They were in Kelly's handwriting, addressed to Poppy's New York City apartment.

"Read them if you want. Throw them away if you want. It doesn't matter anymore. What's done is done."

He got up from the bed with the letters in his hand. "It gutted me when Kelly died," he said. And maybe that was the biggest struggle he'd been having since Poppy had arrived. How could he have loved Kelly, missed her, and still loved Poppy? "It may not have been perfect, but I did love her."

He looked at Poppy for a long moment with the child lying in bed next to her, and his heart swelled with emotion. "If nothing else, he was worth it all."

She smiled as she looked at Keith. "I know."

The letters didn't matter anymore, and yet, as Logan sat on the porch steps, looking up at a clear late March Dakota sky, he couldn't get them out of his mind. Spring was on its way. Pretty soon there'd be more rain. Hopefully, not as much as the ice and rain that left such devastation these past weeks. He'd be able to get out in the field and plow, get on his horse and spend some time with Keith in the warm sun.

And Poppy wouldn't be here.

This was never Kelly's dream, Logan. It was mine.

There was no doubt he was in love with Poppy. But he *had* loved Kelly, too. He couldn't deny it. The irony of it all was he was sure of it now, and he'd never truly been when Kelly was alive. He'd spent half their marriage wishing he could turn back the clock only to realize now that Kelly had given him the biggest gift he'd ever known. His son. Even now that Kelly was gone, she'd always be a part of Keith and a part of him because of it.

The letters were on the kitchen table. He'd been ready to throw them away, just as Poppy had suggested. Kelly had asked Poppy to come back to South Dakota so he could learn the truth and now he knew it. What more did he need to know? And then it hit him. He didn't know why. And the letters on the table held the answers.

He pulled himself up from the porch steps and made his way to the kitchen, not sure if he was prepared for what he'd find. He spent an hour going through letter after letter, piecing together the timeline, knowing for the first time for sure what Poppy had said was true. Kelly had lied to Poppy and fabricated a life that didn't exist here in Rudolph after Poppy had left, long before his shotgun wedding to Kelly. No wonder Poppy had become distant with him. It left Logan wondering if he ever knew his wife at all.

There were missing years, most likely the letters Poppy mentioned that were destroyed by the burst pipes in her apartment. But it warmed Logan's heart that even though these letters had to have hurt Poppy terribly when Kelly had sent them, Poppy, in her sentimental nature, had chosen to keep them because they were from Kelly. This is why Poppy had wanted this house. As much as she thirsted for adventure, she was the sentimental one who wanted to fill her life with good memories.

An hour later Logan sat back outside on the porch and reread the letter that said it all. It was the last letter Kelly had sent in a desperate attempt to gain forgiveness from her friend. It was dated a few weeks before Kelly had passed away.

I know you hate me. I don't blame you. But you don't take my calls, and you won't answer my letters. I am dying, Poppy. And even if you still hate me, I need you to understand. I need you to forgive me.

I stole from you the one thing I always knew you wanted. I'm a terrible friend. I deserve to have terrible things happen to me for what I've done. But I'm not like you, Poppy. I never was. Whenever I was with you, I was invisible. It wasn't just Logan who only saw you. It was every man for miles around. When you were around, I didn't exist.

You have fire in you. Everything about you commands attention, and you don't even have to ask for it. It's just you. For as long as I can remember, I lived in your shadow. But when you left, Logan actually looked at me for the first time. Not like he looked at you. Even at our best I don't think Logan ever looked at me that way. But I wasn't just Poppy Ericksen's tagalong friend anymore. I was his friend, and I thought if I could just keep you from coming back to Rudolph, in time, it could be more.

On the day he packed his truck and was hell-bent on going to get you, I realized I hadn't just lost my best friend, I was losing a man I had secretly loved since I was thirteen. I always knew he loved you. Everyone knew. He was ready to drive away, and I panicked. The lies just came out of my mouth before I could even stop them. But they did stop him. *Logan was crushed and even though I hated myself for lying to him, he didn't leave. He got really drunk that night, and I was afraid he was going to do something stupid and get himself killed like Denny did that night he and Ethan went 4-wheeling. He was that crazy.*

Logan kissed me that night, but I don't even think he knew who he was let alone who he was kissing. He could barely stand. I stayed with him to make sure he was okay, and when he woke up the next day, I told him that we'd made love. Only it was never true.

Logan dropped the pages of the letter onto the porch and tried to squash down his anger, trying to remember the course of events that had spiraled out of control from there. That night hadn't been the only night he'd let himself get stinking drunk. Hawk was away at med school, and Ethan had joined the Navy by then and was training to be a Navy Seal. It had been his brother Sam who'd pulled him up and told him to quit feeling sorry for himself and to just go get Poppy, whatever it took.

So Logan decided to fight for her. His mistake was stopping by Kelly's house to say good-bye. He felt he'd owed her that much for the horrible way he'd treated her when he'd been drunk. She'd cried and told him she was pregnant. She didn't want her baby to grow up without a father. Everything after that moment was a blur.

I was never pregnant. Logan never even touched me until after we were married. But Poppy, please try to understand. I was never going to leave Rudolph. My whole life was here. You always talked about traveling and the adventures you wanted to have before settling down in the old farmhouse you grew up in. You had fire and determination about your life. Logan was always fascinated by everything you said. But where was I going to be? What would I have?

I'm not like you Poppy. I didn't have big dreams and plans. The only big dream I ever had was Logan and he was always yours. Always. I thought I could love him enough for both of us. I thought that in time he would love me too. I couldn't see past that day to something that might be better. I didn't think of how I was hurting you. I only thought that it was my one chance at happiness with Logan. To have my dream. I figured I could have Logan, and you could have any other man you wanted. I just didn't realize that even though every guy within ten miles of here had eyes for you, you never saw anyone but Logan. I never saw how much you truly loved him. I was selfish. And for that I'm sorry.

Please come back, Poppy. I know everything I did drove you away. I know I don't deserve it, and you have every right to hate me, but I need you to forgive me. I need my best friend. I don't know if I can do this without you. Please tell me you forgive me! I'm begging you.

Logan closed the letter and tucked it back into the envelope. There were so many lies, and he was at the core of them all. It was an odd place to be, the object of a tug of war between two best friends. He rubbed the place at the center of his chest where it hurt. Some men would have relished the idea of being loved that deeply by two amazing women. It only left him feeling empty.

Chapter Eight

"I see you rescued the 4-wheeler from the pasture," Poppy said. The ATV they'd driven was parked in front of the porch, still full of mud from their ride the other day.

"Yeah, I filled it with gas and figured I'd give Keith a ride to help ease your leaving here. Right, buddy?"

Keith wouldn't even look at the ATV.

Logan drew in a deep breath and forced a weak smile. "Are you sure your ankle is well enough for you to travel?"

"I'm good to go," Poppy replied, looking down at her feet for a second. "Thank you for cleaning the boots. They give my ankle a lot more stability to walk, so I'll be fine. I should have plenty of time to get to the airport and make my flight."

Keith looked at her and stuck his lip out. "Don't you want to ride with us?"

"I have to go home, Keith. How about I read you a story tonight over the phone before you go to bed," Poppy offered. She added, "If it's okay with your dad, of course."

"That sounds … like fun," Logan said.

That did nothing to appease Keith. Not even the sound of Kate's truck coming up the driveway swayed the little guy's mood.

"Hey, look, little man. Grammie's here."

Keith just held onto Logan's hand and pouted. Poppy thought she'd known heartbreak before. Seeing Keith's reaction to her leaving only shattered it more.

"Keith, I need your help getting Auntie Poppy's big suitcase into her car. Do you want to help me?" Logan coaxed. Reluctantly, he followed his dad.

Poppy took a long look around the yard and then back at the house, fighting off tears she hoped would remain hidden until she was long gone from Rudolph. Kate met her on the porch.

"I'm glad I had a chance to see you before you left."

Poppy hugged Kate warmly. "Me, too."

There was moisture in Kate's eyes when she pulled back. She brushed her thumb across Poppy's chin and smiled. "I hope that my pigheaded son will get some sense into him soon."

Poppy rolled her eyes. "Good luck with that."

"Do you have time for a cup of coffee before you leave?"

"No, I need to get on the road," she said quietly. She had time built into her schedule, but Poppy didn't see the point in prolonging what was already a difficult morning.

"Don't be a stranger."

"I won't."

The sound of the trunk slamming shut drew Poppy's attention.

"Come here, Keith. Give Auntie Poppy a hug. I have to leave."

Logan and Keith made their way over to the porch. Poppy eased herself down the steps, holding the railing and picked Keith up in her arms.

"I don't want you to leave," Keith said.

Poppy closed her eyes and gave Keith a gentle squeeze. "Love you."

With his little arms around her neck, Keith said, "Love you, too."

"I'll take him inside," Kate said.

Poppy handed him to Kate and touched Keith's cheek. Unable to trust her voice, she waved good-bye as she walked toward the car.

"I'll be inside in a minute," Logan said. He walked with Poppy to the car. She was glad that she was able to put weight on her ankle, but she paid special attention to the ruts and dips in the driveway so she wouldn't reinjure herself.

Poppy steeled all her strength for this moment. If she'd thought coming back here was tough, this moment beat it by a long shot.

As they stood there, she wondered if there were any words she could say now that would change things. She wanted so much for Logan to tell her that he loved her and that whatever happened in the past didn't matter. He'd always love her. As she looked into his eyes, remembering all the wonderful love they'd shared before life and lies intruded on them, she decided to make it easy on him.

"I'm never going to regret coming back here, Logan. Or forget a single moment I shared with you. Good or bad, it was real. I hope one day you'll see it that way, too."

"I ... sorry."

She lifted her face to him. "For what? You didn't do anything wrong."

"Looking back, I see that I should have done things different. I didn't realize just how insecure Kelly was until …"

Her eyes widened. "You read the letters."

He nodded. "She was right. The only woman I ever saw when you were around was you. It doesn't change anything that happened. I'll never regret the outcome because I have my son because of what she did. But I least I know why she did it."

Poppy drew in a deep breath and then reached up as best she could to kiss Logan on the mouth. To her relief, he didn't pull back. But he didn't take her into his arms and beg her to stay either. His lips melted into hers. She felt his breath against her skin and the warmth of his body next to hers. This kiss would have to last her a lifetime.

When they parted, she looked into his beautiful blue eyes for a long moment and just gazed at him.

"Take care of yourself and that little boy," she said with a weak smile.

Before he could say more, she opened the car door and slipped inside, shutting the door behind her. She gunned the engine and put the car into reverse before allowing herself to look at Logan one more time. Then she pulled away. Then and only then did she allow her tears to flow. Once again she was leaving Logan and a life she'd dreamed of behind.

♥ ♥ ♥

He was dying. Logan was sure of it. He could only remember one other time when his life felt as hopeless as it did right at that moment.

Kate came up behind him.

"Keith's settled in front of the TV watching his favorite movie."

"He'll be fine," Logan said.

"Sure he will. But you won't be."

He looked at his mom and saw that she was none too happy. "What do you mean?"

"You didn't die with Kelly, Logan. Some people never get a second chance to make things right. Only a fool would let a woman he loved get away twice. And I didn't raise a fool." With that she turned and walked back in the house.

Logan looked back at the car making its way down the driveway. He was a fool. How could he let Poppy leave like this? Years ago they didn't have a choice. But now he did. And he knew exactly what he had to do.

♥ ♥ ♥

Poppy paused at the end of the driveway before pulling out onto the main road. Tears stained her cheeks and blurred her vision. There was no way she could possibly drive all the way to Rapid City crying like she was. As she swiped at her wet face, she heard the sound of an engine. She sniffed and looked down the road to see if a truck was coming. The road was clear so she put her foot on the gas to take the left turn. Before she made it halfway into the road, the ATV came charging through the muddy pasture, spitting up gravel and mud all around and spraying the car with debris before it stopped in the middle of the road.

Startled, Poppy slammed on the breaks just in front of the ATV. Logan climbed off the 4-wheeler and ran to her car. With her heart in her throat, she pushed open the door.

"Are you crazy?" she said. "I could have hit you!"

"Shut up for a second."

"Don't tell me to shut up! You're driving that thing like a maniac. You nearly gave me a heart attack."

"I need to tell you something and don't want you to interrupt while I do," he said, taking her by the hand and helping her out of the car. "Now do you want to hear it or not?"

"What?"

Dragging her into his arms, Logan crushed her against his chest in an embrace. He cupped her face and smiled down at her as his mouth claimed hers, kissing her as soulfully as he had the day they'd made love, leaving her breathless right there on the street. She reached up, daring to pull him ever closer to him. She didn't want to let him go. She never wanted to leave this moment.

She heard a car horn blare nearby, shocking her senses. Logan pulled away slowly and smiled down at her, revealing the deep dimple on his cheek.

"Everything okay?" an elderly man asked smiling as he rolled down his car window.

His wife, sitting next to him in the front seat, smacked him with a rolled newspaper playfully. "Oh, leave them alone and get going."

The man laughed and waved at the two of them, then drove away.

Poppy's heart swelled with joy. "Is that what you wanted to tell me?"

"Yes, and no," he said with a smile. "I have a whole lot more I want to tell you. We have ten years' worth of loving to make up for. I want a lifetime of making love to you like we did the other day. I don't think if I lived to be a hundred I'd get my fill of you Poppy Ericksen. You've ruined me.

"Kelly deserved better than what I gave her ... but so do you. I've been beating myself up for so long about the way I feel about you. The way I've always felt about you. Kelly knew that. She told me in her letter, and she carried the burden of what she'd done to her death. I would have never known the truth if you hadn't come back. I'm grateful for that, not just for me, but for Kelly."

"It's what she'd wanted in the end. For you to know the truth."

"I don't think I would have ever allowed myself to go into Kelly's things because I was afraid of what I'd find. And when I had the truth staring right at me, I felt like I was …"

"Betraying Kelly?"

He nodded. "But now I know it was Kelly's gift to both of us. She set me free from all that guilt I'd been feeling. My marriage to Kelly had been doomed from the start. But I did love her. I'm always going to love her."

Tears filled Poppy's eyes. "I know you will."

"But I also know that I have always been in love with you. Ever since you got here I've been having a hard time reconciling that. But not anymore. I saw you drive away and thought I'd die. And suddenly all the years melted away, and all I knew was I needed to get to you. I should have done it then."

She wrapped her arms around his neck and kissed him, breathing in the scent of him along with the smell of the mud that was splattered on his shirt. But she didn't care. She was in Logan McKinnon's arms.

"So where do we go from here?" she asked.

"I don't want you to feel uncomfortable living in the house I lived in with Kelly. If you want, we'll tear this one down and build a new one."

She frowned. "Tear down the house? Are you out of your mind?"

"Or we could sell this place and get a new one. We can even move to Manhattan. I'll adapt. I just want to be wherever you are."

Tears trickled down Poppy's cheeks. "That's all I've ever wanted, Logan. I love you so much. I don't care where we are. And I don't want the memory of your life with Kelly to be something we run away from. After all, she was Keith's mother, and I want to fill him with as many memories of Kelly that I have so he'll know her and always remember her."

"I'm so happy to hear that. I love you so very much. Marry me, Poppy Ericksen. I don't think I want to live another day without you in it."

She threw her head back and laughed loud. "Logan McKinnon, what the hell took you so long? Of course, I'll marry you … but on one condition."

He looked at her intently. "What's that?"

"We live every day as an adventure. We eat breakfast for dinner sometimes. We sit on the porch roof and look up at the stars on warm nights. We get muddy then sit around on rainy days in our pajamas and watch old movies and …"

He laughed. "You know you're way past one."

"Who cares? I want to live every day as if it was the last day, because if losing Kelly has taught me one thing, it's that you never know when that last day will come."

"Agreed."

He picked her up and spun her around in the middle of the street. When he put her down, he said, "Let's go tell Keith."

She gave him a devilish grin. "I'll race you to the house."

Laughing loud, she climbed into her rental car and Logan climbed on the ATV, both setting out to live the adventure they'd started years ago. Poppy didn't know everything the future held, but she knew for sure that it would be filled with love.

~The End~

BADLAND BRIDE
Dakota Hearts Series Book Two

Chapter One

Army brats weren't wusses. She'd been dealing with tough situations from the moment she'd pushed her way into the world. At least that's what Regis Simpson's daddy always told her. She should've known better than to traipse through mud and rubble without proper boots, no matter how stylish her flats looked in the store window. Her reward was the nice chunk of metal from the rusty fence that had somehow embedded itself into her ankle when she'd slipped.

"You're going to need a tetanus shot for that."

Regis looked up at the man standing over her. He'd just taken her on a thirty minute walk around his property to assess flood damage. It wasn't pretty. Now, as she was sprawled out on the muddy ground, smelling earth and Lord knows what else decaying, she tried to focus on the wetness from the ground seeping into the fabric of her pants rather than the pain in her leg.

"I'm up on my shots," she said, trying her best not to pass out as she pulled her leg away from the twisted fence.

Regis took the man's proffered hands in hers and welcomed his help. She'd already been out to six properties today and couldn't remember all the people she'd talked to.

Tim Bennett. That was this guy's name, right? Relief flooded her. She hated when her brain became overloaded with details. And Mr. Bennett had bigger worries than the damage she'd done to her leg to help keep her straight. Everyone in Rudolph and the surrounding towns in the Badlands of South Dakota were worried about whether or not insurance would cover enough to repair the damage to their property after the worst ice storms and flooding in a hundred years had swept through the area. That's what she did, and the only reason she was on a marathon tour of destruction. And there were days she wondered why she was still doing it after five straight years of living out of a suitcase and calling the local motel in Anytown, USA her home.

"No, you really should have Hawk take a look at that. It looks pretty bad. Might need stitches."

"Hawk? What is he, a local Native American shaman or something?"

Mr. Bennett smiled. "More like the local daredevil. Or he used to be anyway. People around here joke he went into medicine just so he could stitch up his own wounds because the thieving insurance companies cancelled his policy."

The joke fell flat, and Mr. Bennett's smile immediately faltered as if he suddenly remembered who he was speaking to. "Let me see if I can find something clean to wrap that leg."

"I'd appreciate that."

Regis couldn't exactly blame Mr. Bennett for being nervous. It didn't matter what town she was in across America. When a natural disaster struck an area, it caused upheaval and destruction that she needed to help these fine folks fix. She was their hope of a swift recovery ... so long as she approved their claim.

And that, she was sure, was the reason for Mr. Bennett's nervous energy.

While she waited, she carefully tried to put weight on her foot but felt warm moisture seep into her shoe as pain shot up her leg. She quietly let out a colorful stream of expletives that she knew sounded odd coming out of the mouth of someone in her position. But being raised by a single father on Army bases around the world, she heard a thing or two that made even her toes curl.

Mr. Bennett handed Regis a couple of paper towels. "I found these in the car. They're clean."

"Thank you," Regis tried not to wince as she placed the paper towel on her leg. It was no use. She stood and carefully tried to put weight on her foot again. Her ankle throbbed, but she forced herself to walk on it so she could get to her car. Once there, she leaned up against the car door and hiked up her pant leg to get a better look at her injury.

"You're definitely going to need stitches for that," Mr. Bennett said.

Feeling queasy, she asked, "You wouldn't happen to have that Hawk doctor's address on you, would you?"

"No need for an address. Just stay on this road until you get to the center of town. Turn left at the diner and it's right across the street. You can't miss it. It's the only clinic in town."

"Turn left at the diner. That sounds easy enough. Does this Hawk have a real name?"

Mr. Bennett smiled. "His sign says Dr. Keith McKinnon. But I don't know anyone who calls him that."

"Hawk? Right, thanks," Regis muttered to herself as she eased her body into the driver's seat. Once inside, she closed her eyes to the dizziness she felt. She had to drive to town, find this doctor's office and hope this Hawk doctor could take care of her wound quickly. With her long lists of properties to assess, she couldn't afford down time.

As her engine fired up, Mr. Bennett said, "Ah, what about my claim?"

"I'll get back to you on that. I have the information for your paperwork." Despite the cold March wind outside, beads of sweat bubbled up on her forehead.

He looked worried. "Phone service is knocked out."

"I'll be setting up an office at the senior center by the end of the week. You can check in with me there."

That is, she'd have an office if the senior center allowed her the space. She hadn't heard back on that yet. Otherwise, she'd be seeing clients in the motel parking lot.

As she drove towards the center of town, Regis tried not to look at the devastation around her. There were days she felt numb to it, having seen so much in the five years she'd worked at her job. But she couldn't help but feel for the people who were suffering here. She passed a farm that had all its fields washed out. There were ruts in the mud, most likely caused by a tractor that had picked up debris and animals that hadn't made it in the flood. A barn that had once seen its glory days of use was now caved in on one side due to erosion of the foundation from water damage.

She tried not to look as she drove because she knew what everyone else here didn't know. Not everyone would get what they needed. Not everyone would recover from this. And those who'd get bad news, would get it from her.

A series of ice storms, and then an unseasonably high amount of rain, had caused massive flooding throughout South Dakota. The area around the Black Hills had been hit particularly hard. Her office had been inundated with insurance claims from thousands of people reporting property damage. She, as well as a dozen of her colleagues, had been on the road for weeks, examining the damage and submitting paperwork to approve each claim so people could rebuild.

She saw the diner she'd eaten breakfast at that morning and hit her blinker for a left turn. The clinic was easy to miss being nothing more than an old farmhouse that had a fresh coat of paint and a handicap ramp newly installed out front. If not for the felled tree that had been recently cut into pieces and stacked neatly next to the parking lot, if you could call it that, she would have missed the sign.

She parked her car in the empty parking lot. "Maybe this will be quick, and I can get back on the road."

After easing herself out of the car, she limped up the newly built wooden ramp, unpainted and still sporting the color of wood that hadn't been exposed to the elements for long. She winced through the pain as she took each step toward the front door. A small sign hung next to the door giving the clinic's hours. She tried the door, and it wouldn't budge. Her shoulders sagged in defeat.

"What does he do in the middle of the day? Go fishing?"

"Nope, house calls."

Regis swung around to see a tall man walking up behind her on the ramp. He had the Irish blue eyes she'd seen on many models in advertising magazines she'd bought when she was a teenager, and the dark hair that looked a little unruly in the wind, but seemed to fit him perfectly. The light scuff of a beard wasn't more than a day old, but already dark and covering his square jaw.

For a moment, Regis was so taken with this handsome stranger that she'd forgotten why she was there.

♥ ♥ ♥

"Dr. Hawk, or whatever his name actually is, does house calls? I thought that sort of thing went extinct with the dinosaurs. The guy must be a hundred years old."

Hawk fought to keep from smiling. "There are days it seems that way." He then looked at the woman's leg and frowned as he saw the blood staining her pants. "We'd better get you inside so that can be cleaned."

"The door's locked," the woman said, leaning against the rail as he came up beside her. Her face was pale, most probably due to the pain she was experiencing and the loss of blood.

He smiled, looking down into her eyes. "Luckily, I have a key." They were pretty brown eyes, he decided. No, they were hazel. And the fact that he didn't want her to turn away so he could know for sure surprised him.

Standing six feet tall, he towered over her small frame, although he was probably no more than eight inches taller than her. And she smelled like fresh soap as if she'd just taken a shower. But looking at the dirt and blood on her hands, that probably wasn't the case.

"You must rate to have your own key to the doctor's office. When does this Hawk doctor usually come back?"

He slipped the key into the door and turned the handle. Then he smiled as he pushed the door open and held it for her to come inside. "Why don't you have a seat here. It'll just be a minute."

Hawk curled his fingers around the woman's upper arm gently and helped guide her to the chair. As she sat down, a look of relief washed over her face.

"Does that take some pressure off?"

"What?"

"Your leg. Does sitting help?"

As he waited for her to reply, he walked behind the receptionist desk and sifted through the wall organizer that was filled with insurance forms. Nancy was going to have a fit if he had this woman fill out the wrong one.

"Ah, a little."

He felt a muscle pull between his eyebrows as he glanced at the forms. For all his higher education, insurance forms were a mystery to him. Finally, he sighed and dropped the papers on the desk.

"I'm going to need you to fill out some forms, but I'm not sure which one's right at the moment, and my receptionist, Nancy, will have my hide if I have you fill out the wrong form. So why don't we just have a look at your leg first and fill out paperwork later?"

"Your receptionist?"

"Yes. She'll probably be back from lunch before I'm done."

"You? Wait, you're Dr. Hawk?"

His lips curled up just slightly. "It's just Hawk. But if you prefer, you can call me Dr. McKinnon."

Her mouth hung open just slightly. "Oh, I'm ... oh, okay."

"Did someone tell you I was a deranged killer?"

"What? No, of course not, it's just ..."

She was adorable, all flustered with her flub. Hawk couldn't resist teasing her. "They said I was a mean old bastard who was going to cut off your leg?"

She rolled her eyes. "Don't be ridiculous."

"Then what?"

"You aren't ... I wasn't expecting someone so ..." She took a deep breath.

"So ... handsome?"

Color immediately stained her pale cheeks. "Young. You look like you just graduated college."

He chuckled. "So they didn't tell you I was good looking. They told you I was old."

She sighed heavily. "No. Mr. Bennett didn't say anything except your name is Hawk. What kind of person walks around with a name like that anyway?"

"Me," he said. "And I can assure you that you are in good hands. I may not be a crusty old doctor, but I not only went to college, I made it all the way through med school, my internship and a stint at the city hospital in

Sioux Falls before coming back to Rudolph and starting my practice here."

Her shoulders slumped. "I didn't mean to imply—"

"Let's get you cleaned up," he said. "Let me help you—"

He bent down to help her to her feet, and he caught a whiff of her soapy scent again. Normally he didn't notice such things. But he was having a hard time not noticing every little detail about this woman from the slight hook of her nose to the patch of too many freckles on her left cheek.

"No, I can do it."

"Okay, follow me," he said as they made their way down the hall to the first examining room. He opened the door and let her into the well-stocked room first. Then he carefully helped her to climb onto the examining table before going to the sink to wash his hands. When he was done, he put on a white medical jacket that was hanging from a hook on the door, and then turned to her.

"Now that you know my name, why don't you tell me yours?"

"Regis Simpson. But people call me Reggie."

"Why?"

"Why what?"

"Why would people call you Reggie when Regis is such a pretty name?"

Her lips lifted to a sideward grin. "You've got one hell of a bedside manner, Doctor."

"Did it make you forget the throbbing in your leg?"

She thought a second and then chuckled softly. "That's *not* why you said that to me."

"Are you sure about that?" She was easy to tease, and Hawk quickly realized he liked this woman's spunk. But she was here for a reason, and once she was settled on the examining table, he immediately fell into professional mode.

"While I get what I need to clean your leg, why don't you tell me what happened?"

"I got into a fight with a rusty old fence on the other side of town and lost. I had to pull a piece out, but I don't think it's too bad. It just won't stop bleeding. I hope I didn't hit an artery."

Hawk looked up from the stainless steel tray he was putting gauze, saline solution and other supplies on. She was actually worried about it. "If you'd hit an artery you wouldn't have made it over here alive. You *are* bleeding a lot though, so let's have a look."

He pulled the table extender out and helped her lift her leg.

Regis never felt so foolish in her life. Handsome? Yeah, she couldn't deny that. But to ask her that? Was he full of himself of what? Never mind that she'd already been thinking that from the moment she'd seen him walking up the ramp.

"You didn't have a medical bag," she finally said.

He glanced at her. "Excuse me?"

"When you came up to the door you said the doctor does house calls in the middle of the afternoon. But you didn't have a medical bag so I naturally assumed ..."

His face suddenly showed understanding at her fumbled attempt at an explanation. "I keep the bag locked in the truck. You never know when you have to run out quickly, especially now." Turning his focus to her leg, he said, "I'm just going to pull your shoe and sock off so I can see how far down this cut went."

Regis looked above him, behind him and at the posters on the wall warning of germs and the importance of washing your hands as the doctor peeled off her blood-soaked sock and shoe. She closed her eyes to the pain as he turned her ankle.

"Let's clean out this wound and see how bad it is," he said. "Just lift your leg so I can put the towel underneath."

Gripping the table, she did as she was told and turned her head to the side as the cool liquid flowed over and stung her skin.

"You're not going to pass out on me, are you?"

"Not if I can help it."

"Nancy?" he called out, startling her.

A few seconds later, a middle-aged woman wearing a nurse's jacket with cats printed all over it was standing in the doorway.

"I wasn't sure you heard me come in," she said, looking over at Regis's leg and frowning. "Oh, you got yourself a nasty one there. Where'd that happen?"

Regis took a deep breath as the doctor worked on her leg. "Over at the Bennett property."

Sympathy showed on the woman's face. "I heard the whole first floor was flooded."

"It's about that bad," Regis said.

Hawk looked up at the nurse. "I didn't have time to fill out the paperwork for Miss—"

"Simpson. Regis Simpson," she said.

Hawk nodded. "Would you mind getting all that paperwork together while I take care of this wound?"

Nancy shook her head and frowned. But by the motherly look she gave Hawk, Regis knew she was teasing. "Didn't remember which form to fill out, huh? It's a good thing you're not at Sioux City General anymore. You think the other nurses would put up with this?"

"He didn't want me to bleed all over the new carpet."

Nancy chuckled with raised eyebrows. "That was very thoughtful of him. I see you already have this poor girl whipped. I'll get that paperwork."

As Nancy left, Hawk's hands paused on her leg as he looked up at her, giving her a wide smile that reached the depths of his eyes.

"You're getting me in trouble."

"I have a feeling you can do that all by yourself."

She wasn't sure what she'd been expecting from a country doctor, but the man standing next to her was not it. His eyes were the deepest shade of blue Regis had ever seen. He was tall, leanly muscled and had one of those ruggedly handsome faces that would've looked perfect in a cowboy movie. And she couldn't believe she was sitting on an examining table with the hots for her doctor.

Chapter Two

"It's really not as bad as it could have been," Hawk told her.

"How do you figure that when it hurts like hell?"

"You could have broken your leg. You'll have to be more careful out there and wear some sensible shoes. I've been out to the Bennett place since the floods came through. They still have a lot of debris to cleanup and it's tricky stepping."

"I found that out the hard way. I'm more ticked off about the ragged tear in my best pair of dress slacks than this puncture wound."

"Pants can be replaced. By the way, where did the name Regis come from?"

"My parents."

She tilted an eyebrow, and he wondered if it was in challenge or if she were teasing.

He hesitated a moment and then said, "What?"

"I'm just waiting for the standard comment about Regis being a boy's name, and oh, your father must have wanted a boy."

"Is that what everyone gives you? Standard lines?"

She shrugged as if she weren't uncomfortable with the topic. "I'm an insurance adjuster. Everyone wants to see me around here right now, and everyone is always giving me a line they hope will help their claim."

His lips lifted to a grin. "Then I won't make that mistake."

"I appreciate that," she said.

"So is it is true?"

"Is what true?"

"Did your father want a boy?"

Regis paused a fraction of a moment. "Yeah."

He'd hit a raw wound, and it wasn't the one on her leg. He let the name thing go and concentrated on her wounded ankle with gloved fingers gently probing at the damaged flesh. "You're not going to need stitches. But you may end up with a nasty scar."

She blew out a quick breath. "Good. I can add it to all the other ones I got as a kid."

"You're the insurance agent who denied the Proctor family's claim without even looking at the property."

Her sigh made him look up. A wry smile curved her lips. "Does that mean you're not going to treat me?"

Hawk chuckled as he stood. "If I didn't treat people who did things I didn't like, I wouldn't have much of a practice." He gathered a few items from a nearby cabinet and walked back over to her.

"I don't discuss my cases without my clients' permission."

"Evan Proctor said it was a technicality," he said as he began to clean out the wound. Her hands were gripping the edge of the table, but she didn't make a sound of pain, keeping her voice even. "Their policy had lapsed during the time frame of the flood."

"As I said, I don't discuss my cases without—"

"They're people. Not cases. These people lost their valuables, their homes and their livestock."

"I know that. That's why I'm doing everything I can to help them. But unfortunately, some things are beyond my control."

Hawk let the statement slide by, resisting the urge to tell her that there was always something that could be done. But it wasn't his job, and with the weight of the last few weeks bearing down on him, he realized he'd just crossed a very important line.

Once he'd finished cleaning her leg, he looked up at her. "Sorry, it's been a rough couple of weeks around here and many long days."

He'd expected annoyance, which was well earned for his transgression, and yet what he got from Regis Simpson was a sympathetic smile. That somehow made him feel worse.

"I know it's hard to see people you care about hurting. But it'll get better eventually," she said.

"That's what I'm hoping for."

"You asked about my name. Now it's your turn. What's the deal with Hawk?

"No deal. Just about everyone around here has known me since I was a kid, so everyone calls me Hawk."

"What's your name?"

"Didn't you read the sign?"

"There has to be a story that goes with Hawk. What is it about that name you don't like?"

"Nothing. My nephew is named Keith."

"Then why Hawk?"

The image of Wade flashed in his mind, and Hawk immediately felt that familiar pain he always felt when he thought of his older brother. "Your leg is wrapped. Make sure you keep it clean and dry tonight."

"Ah, you don't like talking about it?"

It was clear Regis knew she'd hit on something, but she didn't push further, and for that he was glad. She was new in town. She knew nothing of his family or of their personal tragedies. She dealt in tangible loss. And right now, a whole lot of people in Rudolph needed her help.

He pulled off his gloves and dropped them into the trash. "Are you staying at the motel in town?"

"You're changing the subject."

"I thought the subject was your wounded leg."

"What does my staying at the local motel have to do with my leg?"

From the little he'd seen of her, Regis Simpson was a pistol. And he liked that, Lord help him. He'd been with women in his life, and none of them challenged him. He wasn't a yes-dear man and he didn't want a yes-dear woman or someone who was only interested in being on the arm of a doctor and what his profession could provide.

If he'd cared about any of that, he would have stayed in Sioux City instead of setting up his practice here in Rudolph where it was needed.

"You're going to need some antibiotic to help prevent a Staph infection. I have some antibiotic here, but it's not as strong as I'd like. I am going to call in a script to the pharmacy in the next county. They deliver, and I need an address for them to send it to you. Are there any meds you're allergic to?"

"Ah, no."

"Then I have enough for what you'll need tonight. I'll give you the pharmacy information so you can call and arrange for delivery."

"I can pick it up."

"No you won't. You need to stay off this leg. At least for the night. You need to give it time so it doesn't open up again. And you're going to need a tetanus shot."

"So I've heard."

Her reaction was instantaneous and amusing. He'd never seen an adult look so absolutely petrified at the mention of a shot.

He resisted the urge to laugh at the face she was making. "When was the last time you had a tetanus shot?"

She thought a moment, then shook her head without answering.

Frowning, he said, "Just as I thought. If you can't remember, it's been too long."

"I'm sure I've had one at some point. Maybe before college."

"And how long ago was that?"

"Eleven years."

"I'll finish bandaging your leg. Then we can see about doing that paperwork and getting you up to date on your shots. I'm surprised your boss doesn't require it given the work you do."

"Really, it's okay."

"No, it's not. You said the fence was rusty? Well, even if it's not, it's probably full of bacteria from the flood water. Do you have any idea what kind of pollutants flood waters carry? You don't want to take a chance—"

She started to protest, but he cut her off.

"And neither do I," he said. "It's your choice, but it's really for your own good, and I strongly advise you have it to prevent getting tetanus. Besides, there are too many people depending on you to do your job so they can get on with rebuilding. They'll be plenty mad at me if I don't take good care of you."

She bit her bottom lip until he thought she'd draw blood.

"Something wrong?"

"I don't like shots."

He scratched the back of his neck, fighting the smile pulling at his lips. "No one likes shots. But they're necessary. You had no problem driving here after pulling a hunk of metal out of your leg, but the thought of a shot scares you?"

She tried to glare at him, but the fear in her eyes drained all of the fire from it.

A wave of protectiveness washed over Hawk as he left the room to retrieve the syringe and vial of medicine from the locked cabinet. When he returned to the room, she was white-knuckling the edge of the table.

Tense was only part of what she was feeling. She looked terrified, and her response, given what she had to deal with on a daily basis, intrigued him. Hawk's eyes darted to Regis's pale face. She'd sunk her teeth into her bottom lip and was worrying at it again. He thought of her lips and how many times over the past fifteen minutes he'd thought about kissing them ... and hating himself for thinking that. Not here. Not like this. That's two transgressions in one day with the same woman.

He needed some sleep.

"Are you doing okay, Regis?" he asked.

"Please don't call me Regis."

"It's your name."

"Everyone calls me, Reggie. I never respond to Regis and have never been happy with that name. So, it's Reggie, okay?"

"Okay, Regis," he grinned at the flash of annoyance that cut through her fear. "I'm going to make this quick."

"I told you not to call me – ah!" The middle of her retort was cut off by a yelp as Hawk slid the needle into her arm. "What the hell, Hawk … er, Dr. McKinnon," she growled.

He bit back a laugh. "If you prefer it, to be fair, you can call me Keith."

"I'm thinking of another name right now."

Then he did laugh. She was feisty for sure. And he liked that about her.

While he was sure she was a tough woman, he found her attempt at ferocity to be almost cute. Not that he was about to tell her that. He wasn't stupid. He dropped the syringe into the biohazard container on the floor.

"Are you going to be okay driving?" he asked.

"Sure."

He looked at her intently.

"What?"

"Your face has a little more color. For a while there, I thought you really were going to pass out."

He touched her arm to help her off the table. Her face flushed, and she pulled her arm away. "I'm fine."

"Good. Nancy has that paperwork for you to fill out before you leave."

"I know all about paperwork," she said, chuckling.

"I'm sure you do. I'll make that call to the pharmacy for you."

Hawk walked in the opposite direction that Regis went, and resisted the urge to turn back to look at her. For God's sake, she was a patient. She was here in town to help people he knew needed her to do her job so they could get on with their lives.

Yet, he didn't want to see her leave, and he definitely wanted to see Regis Simpson again. But not like this and not here. He'd fought the urge to ask her out for dinner. He'd find a moment that was right.

When he reached his office door, he turned around and caught her looking over her shoulder at him as she walked down the hall. He'd make that moment come very soon.

Fifteen minutes later, Hawk emerged from his office and walked to the front waiting area. Nancy was sitting behind the computer, inputting information from the paperwork Regis had just handed her. She lifted her eyes from Regis's paperwork only long enough to give him a teasing glance.

"Here is the name of the pharmacy," he said, handing Regis a piece of paper.

"Thank you, Keith."

He ignored the expression on his receptionist's face. Nancy had an opinion about everything, and he was sure he'd hear it once Regis left.

"Make sure you stay off that leg tonight. It's probably going to hurt a lot more once the adrenaline rush wears off."

"I will." Regis was out the door before Hawk could say anything more. And there were a whole lot of things spinning in his head that he wanted to ask her, starting with dinner, and where all that spunk he saw in her came from. He'd do that later.

He finally turned and stole a glance at Nancy.

"Keith?" she echoed.

"Breathe one word, and I'll tell everyone your middle name is Aggy."

Nancy gasped. "You wouldn't dare."

He smiled teasingly. "Only one way you'll find out."

Nancy rolled her eyes and went back to her typing as Hawk walked back to his office, unable to suppress his grin. He had some paperwork of his own to fill out for the Wounded Veterans Center if he was going to get out of here early. He had a house call to make tonight, and he didn't want to be late.

Chapter Three

Motel rooms had been her home for far too long. Regis was so familiar with the blandness of each motel she stayed at that she never really paid attention to details. It only served to remind her about a childhood spending long periods of time in other people's homes on Army bases around the world while her dad was on tour somewhere else. At least now, she could be in the quiet of her own space without having to put on a smile for people she barely knew.

She'd managed to hobble her way out of the car and into her motel room and fire up her laptop so she could check which appointments she was going to miss the rest of the day. She'd have to switch around appointments tomorrow and bump a few to later in the week to keep her already heavy workload manageable. As soon as she'd figured out a workable plan, she called the homeowners who'd given her cell phone numbers with the news. Naturally, some were disappointed they'd have to wait another day or two for the inspections, and it meant she had to stay a little longer in Rudolph to get all her work done. But it couldn't be helped.

Dr. Keith McKinnon had been right about one thing, she felt the pain in her leg more now than she did when she'd initially fallen. With each movement on the bed, pain shot up her leg and brought tears to her eyes.

She finally closed the laptop and pushed it to the side of her bed, debating the need for getting up and grabbing the remote so she could watch television. Before boredom could win out, she heard a knock on the door and decided it must be the pharmacy delivering her prescription.

"Please let there be painkiller in there, too," she whispered. Then she called out, "Just a minute!"

Easing herself up off the bed, she limped to the door, being careful her sweatpants leg didn't fall over her bandage and cause the elastic to squeeze her leg. Even the slightest pressure was enough to send her through the roof. It was a struggle to get up on her tippy toes to look out of the peephole, but when she did, she stepped back, putting weight on her injured leg. Shooting pain nearly leveled her as she opened the door.

"I'd ask how you're doing, but from the look on your face, I'm guessing it's not so good."

Dr. Keith McKinnon stood outside the doorway looking better than he had earlier walking up the handicap ramp at his office. She, on the other hand, looked like road kill. She didn't have to look to know she had a serious case of bedhead from trying to take a nap earlier. Her old sweatpants and sweatshirt were comfy, but so big it made it hard to tell she was female underneath them.

She touched her hair just to make sure it wasn't sticking up. "What are you doing here?"

He lifted the white bag in his left hand. "Your prescription. When I called it into the pharmacy, they said they weren't making runs out this way due to all the flooding and roads being washed out."

She looked at the Styrofoam containers in his other hand. The glorious smell coming from them immediately made her stomach growl. "And what's that?"

"Dinner. For us. That is, if you're up for it."

She stepped aside to give Keith room to walk inside the motel room.

"Am I another house call?"

His voice was gentle as he spoke, making her head light. "No. But since you're from out of town, I knew you didn't have anyone else here to check on you, so I thought I'd make sure you were getting along. I figured you probably hadn't been able to grab a bite to eat yet either."

Warmth spread through her chest. "You wanted to check on me?"

"Sure." He lifted the containers. "Should I put these over on the table?"

She nodded; a sudden feeling of melancholy enveloping her. Keith didn't know how close to the truth he was. It had been a long time since there'd been anyone concerned with checking on her. In fact, she only spoke to her father about once a month because he was always so busy. The fact that Keith thought enough to stop by, and with dinner no less, was a first for her. She wasn't sure how to feel about it.

He was looking at her again.

"I'm not going to pass out," she said.

A low chuckle rumbled from his chest that Regis found enticing.

"No, but you do have this deer-in-the-headlights look about you."

"Do I?"

"Is something wrong? Did I come at a bad time?"

"No, it's just ..." She didn't know exactly how to verbalize the oddness of having Dr. Keith McKinnon in her motel room.

Keith looked around the room, walking a few steps before he turned to her. "Looks okay to me. You didn't leave your dirty towel on the bathroom floor, did you?"

"Of course not. Besides the maid has been through the room today."

"Were you expecting someone else?"

"No. No, that's not it."

His brow narrowed. "Do I make you uncomfortable, Regis?"

Now there was a loaded question. The thing was, Dr. Keith McKinnon *did* make her uncomfortable. But for all the wrong reasons. Regis liked the way he looked at her. She liked the sound of his voice when he said her name. Her real name. She even liked the fact that he refused to call her by the nickname her dad had given her long ago, even though she'd repeatedly corrected him.

"I'm not used to having people in my motel room. It's usually … just my own quiet space."

His dark eyebrows lifted. "Never?"

She shook her head. "I visit ten to fifteen different cities and towns a year. This is a first."

His lips lifted on one side in a way that Regis could only call sexy. The warm feeling in her chest grew.

"I like that. Being a first. But if you would prefer I leave, I will. I don't want you to be uncomfortable."

"I'm not uncomfortable," she said quietly. "You brought me dinner. The least I can do is offer you a seat at my table to enjoy it." She looked back at the small desk and realized there was only one chair. "You can take the chair at the desk, and I'll sit on the bed."

"Good choice. You need to keep your leg elevated."

She hobbled over to the bed and eased down on it while Keith carried the food to the desk.

"I have some sodas in the mini-fridge."

Keith went to the mini-fridge by the dresser and pulled out two cans of soda. "Want a glass?"

"No, it's just one more thing to clean."

He put the cold soda on the nightstand next to her and then handed her one of the Styrofoam containers with a set of plastic utensils and a napkin.

"I thought the diner was closed this time of the night," she said, lifting the lid and fully breathing in the aroma of good home cooking.

"It is. My mother is working down at the shelter again. It's actually the elementary school, but for now it's a working shelter. At least, it's been for the last couple of weeks. Tomorrow everyone should be in temporary housing while they rebuild."

"Your mother owns the diner?"

He smiled with pride. "Since before I was born. Every single one of us McKinnons took our first steps across that dining room floor. Although my mother will swear we all never walked, we just ran."

Regis smiled picturing it. "How many McKinnons are there?"

"Five boys."

She dropped the fork full of food in the container. "Five? Your mother ran a diner and raised five boys at the same time?"

"Amazing, huh?" he said with pride.

They both took a bite of food and were quiet for a few moments. Regis had eaten out of many a Styrofoam container over the years, but there was nothing like home cooking.

"So what about you?" Keith finally asked.

"What about me?"

"Where are you from?"

"Everywhere."

He frowned. "No one place to call home?"

Regis lifted a shoulder. "I'm an Army brat. I've lived on bases all over the world."

"Wow. That must have been quite an adventure for your parents and you."

"Just my dad and me," she said. "My mom didn't like the Army life. Or family life for that matter. She took off when I was six. It was just my dad and me after that. Just me when he was on tour."

He looked shocked, like most people did when she said that. "Who'd take care of you when your father was gone?"

"I usually got placed with another family on base … or two or three while my father was gone. Homecomings were better than times he shipped out. Most families were going through their own trials with a parent gone. It was hard taking care of a snotty kid like me who didn't exactly want to be with them any more than they wanted me to be there."

"You? Snotty?"

"I was a kid. Aren't all kids snotty when they're missing their dad?"

"You have a point. That must have been rough on you though."

"Like anything else, you learn to adapt. At least it made acclimating to my present job easier, since I'm always on the road."

"So where's home?"

She shrugged. "Here right now. Next month, who knows?"

"You're a gypsy."

His voice was as smooth as silk when he said the words, almost as if he liked the intrigue of it.

"I guess you could say that. Except I'm not going to tell your fortune or dance for you."

He raised his eyebrows with a wicked grin. "Now that sounds very enticing. I wouldn't mind seeing you in silk and gems."

Warmth flowed through her as the heat in Keith's eyes flared.

"Do you talk this way to all of your patients, Dr. McKinnon?"

"Hawk."

"I thought you said I could call you Keith?"

His lips tilted to a slight grin, then looked at the container sitting on her lap. "Your dinner is getting cold."

♥ ♥ ♥

After dinner, Keith checked the bandage on Regis's leg.

"Make sure you keep this dry for at least another day. As long as you can walk on it without pain, you can get around. But keep your activity down to a minimum or you'll risk opening up the wound again."

"No can do. I already had to cancel a long list of appointments today. Now I have an even longer list of properties to see tomorrow."

"I talked with my cousin, Ian, earlier. He mentioned you'd called him about rescheduling your inspection of the Center."

She frowned. "Center?"

"It's the old mill by the river. It was being converted to a community center, but there's space for the Wounded Veterans Center there as well as its other functions. Ian is a wounded veteran. My brother, Ethan, is a retired Navy Seal. They've been working to get the old mill transformed into a center for the vets in the area as well as have it funded by regular functions. Dances and weddings and such. My younger brother Logan and his fiancé are hoping to be the first to have their wedding there. It's a pretty spot. Or at least, it was before the floodwaters came in."

"Oh, that's right. I'm sorry. I talked with a lot of people today. I do remember talking to a man named Ian. I didn't make the connection."

"There are quite a few of us in these parts."

"I guess so. I look forward to meeting them while I'm here."

He nodded. "I would like to see you again."

"I don't think I'll really need a follow-up appointment for this. I should be able to wrap this myself now that I've seen you do it twice already." She reached for her cell phone so she could check her calendar. "To be quite honest, I don't think I could fit—"

"I wasn't thinking of an office visit. I was thinking more alone the lines of having dinner again."

She eased the cell phone back into place on the night table. "Excuse me?"

"I enjoyed being with you tonight. I thought you might like a repeat."

♥ ♥ ♥

The deer-in-the-headlights expression was back on her face, Hawk realized. Regis was staring at him, wide-eyed with her lips slightly parted. He waited for her to respond, but he wasn't altogether sure she was even breathing until she finally spoke.

"I don't like to get … involved," she said.

"You're never in one place long enough for that, are you?"

"No."

"You eat alone every night?"

"Most of the time, yes. Sometimes I have dinner with one of my colleagues if they're in the same town, but most of the time we're all too exhausted and have too much paperwork to do."

"Sounds lonely."

"It's the nature of the beast."

"It doesn't have to be. Especially when someone is offering you a home cooked meal."

Her mouth dropped open. "Home cooked?"

"Yeah, my house. Okay,

"Your house."

"Well, not exactly home cooked like my mother's. But I have a pizza stone that needs breaking in. We can be creative."

She shook her head. "I ... when I'm on the job, things get complicated."

"You don't like complicated?"

She sighed slowly, seeming to choose her words carefully. "Sometimes I have to deliver bad news, like with the Proctors. I hate it. It's the worst part of my job. But it's a fact. It makes things easier if I just keep to myself."

A grin tugged at his mouth. "I didn't propose marriage, Regis. Just pizza." He kept his tone matter-of-fact, trying to ignore just how badly he wanted her to say yes. He'd been watching her all night, wondering if the intrigue he'd felt earlier in the day would be gone. She'd greeted him with messy hair, make-up smeared down her cheek, and old gray sweats that were probably two sizes too big and still she looked like the sexiest thing he'd ever seen. He looked at that cluster of freckles on her cheek and wanted to rub his thumb across it as he looked into her eyes.

Hawk watched the choices play across her face. But then she was shaking her head again. "Thank you for the offer, but I have to decline. And thank you for this tonight.

I was wondering if I was going to get to eat more than just Cheetos and peanuts from the vending machine outside."

He forced a smile he didn't feel. "Well, I'm glad we had the chance to talk tonight then."

She started to get up off the bed, but he held her back with his hand.

"I'll let myself out. You stay off your leg at least for tonight. Make sure you come back to the office if your leg gives you trouble."

Hawk had his hand on the doorknob when Regis stopped him.

"Thank you for tonight. I'm not … I don't usually have to depend on people. I'm glad you stopped by."

"It was my pleasure."

Hawk whistled as he left Regis's room and made his way to his truck in the motel parking lot. She'd turned him down, but he could see that she was conflicted. To him, that just meant he'd have to win her over another way. One thing was for sure, he was more intrigued with Regis Simpson than he was when he'd arrived tonight. And that only made him want to see her more. And he would. He was sure of it.

He slammed the truck door closed and turned the key in the ignition, whistling while the engine fired to life. He couldn't recall the last time he'd whistled.

Chapter Four

Her leg was bleeding again. It wasn't even noon, and she'd already managed to get off schedule after brushing up against the fender of her car while taking pictures of a house with roof damage. It should have been a quick appointment, lasting no more than ten minutes to talk to the owner and take pictures. Instead, she needed mending. Again.

Disgusted with herself, Regis pulled her sedan into the clinic parking lot. She killed the engine and drummed her fingers on the steering wheel. She should have gone back to her hotel and just patched her leg up herself. But …

But she was here at the clinic to see Dr. Keith McKinnon again. Yeah, the reason for that wasn't too big of a mind stretch for her. She'd thought of nothing but him since he'd shown up at her motel room last night.

What the hell was she doing? He'd asked her to dinner. And she'd emphatically said no. She never dated men while on the road. They'd get attached. She'd get attached. And then she'd move on to another town. That was the story of her childhood. She didn't want to repeat it in her adult life.

Besides, long distance relationships never worked. She'd learned that one the hard way when she'd held on too long.

"And this is not a date," she muttered, opening the car door. "I'm only here to have my leg wrapped again and then I'll be back on the road."

Oh, why couldn't Keith McKinnon be a crusty old doctor? Instead, she couldn't stop thinking about the drop-dead gorgeous country doctor with a heart of gold she'd only seen in heroes in movies.

Ten minutes later, she was sitting on the same examining table she'd sat on the day before, looking into those deep blue eyes that had haunted her all last night. He'd dispensed with wearing the white jacket he'd put on yesterday, making it hard to see him as the caring doctor he'd been. Instead, strong muscles were clearly visible beneath the fabric of his long sleeved gray shirt. The blue jeans he wore were faded and had stains that clearly had defied laundering.

"Am I keeping you from something?" she asked.

"You just caught me. I was heading over to the mill to help with some of the cleanup."

She nodded. "That's another thing on my list that I'm going to have to reschedule. Again."

Regis fought the tears of frustration she'd been feeling since yesterday's mishap. So many people were counting on her, and she was failing.

"Come on. It's not that bad," Keith said, lifting her chin with his finger. The sympathy she saw in his eyes was more than she could take. She lost the battle with her emotions as the tears she'd been holding back fell down her cheek.

Reaching behind him, Keith grabbed a tissue box and held it out for her. She took two and nodded her thanks.

"I'm so embarrassed," she finally said when she got her emotions in check. "I don't normally blubber like this."

"Why not? It looks like you were overdue."

She shook her head. "I can hear my father in my head tell me to buck up. 'Soldiers don't cry.'" She lowered her voice in that deep way she always did when she mimicked her father's admonition. She hadn't done that in a long time.

"You were a soldier?"

"No, my dad is."

"Oh."

His sudden silence had her looking up at Keith. "What?"

He shrugged as he grabbed a fresh roll of gauze from the cabinet. "I don't know your father, but I do know a lot of people in the military. Male or female, they do cry. How could they not? And plenty of people cry with them. There's nothing wrong with some tears."

His kind words only made Regis feel worse and her tears renewed.

"I can't do what I have to do with this leg."

"The longer you stay off it, the better chance the wound has to heal and stay closed.

"I can't stay off my feet long enough for this to heal."

"You don't have sick time from work?"

"It's not that. I'm sure I can call my office, and they'll send another adjuster out here to replace me. But …"

He cocked his head slightly to one side and waited for her to go on.

"I've been at this a long time," she said. "There are a lot of people who do what I do who aren't thorough."

She glanced up at him, hoping he'd get her meaning. After a second, he nodded.

"It's very noble to be conscientious about your job. In fact, that's something I got from you immediately. You care about what you do. I'm sure not everyone would be as dedicated."

"Thank you. I just want to make sure these people get what they need first." She took a deep breath and used the tissues to wipe her cheeks. "So what's the prognosis? Am I back in the saddle when you get me patched up?"

His slow sigh gave her the answer. "If you want this leg to heal so you can really get around the way you need to, you're going to need to stay off it for at least another day."

"That's not poss—"

"Or every time you bend your foot or rub up against something, you risk re-injuring yourself."

"So warned."

He finished inspecting her leg and then wrapped it up. He dropped his latex gloves in the trash and turned to her.

"Who do you have on your list today?"

"My schedule is in the car."

"Then let's take a look."

Fifteen minutes later they were standing in the clinic parking lot. Regis pulled her tablet from the car and was now scrolling down the list of names of people she'd need to contact.

Keith was standing incredibly close to her. She felt the heat of his body as it shielded her from the March wind, and the light smell of aftershave. She hadn't noticed it earlier, but that was the difference about him today. She'd noticed the light scruff of hair on his jawline yesterday, but now it was cleanly shaven. Just standing so close to him made her head light, making it hard to concentrate.

"You were going to go to the mill today," he said, seemingly unaware of his effect on her.

"That was the plan." The wind whipped her hair around her face. She fought with trying to keep it from obstructing her vision for a few seconds. When it subsided, she noticed Keith was staring intently at her list.

"Okay, then," he said, moving away from her and leaving her in the wind. He opened her driver's side door and reached inside the car, pulling out her camera.

"Okay then what?" she asked.

"We'll take my truck. This is the only camera you use?"

Confused, she said, "Yes. But don't you have appointments?"

"I had them all this morning. I was just about to leave when you came in."

"Doesn't anyone else besides me need a doctor around here?" she said, chuckling.

Keith laughed too, and the sound of it made her smile. Not just a smile on her face, but a smile she felt inside. Good Lord, when was the last time any man had made her feel that way? Ever!

"Hopefully not for the rest of the day. That way we can get through the list."

"You're going to come with me?"

"Yes. If it means you're not going to hurt yourself again. Look, I know the area better than you. I also know the terrain. If there is any place that is too difficult to walk on or can cause you injury, I'll go and take the pictures. Then you won't get too far behind."

She looked up at the strong features of his face, scrutinized the blue eyes she couldn't stop thinking about, just to see if he was kidding. He was serious.

"Why are you doing this?" she asked quietly.

"Why not?"

"You just met me. You don't even really know me."

He nodded and pointed out into the distance. "But I know them. And I do know that doing this right is important to you. So I figure the best way for me to help people I know and care about is to help you. It's a win-win situation. Is there anything wrong with that?"

She drew in a slow breath, unable to find words of gratitude that seemed genuine.

"Thank you," was all she managed.

♥ ♥ ♥

The truck smelled like Regis. They'd been to three properties already on their way to the mill and each time Hawk climbed into the truck, the scent of her filled his head.

"Right over there is the Maitland ranch. That's where I got on my first bull."

Regis gave him a quick glance. "You were a bull rider?"

"I didn't say that. I got on the bull, and it immediately bucked me off. I don't even think I lasted a second. But I did give it a second and third try, mostly because my brother, Wade, dared me to."

"Wade?"

He caught himself. It wasn't often he talked about Wade. And it occurred to him that Wade probably would've been angry at him for closing himself off that way. But even after nearly five years, losing his brother still felt as raw as it did the day they got the news.

"My oldest brother. He's first, then me, then Sam, then the twins, Ethan and Logan." He drove in silence for a few seconds, allowing himself to think about things he hadn't thought of for a long time. "Wade was good at bull riding. He was never serious enough to go pro, but he had no fear of that bull."

Regis smiled at him. "You admired him a lot."

Hawk nodded. "He was the best friend I've ever had." And Hawk had let him down.

His hand went to his chest to feel the small medallion and chain that Wade always wore from the time he was a teenager until before he'd gone on that trip with the Peace Corps that last time.

"I'm an only child," Regis said. "I can't even imagine what it would have been like to grow up with a houseful of boys like you all did. You must have driven your parents crazy."

"We're McKinnons," he said laughing. "I can't imagine what it would have been like growing up without noise and chaos. My parents seemed to thrive on it. You said you lived on military bases growing up. What was that like?"

She shrugged. "Different." She turned her head to look at the side of the road. Hawk didn't push it.

"Did you go to this high school?" she asked as they passed the school.

"Yes. On really hot days in the spring, Sam and I used to skip class and head down to the pond on through the woods with some of the other kids in school. Denny's house was out there." He pointed to a long driveway that disappeared into the woods. "Denny was really Ethan's friend, but we all hung out. And we always got caught when we did."

Laughing, Regis asked, "By who?"

"My dad mostly. And believe me, he wasn't too happy about it. But when the principal would call him at the drilling company and tell him that four of his boys had suddenly disappeared from the school, he wanted to take care of things in person, especially since he knew my mom couldn't leave the diner during the day back then. She has a lot more help running the diner now. But my dad always knew where to find us."

"Drilling company. You mean, as in MW Oil? That big plant I saw a few towns back when I came into Rudolph?"

"That's the one. Started by my father's grandparents and passed down the line."

"Did any of you boys join the family business?"

He made a face and looked at her.

Her beautiful eyes widened. "No?"

"Dad gave up hoping long ago and is now trying to convince my four-year-old nephew that it's up to him."

"No pressure though," she said, with a giggle.

Regis looked on her tablet at the list of properties she had to inspect.

"Do you have the Coleman property on the list?" Hawk asked.

"Yes, but not for today."

"Good."

She gave him a questioning look.

"Bob Coleman isn't always happy to see me."

"Why?"

"I'm not sure he's ever forgiven me for driving his tractor into the side of his barn."

"What?

"Don't listen to any stories about it either. I swear it was a faulty brake. I didn't do it on purpose."

"Were you and your brothers always trouble?"

He chuckled with the memory. "Let's just say people in town knew the name McKinnon. It's a good thing they all loved my mom."

Regis's chuckle turned into a full-blown laugh, and Hawk decided that he'd found his new favorite sound. He wanted to hear it more. But then it changed, and she was quiet again.

"I envy you knowing so much about where you live. Knowing everyone. I barely remember some of the names of people I lived with."

"How many did you live with?"

She drew in a deep breath. "Too many. Every time my father had to leave, I got placed with a new family on base to stay with. It was a lot like living in a foster home, I suppose."

He nodded as if he understood, and yet, Hawk couldn't imagine a life like that.

Since the sun would be setting in an hour, they decided to head over to the mill to inspect the property. Regis had called Ian, but got no answer, so Hawk called his brother Ethan, who agreed to meet them. Ethan's police SUV was parked on the muddied road, and he was standing outside.

"You made it," he said as Hawk parked his truck. "I was worried I'd get a call and have to take off before you got here."

"We got hung up at the Jordan property," Hawk said, getting out of the car.

Regis got out of the truck and limped over to where Ethan and Hawk were standing. Hawk could see that the busy day had taken its toll on her, and she was fading fast.

"Ethan, this is—"

"Reggie Simpson," Ethan said. "We met a few days ago at the diner."

"How are you doing? I didn't realize you were Keith's brother."

Ethan raised his eyebrows. "Keith?"

Hawk shot his brother a warning glare, which earned him a laugh from Ethan. But instead of the normal ribbing he would have gotten, Ethan turned his attention to Regis.

"Keith tells me you were a Navy Seal."

Ethan smiled with pride as he looked at the weathered red façade of the Buxton Mill. "Yes, ma'am. That's why this place is so important."

"Well, let's take a look and see what the damage is."

The terrain was rough on the exterior of the mill. Hawk extended his hand to Regis to give her support as she walked.

"I'm fine," she said in a quiet voice when they got to the stairs by the door. His hand lingered, linked with hers for longer than he needed. But Hawk was in no hurry to let go until Regis pulled away.

"I heard Poppy and Mom talking about a winter wedding here. Seems Poppy has her heart set on having the ceremony in the back by the floor to ceiling windows overlooking the river," Ethan said.

"Winter weather is unpredictable, but it'll be a pretty spot if it snows."

Regis looked around the room. "But there are no floor to ceiling windows here."

"It's all in the new plans that Ian drew up for the place. He's put a lot of time and money into the design and use for the property and has worked with the building commissioner to make sure we can get the permits to get this dream realized."

They walked through the main floor of the Buxton Mill while Hawk and Ethan described the plans for the center. Every so often, Regis snapped pictures with her camera and made notes on her tablet.

"How did you happen to come across this property for a community center?" Regis asked.

"It was a small, family owned business for over a hundred years until about fifteen years ago when the oldest family member died, and the company got squeezed out by the bigger mills in the state. The others were retiring and didn't have a buyer who was interested in doing anything, but tearing it down and putting up condos because of the river location," Ethan explained. "The Buxtons were a family of veterans that went all the way back to World War I and decided they wanted to donate the property to the town for a community center as long as we established space in it for the Wounded Veterans Center."

"That was generous of them," Regis said, stepping back and taking another few pictures as she listened.

"Well, there was back taxes and debt to pay, but we managed to raise the money locally for that," Ethan added. "Ian has been instrumental in working the cause. I think it saved him, to be honest."

Regis lowered the camera and looked at both of them. "Saved him?"

Hawk thought of his cousin and how far he'd come. "He was a mess when he came back from Iraq. But this has given him a reason to get out of bed, and for that alone, I'm grateful to the Buxtons for their gift. Now we just have to get this place up to speed."

They finished their tour of the mill, which took longer than the other properties because of its size and proximity to the river. Just as they were wrapping up, Ethan got a call over the police radio.

"I have a call down at the high school," Ethan said. "I've got to run."

"Are you going to stop in and see Maddie?"

Ethan made a face that gave him his answer.

"She's got to talk to you sometime."

He shook his head. "No she doesn't," he said quietly. To Regis, he added, "Do you need anything else?"

"We're all set here," Regis said. "Thank you for meeting with me."

"No problem. You know where to find me if you have any questions. And you have Ian's number. I'm sure he can answer more than I can. He would have been here today but ..."

"I understand. It was last minute so I appreciate you taking the time."

A few minutes later, Ethan was pulling out of the parking lot in his SUV, and the two of them were alone at the empty mill. They were losing light fast, and the ground was disappearing in the darkness as they walked back to the truck, making it hard to see the ruts in the dried mud. Knowing Regis was already tired, and not wanting her to injure herself again, Hawk took matters into his own hands. In one fell swoop, he scooped Regis up into his arms.

Chapter Five

The last thing Regis had expected when she'd agreed to have Hawk help her today was ending up in his arms. When he'd put a strong arm behind her knees and the other around her waist, she was in the air instantly. His jacket was open, and she was pressed up against his rock hard chest before she could say a word of protest.

"Don't argue," he said. His face was just inches from hers as he carried her effortlessly across the parking lot to the truck.

"This isn't necessary."

"It's just insurance that you don't get hurt again and wind up on my examining room table. I'd much rather see you outside my office than in it."

When they reached the truck, Hawk stood next to the passenger side door and held Regis in his arms, just looking at her. She could feel his warmth, see the mist of his breath against the cold air, and feel his heart beating against her.

"You can put me down now," she said, her heart beating wildly in her chest.

"I don't think so."

"What?"

"I like you right where you are."

"Please put me down, Keith," she said quietly.

His lips lifted to a half grin. "I really like it when you say my name."

"I thought you didn't like people calling you by your given name."

"I like the way you say it. In fact, I like it a lot."

"You do?"

He had a full-blown smile now. "I like you a lot."

"Keith?"

"What?"

"Please put me down."

"I kind of like having you right here in my arms."

She drew in a deep breath. "You don't like me. You only think you like me. You don't even know me."

He chuckled against her eye and whispered, "Then let's get to know each other."

She turned away from him, feeling her resolve wither away. "I don't like to get involved—"

"You don't like complicated. Well, I mean to change that."

He slowly lowered her so her feet were on the ground, but he kept his arm around her and pulled her closer with the other arm.

"I want to kiss you."

"Are you always this direct?"

With his hand, he pushed aside the hair the wind blew in her face, and bent his head so that his mouth was only inches from hers. "Only when I want something very badly."

And then his warm mouth was against hers, and to her surprise, Regis didn't protest. Instead, she melted into the warmth that Keith provided, both in body and spirit. His hands were in her hair, pulling her closer as his mouth devoured hers. And she gave back what was given and wanted more.

She couldn't remember the last time she'd felt so completely undone by a man with just a touch or a look or a kiss. Keith's kisses weren't anything like she'd felt before. He wasn't a man like anyone she'd ever known before.

And it scared her to death and excited every single bit of her at the same time.

He pulled away slowly, with his mouth still just inches from hers.

"I could use a whole lot more of these," he said. Even as the night grew darker, she could see his lips curled into a pleasing smile.

"I don't think that was such a hot idea."

"Regis, I'm plenty hot right now, and I think the idea of kissing the woman who got me there is just fine."

She drew in a slow breath and took a step back, out of his arms. And he let her. He didn't try to keep her where she didn't want to be. Except, she'd liked it a whole lot better when Keith's arms were wrapped around her. And that was just the problem.

"What do you want from me, Keith? This can't go anywhere good."

She couldn't see his eyes or his expression in the darkness, but she could see his frown.

"I don't have a crystal ball. But I do know that I like you. And that hasn't happened for me in a very long time."

Her heart melted with his words. It was as if he were reading her mind.

"I know the feeling."

"Then don't we owe it to ourselves to at least find out what this is?"

Regis had a feeling she'd regret any answer she gave him.

♥ ♥ ♥

"It's only dinner," she mumbled to herself as she drove to the clinic. Regis had managed to get some sleep, and work a full day setting up her space on a table in the large meeting room at the Senior Center next to the FEMA representatives and a number of other insurance adjusters who were in town to help. Despite having a full day of work, she was surprisingly energetic and decided all this energy was the lingering adrenaline rush after the kiss three days ago.

She still couldn't believe she'd kissed Keith. And then actually agreed to have dinner with him tonight, breaking the first rule of being on the road. Of course, he was probably the most persistent man she'd ever met. In the days since they'd kissed at the mill, Keith had made it a point to stop by and see her at the motel to check on her. He never stayed long. He didn't talk about the kiss they'd shared. He just spent time with her and then always asked her to dinner. And she'd always say no. Until last night.

She liked him. Regis couldn't deny it. And he said he felt the same way about her. In fact, Regis really liked the way Keith was not at all shy about admitting his feelings. She'd never been that open with a man before. And while it caught her off guard ... she liked it.

"You're such an idiot, Reggie," she mumbled as she pulled into the parking lot of the clinic next to his truck. Disgusted with herself, she killed the engine and sat in the car looking at the clinic. The light was on inside, and she could see through the window that Nancy was standing inside the waiting room talking to someone. She had her heavy winter coat wrapped around her and her purse hiked up on her shoulder.

"It's just pizza. Even you can handle that." Even as she tried to downplay the importance of this dinner, Regis struggled with the idea of actually going through with it. Still, her palms were sweaty, and her heart was pounding through her chest as she pushed the car door open.

She checked her reflection in the mirror for the umpteenth time since she'd left the motel, unable to stop thinking about the man she was going to meet. It wasn't just that Keith McKinnon was incredibly handsome. He was, and what was so charming was that, despite him teasing her about it the day they met, he didn't seem to realize just how handsome he was. But she had met plenty of good-looking men over the years. The bases she'd lived on all over the world had provided lots of teenage crushes, and one hell of a heartbreak that was difficult to think about even now.

But none of them had ever stuck in her mind the way Keith McKinnon had. There was just something about the man that had kept her awake last night. And it wasn't just the constant replay of the kiss at the mill the other day. It would have been easy to blame her sleepless night on pain in her leg. But that hadn't been the source of her restlessness last night. And as Keith had predicted, her leg was feeling a whole lot better today, to the point where she hardly noticed it at all.

Days ago she'd seen him pull into the parking lot and walk up the ramp toward her. It shouldn't have been a big deal, but the memory made her flush with heat. Just remembering the look on his face and the way she'd reacted … she'd made a fool of herself. And after her reaction to his kiss, she was convinced she was still making a fool of herself.

Regis walked up the ramp until she reached the landing, and then pushed the door open. The warm air from the office hit her in the face as she stepped inside.

Nancy smiled knowingly when she saw her. "There's the girl of the hour."

"Excuse me?"

"Never mind," Keith said. "Nancy was just on her way out."

"Am I late?"

Nancy chuckled. "Depends on whose clock you're looking at. How's that leg?"

"Hasn't fallen off yet."

Nancy laughed harder. "Sense of humor is there? That's always a good sign." She touched Regis on the shoulder as she passed to the door. "Enjoy your evening."

Regis waited for Nancy to step outside before turning to Keith.

"What was that all about?"

"Nothing. Nancy is a good friend of my mother's and the two of them have been trying to get me married off since I was twelve. They're hoping some nice girl will tame me."

"Is that so?"

"That seems to be the plan."

"But you're against the idea. Marriage that is."

He thought about it a second. "No. I just don't believe in putting the cart before the horse. I don't want to get married just to get married."

"That's a recipe for disaster for everyone left behind."

He stopped what he was doing mid-motion. "Sounds like you're talking from personal experience."

She hadn't realized she'd said that last part out loud. "You promised me homemade pizza," she said, changing the subject.

He frowned, and her stomach fell. "I did. But we may have a problem."

"After all your convincing for me to come to dinner, you're backing out?"

"Not a chance. But apparently a pipe burst at the school they're using as an emergency shelter, and while a lot of the displaced people have temporary housing, there are still people there, and they need to be fed."

She looked out the window and saw the diner lights on and the parking lot full of cars. "The diner looks packed."

"Yeah, but the diner isn't big enough to handle it all. Mom said they needed a place for overflow, and the only place big enough to handle it that was close enough to the diner is my place. So my kitchen is in full use. There are a lot of hands helping out tonight."

"We don't have to do this tonight," she said.

He gave her an irresistible half grin. "You're not getting out of this that easy. Ethan called a little while ago and said they're packaging everything up now. All I can say is that I can't vouch for the state of my kitchen until I get there, so consider yourself forewarned."

"Let's go see the damage then."

Keith insisted she drive with him to the house and leave her car in the clinic's parking lot. He was probably afraid she'd bolt when she saw all the cars lined up his driveway.

"Looks like half the town is here," she said.

He chuckled as he pushed the truck door open. "No, just mostly McKinnons and other volunteers that have been helping out since the flood."

"Just a dinner," she muttered as she pushed the car door open.

"What?"

"Nothing."

She ran her fingers through her hair and climbed out of his truck, thankful she'd changed out of her work clothes into a comfortable pair of jeans and a black peasant top. Her leg didn't hurt as much as it did, but she still chose a pair of black running shoes over a dressier high-heeled boot to be on the safe side.

She'd only gone a few steps when a dark-haired man bearing a striking resemblance to Keith came out of the house with a large box in his arms.

He smiled at Keith as they approached.

"I should have known you'd show up just as all the work is finished," he said.

Keith spread his hands as if defeated. "You think I'm stupid? What is the state of my kitchen?"

"It's still there." The man looked at Regis, then at Keith, and then back at Regis. "I'd shake your hand, but they're full. I'm Logan. If I wait for my idiot brother to introduce me, these dinners will spoil. And they're getting heavy."

As if just catching himself, Keith shook his head. "Sorry. Regis Simpson, this is my smart-assed brother. He actually thinks he needs to keep me in line."

"That must come from somewhere," Regis said, smiling at Logan.

Logan laughed, gave Keith a teasing look, and then he eased the box into the back of a truck that already had a few boxes filled with containers. "She's smart. I'd keep her close if I were you."

The screen door to the log cabin opened, and a tall woman walked onto the porch holding a little boy's hand.

"Don't leave without us, Daddy!" the little boy called out as if he were worried about being left behind.

"No worries, little man. I need you to help me carry all this food."

Keith turned to Regis. "This little man about to tackle me is my nephew, Keith." He bent down to pick the little boy up as he launched into his arms, giggling. The bond between the two was evident by the way they connected so lovingly.

"You know, I'm standing here, too," the woman said.

"Sorry, Poppy."

Logan laughed. "Usually I'm getting in trouble for failed introductions. Regis, this is my soon-to-be bride, Poppy Ericksen."

"Not soon enough for me," Poppy said, gazing at Logan with a twinkle in her eye. Regis found herself fighting off the stab of envy in her stomach. They all seemed so close, something she'd never experienced in her lifetime.

"Nice to meet you."

"Ethan told me you were out at the mill assessing the damage," Poppy said.

Regis nodded. "We were there the other day."

"Good. The sooner they get all their paperwork done for the claim, the sooner they can get all the estimates for renovations, and they can start building. I have my heart set on a winter wedding there at the end of the year."

"Congratulations," Regis said. "It looks like it will be a pretty spot."

"Thank you. That's what we're hoping," Logan said, scooping Poppy by the waist and pulling her close to him. "We need to get this food over to the school so they can start feeding people."

Keith glanced into the back of the truck. "Looks like you've got a full load. That's good."

"Ethan already took off with a bunch of boxes. He's waiting for us at the school," Poppy said. She kissed Keith on the cheek and said, "Make sure you ask your mother why she can't stop smiling."

He looked at Poppy, then quickly looked at Logan. " It's too soon for you …"

"To be expecting? Jeez, give us a little time why don't you," Poppy said, chuckling as she shook her head.

"Then what is it?"

Logan took his son in his arms and carried him over to the open truck door to help him into his car seat. "Ask Mom."

They said their good-byes as they walked to the log home. As the pick-up rumbled away, Keith led Regis up the stairs just as the door opened again. A man and woman emerged, carrying the same type of containers Keith's brother had. The woman gave them a half-smile that spoke of long days and fatigue. Regis hoped she wasn't someone whose claim she had to investigate. But in all likelihood, she either had already or her name was on a long list of people she needed to visit.

It wasn't until Keith started to introduce them that Regis remembered they'd already met.

Chapter Six

"Regis, I'd like to introduce you to—"
"Ali Hubbard," she finished for him, feeling relief wash over her with the memory. "I was out to see you last week."

"I wondered if you'd remember," Ali said. "All our faces and names must blend together after a while."

"Sometimes it feels that way. But I pay close attention and take great notes to make sure I don't miss anything."

Yes, she *did* remember the details. Ali and James Hubbard. Ten acres on the outskirts of town. Lost half of their livestock and their barn. Regis had approved the claim her first day in town and submitted the paperwork to the insurance company. She was now waiting for their final payout decision.

She let out an easy breath with the recollection. The claims that were seamless didn't stress her out. The denied claims were the worst, and the reason she liked to get into a town, do her job, and get out without any complication. The denied claims broke her heart, but not nearly as much as it did the homeowners. She had to focus on the ones she could help.

Keith held open the door, and they both slipped inside. She stood for a moment, overwhelmed by all the activity around her. It was as if Keith had planned a party especially for her. The room was filled with people of all ages. Some she recognized from when she ate at the diner. Some were people she didn't know. Some she could tell definitely had McKinnon blood in them just by their strong resemblance to each other. To her relief, all of them were too busy putting filled containers of food into bigger boxes to notice her.

She followed Keith through the living room to the kitchen. At the oven was an older woman wearing a blue and white checkered apron and matching oven mitts. Her salt and pepper hair was cut short, framing an oval face that was pleasant and familiar.

"Ah, you made it!" the woman said with a warm smile. "Don't worry, we'll be cleaned up in about 10 minutes. All the meals are being served over at the school. I just need to wrap up the left overs and bring them over to the diner's freezer."

"Mom," Keith addressed the woman in the apron and bent his head to give her a kiss, which she warmly accepted. "I want you to meet …"

"Reggie Simpson," the woman said, finishing his sentence.

Keith's eyes narrowed as he glanced back at her.

Regis smiled. "I told you everyone calls me Reggie. It's nice to see you again, Mrs. McKinnon."

His mother turned to Keith and gave her son an insulted look. "I may be a little absent-minded at times when it comes to where I put my car keys, but I'm not about to forget someone I've fed breakfast to for the past four days." With a wink, she said, "You can call me Kate."

Regis's greeting was sincere. She'd liked the older woman almost immediately despite their limited interaction. Kate ran her diner with a brisk efficiency and, though she came across as gruff sometimes, she had a bit of a soft side. Regis had seen the woman give a harsh word to a man who'd been unreasonably impatient with one of her servers during the rush hour, and then slip an extra cookie to a little boy who'd just been told that his dog had died.

Kate set a pie on the counter and took off the mitts. "And you'll have to ignore my son. Hawk seems to think I'd lose my head if it weren't attached."

"Mom," Keith countered. "Did you or did you not put a spoon in your pocket at work and forget about it until you found it in the washer?"

Kate made a dismissive noise. "When you've got as much on your mind as I do, that's normal."

"And your excuse for spending twenty minutes looking for your glasses when you were wearing them?"

Regis couldn't help but enjoy the playful bickering as Kate and Keith wiped down the counter together, one on each side.

"Excuse me," Regis said, not really wanting to interrupt. But she felt bad just standing there while they worked. "How can I help?"

"You can have a seat," Kate answered. "You're a guest."

"Please," Regis pressed. "I can't just let you do all the work."

"Very well," Kate said, ignoring Keith's exasperated sigh. "I'll take out the last of the food and you can wash the dishes while Hawk puts them away." She paused, giving Keith a meaningful look. "I'll get everyone on their way. We should all be out of your hair soon. By the way, honey, I put some leftovers in containers in your fridge. They should be good for a few days."

"That's an awfully big smile on your face, Ma," Keith said.

Kate's smile got bigger. "Yes, it is. Sam is coming home."

Keith's face brightened. "You're going to have all your boys in one place at the same time."

Kate's smile faltered just a little. "Well, not all. Only God's going to provide that. But I'll take my four boys together here in Rudolph for as long as I can have them."

"How long is he staying this time?"

"At least the whole summer. He'll be working to clear some of the damaged areas down here because the threat of fire will be higher this summer after all this flooding left debris everywhere." Kate was almost giddy with excitement as she talked.

"Ah, so that's the reason for the smile," Keith said. He hugged his mom and then turned to face Regis as he spoke. "My brother Sam works with a Hotshot fire crew out of Colorado. But he's like you. He goes where the action is."

"And this summer, I aim to enjoy having you all home." Kate turned to Regis. "Thanks for the help, dear. Enjoy your evening."

Kate picked up the pie from the counter and headed out into the other room. A few seconds later, Regis heard the door shut and then quiet. After all that commotion, she was finally alone with Keith.

Regis walked over to the sink and turned on the faucet, feeling the water with her hand until it got to a hot enough temperature to wash dishes. "Your mom's great," she said as Keith came up alongside her.

"Yeah, she is." The three words were full of love and again, that feeling of envy filled her. After a moment, Keith continued. "You know, you really don't have to wash dishes. You've had as long a day as everyone else, and I promised you dinner."

"This is fine," Regis assured him as she began to wash a mixing bowl.

She was thankful that her back was to Keith so she didn't have to see his weak in the knees kind of smile. But to top all that, he had a wonderful mother whom he clearly adored, and was committed to doing charity work in his community. If she'd been unable to get him out of her mind before, today had just made it ten times worse. She shoved the thought aside and forced herself to concentrate on the slippery bowl in her hand.

"Leave these," Keith said, pulling her from her thoughts and making her jump. He was a lot closer than she'd realized. She could smell the crisp scent of him, all male and one hundred percent appealing. "You came over so I could feed you, not so you could wash dishes."

"It's fine," Regis smiled. "It's nice to be doing something so simple. Gets my mind off of things."

"You'll have to tell me about those 'things' later. But to be honest, I'm starved, so we might as well start those pizzas or we're never going to eat."

"I have a better idea," she said, turning the faucet off.

"What's that?"

"Leftovers. Your mom just said she left you some leftovers in the refrigerator. They're probably still warm, and if they're not, we can just heat them up quickly."

"That's cheating." His answer brought a bubble of laughter from her. "My mom made that, not me. This was supposed to be something special."

"Look, I'm starved, too. I don't know if I can wait for pizza when I know your mom's home cooking is on the other side of that door. And you and I both know her cooking is good. We can do pizza another night."

"Another night, huh? Thinking ahead. I like that."

"Well, let's get through this one first."

Keith pulled her into his arms and gave her a warm hug that made her head spin. When he released her, he said, "You're a woman after my own heart. I'll get a fire going in the living room if you want to heat up some of that food."

"That sounds like a plan."

Keith pulled two dishes out of the cabinet and put them on the counter. Regis waved him away with her hands.

"I can find everything we need. Go make that fire."

Twenty minutes later, they were sitting cross-legged on a blanket in front of the floor to ceiling stone fireplace eating the dinner Kate had made. There was a corked bottle of wine resting against the sofa next to Keith and a half-full glass of wine that Regis was drinking with dinner. If not for the food she was eating, the wine would surely be going to her head and making her sleepy.

"I don't know how your mom manages to feed so many people like this."

"She doesn't do it alone. There are a whole lot of people who are working round the clock trying to set everything to right around here."

"Like you."

Hawk shrugged, embarrassed. "After the flood, there were so many families that lost so much. The need grew, so I just helped fill in like everyone else. It's the least we can do."

"How bad was it?" Regis asked.

"I watched the water coming down off of the higher points." Hawk looked down at his hands, lost in a memory that must seem so vivid to him. This was his home. It wasn't just some other place that he saw on the news. "This part of town is high enough that I wasn't in any real danger, but Logan's place is on lower ground, and he was there alone with Keith when the flood waters came in fast and furious. It covered most of his pastures. He'd moved his animals so his damage was minimal. But it managed to get all the way up to the barn, which was close enough.

"When the rain stopped, I went out with a lot of others to try to help rescue people who were stuck. It's weird the images that stick with you during something like this. I saw the Hardwicks rowing a canoe across their field. The Joyners' boy was in a tree for almost two hours before rescuers could get to him." Hawk took a deep breath and tossed his paper napkin into the fire. "I think over the following week, I set a dozen broken bones, sewed up hundreds of cuts and gave tetanus shots to half the town."

"This is one of the worst disaster areas I've seen," Reggie said. "Definitely the worst flood. Thank you again for helping me the other day. I'm not sure I could have gotten through all the properties I did without your help."

Regis looked up from her plate and her stomach clenched. Keith was finished eating and was leaning against the sofa with a beer in his hand. The heat in his eyes was unmistakable. It had been a long time since a man had looked at her like that.

"What are you looking at?"

His smile widened. "You. I like looking at you."

She put down her fork. "I can see that. What I can't understand is why?"

"You have a little hook nose. Did you know that? And there is one little cluster of freckles that are bunched up high on one of your cheeks."

Her hand immediately went to the place he spoke of. Usually she spent time to cover up that spot. It had plagued her when she was a teenager. But she was so busy these days she hardly noticed it.

Keith leaned over and pulled her hand away. "I like it."

She giggled. "And you're strange, Keith McKinnon."

"And I like very much the way you say my name."

She was blushing again. It amazed Hawk how easily he could get Regis to blush about the simplest things. The woman loved to put up a tough front, but inside she was as smooth as silk. She had a big heart, and he wanted so much to know that heart in every way.

"Why doesn't anyone but your nephew call you Keith? Even your mother called you Hawk."

"There's no real mystery really."

"Then tell me the story. Why does everyone call you Hawk?"

"It goes way back," he said. "I was on a scouts' camping trip with my brother, Wade. I must have been six or seven at the time. My dad was one of the scout leaders back then. Anyway, we'd gone on what seemed like a long hike down in the Black Hills. When we got back up to base camp, the other scout leader noticed he wasn't wearing his wedding ring. Anyway, we all looked around the ground at camp for about an hour, and no one could find it. But I'd remembered seeing something when we were hiking, so I decided to investigate."

"You all went back out on the trail after being there all day?"

"No. Just me."

"At six or seven? On your own?"

"Seemed like a good plan at the time. Anyway, I hiked down the trail and went back to the place where I'd seen the sun was hitting this shiny thing below, and sure enough, it was a wedding ring. I felt like I'd struck a vein of gold. I didn't realize they'd sent a search team out to find me. And when we all got back to base camp, my father was ripping mad. But I told my story about how I'd seen the ring up from high on the trail. Then I proudly pulled the ring out of my pocket and gave it to the scout leader."

"Aw, he must have been so happy to get his ring back."

Hawk couldn't help but laugh. "It wasn't his."

"What?"

"It was someone else's wedding ring. We found out when we got home that the other scout leader found his ring at home on his nightstand."

"He'd never even lost his ring?"

Keith shook his head as he thought of how Wade tried to defend him. "Wade used to tell the story about how I had eyes like a hawk to find that little wedding ring from high up on the trail, and if anyone was missing anything, they should come to me first because I'd find it. The nickname stuck with my friends and eventually with my family. I think my mom just gave up calling me Keith because it was easier to get me to answer to Hawk. Not even my teachers called me Keith. It was usually, 'Mr. McKinnon' in response to something I was getting in trouble for. I'm surprised I ever made it out of high school. Even my patients call me Hawk since most of them have known me my entire life. And if they haven't, they call me Doc."

"And with your nephew?"

His chest filled with pride. "Well, that's special between the two of us."

She shifted in place and shrugged. "I didn't realize I was treading on sacred ground."

"But I like the way *you* say my name," he said. "Your eyes sparkle when you say it."

Her mouth dropped open. "They do not."

"And your voice changes." A tiny voice in the back of Hawk's mind wondered what it would be like to hear

Regis say his name when they were making love. And the two of them making love was something he'd thought a whole lot about ever since he'd kissed Regis the other night at the mill.

She was looking at him intently, and he wondered if his thoughts were giving him away. And yet, she didn't look away or blush. She just studied his face and then ... there it was in her eyes. The sparkle.

"Come here," he said, moving closer to her until he could feel the heat of her body more than the heat of the fire. "I like having you close by."

"Oh, really?" she teased with a smile.

"I like you. A lot."

She drew in a deep breath and looked into his eyes. He reached up and touched her hair, pushing a few silky strands away from her forehead. He let his hands trail down the side of her cheek until he found that adorable cluster of freckles that had consumed his thoughts for days. He brushed his thumb over it and then bent his head to place a soft kiss on her cheek. But before he could do it, Regis lifted her face to him with her mouth slightly parted.

"Not yet," he said, when it was clear her mouth was seeking his. "I want to look at you. Discover you. Know all of you."

The flame of fire that lit her eyes sent sparks flying through him, settling deep in his chest and lighting a fire below his belly. He wanted her more than he wanted his next breath and couldn't think of anything else.

As Hawk moved to give her what she wanted, what he wanted, Regis shifted closer to him and then winced. He pulled back quickly. "Did I hurt you?"

She reached up and wrapped her arm around his shoulder as if she didn't want him to move too far away. "I just pressed my leg against the ground. Forget it." Then she lifted her face to him as she did earlier, wanting him as much as he wanted her. His mouth claimed her instantly, playing, teasing, tasting and then devouring until he thought he'd lost his mind.

As he wrapped one arm around her waist and placed his hand at the nape of her neck, Regis's hand made a slow journey from his stomach and up his chest until she abruptly stopped.

Pulling back, he saw her confused expression as she touched his chest. Not wanting the distraction, he reached inside his shirt and pulled out the chain and medallion he always wore.

"Is it going to bother you?"

She shook her head and touched the cross and medallion with her fingers. "I just wondered what it was."

Relieved Hawk went back to the very thing that was driving him crazy. As he kissed her cheek, he breathed in the sweet scent of her and made a trail of kisses along her face until he nestled his face against her neck and kissed her there. He heard her soft moan of pleasure and it only surged him on.

"Keith?"

With a ragged breath, he dragged himself from the source of his pleasure to look at her. He couldn't remember the last time he was out of his mind wanting a woman, and now, he realized he'd never wanted a woman more than he wanted Regis right now.

♥ ♥ ♥

She was coming completely unglued by Keith's every touch. Regis couldn't think. She couldn't breathe. She dug her fingers into his shoulders, and for a second, she questioned whether she should even be considering getting involved with Keith McKinnon, much less making love with him. And she hoped with every fiber of her being that this was leading to that because she couldn't think of anything other than getting gloriously naked with this man.

As he gazed at her with the same desire that was like a drug to her, his eyes were questioning. There were no more questions in her mind. With her fingers, she pulled at the buttons of her shirt. He watched her attentively as each button slipped out of place until her shirt was fully free, and she pushed it aside. He freed her the rest of the way by slipping it off her shoulders and dropping it to the floor. She undid the front clasp of her bra under his watchful eye and marveled at the blaze of fire that ignited in his eyes as her breasts fell free of their restraints.

"I don't know how much more of this I can handle," he said, slipping out of his shirt and tossing it somewhere else in the room. Regis giggled as they rid themselves of the rest of their clothes, pushing them aside so they had the full spread of the blanket Keith had laid out in front of the fire for them to lay on.

And when they lay next to each other, hot flesh against hot flesh, Regis thought she'd lose her mind again. His hands were everywhere, stroking her skin, touching her in places that made her throw back her head in pure pleasure. And then he explored her more, this time with his mouth. He kissed her, leaving a moist trail down her neck, to her breasts as he stroked one breast with his wide palm and then drove her crazy by flicking her nipple with his tongue.

"Oh, I want you inside me," she said, not sure where she'd had the strength to even utter the words aloud. She reached between them, stroked him and wrapped her leg around him. He threw his head back with a gasp, breathing heavy, and then with determination, he kissed her with such passion and fire that she lost all sense of where she was. All she knew was their two bodies entwined, touching each other, loving each other.

And when he entered her with such force and hunger, all it took was a few strokes to lift her higher until she reached her peak and tumbled over the edge. She was still feeling the incredible pleasure he'd brought her when he rocked his hip harder. He buried his face in her neck and breathed harder until he reached his orgasm with an intensity that had him gasping for breath and clinging to her.

In his arms, Regis closed her eyes and wrapped her arms and legs around Keith, not wanting to let go of the beautiful connection they'd created. And as he pulled away from her and gazed into her eyes with such longing, she wondered if it was possible to ever get her fill of Keith McKinnon.

Chapter Seven

The fire was warm against her naked skin. Keith's body nestled up against hers made it all the warmer. He'd pulled a small blanket that had been draped over the chair by the fireplace and loosely placed it over them. Content, she watched the changing colors of the fire licking the burning logs as she rested her head on Keith's shoulder. With his arm wrapped around, he held her close.

She played with the gold medallion and cross he was wearing.

"Where did you get these?"

He glanced down and took the medallion between his fingers. "This was Wade's. Remember that ring I found in the canyon?"

"Yeah."

"Wade melted it down and made it into this. If you noticed, there are only markings on one side of the medallion. He always wore it, too."

"How did you get it?"

Keith drew in a deep breath, expanding his chest. She felt the rise and fall of it and the heavy thump of his heartbeat against her ear as she lay there.

"Wade was leaving for the Peace Corps. He'd been gone for a while and was back for a visit before heading out again. As you can imagine, my mother wasn't too pleased."

"She likes having her boys around."

"Could you tell?"

Regis chuckled.

"Anyway, Wade called all of us who were still stateside and wanted to meet for a drink before he left. Ethan was overseas in the military. Sam was in Arizona, I think, fighting some monster fire that had broken out there. Logan, well, he was dealing with his life back then, which was …difficult."

"And you?"

"I was doing my residency in Sioux City. Wade was in Aberdeen, just a few hours from Sioux City."

Keith was quiet and just rolled the medallion between his fingers.

"Logan went to have a drink with Wade, and I didn't. Next time I saw Logan, he gave me the chain with the medallion and this cross and told me Wade wanted me to hold onto it until he came back. I put it around my neck, and the next day we found out about the tsunami that hit the island he was working on. They never found him."

She gasped and lifted her head to look at Keith. The unshed tears in his eyes were illuminated by the dying fire.

"I've never taken this off since," he said, looking directly at her. "I've never told anyone else that story."

She sat up and touched his chest in an effort to comfort him. She didn't care that she was naked and her breasts were fully exposed in probably the most unflattering position.

"What about the cross?" she asked.

"That's the odd thing. I don't know anything about this cross. I knew so much about my brother. Of all my brothers, I was closest to Wade. But I don't know how he got it or why he wore it. He used to only have the medallion on the chain. But this is the way Wade gave it to Logan, so I kept it that way. It makes me feel like ... he's close by somehow."

She lay back down against Keith, and he pulled her close to him.

"Like a part of him is always with you," she added.

Keith lifted his head a fraction and looked down at her, but said nothing. Then he lay back again.

"I have my mother's hairbrush," she finally said. "It's nothing special. It's just a big silver brush. I don't even know if it's real silver or just plated. She couldn't take living on bases and moving all around the world."

"With your dad gone so much, I'm surprised she didn't take you with her."

"Yeah, well, she didn't like family life so much either, and having a six-year-old in tow didn't fit into the next phase of her life."

He cursed quietly and shook his head. "Sorry," he said.

"Why? Because of my mother or your foul mouth?" she said chuckling. "Remember, I lived on Army bases.

You couldn't possibly say something I haven't already heard."

Keith chuckled too and then became quiet again.

"It doesn't really matter though. It's just a hairbrush," she said. "I just … with all the moving, I was never able to let it go."

He squeezed her harder until she thought they couldn't get closer. And still she wanted more. She wanted to feel that connection she'd felt when they'd made love.

She lifted up on her side and put her arm around him. "Keith?"

"Hmm?" he said, his voice groggy.

"The fire is dying."

"Do you want another blanket?"

She smiled and kissed him slowly. "I had something else in mind."

She felt his smile against her lips and felt the thundering of his heartbeat beneath her palm. Then he said, "I like the way you think."

♥ ♥ ♥

The next few weeks had been the happiest Regis had ever known. She spent the mornings working in the senior center with a long line of people filing in to ask questions and fill out paperwork. Some afternoons she'd go on the road with Keith and visit properties. She'd listen to the stories about the people she'd meet and at night, the two of them would lock themselves in his log home and make love.

Soon the number of people needing help grew shorter, and somewhere in the back of Regis's mind, she knew her time in Rudolph was close to coming to an end. But she'd decided to relish each and every moment she had with Keith for as long as she possibly could.

And then came the afternoon when she knew all that love and beauty was in jeopardy. She answered her cell phone call from her manager as she stepped into the motel room, wondering why she even bothered to keep it since she'd been spending every night for the past two weeks with Keith.

"Is there a problem?" she asked Mike.

He hesitated a fraction. "You're doing great there. I'm just wondering why you've sent this claim for the Buxton Mills through with a recommendation for full replacement when it's clear it was flood damage."

She dropped her briefcase on the bed and sat down next to it. "The roof and siding show that the ice storm did some damage to the property. I have pictures to support that."

"I see them, and I don't dispute that. But I also see the water line on the inside of the property showing that there was a flood."

She bit her bottom lip. "There was. The property is on the river. But the ice and rain did the damage to the structure."

Mike's heavy sigh sounded distorted through the phone. "You're one of the most thorough adjusters I have, Regis. But this one is cut and dry. They have flood insurance, so the most we can approve for this is what is listed in their policy. We can repair the roof although I have my doubts it was the storm that damaged that and the siding. My records show this property has been empty for quite some time."

"The amount of the payout for those won't be enough to cover the structural damage."

"You need a vacation, Regis. You're getting attached again. I'm sorry, but I can't approve the full amount of this claim. If you'd prefer it, I'll send the letter."

She closed her eyes to the disappointment filling her. "No, I'll do it."

"Fine. Regis?"

"Yes?"

"Why don't you pack up. I'm sure you're tired and could use a break. I'm not kidding about the vacation."

"I'm not done here."

"End of the week you are. I'll bring in someone else to give you a break."

"But—" she started to argue, but he'd already hung up.

She was leaving. But before she could do that, she had to break the bad news to some people who'd counted on her.

♥ ♥ ♥

"Are you all right?" Keith's voice brought Regis out of her reverie as she sat at the kitchen table and cradled her morning coffee in her hand. She tried not to read too much into the concern in his voice. Things were complicated enough as it was. She decided it was probably a good idea to keep things simple. There was no reason to bring up the reasons for her insomnia.

"I didn't sleep well last night."

"I noticed."

"I'm sorry. Did I keep you awake?"

"No, but clearly something kept you awake. What was it?"

She shrugged. She hadn't written up the letter to the town yet about the outcome of the claim for the Buxton Mill. She wanted to write it and then tell Ian McKinnon personally. He'd worked hard on plans to develop the property for the town that he deserved to hear it from her first.

"You're awfully quiet," Keith finally broke the silence, bringing his empty coffee cup to the sink. "Something is bothering you."

Regis glanced over at Keith's handsome face. When had she become this attached to seeing it, having it bring her comfort.

"I have a lot of work to do before I leave."

His expression fell. "You're leaving?"

"End of the week. I got the call from my supervisor yesterday."

He opened his mouth to say something, but then stopped.

"I knew last night," she said, answering the question he didn't put into words. "I just didn't know ... how to tell you. I didn't want to talk about it." She abruptly got up from the table, dumped the rest of her coffee in the sink and turned on the faucet to rinse the sink and her cup.

"Stop," Keith said.

She didn't look at him. "I don't want to leave these dishes in the sink."

"Stop," he said again, turning off the water and pulling her around to face him.

"We knew this day was going to come eventually," she said, looking up at him. The light in his blue eyes had faded with his disappointment.

"Did we?

A cynical laugh escaped her lips. "How could you not know that I'd be leaving?"

"I don't know. I didn't really think much about it. I just thought about how I was feeling. How I thought we were both feeling."

She fought tears as he pulled her into his arms. "Right now, I'm feeling rotten. To make matters worse, my boss is insisting on my taking a vacation."

With raised eyebrows, Keith said, "Well, there's an excuse for you to stay longer."

She pulled out of his arms and went back to the sink. "I can't even think that far. There is still so much for me to do this week."

"Okay, here's a radical idea."

She stopped washing a coffee cup and glanced at him.

"Stay."

"What?"

"Finish out your week and then just stay. You said you have vacation. So take a vacation right here. You don't have to run off to another town, do you?"

"Well, no."

"Where do you go when you leave a town you've been working in?"

"I have a simple apartment in Chicago. By simple, I mean utilitarian. It looks a lot like my motel room except it has a small kitchen. I'm not there very often. I'm sure once I get home Mike will find another town for me to go to. He usually keeps me busy."

Keith leaned against the counter as she finished rinsing the last dish and put it in the strainer to dry. She turned off the water and dried her hands before looking at Keith again.

When she did, she saw emotion in his eyes that she'd never seen. Not even when they'd made love. A lump of emotion formed in her throat that she couldn't swallow down.

"Stay," he said in a soft voice that was almost pleading. Her bottom lip began to quiver, and she clamped it down with her teeth to keep it steady.

"This isn't something we should talk about this morning."

He looked at her for a lingering moment as if studying the lines on her face.

"Okay, we'll talk about it tonight then."

She nodded and reached up to kiss him. He tasted of coffee and smelled like the cinnamon bagels they'd had for breakfast. His tongue brushed against her lips, and she gasped. The hand at the small of her back flexed, pressing her closer to him as he tilted his head, deepening the kiss until she was lost in him again.

Everything that had been circling in her head since last night vanished. All she thought about was the way it felt when this incredible man kissed her. He'd turned her world inside out. And yet all that disappeared when she was in Keith's arms. There was absolutely no confusion about the way his mouth felt against hers, the way his lips moved, how his tongue teased at the seam of her mouth. She had no doubts about whether or not she wanted him to keep kissing her, about how right it felt to have him holding her.

When they finally broke apart, their breath was coming in pants, and she could feel Keith's heart beating as furiously as her own. He kept his arms around her and looked down at her.

"I'll see you tonight," he said with a smile.

And for the first time in the past two weeks, Regis dreaded it.

Chapter Eight

"This is the second time I've caught you daydreaming," Nancy said, standing in the doorway to Hawk's office.

"I'm not daydreaming," he said.

"Yeah? Well, whatever it is, if you don't snap out of it, I'll be forced to do something drastic."

"Like what?"

"Call your mother." She chuckled at the look he gave her, and then tapped her fingers on the doorjamb. "Seriously, you've got a patient in examining room one who is waiting for you."

"I'll be right there."

Ever since Regis left his house yesterday morning, he knew she was pulling away from him. She told him she was going to be finished with her work in Rudolph by the end of the week. But Hawk didn't think she'd avoid him before she had to leave. But then, just as he was expecting her to come to his house last night after work, she'd called and said she had too much paperwork, and thought it was better for her to stay at the motel.

He'd spent many nights alone in that big log cabin since he'd come back to Rudolph after med school. But last night was the first night in over two weeks that he'd spent the night without Regis snuggled up, warm, and naked next to him. And he didn't like it one bit.

He got up from behind his desk and walked the few strides to the examining room, pulling the folder from the wall file and checking the contents. Concerned, he knocked on the door and went inside.

Ian McKinnon sat in a chair by the window instead of the examining table. And he didn't look happy, which was great concern to Hawk.

"I didn't expect to see you here today."

"I didn't plan on coming." He turned his hand. That's when Hawk saw the white rag stained with red. "I slammed the glass on the counter and cut myself."

"On purpose?"

"The slamming of the glass was on purpose. The glass breaking was just Murphy's Law."

Hawk washed his hands and dried them quickly before putting on latex gloves. Ian sat in the same chair by the window. Hawk sat in his seat and rolled it closer to his cousin to examine the wound.

"You may need a stitch or two," he said.

"Terrific," Ian said.

"What set this off?"

"The phone call I got last night from your girlfriend."

Hawk stopped examining the wound and looked at Ian. Dark circles were evident under his eyes.

"Regis called you? What for?"

"The claim for the mill wasn't fully approved. What they're giving us is a joke. We can forget getting the mill rehabbed for the center. There isn't enough money to fix what needs to be repaired. The engineer said the flood water caused structural damage to the foundation of the building and needs to be completely repaired or the building will have to be torn down. Except, the insurance company is only giving us cleanup cost for the building."

"What about FEMA aid?"

"What? In two years? The repairs need to be made within a certain period of time. Without enough money to repair the foundation the floods destroyed, the town will order the building to be completely torn down. That means no more Wounded Veterans Center. "

Now it all made sense to him. "I'll talk to her."

"She can't do anything. At least, that's what she said. It came from higher up. Oh, and she's really sorry."

Hawk squashed down his anger as best he could. Why hadn't Regis come and told him about the claim for the mill herself? Why was he getting it second-hand?

"Let's put that aside for now and get you stitched up."

"What's the hurry? It's not like I have anything pressing to do with my day now that the project at the mill is all but dead."

Ian might be ready to give up. But Hawk was a long way from giving up the fight.

♥ ♥ ♥

The community center was busier than it had been in days now that a full FEMA staff had set up camp there. People were coming in and out of the room from morning until late afternoon. Regis was glad she'd gotten most of the paperwork for her claims finished. Now she was just fielding questions and dealing with disgruntled customers who weren't happy.

She was tired, physically from lack of sleep, and emotionally from dealing with a heart so heavy, it physically hurt. She'd hated sleeping alone last night. Regis hated even more that each time she rolled over, she'd searched for Keith's warm body. Not finding him there left her cold.

She forced herself to be in the present and not the past. She had too much work to do to spend time pining over a man who'd be part of her past very soon.

The main area of the community room was full of people. Some were filling out paperwork, others were lined up in front of a table. Off to one side, a group of older kids watched their younger siblings playing while harried parents waited for their turn in line with the FEMA reps. Luckily, no one was lining up in front of her table needing help. It gave her some time to go through paperwork that needed to be finalized and filed by the end of the week before she left.

She heard a familiar voice greet someone in the crowd and lifted her gaze from the computer screen long enough to see Keith charging her way. The look on his face made her stomach drop.

"Can I talk to you a minute in private?" He didn't bother with preliminaries as he stepped behind the table.

Regis looked up, startled. She braced herself for what she knew was coming.

"Can it wait until later? I really want to finish this paperwork before the end of the day. Maybe we could have dinner out somewhere tonight," she said.

"This is important," Hawk insisted. "There is an empty room down the hall. We can talk there."

"All right." She quickly asked the agent at the next table to watch her computer while she stepped away, a courtesy they did for each other during the day when it got busy and promised to be quick.

She followed Keith to an empty room down the hall and waited for him to shut the door behind her. She didn't wait for him to get to what was on his mind.

"I didn't tell you because I thought Ian should know first."

"That was very thoughtful of you. But that doesn't change the fact that the Buxton Mill claim has been denied."

"It wasn't denied. It just wasn't approved for the full amount."

"It may as well have been denied for all the good that tiny settlement will do for the cause."

"Keith," Regis shifted, uncomfortable with his question. "You know that I'm not really supposed to discuss my cases."

"Ian isn't a case," he spat out the word. "You should have seen him, Regis. He's given up. That center was a lifeline for him and now ..."

She closed her eyes and tried to steady her nerves. This had been her fear.

"I did everything I could do, Keith. These things aren't always as cut and dry as you think. Every claim has certain criteria that need to be met if it's going to be approved. I skated on thin ice with my report, but I got called on it by my manager. The pictures clearly show flood damage inside the building. That water level was enough to show that it was flood water, not the rain, wind or ice that damaged the property. I can only pay out for how the policy reads. Believe me, I wish the damage had been done by wind and ice. It would have been easier to approve more for the claim."

"The engineer said the foundation needs to completely be replaced or the building needs to be demolished. If you read the report."

"I had the engineer's report. Ian gave it to me. But, unfortunately, the engineer also said that the foundation showed signs of wear before the storms. The building was aging. The insurance company won't pay out for an aging property that was already in disrepair."

"So that's it?"

Lisa Mondello

"There's nothing else I can do."

Keith paced in front of her, clearly upset by what his cousin was going through. Then he stopped and looked at her directly.

"Is that why you didn't stay with me last night?"

She drew in a slow breath. "I needed to call Ian and prepare the letter to the town. I wanted to make sure it was thorough."

"That's an excuse. You could have done that at my place."

"You know I wouldn't have worked if I had stayed at your house last night." She smiled up at him and was taken aback when he didn't respond in kind.

"If we can't get the money to repair Buxton Mill, it'll have to be demolished. The town won't let it stand in that condition while we raise money."

She'd never felt so helpless in her life or wanted to do something more than what she could do for anyone. "I know. And I'm sorry."

"Are you?"

His accusation was like a slap to the face. "What the hell is that supposed to mean?"

"You blow into town, take a quick look at a policy or a property and decide the fate of people's lives. And then you get the hell out of town again and leave the people left behind to pick up the pieces."

Anger surged in her. "Yes, that's what I do. That's all I do. But in doing that I'm trying to help people just like

254

you do, Keith. It may not be the same, but I can help some people. There are times when I can't. Sometimes my hands are tied."

He paced in front of her again. "Ethan served eight years in the Navy, Regis. Ian did two tours in Iraq, lost his leg and nearly lost his life. This center was important to the soldiers in this community coming home from service overseas. It was supposed to be a place where they could come together and deal with whatever they experienced while serving this country. They need this center."

"Do you think I don't know that? Believe me, I have been around active military and veterans my entire life. But it doesn't change what I can and can't do for the center."

Keith ran his hand over his head in frustration. "Jeez, Logan and Poppy were talking about getting married there. Now that's not going to happen either."

She took in the heavy slump of Keith's shoulders and felt it herself. She was losing this battle. And maybe it was never a battle that could be won. This is what she'd always dreaded, falling for someone and then having to disappoint them.

Keith pierced her with a pleading look. "They'll never get the building inspector to approve repairs without the money. And without the money the mill will have to be demolished and that'll be the end of the community center for the veterans. They need help."

"I know." She glanced at the door and thought about all the people waiting in line. Every one of them was feeling as desperate as Keith felt.

"I can't help everyone. But I can help some of the people in there," she said, pointing out the door. "I need to get back to doing that."

Keith nodded. "You're right. Okay."

"I'll understand if you don't want me to come over tonight."

"No, I do."

With a wary smile, she said. "I'll see you then."

♥ ♥ ♥

Hawk watched Regis walk down the hallway until she disappeared in the room that was mulling with activity. Every emotion inside him was raw and conflicted, making it hard for him to even think. Deep down he knew this wasn't Regis's fault. She didn't make the rules, and there were a whole lot of rules that were stacked against them.

But part of his frustration went deeper than the center. She hadn't told him what was going on. Instead, she'd avoided him last night. She was leaving. She'd said as much the other day at breakfast. And that was the harder pill for him to swallow than losing out on insurance claim money for the mill. It was losing Regis that was eating him up inside.

If he was going to fight, then the fight started there.

Chapter Nine

Regis sat in her car in front of Keith's house for a minute, hoping that tonight would turn out better than this afternoon had. She'd reminded herself a thousand times over the course of the afternoon why she didn't get involved. It was for this. There was always going to be someone leaving. And leaving was just as hard when you cared about someone as being left behind.

But she wouldn't deny herself the chance to spend as much time as she could with Keith before she left Rudolph. She hoped he felt the same.

She checked her hair and make-up again in her rearview mirror and tried to push away the memory of her confrontation with Keith earlier. She'd known he would be upset about the Buxton Mill claim. But she had no idea how deep his feelings for it went. She only hoped they could get past that tonight.

The moment she entered the house, it was clear that her hopes had been in vain. A meal was set out on the table, and the lights were low, but the normal easiness of their nights together was gone. Instead, Keith sat at one end of the table and ate his dinner while she silently ate hers.

Regis looked down at her plate, trying to figure out what she could say that would fix this. She picked at her food, pushing it around on her plate with her fork, unable to eat any of it. Her stomach was in knots, waiting for Keith to say something, anything that would indicate what he was thinking. But she already knew. She'd been through many nights like this right before her father would ship out on a tour.

"Maybe this wasn't such a good idea," she finally said.

Keith looked at her then, questions clouding his handsome face. "What? You coming here or us?"

"Both."

"You can't mean that."

She didn't. She couldn't imagine not having spent these last few weeks with Keith, and yet, part of her wished she hadn't. It would be so much easier to leave.

"I'm leaving in two days, Keith. It's not going to get any easier."

"Then stay," Keith said. There was more there, in his eyes and in his voice. But he said no more.

She shook her head slowly. "I'm no good in one place."

"That's an excuse not to face what you feel."

"Really?"

Frustration shadowed his normal happy-go-lucky expression. He got up from the table and dropped his plate into the sink, the sound of it jarring her.

"You've spent a lifetime leaving people behind, Regis. Aren't you tired yet?"

"Correction. People left me behind."

"And you followed suit."

She started to protest, to argue the same clichéd points she'd convinced herself of all these years. But those arguments were bogus. They just fell flat in her mind, and she knew she'd lose as soon as the words came out of her mouth.

She did leave. Just like her mother had. Just like everyone else who'd left her behind. It was easier that way.

"Stay," he said again. This time, his eyes were pleading. "Stay long enough to see if something is real. To see if there's anything here worth holding on to."

Her bottom lip threatened to betray her with a slight quiver. "That's easy for you to say. To imagine. You have this fantastic family and wonderful friends you've known since the cradle. Everyone in this town has memories that go all the way back to the dinosaurs." She laughed at the absurdity of her statement, but at its core, Regis had meant it.

Hope filled his eyes. "You could have that, too."

She shook her head quickly. "How? All I have are faces. I don't even remember the names anymore. They're all blurred into one."

"Then stay and let someone love you. Let someone leave an imprint on your heart. I want so much to do that. You have no idea."

"You say that because you've never had anyone you loved leave you before. I have."

"That's where you're wrong. My best friend left me, and he's never coming back."

Her heart stopped just seeing the anguish on Keith's face.

"Do you know what the last thing was that I said to Wade? 'I can't.' Those are two words I regret more than anything."

"You couldn't know what was going to happen."

He nodded. "No, but it doesn't change what did. All he wanted to do was have a few beers with his brothers before he left for his tour with the Peace Corps. I was in the middle of my residency in Sioux City, working eighty hours a week. I didn't want to lose precious sleep to drive the few hours to meet him halfway between Sioux City and Aberdeen and then drive back.

"Regis, I think about that phone call with Wade all the time. I would change that in a heartbeat if I could. I missed my opportunity to say good-bye to my brother. Of course, I never would have known at the time it was my last chance. But if I'd known, I would have driven all night and worked all day to have that last laugh or last hug from him before he boarded that plane."

"I understand your loss. But there's a difference. Wade didn't leave you on purpose. My mother did. She just … left."

"This isn't about loss, Regis. It's about risk. I was so focused on becoming a doctor and doing well at my residency that I didn't risk stepping out of my comfort zone to do something that was probably one of the most important moments of my life; my opportunity to see my brother one last time. I would have been fine. I'd pulled all-nighters before, working two days straight without sleep."

"This isn't the same thing."

"Then why are you leaving? Why not stay and take a risk? You and I both know there's something special here. I've never felt the way I feel about you before. No other woman in my life has even come close. Even though you're too stubborn to admit it, I have a feeling you feel the same. Except the closer we get, the more you want to run. That's the real reason why you didn't want to stay last night."

Tears filled her eyes. "I'm no good in one place."

"How do you know that? You don't even let yourself get close to finding out."

She sighed. "I just know."

"What are you so afraid of? Needing someone?"

"I don't need anyone," she said. It was a standard line and one she let herself believe for a long time. And she knew this time she was lying to herself.

"Then you're in better shape than me because I need you."

She shook her head. "How is that possible?"

"It's true. I've spent my entire adult life pushing forward with tunnel vision. But one thing became crystal clear to me yesterday when I woke up and you weren't next to me. I need you, Regis. And I thought, 'What if she doesn't come back. Ever.' I couldn't handle that. And suddenly I didn't know how I was going to get through the day."

"This can't end good, Keith. I'm leaving in two days."

"Then don't leave. Stay with me, Regis. Stay and find out if what we have is more than just a passing fling."

She jolted back at his words. "Fling? Do you really think that's what this has been for me?"

"How would I know anything? You're pulling away again. You've got so much armor guarding your heart that I can't get in to see it. Where is your heart, Regis? I want to love you. Let me love you."

The tears she'd been holding back were falling now. "You're not the only one who lost someone, Keith."

"I know your mother hurt you."

"I'm not talking about my mother. Or my father's endless tours and being left behind." She sighed. "I can't even believe I'm telling you this."

"Tell me," he said, pulling her closer. But she needed her distance and turned toward the table, sitting down before he spoke.

"I told you I've lived on bases all over the world. Well, as you can imagine, there weren't a whole lot of eligible guys to date other than young military men. I'd met someone when I was eighteen. His name was David, and he was a year older than me. My father was gone, and I was staying with a family on base when we met. I'd been getting ready to leave for college, but I stayed because of David. I thought I was in love with him. I'd had crushes on servicemen before, but this was different. He was my first kiss, my first love, my first everything."

She shrugged, sure that Keith understood her meaning. When he didn't say anything, she went on.

"David was sent to Iraq early on. We wrote. Talked to each other whenever we could. And then I didn't hear from him for a while. Everyone told me not to worry because he was probably in some remote place, and the mail would catch up eventually. It did. I got a letter from his sister in the States telling me he'd been killed."

Empathy showed on Keith's face, making her want to weep. "You loved him," he said.

She nodded. She hadn't known at the time, but she'd realized too late just how much she had loved David.

"You see, I've spent a lifetime of seeing people go, living with families who were suffering through waiting for people to come home, and sometimes they never did. You ask me where my heart is? It broke a long time ago. How many times can a heart break before it never heals, Keith? And you want me to risk it again?"

She couldn't hold back the tears. "This was a bad idea." She went into the living room, grabbed her coat and purse and headed for the door.

"Where are you going?"

"Back to the motel."

"You don't have to do that."

But she was already out the door.

♥ ♥ ♥

The mattress was lumpy. Regis turned her pillow over and rolled over to her side with a sigh. It was no use. It wasn't a lumpy mattress or a flat pillow keeping her awake tonight. Try as she may, she couldn't get her brain to turn off.

Keith was right. She was always running away. Leaving before someone left her. She'd spent years trying to convince herself that she did her job with such dedication because she was passionate about helping people. That's what drove her. Surely Keith could understand that. Why else would he have become a doctor?

As a fresh wave of pain washed over her, she pulled her knees up to her chest and wrapped her arms around them, as if holding them tightly to her would keep her together. For years after David had died, Regis had sworn she'd never allow herself to fall in love like that again.

And she hadn't. She never got involved with men when she was on the road, and she was always on the road.

But Keith had worn her down. His gentle smile and easy way had pulled her in right from the start. She didn't understand it. She'd only known Keith for a few weeks. She spent countless nights alone in motel rooms over the years. And yet, the one thing she knew for sure was that she missed being next to Keith as she slept. She missed the way his hand found her under the blanket and rested on her hip. She missed the way she could feel his warm breath on the back of her neck as he nuzzled against it. And the way his mouth moved perfectly with hers when he kissed her.

Regis turned her face into her pillow and let out a scream of frustration. Every time she closed her eyes, she saw that thick dark hair and remembered how soft it had been between her fingers, saw those amazing eyes and how they'd warmed whenever he'd looked at her.

She'd told him all about David, and he'd known immediately how much she'd loved him. And then realization dawned on Regis like a smack to the head. She shook her head and whispered into the darkness. "That's not possible. I barely know him. We've only been together a few weeks."

Images flashed through her mind in rapid succession.

Deep blue eyes filled with concern as they took in the blood on her leg.

Strong fingers moving gently against her injured flesh.

A warm smile that had greeted her at the door to this very room, just to check on her.

His hand in hers, guiding her as they walked over difficult terrain.

The safety of being wrapped in his arms.

The pain of not having him here with her now.

And then it struck her hard. "What the hell did you do, Reg?" She'd gone and fallen in love with him.

Chapter Ten

Regis woke up before her alarm went off; before the sun had even fully breached the horizon. The sky still had that hazy gray, streaked with orange and red that came with morning. She hadn't slept much, but she knew she'd never get back to sleep. Besides, she needed to get to Keith's house before he left for the clinic. What she had to say was important and didn't need to be done in a public place. She grabbed the first clean pair of pants she could get her hands on and yanked on a blouse, buttoning it as she went to her door.

After a quick stop at the diner to grab two coffees, she headed over to Keith's house. But instead of pulling down the driveway, she saw his truck parked in front of the clinic. The light was on inside, but surely it was too early for Nancy to be at work. She parked the car, grabbed the two coffees and walked up the frost-covered ramp to the front door.

The warmth that surged through her the moment she pushed through the door and saw Keith confirmed what she'd been trying to deny. She was in love.

Keith raised his head from whatever he was reading as he sat in the seat normally occupied by Nancy, surprise written on his face at the sight of her. For a split second,

Regis felt a twinge of guilt at how ragged he looked, knowing she'd probably caused it. He didn't appear to have gotten any more sleep than she had. Although dressed in a clean shirt and jeans, his hair was tousled more than usual as if he'd spent the last hour pulling his fingers through it with frustration.

Still, the way he looked at her, as if he were drinking her in, made him look incredibly sexy despite his obvious fatigue. Then he smiled. "Are one of those coffees mine?"

A small laugh escaped her lips as she held out the cup, which he reached for through the window that separated Nancy's desk from the waiting room. "Just how you like it. But I didn't make it. Your mother did. I stopped by the diner."

He took a sip of satisfaction. "I needed this."

"I was going to stop by your house. You don't normally come to the clinic this early."

"I couldn't sleep. Seems like that's contagious."

"Can we talk in private?"

He glanced around the room. "No one is here but us, Regis."

She sighed, knowing she was stalling.

"Whatever it is you want to tell me, just say it," he said. "I'm here."

Her bottom lip quivered against all her efforts to stop it. "I know. I'm not used to that."

"Just say it," he urged.

She took a deep, cleansing breath. "I know I've been pushing you away these last few days. I don't know how to do it any other way. I've never had any one place to call home before. I've been running so long, I don't know how to stop."

"This could be your home. Give yourself a reason to love something and dig some roots."

She put her coffee cup down on the table. "It's not that easy."

"It could be." He walked out from behind the desk and came into the waiting room, standing close to her, but not close enough.

Her heart thumped in her chest. "I deal with harsh realities all the time, but the biggest one is how I feel about you. I feel like I'm falling without a safety net. "

"That's what falling in love is. You're not alone." With one quick stride, he was standing in front of her and scooping her into his arms. Here she felt alive and whole. In his arms, she felt the earth beneath her feet.

"We started this, Regis," Keith said, gazing down into her eyes. "Let's finish it. Let's find out how far we can take this. When I went to see you yesterday, I was angry. But I realized last night that it wasn't just about the Buxton Mill claim. We'll figure something out about that. It was because you were leaving, and I didn't know how to feel about that. I've never felt like this before. Since the moment I saw you standing in front of the clinic door, you've been throwing me for a loop. I never knew what love was like. With Logan and Poppy, I saw it. It was real. But I'd never had that before until I met you. I love you, Regis. I'm sure of it."

"I love you, too. I don't know how it happened, but I do."

He kissed her lips, her face and her eyes as he dug his fingers in her hair, setting her soul on fire. It scared her to death and yet, it was everything she wanted.

She heard Nancy clear her throat. *Loudly.*

Keith pulled away from her abruptly and looked up with surprise. When Regis turned, she saw Nancy standing at the door with her coat still on, wearing a grin of amusement. "It's a bit early in the day, isn't it?"

Regis felt her face flame, but Keith wasn't fazed. "Why don't you go to the diner and have a long breakfast. Tell my mother it's on me."

"Oh, Hawk, your mother and I will have plenty to talk about," Nancy said, laughing as she left the office.

Regis giggled. "You do know what they're going to talk about, don't you?"

"I'd hate to disappoint them. I don't expect you to say yes to marriage, Regis. But I can't deny that I hope one day that's what you'll want. All I know is that I don't want you to leave. Please tell me you'll stay."

"I'm almost done with my work here," she said. "I do have that vacation my boss promised—"

"Great," he said, cutting her off. "I'll take however much time I can get with you."

"And then I'll probably be unemployed."

Confusion pulled at his handsome features.

"I think I've figured out a way to help the Buxton Mill center cause."

"Really?"

"I contacted one of the families I lived with on base and mentioned what Ethan and Ian have been trying to do here. It seems there are a lot of groups all over the country who are trying to do the same thing. I've got some great ideas to raise money. It won't be easy, but we may be able to raise the cash needed to make the repairs to the center and even get a grant to complete the renovation. Of course, it puts me out of a job because it'll be a job in itself to facilitate it all. But who knows, we could create a foundation that could grow beyond the Buxton Mills site."

"If it keeps you here in my arms, I'm game if you are."

"We could organize volunteer groups from other counties to come in and do the work in exchange for other services. It would eliminate a lot of red tape. And you know, we could even do that for other people in town to help get the building process started faster."

Keith was staring at her, and she wasn't sure he'd heard a word she'd said.

"Do you think it's too much?" she asked.

He laced his fingers with hers. "I think it's perfect."

She reached up on her toes to kiss him on the mouth. With her lips on his and his fingers entwined with hers, everything felt right.

"I love you Keith McKinnon. But I have only one problem."

A crease pulled at his brow. "What's that?"

"If I don't have a real job anymore, I can't exactly afford to live in the motel."

His smile widened. "Regis Simpson, you will always have a home with me. And I'm going to love you so well you'll never want to leave again."

Regis threw her arms around his neck, hot tears spilling down her cheeks. She buried her face in Keith's neck.

Then he whispered in her ear. "No more leaving. You're home for good."

"I'm going to hold you to that."

Keith's kiss was like a promise full of love and commitment to their future that they would be together always. And for the first time in her life, Regis believed it.

~The End~

DAKOTA HEAT
Dakota Hearts Series Book Three

Chapter One

"You've got to be kidding." Summer Bigelow glared at the police chief of the Providence Police Department as she sat back against the chair. She'd thought the parking ticket she'd found on her windshield this morning was a bad start to the day, and it could only get better from there.

She'd been wrong.

Matt Jorgensen looked at her with sympathy. "You're one of the best dispatchers I have, Summer. I'm not disputing that."

"Then why?" she said.

Matt raised his voice over hers. "But I'm not going to risk your life to some crazy stalker who has already killed four women."

Summer's mouth dropped open. She forced air into her lungs as she looked at the two detectives sitting in the office with them. Jake Santos and Kevin Gordon had been working this case right from the beginning and had been doing drive-by checks on her ever since the killer had called into her line.

"There was a fourth?"

The grim look they both offered was answer enough.

"Last time he called in, he reported there was a fourth," Jake said. "A kid discovered her taking a shortcut through a parking lot on the way to school this morning."

"But he called in last week. He said ..." Summer fought to think through the chain of events that had transpired over the last two weeks.

Kevin Gordon got up from his seat and walked in front of her, sitting on the desk. She knew his wife had been stalked by her ex-husband a few years ago and was nearly killed.

"You have to take this serious. We are. With Daria, we knew her ex-husband was after her, and she didn't leave town. We were watching him, and he still managed to slip through our fingers. I thank God every day we found Daria in time. We don't know who this serial killer is or where he'll be next. All we know for sure is that based on his last phone call, he's fixated on you."

"Look at you," Matt said, throwing his pen on the blotter on his desk. "It's been a week since that nutcase called in, and I can already see the toll it's taking on you. You've got dark circles under your eyes, and you look like you haven't slept at all. And don't blame Bobbi's lumpy couch, either. You walk down the hall, and I see you looking over your shoulder. That's no way to live, Summer."

"He doesn't know my name. Bobbi said I could stay at her place as long as I need to while you watch my apartment. How could he possibly find me?"

Jake handed her a folded newspaper. "We found this on your doorstep this morning. He could be anyone you talk to on the street, Summer. Anyone."

She opened the *Providence Journal Bulletin*. In red marker, the words YOU'RE NEXT were boldly scribbled on the page. Taped to the top was a picture of Summer walking out of Bobbi's apartment. The picture had the mark of a bullseye over her face.

Summer swayed in her seat. *The serial killer had been stalking her, and she'd never even known.* The growing ball of fear she'd walked around with for the past week burned in her stomach.

She thought to this morning when she'd found the parking ticket on her car in front of Bobbi's apartment building. A nice man had stopped his walk when she'd ranted in frustration over what was happening and told her the day would get better. It could have been him. *It could be anyone.* How would she know?

"For your own safety," Matt said. "You *are* going to be leaving Providence today. I'm not arguing the point."

"But … You're sending me to the middle of no man's land."

"South Dakota isn't exactly the South Pole. You'll be working fire dispatch. It's a good cover. I've already briefed the superintendent in charge of the fire unit in the area."

"Fire dispatch."

Matt looked at her file. "You've been trained in it. It's a perfect cover. If the killer continues looking for you, he won't be looking for a fire dispatcher."

"Why would he look for me in South Dakota? What the hell is even in South Dakota?"

Kevin's voice was sobering. "Safety."

♥ ♥ ♥

"You're an accident waiting to happen, Sam McKinnon!" Kate McKinnon grabbed the knife out of her son's hand and scowled.

"What am I doing wrong?" Sam asked, chuckling.

Kate grunted with exaggeration. "There are too many things for me to list. Sit down and let me make you a meal, will you? You've been gone for over a year. Can I at least enjoy having you home for five minutes before you blow up my kitchen again?"

"Hey, I told you that was an accident. What did Logan tell you?" Sam said, stepping back against the wall while his mom moved into his spot by the counter.

She waved him off. "Yeah, yeah, never mind. It wasn't always Logan and Ethan creating all the trouble around here. You and your cousin, Ian, were always an unpredictable pair, too." Despite her irritation, Kate chuckled quietly, clearly thrilled to have Sam home after so long.

"I don't have time for one of your famous breakfasts, Ma. I have to meet the new fire crew in an hour."

"You'll be out the door in twenty minutes. Geesh, I wish you'd been this eager to go to school when you were younger."

Kate busied herself whisking scrambled eggs in a cast iron fry pan with one hand while pulling a toasted bagel out of the toaster and dropping it on a clean white plate. She glanced up at Sam with that look she always gave him when she wanted to ask something but wasn't sure if she should.

"What?"

"Speaking of Ian, have you talked to him yet?"

His stomach dropped. His cousin, a wounded military hero, had talked about becoming a Hotshot fireman once he was done with his military service. But a mortar blast in Afghanistan had left him without a leg and struggling to find his way again back home.

"I just got home last night. Haven't had a chance."

Kate smiled weakly. "He'll be happy to see you. Just don't avoid him because you think it's too painful for him. He'd hate that."

Sam leaned back in his chair. His brother Ethan had told him as much. Ethan, a former Navy Seal, understood what Ian was going through more than any of them.

"I'll make sure I stop by on my way home today."

Smiling, Kate placed a full plate of food in front of Sam along with a full glass of orange juice.

"If you keep feeding me like this, Ma, I'll be so fat I won't be able to get any of my fire gear on by the end of the week."

There was a twinkle of happiness in her eyes as his mother smiled down at him. "If that's what it takes to keep my boy home in Rudolph, I'm game. If I can manage to find you a girl, even better."

The girl was new. Sam walked around the Interagency Fire Crew basecamp with familiarity. He saw faces he recognized from working in different locations over the past few years. But the girl … Yeah, she was new. He doubted he would forget the soft blonde color of her hair or the slight tilt of her head as she read through paperwork, pretending she didn't notice the people around her.

He grabbed two water bottles from the bucket full of ice in the back of the Quonset hut and walked toward her. She didn't look up until he held the water bottle in front of her.

Blue eyes met his with a mixture of irritation and surprise.

"You're dropping ice pieces on my paperwork," she said.

He noticed the smooth as silk sound of her voice before the water splatter on the top page of her paperwork. He immediately pulled the water bottle back a few inches.

"Sorry. I thought you might like something to drink."

Her face softened as quickly as it had shown irritation. She reached her hand out and took the water bottle, and then placed it on the bench next to her before shaking her hand of the residual moisture the bottle left behind. "Thank you."

"You're new here," he said as he sat down next to her.

Not looking up, she said, "So are you."

She smelled like soap and lavender. After breathing in smoke and dirt for so long, it was refreshing to breathe in the sweet scents of a woman.

"Not exactly. I grew up in Rudolph."

That earned him a lingering second glance. One that afforded him a few seconds to really look into her eyes, at her face.

"Really?"

"My whole life."

She glanced around quickly. "When I got in last night I was told the basecamp here was new this year. I didn't realize South Dakota had a dedicated fire basecamp."

Sam had never worked fire duty in his home state before. And he'd never come to a new location and been so familiar with faces as well as the location. His reason for wanting to come back to South Dakota this year was personal.

A lot of his friends who worked with the Interagency Fire Crew were still reeling after the deaths of nineteen Hotshot firemen in Arizona last summer. Some had quit fighting fires altogether at the urging of their family. Sam's own mother had tried her best to do the same during many phone calls since the tragedy, but Kate McKinnon settled for having him come home to Rudolph to work.

"This was just constructed this year. The Black Hills are a hot spot this year because of all the flood and ice damage that occurred over the winter. When I found out they were setting up a base here to do fire control for the season, I put in a request to work here."

She nodded. "Must be nice to be home. At least for the season."

She glanced down at her paperwork again.

He chuckled at how quickly she fell into her reading again. "You're looking at that like you're cramming for a final exam."

She shrugged. "I feel I am. This is my first season working fire dispatch anywhere."

"Ah, then that explains it."

"Must feel good to be home after—"

"Summer?"

Both Sam and the girl looked up to see the chief calling out from across the tent. The girl quickly collected her paperwork and stuffed it in a folder.

"Be right there," she called out. She turned to Sam, lifting the bottled water in her hand. "Thanks for the water."

"No problem."

But she was already trotting over to the superintendent's office. He hadn't even had a chance to get her name. But he would before the day was done. This was one woman he had a feeling he wanted to get to know.

♥ ♥ ♥

Adam White sat down at his desk and glanced at the folder Summer had handed him. She'd been given strict orders to report immediately to the superintendent of the Interagency Fire Crew she'd been assigned to on her first day on the job.

Summer hated first days on the job. The butterflies that had been souring her stomach for the past two days as she drove from Providence to Rudolph were only getting worst. She'd barely had enough time to get herself settled in the basecamp housing let alone look at the portfolio of information she'd been given when she'd been booted out of the police station.

She'd left her meeting with the chief to find Bobbi had already packed her bags and loaded them in her car. Matt had handed her an itinerary and given her an envelope full of petty cash, courtesy of an officer collection at the precinct. It didn't take a genius to know

Bobbi had been behind it. Her friend had been worried sick about her ever since the call came in on her phone line from the serial killer, telling her he was watching her.

When she'd counted the money, she'd gasped, not knowing whether to be flattered that the officers in the department cared that much about her well-being, or be offended that they wanted her out of town so badly. Since Bobbi had been on duty when she left, Summer hadn't had time to thank her friend for all she'd done for her before Summer left the city.

Adam finally closed the folder and handed it to her. "Did you find everything you need last night?"

"Uh, yeah. I guess."

"Good. It's the dormitory is rudimentary but has everything you'll need for the time being. I was told that some of the local rooms at the motel in town might open up soon now that some of the emergency crew that came into town over the winter will be leaving. You might find it more comfortable there."

"No, it's fine."

"We have briefings every day in the room you were in earlier. Most of the fire crew is required to do an hour of physical training every day, but that's not necessary for your job in dispatch. But feel free to use to the equipment in the Quonset hut if you want. I just ask that you wait until most of the crew has done their daily workout."

"Sure."

Adam stood up from his seat behind the desk and glanced quickly out the window at the crew of fire fighters who had already arrived. The briefing room she'd sat in earlier would soon be full of Hotshot fire fighters.

"Matt and I go way back to college. I was glad to get his call about you doing dispatch for us this fire season. Even though this is your first season in fire dispatch, Matt has high regard for your instinct and dedication. I think you'll do fine here."

"Thank you."

Despite being close to the same age as the police chief in Providence, Adam looked older, with salt and pepper hair and deep creases around his eyes. She guessed him to be close to forty, or maybe a few years beyond. As he looked at her, his forehead creased.

"What are you holding back?" she said.

He chuckled. "Matt warned me about you. Very direct. That's good. I just wanted to say that no one knows about what's going on back in Providence but me. Matt would like it to stay that way. I'll be checking in with him each week just for peace of mind. He'll keep me abreast of what is going on there if anything happens in the meantime. All I want you to do is concentrate on settling in. I see you've already met our squad leader, Sam McKinnon."

"Excuse me?"

"The man you were talking to in the briefing room when I first arrived."

How could she forget? Summer forced herself to be as nonchalant as she could. "Oh, him."

Adam chuckled.

"What?"

"I'm not sure he's used to that kind of brush off from women. He's got the reputation of being a bit of a charmer with the ladies. Don't say you didn't notice."

Her mouth dropped open. "He only handed me a bottle of water. We didn't even have a chance to exchange names before you called me in here."

Adam smiled knowingly.

"I'm sure that will change. Sam likes to know the people he's working with. It doesn't surprise me at all he sought you out before I had a chance to introduce you to the crew. He is one of the best Hotshots I've worked with. He doesn't let anything get in the way of doing his job safely."

She nodded. "Then I guess we'll get along fine."

Chapter Two

The sun was setting over the hills when Sam turned onto the lane that led away from the basecamp in Rudolph. It had been a long day. First days always were. And they'd get longer as fire season got busier for all of them.

No matter how many times he'd tried to get a moment to talk to Summer Bigelow, his efforts were thwarted. A new crew member had a question. Adam needed supply orders to make sure they had enough equipment stocked and ready to go before the prescribed burns they were planning got underway.

And every time he'd had a free moment again, Summer Bigelow was nowhere to be found. He'd only learned her name when Adam had announced her as a new dispatcher at the briefing. He'd given one last look around the makeshift building that housed basecamp and then decided to head back home.

He could feel the fatigue climb up his arms and legs, sneaking its way into his back as he climbed into his SUV. Anticipation that a meal would be waiting for him at home made sudden hunger roar in his belly as he drove. The rumbling only grew louder as he focused on the quiet sense of comfort that being home gave him as he drove down familiar streets of his hometown.

A small Honda sitting cock-eyed on the shoulder of the road caught his attention and had him pulling over. His hunger forgotten, he put his SUV into park and killed the engine before climbing out in search of the driver of the car. The trunk of the car was open and a duffel bag and suitcase were scattered on the ground as if whoever had put them there was searching for the right tool.

"Need any help?"

He saw the blonde mane of hair fly up quickly, covering the woman's face. But he knew exactly who it was. She shook her head to clear the strands of hair from her face. The terrified look on her face shocked him until her eyes showed recognition.

"You," she said. "No, I've got it." Summer grunted as she struggled with the tire wrench.

"You sure about that?"

With one big push, she lost her balance and fell back against the ground, the force pushing her hair away from her face.

Her face turned flush. He wasn't sure if it was from embarrassment or exertion.

"Well, maybe not. There's always one stubborn lug nut ..."

"And you're determined to conquer it."

"Damn right," she said, chuckling softly. Smooth. Musical. He liked her laugh and the mellow sound of her voice.

"Gotta love an independent woman."

"What?"

"Nothing." Sam extended a hand to help her up to her feet.

"I'm all set." As Summer got to her feet, Sam watched her wipe the back of her jeans with her hand. His eyes were immediately drawn to the shapely curve of her buttocks and he suddenly had a longing to run his hand over the same path her hand had just traveled.

He cleared his throat. "Let me give it a try."

"I told you. It's stuck."

Sam took the tire wrench and placed it into position. He put a little force behind his push. One, two pushes and then the bolt turned.

With a grin of satisfaction, he said, "There you go."

Her shocked look had him laughing.

"You weakened it. I just finished it off."

Summer rolled her eyes. "You don't have to make me feel better. Thanks for the muscle but I can take over from here."

He stood up and let Summer take his place by the flat tire. She lifted it off and set it aside. Sam took the spare tire she'd propped up against the side of the car and rolled it over to her and said, "We didn't have a chance to be properly introduced this morning. I'm Sam McKinnon."

She glanced up at him before picking up the tire and placing it in position on the car. "I know. Adam mentioned it."

"He did."

"And you were there when he introduced me to the crew this morning, so I'm guessing you know my name."

He grinned. "Yes, I do. Summer Bigelow. You're a long way from your home in Providence, Rhode Island."

She stopped what she was doing and stared up at him with a deer-in-headlights look that left him cold. "How'd you find that out?"

"You have Rhode Island plates. Providence was just a lucky guess."

She began turning lug nuts to secure the tire. "Oh."

"You sure you don't want me to help you with that?"

"Changing a flat tire was one of the first things my father taught me when I learned to drive. He said I had no business operating a motor vehicle if I couldn't get myself out of a flat tire." She tightened the lug nuts with the tire wrench, giving a grunt for added emphasis with each turn. "Damn lug nuts get me every time. Please don't tell anyone you had to help me. I'll never be able to show my face amongst the guys."

He raised his hand as if making an oath. "Your secret is safe with me."

Sam picked up the flat tire, rolled it to the back of the car and dropped it into the trunk. Once he had that securely in place, he picked up the duffel bag and suitcase.

"Leaving us already?" he asked.

The little Honda slowly floated back to right as Summer released the jack. When she was done, she stood up, wiping her hands on her backside again. Damn, that simple move drew his attention away from his question and had him forgetting what he'd asked.

"No, just moving house," she said. "I stayed at the base dormitory last night."

"Which is a Crew Haul that consists of a cot in a tin can trailer. Yes, I know it well."

She chuckled. "I'm sure you do. But I was thankful for a place to sleep after my long drive. I could have slept on the ground and still slept. I got a call this afternoon about the…an open room at a motel around here so I'm going to stay there. That is if I can find the motel."

Standing by the car, Sam got a really good look at Summer for the first time. His throat went dry, looking at the blue of her eyes and the soft color of her medium length blonde hair against the setting sun behind them. She had her hair pulled back in a messy ponytail as if she'd haphazardly tied it when she'd discovered the flat tire. Her round face and high cheekbones made her look more delicate than he imagined she was. Her pink lips were pursed just a little as she looked up at him as if waiting for a response.

"The motel is near the center of Rudolph, next to the diner and across the street from the clinic where my brother, Hawk, works as a doctor. If you follow me, you can't miss it."

Summer smiled up at him, and it actually stole his breath away. Good Lord, when was the last time he'd gone weak in the knees over a female smiling at him? But there was something there … a hesitation that didn't seem quite right.

A few shorter strands fell across her face, and she nervously pushed them behind her ears as she spoke. "Thanks, but I'm not sure of the name of the motel. I'm sure I can find it on my own."

"There's only one motel in Rudolph. It's not hard to find. Just a few turns off this road. I'm going that way anyway."

She seemed to weigh his offer, but her hesitation had him wondering why. "I appreciate that. My GPS started giving me fits somewhere between South Bend and Des Moines and hasn't recovered since. So I'm not trusting it to find my way around these back roads."

Sam pointed to his SUV. "I'm stopping in the diner for a bite to eat. Do you want to join me?"

Her mouth dropped open, her lips still pursed in that way she did earlier. He liked it, and it made him want to bend his head and brush his mouth on hers just to taste how sweet those lips really were.

"Oh, I don't think so," she said. "I need to unpack and go through my notes and—"

He raised an eyebrow. "Are you always this dedicated to your work?

"Yes," she answered quickly.

With a slow smile, he said, "I like that. But all work and no play is not good."

"Something tells me you get your share of play time in."

Sam laughed at that. "Just don't listen to any rumors. I swear they're all lies. I will have lots of distraction now that I'm home, though."

"Yeah. Okay, well it was nice to formally meet you, Sam McKinnon. I'm sure we'll see lots of each other."

His fingers curled around hers as her hand slipped perfectly into his. "I'm counting on it."

Sam stared at her wordlessly for a long moment before realizing that she was standing by the driver's side, door ajar with one foot inside and the other on the road.

"We should get off the side of the road like this," she said, the words rolling off her tongue quickly.

"Right."

A moment later, Sam was left watching Summer Bigelow from his rearview mirror. There was a cautiousness about her that she tried to hide. But the fear in her eyes as she popped her head up from behind the car, along with the relief in recognizing him had Sam wondering what was really scaring her.

The few minutes that he'd spent with Summer had told him two things. She was not here because she'd planned to be here. And the expression that had come over her when he'd offered to bring her to the motel was enough proof for him that she afraid of something or someone.

As he drove, Sam wondered just what would make a woman like Summer that frightened. But what concerned him most was that he didn't just want to know what demons she feared enough to be that scared when she'd seen him. He suddenly wondered why he seemed to be so curious about the woman at all.

Chapter Three

"You want me to spend the entire day with Samuel McKinnon?" Summer asked before she could stop herself.

"You have a problem with that?" Adam asked, clearly surprised.

"No, of course not," Summer replied, forcing her expression to remain impassive even as she felt heat rising in her cheeks. Of course, she had a problem with that. After yesterday's embarrassing fiasco, she'd done nothing but dream up ways to avoid the sinfully handsome fireman so as not to relive yesterday's humiliation.

She'd been genuinely terrified when she'd pulled over to the shoulder of the road with that flat tire. She couldn't believe she'd managed to drive all the way from Providence to Rudolph without incident. Then her first day in Rudolph, she was left stranded by the side of an empty road with a flat.

During those long moments when she'd climbed out of her car and pulled out the spare tire and jack, all Summer could think about were those pictures of her taken by the serial killer. Her mind ran rampant, and every little noise in the woods behind her sounded ominous. She'd been so preoccupied with that stubborn lug nut that she hadn't even heard Sam's car or his approach.

Then she proceeded to make a colossal fool of herself. The man probably thought she'd been breathless because of him. And worst of all ... she *had* stared at him with total girl crush. Totally uncool. Completely humiliating.

But how could she not? Sam McKinnon was the very definition of a chiseled Greek god. She was sure his name was right next to *warrior protector* in the dictionary. All the Hotshots were required to workout daily to stay fit for the rigorous activity they dealt with during fire season. But Sam McKinnon ... Lord help her.

"Summer?"

Her head snapped up as she looked at Adam again, realizing she hadn't heard a word he'd just said.

He leaned back in his chair. "It's understandable that you'd be distracted by what's happening in Providence. But I need you to focus here. You *are* safe here. You can be sure of that."

"I know. I'm sorry."

Adam turned his head with the hard rap of knuckles on the office door.

"Come in."

The door opened, and Sam McKinnon took up every inch of space in the doorway. No wonder she'd taken him for a warrior protector.

Sam nodded a hello to both of them.

"You've met our new dispatcher, Summer Bigelow?" Adam asked.

"Yes," Sam said, sitting in the seat next to Summer. "I take it you had no problem with the tire this morning?"

"I'm still using the spare, but it's working."

"Spare?" Adam asked.

"I had a flat tire last night on the way to the motel. Sam stopped when he saw me changing the tire."

"Since the two of you have already had a chance to get to know each other a little, you'll feel more comfortable working alongside each other today. Sam will get you up to speed on the operation here. We never know when fire season is going to go into full swing, and we have a lot of clean up and prescribed burns to do in the area."

She drew in a deep breath as she folded her hands in her lap. "Sure."

Sam was staring at her, into her eyes as if he were searching for some deep secret.

She wove her fingers together. "Is everything okay?" she asked.

"I figured you'd get a decent night's sleep in a real bed, but you look like you didn't sleep at all last night."

"Thank you," she said dryly.

"I didn't mean you look bad. You just look more worn out than you did yesterday morning after that long drive."

"Oh, that's so much better. I can't wait for you to really turn on the charm."

He chuckled, shaking his head. "This isn't coming out right at all. I've lost all points I gained helping you with that lug nut."

She lifted her eyebrows.

Sam made a face that showed he knew he was busted. "And I just blew that secret, too."

"Maybe you should quit while you're ahead," Adam said, chuckling.

"You thought he was ahead?" she remarked.

"Guess not," Sam said with a shake of his head as Adam laughed louder. His face grew serious. "It's just that you seemed pretty terrified when I came up on you by the side of the road. I hope I didn't scare you too much."

Summer darted a glance at Adam, whose eyes had narrowed. She had been reliving the nightmare of seeing those photos the serial killer had taken of her as she struggled with the car tire. Her imagination had run rampant as she found herself alone on the side of the road, wondering if anyone was watching her. She'd nearly jumped out of her skin when she'd suddenly realized she wasn't alone and hadn't heard anyone approach.

But then she'd turned and seen Sam standing there, looking so commanding, and her fear melted away. His eyes, although a steely gray in the fading light, had been kind and filled with concern as they'd run over her face. His smile and deep, reassuring voice, made her trust him almost instantly.

"No," she said quickly. "You just … I didn't hear you stop. I'm fine. Really."

Sam looked at Adam, then at Summer.

Adam cleared his throat. "I assumed you might feel more comfortable at the motel, but maybe staying here in the dormitory will be better until you get more comfortable with the area. You'll have people you know all around you. These roads aren't well lit like the city roads in Providence you're used to."

"Don't be ridiculous. The motel is fine for now. And once I settle in a little more, I plan on finding a rental in the area. I'll be fine."

"Well, then Sam is your man," Adam said, gesturing with his hand to Sam. "He's the only one on the crew who knows the area."

"I don't know of any rentals off hand. But I know a lady who knows just about everything going on in town. If there is a rental, she'll know about it. I can introduce you to her."

Adam chuckled, making Summer wonder just who this "her" was to Sam. She didn't need to know. She only needed to find a comfortable place to live.

"If you happen to see this *lady friend* of yours, I'd appreciate finding out if she knows of any vacancies in town," Summer said. When the silence dragged on, she added, "So where do we start?"

♥ ♥ ♥

They'd spent the afternoon going over the basics of Hotshot gear and the running of the basecamp.

"Everyone will spend the first two weeks getting trained and tested to make sure they're up to standards. At some point, I'll get you up to speed on the maps of the area and take an afternoon or two to drive out to the area the fire crew will be doing some clearing and prescribed burns."

"I didn't realize I'd be going out in the field," Summer said as they walked toward the dispatch center along the already trampled patch of grass in the large pasture where the makeshift agency basecamp had been set up.

"It's not really necessary as long as you understand the maps and how to relay information."

"I've been certified in fire dispatch."

He glanced at her, his lips slightly lifted as he said, "You don't have to convince me. You came very well recommended by your chief back in Providence."

Summer stopped walking. "How do you know that?"

Sam turned and looked back at her. "Because I talked to him on the phone. Matt is his name, right?"

Color stained her face.

"I like to know who I'm working with," he added, his eyebrows slightly knitted on his forehead. "Out in those hills I'm responsible for the lives of my crew. Surely you can understand that."

"Of course." She was being ridiculous. And the way Sam seemed to look at her with such depth told her he wasn't buying her cool act every time she tried to recover. The last thing she needed was to act like she was an inept idiot and have him lose confidence in her ability.

"There are aerial view maps here, right?" she asked.

"Yes. You'll find them in the dispatch office, which is down the hall from Adam's office. But the Black Hills are unique and this land was overrun with floods and damage from the ice storms this past winter. I find it's always good to have a visual of the area we'll be working as it looks right now. It doesn't prepare any of us for the uncertainties. But being as prepared as we can be makes our job safer. The map can only give you so much information."

"I understand."

"Do you?"

She stared up at Sam for a brief moment, wondering whether or not it was a simple question or a challenge.

She pushed an errant strand of hair away from her face that the wind had blown around. "You don't trust me?"

"Trust? I don't know you well enough yet. Like I said, you come here highly recommended."

"Then there shouldn't be a problem."

She smiled even though she didn't feel it. His probing stare was definitely a challenge.

"What I don't understand is why a woman who is so admired in her job back in a big city like Providence ..."

Summer sputtered. "Big city? Hardly."

He shrugged. "Okay, a city. I've never been to Providence. But it certainly isn't Rudolph or any of the other small towns in South Dakota that I know. Why here when you could have gone anywhere, especially when Matt had such high praise for you?"

She chose her words carefully. "I have never done fire dispatch before. Why not South Dakota?"

He made a face that Summer found incredibly adorable, and at the same time, hated that she did. Thoughts of Sam McKinnon had consumed her mind ever since she'd met the man. She wasn't staying in South Dakota. And from what Adam told her, neither was he. Smokejumpers and Hotshots didn't work in her little state of Rhode Island, so the likelihood of anything other than a quick fling happening between them was zero. And since Summer wasn't into cheap, meaningless sex, no matter how gorgeous a man Sam McKinnon was, they were at less than zero.

Still, she couldn't ignore the way his warm eyes seemed to caress her as he gazed at her.

It had to be her imagination. And lately she'd found that her imagination was as wild as the crazy turn her life had taken.

"Let's go. I'll show you your home away from home for the next six months," he said, placing a gentle hand on her shoulder to lead her toward the dispatch office.

Her feeble explanation seemed to satisfy Sam, which brought a weird sense of relief and disappointment. Only Adam knew of the danger Summer had faced in Providence and her real reason for ending up here in Rudolph. It was safer that way, and yet part of her wanted to confide in Sam. She didn't know why.

It was crazy. She'd only just met the man. And yet something about him told her she'd be safe with him.

Warrior protector.

She'd been watching too many movies, Summer thought with a smile as she walked alongside Sam. And then it hit her. For the size of him and the length of his legs, Sam McKinnon should be walking strides ahead of her. She should be running to keep up. And yet Sam was walking by her side.

She liked that.

Chapter Four

They'd spent the first week having every member of the team tested for fitness, stamina and knowledge of the procedures the Hotshots would use all fire season. Many of the members of his crew were veteran Hotshots, but Sam had a few new members that he wanted to pay close attention to in order to make sure they were fully prepared for the unexpected.

As they did at the start of every day, the entire crew of Hotshots, Smokejumpers and dispatchers met in the Quonset hut for a morning briefing. Mornings were cool, but as the day progressed, the Quonset hut would get warmer under the baking sun.

As he held his cup of coffee in his hand, Sam glanced at Summer for what seemed like the hundredth time during the briefing. He tried not to, he wanted to listen to Adam as he discussed the success of the drills and the strategies he'd put in place to deal with the fire season. But he found it difficult to focus on the superintendent.

He had heard all of it before, he knew the drill well enough to act in his sleep, but Sam also knew that it was a dangerous thing to get lazy and think there wasn't anything left to learn. There were no typical days in his job. Every day could bring something unexpected. So he forced himself not to be distracted.

And Summer had definitely become a distraction over the last week since he'd arrived home to Rudolph. So much so that even his brother, Ethan, had noticed his preoccupation at dinner, choosing to rib him about already finding a lady friend for the summer.

Being that Sam already had a reputation with the women folk in Rudolph, he just took the teasing from his brother and didn't elaborate. Summer Bigelow didn't appear nearly as interested in him as he was in her.

As he turned to look at her, he saw her face lifted to the front of the room, focusing on every word that Adam was saying, just like she had been every time he glanced her way. He still had no idea what this woman was all about or why she was here in South Dakota. Everything inside Sam told him something was driving Summer and it wasn't love of the job. He couldn't shake that look on her face when he'd seen her on the side of the road a week ago. It was almost as if she were running from something. But from what?

"I know I'm not saying anything new," Adam said, the words grabbing Sam's attention. "But a recap never hurt anyone. And since we have some new faces in our crew this season, I'd say it's necessary."

Sam watched as Adam turned to Summer. He spoke to her quietly, his voice soft enough to not even reach the people standing closest to him. A moment later, Summer nodded and smiled and Adam turned back to the group.

"That's all for now," Adam said. "I'll leave you to your responsibilities."

As the group dispersed, Sam tried to move to the front of the room where Summer had been sitting. A wall of men surrounded her before he could get close. Sam fell back, watching with a twinge of envy as some of the crew talked to Summer. She smiled up at each of them as they spoke to her. He could understand their reaction. Through the years, there'd been no shortage of pretty women in Sam's life, but Summer Bigelow was one of the most beautiful women he had ever seen and the male to female ratio at basecamp was way off balance.

"Sam?"

He turned with the sound of a familiar voice behind him, one that he couldn't ignore.

Ian McKinnon was more like another brother to Sam than a cousin. Having grown up in Rudolph all their lives, they'd had the chance to grow up, make mischief and dream big together. Sam had realized his dream of being a Hotshot. That dream had been robbed from Ian while in the military.

"I'm glad you stopped by," Sam said, shaking Ian's hand. He glanced over to where Summer had been sitting just in time to see her leaving the Quonset hut.

Ian chuckled. "Looks like I came at a bad time."

Sam waved him off. "Nah, your timing was perfect."

"I can't stay long. I need to get back to the work on the Veteran's Center."

"Adam just finished his meeting. Let me introduce you to some of the guys and then I'll bring you over to meet Adam."

They spent the next fifteen minutes meeting crew members and walking around basecamp. His brother, Hawk, the resident doctor in Rudolph, had told him that Ian's limp had lessened considerably from the time he'd first gotten his prosthetic limb to now. But to Sam, each step Ian took was a reminder of how close they'd come to losing him. It had to pain Ian being amongst people who were looking forward to working a job Ian had dreamed of doing himself. For the first time Sam questioned urging his cousin to meet Adam White and talk about his future possibilities working in some capacity with the Interagency Fire Crew.

As they approached the dispatch office, Ian stopped Sam. Summer was standing by Adam's office door. The smile was gone and was replaced with the deer-in-headlights expression he'd seen on her at the side of the road last week.

"Everything okay?" Sam said as she breezed by them quickly.

Summer drew in a deep breath as she turned and focused on his face. As recognition set in, she said, "Yes, of course."

Before he could introduce Ian, Summer turned on her heels and headed to the dispatch room, leaving both Sam and Ian wondering what had just transpired.

"I can handle this on my own," Ian said, motioning to Adam's closed office door. "You've got someplace else you need to be."

Sam shook Ian's extended hand. "I'm glad you came down. Let me know how things go."

♥ ♥ ♥

"You look like you're all settled in."

The deep sound of Sam McKinnon's voice was both startling and comforting. Summer glanced down at her hand and saw it shaking. She stuffed her hand into the pocket of her jeans and turned in her chair.

"I should be. I've been here a week."

"You've been ignoring me."

Her mouth dropped open when she saw Sam was actually serious. She didn't know exactly how to take Sam McKinnon. In the week she'd been here, she'd heard stories, especially from one particular waitress at the diner near the motel, who clearly still carried a torch for the man.

"I've been busy," she said.

He dragged a chair from one of the other desks and turned it around, straddling it as he sat down.

"I thought we hit it off that first day."

"From what I hear you hit it off with all the women. No thank you. I'm not sticking around long enough to make it worth your while."

He raised an eyebrow. "Fire season hasn't even started yet."

She'd fumbled, but recovered quickly. "I'll be here this season. But you won't be seeing me after that."

A satisfied smile that she couldn't ignore touched his lips. "You've been talking about me? I'm flattered."

She sputtered. "It's hard to work here and not have you end up in the conversation down at the diner."

"So you've met my mother," he said with a smile.

She nodded, finding it hard not to smile with him. Summer had immediately taken a liking to Kate McKinnon. There was something about her that was so familiar that it made it hard for Summer not to miss her mother now that so much had changed in her life.

When Summer had arrived in Rudolph, she'd called her parents in Florida. But instead of relaying her reasons for coming to South Dakota, she'd simply told her parents she'd decided to test her training in fire dispatch for a change of pace. Thankfully, they hadn't questioned her.

"Your mom is very nice. And she's obviously thrilled you're home. So much so that I think she's forgotten she has other sons."

Sam cocked his head to one side. "I can't help it if I'm the favorite," he said quietly.

Summer chuckled while shaking her head. "You're so full of yourself."

"Some women find that charming."

Her smile faltered. "Well, I'm not like most women."

"I knew that the moment I met you."

He was looking directly into her eyes, probing as if he could read her mind. Her head went dizzy, and her heartbeat quickened.

"I told you you're wasting your time. After fire season, I'm heading back to Providence to resume my old job. And from what I hear, you're only here for the season anyway, and then you'll be off to some other location next season. Surely there is some old flame of yours you can play with while you're home."

"You remind me of that quote from Hamlet. 'The lady doth protest too much, methinks.'"

"Wow, you didn't strike me as a fan of Shakespeare."

"I'm a man of many mysteries. I think my passion for his work is the only thing that helped me graduate from high school. Shocked the hell out of my father."

Now Summer was impressed and more than a little intrigued.

"Who would have thought?"

Sam got up from the chair slowly and silently placed it back at the workstation he'd taken it from.

"The color has returned to your face," he said quietly, giving her a thoughtful look that caught her off guard. "Whatever ghost you saw has vanished."

Her heart hammered in her chest. "I don't know what you mean."

"Sure you do. If it comes back, whatever it is, I'll be here. You're not alone."

As Sam walked away, tears filled Summer's eyes. Based on what Adam just told her, her ghost still hadn't been found, and that's what chilled her to the core.

People were laughing outside her window. She'd kept the window open to catch some of the cool breeze blowing over the field. She'd lived in the city so long that she'd forgotten the smell of clean, wide open spaces. Now she wanted to shut herself inside.

What scared her more than anything was that she didn't want Sam McKinnon to walk away.

Chapter Five

"Sam?" Summer ran down the steps of the dispatch office, pulling her light spring jacket on as she ran.

The sun was setting behind Sam as he walked to his SUV in the parking lot. When he heard her calling, he stopped and waited for her.

"Did I forget something?" he asked.

A little out of breath from running, she said, "You mentioned last week that you had a ... *friend* who could help me find a rental in the area. I was wondering if you could introduce me to her."

"Ah, the lady friend." Sam smiled down at her in that way he did when he was teasing. It grated on Summer's nerves more than she wanted to admit, but she refused to give him the satisfaction of knowing how he got to her.

"Yes. If you have her number, I can call myself."

"That won't be necessary. You've already met her."

Her eyes widened. "I have?"

"Sure. It's my mother."

A smile pulled at Summer's lips despite the realization that Sam had indeed been playing her.

"My mother knows everything going on in this town. She owns the diner. That's akin to being a bartender or psychiatrist in a small town. People tell her everything. You should hear the stories she's told us at dinner."

Summer laughed.

"Come on. I'm heading home for dinner now. She's always up for setting an extra plate at the table."

"Are you sure?"

"Of course. But ..."

"What?"

"She's also determined to marry off her single boys. And since both Logan and Hawk are both off the market, she's turned her attention to me and my brother, Ethan. Don't say I didn't warn you."

"I've never seen anything like it," Ethan said, accepting a bowl of mashed potatoes from his father and then dropping a big spoonful in his plate. He passed the plate over to Summer and then continued talking about the damaged areas of forest surrounding the river. "It looks as if a tornado ripped through the area. Trees are flattened, and if a tree is still standing, the limbs are gone."

Donald McKinnon shook his head. "All my life I've never seen anything like it either. That's the power of all that floodwater and everything it took down the river with it."

"That's why this area is so vulnerable right now," Sam said. "So much of the debris is compacted. It's like a tinderbox. It only needs the heat of the sun or a small spark to ignite it. It needs to be cleaned up before the summer heat or a lightning storm strikes or we'll have wildfires all over the place."

Kate sat down at the table with a sigh now that the last bowl of food had been placed in the center.

"You look tired, Mom," Sam said.

"Worried. After what happened to all those fire fighters in Arizona, I haven't stopped worrying about you, Sam. I know you and Ian have always had an affinity for being fire fighters. But … I just worry."

"That's understandable, Mrs. McKinnon," Summer said.

Kate gave her a glance with raised eyebrows, reminding her that Summer had been instructed to call her by her first name.

"Sorry. Kate. When I told my mother I was going into criminal justice because I wanted to become a state police officer, she nearly fainted. Even after I'd gotten my acceptance letter to Johnson and Wales, she tried to talk me out of it. She wanted me to be a chef."

"Well, there's nothing wrong with being a chef," Kate said. Then she glanced over at Ethan and added, "I gave up trying to talk my boys out of doing dangerous jobs a long time ago. I just learned to pray a lot, especially when Ethan was a Navy Seal." To Ethan she said, "I was almost glad I didn't know where you were in the world or what you were doing."

"You're right. You wouldn't have wanted to know," Ethan said. "And I couldn't have told you anyway."

She turned her attention to Summer and said, "My son Keith—everyone calls him Hawk, even his patients— became a doctor. He has a practice right here in town. Logan, Ethan's twin brother, is the only other one who settled down to do a relatively safe job. Although he's given me reason enough to worry over the years."

Sam quietly said, "Logan's wife died a little over a year ago."

"Oh, I'm sorry to hear that."

"It was rough going for him and their little boy, but I hear all that has changed now that Poppy is back in town."

Kate smiled bright. "Poppy sure is a ray a sunshine for my Logan. Sometimes the universe rights itself when it's upside down. She sure did that."

Sam leaned into Summer. "Logan always had a thing for Poppy in high school. I'm sure you'll meet both of them while you're here."

Summer couldn't help but notice how amazing Sam smelled. He'd taken a quick shower before dinner while Summer helped Kate make a salad in the kitchen. He smelled of a mixture of musk and soap that filled her head. It was hard for Summer to concentrate on the good meal that Kate had prepared for the family with Sam seated so close to her. She could almost feel the heat of his body penetrating her skin, and they weren't even touching.

Summer welcomed Ethan's curious question to pull her attention away from her strong reaction to Sam.

"How did you go from wanting to be a police officer to being a dispatcher?"

"It's sort of a long story, and one I'm sure my mother would rather had not have happened at all, despite her not wanting me to be a police officer."

"Tell us," Kate said.

As they ate, Summer recalled the incident that had been the turning point in her decision to become a dispatcher.

"My senior year of high school I was home alone one night. My parents were out at some dinner party in Massachusetts and weren't supposed to be home until very late. Anyway, I was in my bedroom and heard voices downstairs. I knew it wasn't my parents, and since I was upstairs, I had no way to get out of the house without going through the living room. I was pretty sure they were down there and would see me."

She leaned back in her chair, surprised she was being so open about a memory that had haunted her for years. All eyes at the table were on her as she recollected what happened.

"I crawled into my closet with the phone and called 911. I could hear the burglars downstairs, but when their voices became louder, I started to hyperventilate. I was sure they were going to find me in the closet and do God only knows what to me when they did. The female dispatcher on the other end of the line became my lifeline. She talked to me calmly and told me everything would be okay, that the police were on their way. It probably only took the police about five minutes to get there, but it felt like an eternity."

"You must have been so terrified," Donald said.

"I was. I heard their voices in the upstairs hall and then the dispatcher—her name was Elaine—told me the officers had arrived at the house. One of the burglars ran out the kitchen door when he saw the cruiser outside. The other guy hid in my room and closed the door. For the longest time all I could hear was my heart pounding and the sound of Elaine's voice reassuring me on the phone. The guy in my room eventually gave up and was arrested.

"I was so shocked when I met Elaine the next day when I went to the police station. She was this little woman who was barely five feet tall and about ninety-five pounds. But while I was on the phone with her she was a giant, larger than life. I knew then how powerful that lifeline was for someone in need. So I trained to be a dispatcher, and my best friend, Bobbi Collins, went to Johnson and Wales and eventually became a police officer."

"Wow, that's quite an experience," Sam said.

"I told my story. Why did you want to become a fire fighter?" Summer asked.

"Sam had a fondness for blowing things up when he was a kid," Kate said dryly.

Ethan laughed. "Yeah, he figured he'd better learn how to put fires out since he was so good at starting them."

They all laughed and Summer found the tension that had plagued her since she'd left Providence was finally draining away. It was the first time she'd felt completely comfortable and safe since she'd arrived in Rudolph and gave her hope that she might just be able to get through this after all.

An hour later, Summer was saying her good-byes, and Sam was walking her to her car. The smell of cool spring night wrapped around her, and the sound of frogs mating in a nearby pond filled the air.

"You didn't have to walk me out," Summer said when she reached the car.

Sam leaned in close, and she could smell the familiar scent of musk and soap that had tickled her senses earlier at the dinner table.

"I know. But how else was I going to kiss you if I didn't?" he asked.

Summer swallowed to help keep herself from responding impulsively. She couldn't deny she'd thought about kissing Sam McKinnon. How could she not? The man was a teenage dream. But she refused to be his plaything.

"You're so damned sure of yourself, McKinnon. What makes you think I even want you to kiss me?"

"Don't worry. I'm not going to take from you what isn't offered. I'm not like that."

"And I'm not the kind of woman who throws herself at a handsome man."

His eyebrows raised playfully as he bent his head, giving her ample access to reach up and kiss his mouth if she'd wanted to.

"You think I'm handsome, huh?"

She rolled her eyes and took a small step away from him, hating herself for doing so as much as admitting the obvious. Summer could see how the waitress at the diner had become so enamored with the man in high school.

"Don't tell me I'm the first to say that to you, Sam McKinnon, because you'd be lying."

"You're the prettiest girl who ever said that to me."

"That was strike two."

His eyes narrowed. "How did I already get to two? Seems to me, you're the one who is playing."

"How do you figure that?"

"You can't tell me you don't know how beautiful you are. And you are so very beautiful. Every male Hotshot in that briefing room can't take their eyes off you, including me."

She'd noticed the attention of the other men. And yet, the only person Summer cared was paying any attention to her at all was Sam.

Abruptly, he backed up and drew in a short breath. "Tomorrow is my day off. Yours too I think."

Confused by the sudden subject change, Summer blinked. "Uh, yes."

"I mentioned to my mother that you were looking for rentals in the area. She said she'd check around, but wasn't sure since most of the available rentals are filled with people who are still displaced after the floods last winter. The fact that you got a motel room at all is a huge deal. Most of the guys from out of town are still bunking in the basecamp dormitory."

"Oh, well, then I guess I'm lucky to have the room I have."

"Yeah. The only other room, other than the ones here in my parents' house, is the room over the garage." Sam pointed to the dark windows above the two-car garage. "It used to be my brother Wade's room. But since he's been gone, well, my mother can't bring herself to clear it out."

"Gone?"

"He was presumed dead in a tsunami that hit an island off the coast of Asia where he was working as a Peace Corp worker."

"Oh, I'm sorry."

Sam sighed as he shrugged. "Even after nearly five years it still feels a little surreal. I keep expecting him to run up the driveway and put me in a headlock like he used to do when we were kids."

"Something tells me you deserved it."

Sam chuckled. "Yeah, I probably did. It's one of the reasons why my mom is always so worried about Ethan and me."

"Of course. She already lost one son. Who could go through that heartache and survive twice?"

"Exactly. Anyway, as I was saying, I have tomorrow off. I was thinking of riding out to the areas where we'll be doing some prescribed burns next week, just to get a feel for the damage to the land. I know the area, but I also know it's changed quite a bit since the winter. Would you like to go?"

It was her day off, and the thought of spending the day holed up in her motel room or doing laundry seemed depressing.

Summer held Sam's gaze, biting her lower lip unconsciously as she considered his proposal. "Sure," she said before she could talk herself out of it.

"Okay. I'll pick you up at the motel early then?"

She nodded.

His dark eyes were warm as he smiled at her. "Goodnight, Summer," he said softly.

"Goodnight, Sam."

As she climbed into her car and turned the key to the ignition, Summer watched Sam walk back to the house. She couldn't drag her gaze away from him. The way he moved with each step, the tone of his voice, and the way he made her feel just being near him enveloped her like a warm blanket.

As she pulled out of the driveway, disappointment tugged at her gut, replacing the warmth she'd felt.

Sam had forgotten about the kiss.

Chapter Six

They'd spent the day driving through the most beautiful country Summer had ever seen. With everything Providence had to offer, Summer had never seen hills and space like she had seen here. She talked of her childhood in Providence, and Sam entertained her with stories of the childhood antics of the McKinnon clan. Of that, there were many, making Summer laugh until she cried. They were a close bunch and the loss of their older brother, Wade, had devastated them all.

"When we got word about Wade, Mom closed down the diner, and I don't think she got out of bed for a week after the memorial service," Sam said as he parked the SUV in a parking lot near a scenic trail for hikers.

"Where were you?"

"I was based out of Colorado at the time. My father threw himself even deeper into work at the oil company. I'd never seen my parents so divided. They've always been devoted to the family, always there for us. But this happened and ... I really didn't think they were going to make it."

"How'd they get through it?"

"Kelly found out she was pregnant. Kelly was Logan's wife. She died just over a year ago. They have a little boy named Keith, named after my brother Hawk."

Summer chuckled wryly. "How did he get the name Hawk?"

"It's a long story," he said, getting out of the SUV. She did the same and took in a deep breath of mountain air. The sun was high in the sky and warm against her face.

"So having a grandchild changed everything for them?"

"Pretty much. Having Keith come into the family gave my parents a reason to get up in the morning again. It'll never take the sting out of losing Wade. But it did change them, and they got through it."

They fell in step as they walked down the hiking trail.

"I hope one day I can be as lucky in love as my parents."

"You?"

Sam gave her a sidelong glance. "Why not me?"

"From what I hear from Michelle, there is no chance of Sam McKinnon ever settling down."

"Michelle?"

"Oh, you forgot her already? Waitress at your mother's diner? She told me all about how you broke her heart in high school. And that's not the only broken heart in town by her recollection."

"Ah, Michelle. She was a nice girl. Not my type though."

"Really?"

"Besides I hear she's gotten over me just fine."

"She told me she's engaged. But she carried quite a torch for you."

"You jealous?"

"Me? Why would I be jealous?"

He chuckled, the sun making his eyes twinkle just a bit. "I wouldn't mind if you were."

"I don't have time for a broken heart, thank you very much."

"And yet you're here with me now. With all that talk, it seems to me you'd have run in the other direction when I asked you to come today."

Damn that Sam McKinnon. He always seemed to have a way of backing her up in a corner about her feelings.

She thought a second before she replied. "You were the one who suggested I come see the area before fire season got into full swing."

"That's only because I wanted to be alone with you."

She snapped her gaze at him as he laughed.

They reached the top of the trail, which opened up to a magnificent view of the rock formations on the hills beyond the canyon.

"Wow, a person can really get lost out here," Summer said, taking in the breathtaking view.

"Some do. Not me, mind you. But some people do."

She gave Sam a playful smack on the arm. "You're so full of yourself."

"You love that about me."

"There you go again. So sure of yourself."

Sam took her hand in his and walked with her up a pass toward the top of the cliff to get a better view of the canyon below. She didn't pull back, surprised at just how easy it was to feel connected to this man and how much she wanted more of him. It was easy to be with Sam, easy to feel comfortable and say what was on her mind. And it was easy for her to forget her reason for being in South Dakota in the first place. All her fears felt so far away when she was with Sam.

"There is a blessing and a curse in those rock formations."

"How do you mean?"

Sam pointed to the red rock formations on the opposite side of the canyon. "They'll stop a fire from spreading past that point. But they'll trap a man in that canyon just as easily if all access below is blocked. We'll need two spotters when we work down there this week in case the wind shifts. And in the canyons, the wind shifts rapidly."

Being here with Sam was both an education and a comfort. He knew his job well and took all precautions to make sure his crew was safe. He wouldn't risk their lives.

"When do the prescribed burns start?" she asked.

"Next week. We have a lot of work to do this season. The NOAA has warned that this area is a hot spot if the heat lightning we've been experiencing sets off a fire. Once we get underway, we'll probably be holed up in our Crew Hauls for days until the work is done."

And she'd be back at the basecamp that would act as a satellite base for the Hotshots, Smokejumpers and fuel haulers. That was where her job was. That's where safety was. Sam would be out here where all the danger would be.

But for today, she was here with Sam, and there was no danger for either of them. It was just the two of them on this gloriously perfect sunny day.

"What?" he said, looking at her curiously.

"I didn't say anything."

"No, but you're smiling."

She raised an eyebrow. "You don't like my smile?"

He dragged her into his arms and enveloped her. "On the contrary, Summer. There is a whole lot about you that I am crazy about. I don't see it nearly often enough, but I love your smile. In fact, that first day when you were meeting the rest of the crew, I was out of my mind with envy at the way you smiled at each and every one of the men talking to you. You just scowled at me for dripping water on your paperwork."

She laughed. "That's because I didn't want you to know what I was really feeling."

"Oh? And what was that?"

Heat crept up her cheeks as she turned away. But Sam moved so he could look at her face straight on.

"Don't do that. I love it when you blush. I love it when you smile. I love your amazing blue eyes. And I love hearing your voice when you talk to me over the radio."

"What?"

"It's sexy."

"It is not! For Pete's sake, I'm talking to the other fire fighters, too. Not just you."

"I know, but when you say my name it's sexy." Her cheeks flamed hotter as Sam bent his head, brushed the tip of his nose against hers and whispered against her lips. "I love hearing you say my name."

Her head was swimming, making her dizzy with emotion and desire for this incredible man. Her heart hammered in her chest as Sam held her close. He'd opened up his heart and shared with her some of his deepest personal pain. The man she'd come to know this past week didn't jive with the stories she'd heard from the crew or from the talk down at the diner.

Sam was a gentle and loving family man. Not the womanizing loner destined to never settle down. Through his own admission, he wanted the kind of love and happiness his parents shared. It was hard to believe he was the same man people were talking about.

Summer wanted so much to open up to him. Adam was the only one who knew about what happened in

Providence. She felt so safe here in Sam's arms that she didn't want the feeling to end.

"Sam?"

"Ssh," he said, taking her hand and placing it against his chest. She felt his heart beating just as wildly as her own.

"This is what you do to me, Summer. I look at you, and it takes my breath away. My heart starts beating right out of my chest. I know you don't believe me, but your heart is safe with me."

He was impossibly close, and before she could think of anything else, his lips brushed against hers. She wrapped her arms around his neck and weaved her hands together, not wanting to break this connection they'd made. As his tongue darted out, parting her lips, she melted in his arms as he drew her closer still. The heat of his body enveloped her.

He pulled back just a little, just enough for them to catch their breath as he gazed directly into her eyes. The overhead sun cast a silhouette above him. Sam smiled down at her and then kissed her again, wrapping his arms tighter around her waist so her body was pressed firmly against the length of him.

Summer's whole body was on fire and alive. She melted in his arms, feeling every stroke of his tongue and intake of breath as he kissed her. And when they parted, breathing raggedly and their bodies trembling, she saw their kiss had affected Sam as much as it had her.

With a smile he whispered, "You were about to say something?"

"Forget it and kiss me again."

And he did, leaving her as breathless and shaky as he had with the first kiss.

♥ ♥ ♥

The next week was spent with most of the Hotshot crew out in the field while Summer stayed holed up at the basecamp office. The Smokejumpers and dedicated EMTs had arrived, and she kept herself busy getting to know the new crew. She hadn't received a call from Providence. That and having Sam gone for most of the week had put her on edge.

Summer worked dispatch, relaying information as needed to the fire crew out doing prescribed burns to clear the felled trees that the flood had left behind. Adam marked the maps, and Summer quickly came up to speed on where the crew were at all times.

She got so she could tell the voices of the men apart when they talked over the radio. She followed it all and listened for Sam's voice. And when she'd hear him, her heart smiled. She knew he was safe. It got so she hated going back to the motel alone, leaving her connection with Sam behind.

After having lunch at the Quonset hut that housed the exercise room and the cafeteria, Summer headed back to her desk in the dispatch office and checked her phone to see if her parents or Bobbi had called. They hadn't, but there was a new voice message. When she dialed her voicemail, she couldn't hear the message the caller left. However, she did recognize the telephone number. It was Matt Jorgensen.

Summer's thoughts drifted back to Providence, to the time when she had been alone in her closet, listening to Elaine's voice over the phone. And then to Matt's office, looking at the picture taped to the newspaper and the red bullseye over her face. And all that fear that Sam McKinnon had managed to wash away came crashing down upon her.

Summer wanted nothing more than for someone to be with her so that she didn't have to handle this alone, so someone could talk her down from the ledge she suddenly felt like she was dangling on again.

But that wasn't true. She didn't want someone. She wanted Sam. No matter how far away from Providence she was, she'd only truly felt safe when she was with Sam McKinnon. And he had no idea what was going on.

Summer grabbed her purse and hurried to Adam's office, knocking on his door with a shaky hand.

"It's open," Adam said.

She pushed through the door and sat in the chair on the opposite side of the desk.

"Matt called me," she said quickly. "I'm sure it's nothing, but I couldn't make out the voice message. Did he call you?"

Adam shook his head. "I've been busy all day, but I haven't received any messages."

"I should probably call him back."

"Say no more. If you want to take off for the day, go ahead. Things are pretty quiet here. The crew is scheduled to come back to base for a break, and Derek has the radio covered for now."

"Thank you." Summer quickly got up and headed to the door.

"You will let me know if there's been a change, won't you?"

Summer turned back to Adam. "You'll be the first to know."

Chapter Seven

Sam was filthy, still covered in sweat, soot, and dirt from his work in the field when he walked into the main office. It had been four days since he'd last seen Summer and the first thing he wanted to do was see her smiling face light up the room for him. He'd already cleaned and put his equipment away in the cargo hold of the utility trucks. All that was left was a shower and shave, and that could wait until he caught a glimpse of Summer.

He walked into the dispatch room and found her office area empty. The other dispatcher in the room, Derek, lifted his head from his desk when he saw Sam approach.

"Looking for Summer? She went home," Derek said.

"Was she sick?"

Derek shrugged. "I saw her at lunch and when I came back Adam told me she'd taken the rest of the day off."

Sam thought about their last conversation. Money was tight for her staying at the motel. Maybe she'd found a rental somewhere in town and needed to move in.

Disappointed, he decided to get in that shower and clean up before heading over to the motel. If she had gotten a rental, he might be able to catch her before she left.

He thought back to the last few days, hearing her voice over the radio as they worked. Although she shared responsibilities with the other dispatchers, Summer had been on the radio a lot, keeping the team coordinated as they moved on the ground and through the area where they'd been doing prescribed burns all week.

She was a natural at her job and Sam knew she'd be an asset to the crew this season. She had remembered every single Hotshot's name, managing to recognize them by voice even over the radio and relay what they needed exactly when they'd needed it. Every time her voice came over the radio, he could picture her face as she said the words he was hearing. He could picture her lips moving, the raising of her eyebrows, the clicking of her nails on the table—a habit that surfaced every time she attempted to curtail her anxiety—the narrowing of her eyes as she enunciated the names of the locations that they needed to move towards, and every little nuance that he'd noticed every time he saw her.

But more than that, Sam just liked listening to her smooth as silk voice. Even after a long day of work, he lay awake in the cot in the Crew Haul they used for the fire fighters while out in the field, he thought of her voice and how it soothed him.

He finished his shower quickly. Seeing Summer was the very thing that he had been waiting for the entire day. He wanted to look into her bright blue eyes as they twinkled when she smiled. He wanted to hear her soft voice as she told him about her day. He wanted to discover every little thing about her and then he wanted to hold her in his arms and feel her against him as she'd been when he'd kissed her on the trail over the canyon.

That kiss had kept him going this week when his legs and arms were tired from work. He wanted more of it. More of her. He wanted to see the intensity of her stare as she looked at him. He felt himself grow hard just thinking about it. And he suddenly couldn't get to the motel fast enough.

Twenty minutes later, he was driving through town and spotted Ethan's police cruiser parked in the space next to Summer's car in the motel parking lot. Sam's stomach dropped as he pulled into the parking lot and found an empty parking spot on the other end of the lot.

As he rushed to Summer's room, Ethan was just coming out the door and spotted him.

Relief washed over Ethan's face. "Good. I'm glad you're here."

"What is it? Is Summer okay?"

Sam took in the official look on Ethan's face and knew it meant his brother wasn't going to disclose anything he couldn't. He knew Ethan well and knew what drove him to be a great police officer, and an even greater Navy Seal.

"She's fine."

But nothing about the sound of Ethan's voice made Sam believe his words. Fear struck the core of him, leaving him cold. He tried to move past Ethan, but his brother held him back.

"I think it's best if we find her a place to stay that's safe. I'm going to talk to Mom and Dad about Wade's room. I think even Mom will understand."

"Safe from what?"

"She'll tell you. Let me talk to Mom and Dad first. I'll call later when I know more."

Summer sat on the floor, squeezed inside a gap between the wall and the bed. She was hugging her knees to her chest as she wrapped her arms around her legs trying not to hyperventilate. Her breathing was ragged and her eyes were heavy with unshed tears. But she knew they'd come eventually. Right now she was in shock.

The door to the motel room opened, and she saw the silhouette of a man. She blinked her eyes fast to focus, to squash down the panic filling her.

"Summer?"

The familiar voice filled her with relief and was all she needed to let go of her fear. The tears fell heavy along with sobs she couldn't hold back. "Sam?"

The look on Sam's face when he ran to her was one of pure terror. He rushed inside and fell to his knees by her side. "It's okay, baby. It's all going to be okay," he said, keeping his voice calm as he raised his hand to cup her cheek.

Summer looked at him for a long, silent moment before throwing her arms around him. "Sam," she whispered, burying her head in his chest as she began to shiver in spite of the heat. "He's coming after me, Sam."

"Who?" Sam asked. He sat down on the floor and leaned his back against the bed. Picking Summer up as if she were a feather, he settled her into his lap and wrapped his arms around her, encasing her with his warmth.

Her warrior protector.

"Tell me who's coming after you?"

"He's going to find me," Summer whispered against his cheek as tears of fear spilled from her eyes again.

"No one is going to find you, Summer. I'm here. I have you," he said, his tone soothing as he gently stroked her hair. "You're safe here. I promise no one will hurt you."

A long moment passed as Summer stayed quiet. She was no longer crying. Slowly, with every passing second, her shivers subsided. She turned, laying her head against Sam's chest as she took a deep breath.

"I didn't leave Providence because I wanted to be a fire dispatcher," she finally said, her tone defeated. "I was forced to leave."

"What are you talking about? Who forced you?"

"The chief of police in the precinct where I worked as a dispatcher. Matt Jorgensen."

She took a deep breath, wanting so much to release this burden that she'd carried for so long, wanting to share it with Sam.

"About two months ago, the police found the body of a murdered woman. At that time, they treated it as a random act of violence and investigated it as an individual homicide. But then a second woman's body was found. The MO matched the first murder."

Summer pulled back and raised her head to look at Sam. "I got involved when the third woman called into 911. She'd called and then hung up before I could get her information. I put through the information like any other call because the address comes up automatically when someone calls the 911 line. I tried to call back while the officers were on their way, hoping to get the woman on the phone so I could tell her that help was on the way." She closed her eyes and took another deep breath. "But *he* answered the phone. He threatened to come after me."

Sam muttered a curse under his breath and squeezed her tighter. Fresh tears fell down her cheek.

"When the police broke through the door, the woman was dead. Same MO except the killer actually talked to me on the phone and threatened me," she said, a silent shudder running through her at the thought of the madman who was now targeting her.

"So the police chief sent you here?"

"Not at first. We didn't think there was any way for the killer to know which 911 operator he'd spoken to.

Being a city, Providence has a lot of 911 dispatchers. But to be safe, I stayed with my friend Bobbi. I mentioned last week that she'd become a police officer."

Sam nodded, recalling the conversation at dinner.

"But a week later, a fourth body was found on the same morning a newspaper was delivered to my apartment doorstep. Sam, he knew where I lived. He put a picture of me coming out of Bobbi's apartment inside the newspaper and put a red bullseye on it. They'd had a car watching my apartment, and he still managed to get inside. That's when Matt told me to leave. Matt went to college with Adam White. They arranged the whole thing."

"Adam knew about this?"

Summer could feel the rise of anger in Sam by the way his body stiffened.

"I didn't want anyone to know. Adam thought it would be easier if no one in the crew knew. You all have a job to do that is bigger and more dangerous than—"

"Than a serial killer coming after you?"

"They all thought I'd be safe here. I began to believe it to until ..."

She pulled herself from Sam's arms and stood. Sam did the same.

"Until what?"

"A woman's body was found along the same route I took coming to Rudolph, just a few hours away from here in Montgomery."

"Was it him?"

"Ethan is checking it out. Matt told him the MO was very similar, and there have been no other murders in Providence since I left. It could be him. It might just be a random killing that is unrelated. But … I'm scared Sam. He was at the front door of my apartment. He got a picture of me. He knows what I look like. What if he followed me here? For all I know he could be in Rudolph right now."

Sam felt as if he'd been hit by a truck. His mouth went dry as he took in each word Summer said. He felt an unbearable coldness spread through his entire body as he realized what everything she'd said actually meant. Someone wanted Summer dead.

The helplessness and fear in Summer's eyes made his body throb with restrained anger.

"I'll be okay," she added. "But I'm better now."

Sam stared at Summer for a long moment, wanting to wipe away all that fear she felt. She was trying so hard not to be afraid. But how could she not be with a monster hunting her? And it terrified Sam just as much to know that monster was still out there.

"I'm not going anywhere, Summer," he said, pulling her close again. "No one is going to touch you."

"You can't make that promise, Sam. You can't be everywhere. You have a job to do. And you can't be thinking about me while you're out facing a wall of fire that's out of control. I should just leave here. Go somewhere else where he won't find me."

"You did that here. Look, we don't know yet if that murder in Montgomery is from the same guy. I'm sure the police chief in Providence just wants to be cautious, which is good. Ethan will check it out. In the meantime, you're safe right here in my arms. And I'm not letting you go."

It took about an hour for Summer to settle down. She'd gone from being quiet to jumping at every noise she heard outside her door. When she finally fell asleep in his arms, Sam called Ethan's cell phone.

"How is she?" Ethan asked.

"Sleeping," he said quietly, watching the rise and fall of Summer's body against his to make sure he didn't rouse her.

"I talked it over with Mom and Dad. Logan and Hawk are coming over tomorrow to help clear out some of Wade's things in the room over the garage. I'm sure you'd feel more comfortable knowing Summer is close-by while you're out working a burn."

He closed his eyes. He didn't want to leave her at all. But the reality of it was, he had to. He couldn't be a man who would come home to her every night to sleep next to her and make sure she was safe. That was the reality of the job he loved and did well. It's one of the reasons he'd never settled down before now. It took a special woman to understand what it took to be a Hotshot and live that kind of life, never knowing where you were going or when you'd be home. Being gone for weeks on end, fighting a monster fire that threatened to destroy people's homes and lives, was part of the normal course of his life. What woman wanted an empty bed every night?

But he could be here for Summer tonight, and God help him he'd make sure she was watched over when he couldn't.

"Sam?"

"Yeah?"

"I talked to Matt Jorgensen of the Providence PD. He's going to keep me up to date on anything at all that happens with this case. Summer is going to be fine."

"How'd Mom take it?"

Ethan hesitated. "She said Wade's room has been dark long enough. It's time to put some light back up there."

"Ethan?"

"Yeah?"

"Thanks."

He hung up and put his cell phone on the nightstand by the bed. Pulling the blanket up over Summer, he snuggled next to her. She felt so right next to him. She was sleeping soundly, most probably because of emotional exhaustion. But Sam knew the last thing he'd get was sleep tonight. Not when a killer had put a bullseye on Summer.

Chapter Eight

Kate McKinnon was sitting in the middle of the empty bedroom above her garage when Summer walked in carrying her suitcase. Summer had finally met the two remaining McKinnon brothers, Logan and Hawk as they were leaving after helping their mother straighten the room of their eldest brother's belongings.

Kate glanced up at Summer and said, "Let me help you with that, dear."

"That's okay. It's just a few suitcases." The sheen of moisture in Kate's eyes showed how much emotion she was trying to hold back being in the room.

"I'm sorry for forcing you to do this, Kate. I told Sam I'd be fine at the motel. He told me this was Wade's room and how hard it was for all of you when you lost him. I don't want to make things more difficult for you."

Kate waved her off with a weak smile. "Don't be silly. There's no safer place for you to be than fifty feet from that house," she said, pointing across the driveway. "Sam has a very dangerous job, and he won't be able to do it safely if he worries about the woman he loves."

"Oh, I think you … Sam doesn't …"

"Love you?" Kate said with a chuckle. "Dear, I know my boys better than they think I do. And I know when one of them is in love. He may not know it yet, but he definitely is. Logan was always madly in love with Poppy. Now he's happy and planning a wedding that should have taken place years ago. Hawk, well, I saw that one coming long before he did. It was if he and Regis were cut from the same cloth. It's only a matter of time before the two of them will be announcing wedding plans and I couldn't be happier. And Sam? I thought I was happy enough to have my son home for the season. But when I see him with you, I know he's found someone special."

Summer started to protest as Kate lifted from her seat.

"Don't bother to deny it. I see the way you look at him too. He told you about Wade? Sam never talks about Wade to anyone. Not that I know of anyway. That's something."

"I ... don't know what to say," Summer said.

"You don't have to say anything. You'll be safe here. Ethan and my husband, Donald, will be right across the driveway in the house every night. And Sam? Well, I know he spent last night with you."

Summer's cheeks flamed.

Kate chuckled at her reaction. "It's none of my business. He's a grown man, and you're a grown woman. And I'm just a mother who wants her boys to be happy. I think you make Sam happy, and for that I'm grateful. I think even Wade would approve of giving up this room for you."

Summer wanted to cry. "That's very kind of you."

Sam appeared in the doorway with her other suitcase. He looked at both of them. "Everything okay?"

"What took you so long?" Kate said, winking at Summer.

"I was talking to Hawk and Logan."

"Well, I'm not cooking dinner tonight. Daddy is taking me out for dinner and dancing. Who knows, maybe we'll find a hotel room and have a little … you know."

"I don't need to hear this, Mom."

Kate rolled her eyes. "Boys. Feel free to make use of the kitchen." She gave Sam a squeeze. "Just don't blow anything up."

"You're never going to let me forget that, are you?" Sam said as Kate walked out the door, laughing.

"What's that all about?"

"Ian and I did a little experiment in the kitchen when we were about ten years old and … let's just say it didn't exactly turn out as planned."

"Oh, no."

Sam shrugged. "As I recall, the fire department did come to the house, and there were some kitchen cabinets that needed to be replaced. But that was a long time ago."

Summer laughed. "I think I'm going to like it here."

She turned to look at Sam and instantly knew that staying here so close to him was going to be a mistake. Her breath caught in her throat as she looked into the gray eyes that gazed down at her. She wanted to be with Sam. She wanted to feel the strength of his embrace again as she had last night when he'd held her. She wanted to feel him against her as he kissed her lips. She wanted him to hold her in an embrace that left only them as the world melted away.

And she wanted to feel his warm breath on her skin as he made love to her.

The realization struck her hard. She only hoped that when all the drama of this crisis was over, she could return home with her heart still intact. Sam McKinnon was a man who loved his job and was always leaving, chasing another fire. She was a woman who loved her job, loved her city, and was now falling for Sam McKinnon. She was sure of it. But the decision to stay here or go home wouldn't matter. Either way, Sam would be moving on to another town, another fire. It didn't matter where. It would be without her.

♥ ♥ ♥

The headlights in the driveway sent fingers of light stretching across the ceiling of his bedroom before it went dark again. Sam had passed the night tossing and turning, unable to forget the fact that Summer was only a few steps away from where he was.

He heard his parents talking as they came into the house, and then a few minutes later as they climbed the stairs to their bedroom. Sam waited a few minutes before getting out of bed. He looked out the window toward the garage and saw that the light in the room above the garage was still on. Summer was awake too. Either that or she'd fallen asleep with the light on.

He quickly pulled on his sweatpants and a tee-shirt and walked through the house barefoot to the front door and then across the driveway. For a second, he paused at the bottom of the stairs leading up to the room above the garage. Summer may be sleeping. If she'd managed to calm herself enough to sleep, he didn't want to disturb her. He just needed to see for himself that she was fine.

Having her in his arms last night and waking up with her this morning was the only thing that calmed his nerves. Watching her, taking in the rise and fall of her body against his, touching her full lips with his fingers as she slept ... he needed that again. He needed to have that connection again.

To his surprise, when he reached the top of the stairs, the door opened. Summer stood in the doorway wearing a fluffy pink terry robe that looked two sizes too big for her frame. Her hair was tousled on one side as if she'd been tossing in bed.

"You couldn't sleep either?" she asked.

Sam shook his head. Stepping aside, Summer opened the door wider so he could come inside.

"I usually make myself a cup of tea when I can't sleep," she said.

"Do you want to go over to the kitchen? I'm sure there's some tea—"

"No, I don't want tea," she said. Her voice, slightly rough from fatigue, caressed him as much as the cool night breeze he'd felt as he'd walked over.

She shut the door behind him. He stood in front of the oversized chair in the corner of the room that he and Wade had struggled mightily to get up the stairs and through the door years ago.

He'd known exactly what he wanted when he'd left the house. He wanted Summer in any way he could have her. He'd wanted so much to make love to her last night, but it wasn't right. She was upset. She needed his comfort and his strength, not a man to take advantage of her vulnerability. His body still ached from wanting her, and yet he was at war with his desire for her and his need to protect her from all the uncertainty surrounding her right now.

But right now, the woman standing in front of him wasn't gazing at him with fear in her eyes. All he saw was the same red hot desire that was burning inside him.

♥ ♥ ♥

Summer could feel the same heat blazing in Sam's eyes that was burning within her. Whatever doubts she had about loving Sam McKinnon were long gone. She'd live with whatever heartache that remained when it ended. All she knew now was that Sam wanted her just as she wanted him.

She raised herself on her tiptoes and brought her lips to his. Sam's lips caressed hers softly, gently until her body was tingling with anticipation. His hands grazed her back, but the heat of his hands couldn't penetrate through the fabric of her thick terry robe. She wanted his heat. She wanted it all.

His lips left her mouth and made a trail of kisses along her neck until he nuzzled his face between her neck and the terry robe, tickling her with his breath and his kisses. She pulled the fabric back to give him more access. He brought his lips back to hers and pulled her closer to him, their bodies fitting against each other like they were meant to be. And when his tongue dipped into her mouth to stroke hers, she couldn't hold back the moan of pleasure that erupted from within her.

Sam went rigid against her, and her heart almost stopped. Holding her waist, Sam pulled back and looked down at her. Summer looked up at him, trying to hold back the twinge of fear that was beginning to build within her.

"Summer, I ..." Sam said, hesitating. "I want you so much right now. I've wanted you. But ..." And then he whispered, "I need *you* to be sure. I need to know that you want this as much as I do."

Summer said nothing as she looked at the concern flashing in his eyes – concern for her, mixed with restrained desire. And she knew, without a doubt, what she really wanted. Leaning in, she kissed him softly, feeling the rigidity of his body melt away to be replaced with the building tension of his arousal.

Cupping her face, he said softly, "You're an amazing woman, Summer Bigelow. Last night I damn near died lying in that bed with you for wanting you so much. I know you've heard talk—"

"Ssh," she said, placing a finger against his lips. "You talk too much."

"I don't want you to think I'm the bastard others have made me out to be. Not where you're concerned anyway."

"Last night you were a gentleman," she said, looking up at him, trying to show him just how sincere she was about the way he'd treated her. "And there's nothing sexier than a gentleman."

His lips lifted to a sexy grin that made her knees weak.

"Sam," she whispered against his lips. "Make love to me."

Sam pulled back to look at her, and Summer held his gaze, hoping he'd feel the depth of her emotions. A moment later, he picked her up and crossed the distance to her bed in two strides. Laying her down on the soft covers, he climbed on top of her, pressing his body against hers so she could feel his arousal.

There was too much between them. She pulled back the robe and watched as flames ignited in his eyes at the sight of her nakedness.

"You didn't think it was just you wanting this, did you?" she asked with a smile. "I was waiting for you."

As he claimed her mouth with scorching desire, the world slipped away. Summer could feel nothing but Sam as she gave in to the rough feel of his calloused hands as they teased her breast, and the passion in his kisses as his mouth claimed her swollen nipple. She cried out in exquisite pleasure.

Pulling at his tee-shirt, she whispered, "We need this off. Now."

They rid themselves of the rest of their clothes and joined together, hot flesh against hot flesh. Her hands roamed his body, exploring, discovering places that drove Sam wild. And he did the same, using his mouth, his hands, his fingers, until Summer thought she'd die.

And when he finally entered her, Summer cried out from the depths of her soul at the beauty of their joining. He moved inside her, and she joined in his rhythm perfectly, breathing hard, matching him with every sigh and moan until they both reached the pinnacle of their pleasure. Pure pleasure exploded inside her as she threw her head back and urged Sam to claim all of her. And then everything seemed to shatter inside her until she floated back to a place where she could regain her composure.

Sam followed moments later, his body tightening around her, inside her until his orgasm claimed him, and he fell against her body, completely spent from their lovemaking.

And even as she continued to ignore it, a voice from deep within her said what she'd always known. She had fallen helplessly in love with Samuel McKinnon.

Chapter Nine

Summer blinked as sunlight streamed through the sheer drapes that covered the windows of her bedroom. Sam's warm, naked body was snuggled against her. Her own body was still achy from making love the night before, a beautiful reminder of a memory that would stay with her long after she left Rudolph.

It had been three weeks since Matt had told her about the murder of the woman in Montgomery. Despite the fear that had sent her here, Summer was finally able to put her guard down and just allow herself to live and feel in the moment.

She and Sam spent every precious moment they could together. She loved waking up with sunlight streaming through her window and spending the day naked and loved by Sam McKinnon. Here in the room above the garage, Summer had found more peace and happiness than she'd had in a long time.

Each day Summer worked dispatch while Sam was out in the field with the crew. Some days were longer than others. Sometimes she'd come back to her room alone and Sam would spend the night in the Crew Haul with the others crewmembers while he finished his shift. He'd come back to basecamp and shower off all the dirt and soot fighting fires had deposited on him, and then they'd go back to her room and make love again.

Summer cracked her eyes open as moonlight streamed through the window. It had only been a few hours since they'd made love, and still she could feel every touch of Sam's hands on her body.

A shy smile curved her lips as she recalled every intimate detail of the night. She turned to see Sam fast asleep, his arm outstretched as he lay on his back. Shifting closer to him, she laid her head on his chest and listened to his heart beating. Strong. Steady. Comforting.

Sam instinctively moved, pulling her against him as he turned onto his side. Summer felt a deep sense of contentment within her as her eyelids drifted shut.

The shrill ring of Sam's cell phone jolted her awake before she could fall fully asleep. Instantly awake, Sam grabbed the phone off the table next to him as he sat up.

"Adam?" he said, his voice gruff with sleep.

Summer watched as Sam listened to whatever Adam was saying. His expression was grim. "I'll be right there," he finally said and disconnected the line.

"What's going on?" Summer asked, suddenly apprehensive.

"Adam needs me to come in. The wind shifted. The containment field is now gone, and in the last two hours the fire has doubled in size and spread fast."

"Tomorrow is your day off."

"Today. But the crew that's out there has been out all night. We have more Hotshots and Smokejumpers coming in tomorrow. Right now, Adam needs me."

♥ ♥ ♥

Sam watched Summer as she stared at the kettle, waiting for it to switch off. She was wearing a loose tee-shirt and a pair of shorts – clothes meant for comfort. And yet, he had never seen anyone look more beautiful.

He wanted to hold her to himself, to keep the world and all its dangers away from her, to feel her soft skin under his fingers, to feel her tongue as it brushed against his and to feel her around him as he gazed into the depths of her beautiful blue eyes.

The click of the kettle resounded in the silent night, snapping Sam back to reality. He watched Summer as she moved around preparing the tea and a pot of coffee. And he realized that although he wanted Summer, his first priority was to keep her safe and to keep his mind on the work he had ahead of him.

"You promise you'll stay here every night. No taking risks. No going off without protection."

"Ethan is here at night, and there are a whole slew of people at the basecamp during the day. I'll either be there or here. I don't want you worrying about me."

Sam sighed. "At least Mom hasn't woken up."

He didn't need to see the worried look on her face or allow himself to be distracted by it.

"Here you go," Summer said, placing the travel mug full of coffee in his hand.

"Thanks." He took in the gravity of her heavy sigh. "You know, you didn't have to get up. You're not due at the basecamp for another few hours. You need the sleep."

Throwing her arms around him, she hugged him tight.

"I'm not going to let you leave without this," she said.

Sam stood stunned for a moment before draping his arms around her waist. He'd seen her terrified before. But this time it was for his safety, and he hated that.

"I'm glad," he said, his voice soft as her scent took over him. She smelled of flowers and nature, and the scent took him back to when he'd kissed her.

He pulled away from her just enough to look into her eyes and knew, in that moment that he had lost the battle he had been fighting against his own desires. He'd never worried about going out on a fire for days. But seeing the worried look in Summer's eyes, worry that she held for him, not the maniac that had made her flee from her home, caught him off guard.

He suddenly realized just what his mother had been battling for years. But where Kate didn't mince words about her worry, Summer kept it to herself. Everything she felt was written in her expression.

"You are so beautiful," he said.

Smiling weakly, she said, "I look a mess."

"A beautiful mess."

And at the same time, he felt a pull to stay that he'd never felt before. This fire was a monster of a different kind, one that Sam knew they'd be fighting for days if the wind in the canyon didn't cooperate. That meant he could conceivably be out in the field for a week or more, leaving Summer alone.

He knew Ethan would be here at night, and there would be protection while Summer was at basecamp. But they couldn't account for every moment of the day. He didn't want to spend the night in a Crew Haul truck. He wanted to feel Summer's naked and warm body against his every night.

For the first time since he'd become a fire fighter, Sam hated his job.

♥ ♥ ♥

Days were long. After three days of fighting a monster fire that the canyon winds fed with wind, the crews were getting tired. Sam and his team had come back to basecamp for a day of rest and were already going out again. Luckily, Adam had called for more Hotshots and Smokejumpers from out of state to come in and help battle the blaze.

Summer held her breath while she focused on her job, thankful for the need to throw herself into something that would keep her mind off Sam directly. She poured over maps, fed information into the radio, and only felt a little relief when Sam's voice would come back over the radio.

The EMTs had taken care of several fire fighters who'd become over exhausted and overheated by the flames and long days. They'd rest for a day and put themselves right back on the roster to go back out in the field. Each morning during the briefing they listened to Adam talk about spread and containment or hot spots that the NOAA predicted. This morning, it had been a new spot that flared up fast and threatened to join the other fire Sam and his crew had been fighting.

"It could be a 'perfect storm'," Adam was saying. "If we don't get this one under control, it'll create a wall of fire so big it'll threaten homes on the outskirts of town. We've already evacuated most of the homes in line with the fire. But there will probably be more evacuations over the coming days."

Sam was already in his gear, ready to jump into the utility transport with the rest of his crew.

"Ethan is out evacuating people. Promise me you'll stay safe."

Summer reached up on her toes and kissed him. "You, too. When do you think you'll be back?" Summer asked fear balling in the pit of her stomach at the thought of Sam in the middle of a roaring, uncontrollable fire.

"You heard Adam. It's fixing to be a giant," Sam said, his gaze burning into Summer's as he turned back. "And it's growing. Those canyon winds never let up this time of year. Don't look so worried. I'm going to be fine."

"You'd better be. I want you to come back to me, Sam McKinnon. I'm not done loving you."

His eyes widened with her words. "How can I resist that?"

Dipping his head, he brushed his lips across her temple. With a reassuring smile, he stepped away and rushed to the truck.

Summer stood rooted to her spot, her eyes following the truck as it left until she could see nothing but a cloud of dust. Sam was gone, and she had no idea if he would make it back to her safe and sound. And for the first time in her life, in spite of everything that was happening to her, she realized what true fear felt like.

"Summer!" Derek called out. "Let's get to it."

She followed Derek to the dispatch room. There were maps to mark and fuel orders to make so that the tankers could drop retardant where needed. They all had work to do. She had to stop thinking about Sam and do her job for the sake of all the fire fighters out there today.

Chapter Ten

Summer got up from bed for the umpteenth time and paced the floor. Why had she made that ridiculous promise to Sam that she'd sleep at the house instead of basecamp?

She'd spent the last hour revisiting every moment she'd shared with Sam. From the first time they'd kissed, Summer had known she wanted much more. She wanted the warmth and safety that Sam's arms offered, she wanted his lips to caress her skin, she wanted his fingers to explore her body, and she wanted to feel him joined to her as they made love.

She couldn't forget the feel of his lips on hers and the soft brush of his tongue against her lips. And it only made her want him more with each passing day.

Every moment Sam was gone, memories of him haunted Summer. Her only lifeline was the radio and hearing Sam's voice come through. And then relief would wash over her that he was safe.

Summer walked to the window and pushed back the drapes, giving her a hazy view of the night sky. As she stared out the window, Summer thought of Sam and the monster fire he and the rest of the crew were facing. She didn't want to be back in her room, safe and sound in a warm bed without Sam. She wanted to be at the basecamp, listening to the radio and making sure the man she'd fallen helplessly in love with was safe and would come home to her.

Home. This wasn't her home. It was Sam's. And only when he was in Rudolph. When all was said and done, she'd be going back to Providence. Alone. And Sam would go off somewhere else.

A light in the kitchen turned on in the main house. Someone was awake. And Summer had a good idea who it was.

♥ ♥ ♥

"Sometimes I think it's worse when he's home," Kate said, sitting at the table with a cup of tea in front of her.

She hadn't taken a sip. Neither had Summer.

"Donald can sleep through anything. Me? I'm a zombie. When Sam is in Colorado or California or wherever he goes, I worry when I listen to the news. But here …"

"You can't get away from it," Summer said. "You know when he's out there."

Kate nodded. "Ethan said there has been no word about the serial killer in Providence. No lead on where he is."

Summer drew in a deep breath, thankful for the change of subject and finding it odd that she'd rather talk about a serial killer hunting her than a monster fire Sam was in the middle of. "But there haven't been any more killings, so that's a good thing."

"What will you do if they don't find him? Where will you go?"

She hadn't thought that far ahead. "I guess I always assumed they'd find him. But if they don't ... I guess I could always move to Florida with my parents."

"What about Sam?"

"What about him?"

"You two have become quite close."

Summer smiled. She couldn't deny it, nor did she want to hide her feelings from Kate. She genuinely liked the woman and felt comfortable with her.

"Sam hasn't even told me he loves me."

"But you love him."

Feeling the weight of emotion deep in her chest, Summer nodded.

"I don't even know what I'm doing here when all I want to do is be on the other end of that radio so I can hear what's going on. It's killing me."

Kate smiled slowly, fatigue pulling at her tired eyes. "So what's keeping you?"

Summer didn't have an answer to that. There were probably a thousand good reasons why she should stay put in her room. Ethan and Donald were asleep upstairs. She'd promised Sam she wouldn't take any chances or venture out on her own. But she knew she was safer at basecamp than anywhere else.

Summer put her hands on the table and stood up. "Absolutely nothing."

♥ ♥ ♥

It took Sam and the other Hotshots three days to bring the fire under control. Summer hadn't left the base for a single moment in those three days. Ethan had a guard stationed outside the dispatch office just in case because all of the activity at basecamp and the new faces of fire fighters coming in from out of state made it difficult to keep track of who did and didn't belong there.

Summer barely noticed him. But always remembered to get a cup of coffee or a plate of food from the mess hall for him so he wouldn't starve.

Ethan gave her daily updates on the serial killer investigation and the murder in Montgomery. But none of that mattered to Summer. Her fear no longer stemmed from the fact that a serial killer had been fixated on her, forcing her to leave her home. Now that fear was rooted in the fact that she could lose Sam to something far deadlier. And she knew that if she lost him, she would lose herself.

She could no longer ignore the voice that had gone from a soft whisper to a deafening shout. She was in love with Sam. And she couldn't bear to lose him.

She was eighteen hours into her shift when Sam's voice crackled over the radio. Summer jumped to her feet as she jotted down the message that she had to relay to Adam. And it was when Sam clicked off the radio that something within Summer shattered. She bolted from the chair and ran to Adam's office, pushing through the door without knocking.

Adam's face went ashen when he saw her with the paper in her hand.

"That bad?"

Tears welled up in her eyes. "Worse."

Chapter Eleven

"I'll take over," Derek said. "You need a break."

"No, I don't," Summer said. "I don't get a break until Sam and the others radio in that they're in the clear."

"Look at you. You're shivering and it's ninety degrees out there."

"I'm fine."

Behind her, Summer could feel Adam's eyes on her back. All it would take was for Adam to pull her off the desk, and her connection to Sam would be gone. She turned to him and saw the concerned look on his face.

"I made the call for another two air tankers to come in and another supply of fire retardant. But they're still an hour away."

"What about the Smokejumpers?"

Derek looked at the notes, "They're out. They made it to the river and are cleared."

Summer took a deep breath, then swallowed hard. "The wind has picked up again. The new burn that was started by the heat lightning has grown. I've been in constant contact with the crew. All twenty are accounted for. The rock still has them boxed in at the base of the canyon wall, and the fire is building on the canyon floor. But Sam put two men on lookout, and they still have eyes on the rest of the crew. They're all safe for now. There's not enough of a clearing for a safe escape route out of the canyon floor yet. We need the air tankers to drop enough retardant to knock out one of the lines of fire to give them a clear path out. I already have the helicopter pilots on alert to fly in and retrieve them when they get in the clear." She took a deep breath and waited for Adam's instruction.

"It's going to be a rough place for the air tankers to get into low enough to drop the retardant. Let's hope they get here soon. Derek, how long have you been at the desk?"

"About thirty-six hours."

"Summer?"

"Just over twenty-four." It was probably a little more than that, but Summer knew where Adam was going with this, and there was no way she was leaving her only connection to Sam.

"Okay, Derek, get some rest and then relieve Summer in the morning. It's going to be a long night, and I need you two rested. I have called for more dispatchers to give you both relief. They should be here in the morning."

Both Adam and Derek left the dispatch room, and Summer was alone. She couldn't cry. Couldn't feel anything because if she did it would break her concentration, and she needed to stay focused on the voices coming in over the radio.

Closing her eyes, she said a silent prayer for the safety of Sam and the rest of the fire crew. A firm hand on her shoulder nearly had her jumping out of her skin. It was nearly two-thirty in the morning. Everyone was either out in the field working or getting sleep so they could do battle on this mammoth fire as soon as the sun came up. She was supposed to be alone. And yet the squeeze of pressure on her shoulder proved she wasn't.

She turned around quickly and nearly wept. Looking down at her were the warm eyes of a man who understood exactly what she was going through.

Donald McKinnon settled into the seat next to her. "Ethan, Logan and Hawk are home with Kate. I thought it might be easier for us to get through this night if we do it together. You're not alone."

Summer thought back to the day Sam sat in that chair and said those very words to her. *You're not alone.* She placed her hand over Donald's and welcomed him with a trembling smile.

They were cursed by the beauty and trappings of the canyon walls. Sam kept his eyes on his crew to make sure no one was failing, and everyone was accounted for. They were sitting in a bowl of heat on the canyon floor thanks to a disastrous explosion of felled trees ignited by the heat lightning they'd experienced earlier. It gave them no time to escape before the wall of fast moving fire closed them in.

The LCES had been in place and was now fractured by a force beyond their control. Sam was infinitely glad he'd opted for two lookout men on the hill. At least two of the twenty man crew were in a clearing and had a way out of this fire storm. He knew the men would not leave their lookout positions unless the fire forced them to. They were in constant communication with the crew and with the basecamp. The lookouts would scout escape routes and safety zones should they become available until the air tankers arrived.

"Sam?" the lookout crew member named Barry called out over the radio.

"Go head," he said into the radio.

"Basecamp gives ETA of the air tankers at thirty minutes."

Sam cursed under his breath. The smoke around them was getting thicker. They were all well suited up with gear. But thirty minutes was an eternity.

"Sam? The wind is shifting your way."

He looked up at the sky to see if he could tell which way the smoke was moving above them, thankful the moon was bright tonight. As he feared, the wind was moving them closer to the canyon wall.

"You're going to feel a blast of heat soon if you aren't already. It's moving fast," Barry said.

"Where the hell are those air tankers?" Sam said. "Okay, everyone, get in your fire shelters!"

Upon command, the crew dropped their gear and pulled out the silver blankets, wrapped up like a brick in their packs, opened them up and crawled inside as instructed. Once inside, the air closest to the ground would be cooler and cleaner. It gave them at least a fighting chance of survival if a heat blast blew over them and coiled around the base of the canyon wall, baking them where they lay.

Sam climbed into the fire shelter and prayed. The shelter would provide some protection against the heat, but only to five hundred degrees before the fabric started disintegrating, and the heat inside the shelter rose beyond a temperature their lungs could handle.

There'd been many fires throughout his years as a Hotshot where Sam thought things were touch and go. He'd been in close calls just like the rest of his crew. But this was the first time he truly believed he might not make it home alive. He thought of his parents and his brother, Wade, and how his family would survive another heartbreak.

As the roar of the wind whipped over him, he pressed his face to the ground and thoughts of Summer drifted to his mind. Good Lord, what must she be going through knowing every detail of what was transpiring? He closed his eyes and tried to remember the sweet scent of her hair, and the feel of her skin, and the taste of her mouth as he kissed her.

Fear bubbled up inside him. He had a crew of men lying on the ground praying for hope along with him. But he knew that Summer was sitting there at the other end of the radio.

His lifeline.

"Basecamp?" he said into the radio.

"Go ahead, Sam," Summer said.

"The crew is in their fire shelters. I have two lookouts on the ridge above the canyon. They've confirmed they're out of harm's way."

"Got that."

Hot tears stung his eyes. He wanted to hear her voice. If he was going to die tonight then Sam wanted Summer's voice to be the last thing he heard. He needed the comfort of her smooth voice, to remember that look on her face before she reached up on her toes and kissed him. He needed it like a drug he had to have to survive.

"Talk to me, Summer," he said quietly, pulling in a breath of air that was growing hotter by the second. He knew she couldn't say what he wanted her to say that she loved him as much as he loved her. And he did. He'd never thought he'd ever feel this way about a woman, but now he knew without a doubt that he loved Summer Bigelow.

"The air tankers are on their way. ETA ten minutes," she said. He knew her so well that even though her voice sounded steady, she was as scared as he was at that moment. "Um, another fire crew is attacking the fire on the west ridge above where you are. Barry thinks it's the safest route for all of you to climb out of the canyon and the best location for the air tankers to make the drop of retardant."

"I love you." He didn't know how much time he had left, and he didn't care who heard him.

The radio was silent for a few seconds. But when she finally spoke, her voice cracked. "I want to be in your arms looking straight at you the next time you say that, Sam."

A nervous chuckled bubbled up his throat. "It's a deal."

"The tankers just radioed in. They are almost in place. Once they make the drop, Barry will give you the all clear if they're able to create an escape route. Hang on, Sam. We have the helicopters on their way to pick up the crew."

Relief enveloped him.

"And Sam?"

"Yeah?"

"I'm going be right here when you get back. Just make sure you come home to me."

He heard the roar of flames above him mixed in with the sound of the air tankers flying overhead. The noise was so loud that he could barely hear the radio. He only hoped the tankers were able to drop enough retardant to snuff out the fire before the blazing heat of the fire got to the crew.

Chapter Twelve

The sky was still an inky black when the helicopters landed in the parking lot of basecamp. The entire crew had made it out of the canyon alive, and now Sam was more exhausted than he'd ever been in his life.

He'd gotten no sleep in three days as he'd fought one of the fiercest fires he'd ever faced. The team had been stretched to every limit and beyond and yet, they'd returned alive. Each member of the team was covered in soot and dirt, tired enough to fall asleep on their feet as the adrenaline that had kept them going began to wear off. Sam would have been too. But he needed to see Summer first.

He had waited every minute of every hour of those three days to hear her voice over the radio. When he heard her voice, he knew that she was safe, that the madman who was trying to reach her hadn't been successful.

Now, he was finally back and could hold her in his arms without fear of losing her.

One by one, the crew jumped from the helicopter and walked with all their gear to the Quonset hut where the medic office was set up. They'd all be given a quick once over by a medic and then sent to the shower for a good cleaning.

But he had barely taken a couple of steps when the door to the Quonset hut was thrown open. Summer stepped out into the path of men filing in toward the Quonset hut, her eyes frantically searching until she saw him.

Sam saw her eyes light up for a brief second before she flew into his arms. He draped his arms around her waist and held her against him, cherishing the fact that he could hold her in his arms at all. Summer held on to him like she'd never let go. And that was just fine by Sam. He could take a million years of just holding her close like this.

But then she pulled back and stepped out of his arms. Her eyes were shining with tears of relief as she held his gaze. That's when he saw his father standing behind Summer.

"Good to have you back home, son," Donald said, pulling Sam into his arms for a tight embrace. "I've already called your mother, and she knows you're safe. Your brothers are at the house waiting for you to come home. All except for Hawk. He's helping out in the medic room here. You'll see him in a few minutes."

Sam looked at the two of them silently for a moment. He had been filled with fear that he might never see any of them again.

"If you want, I'll wait and drive you both home. I'm sure you're both exhausted."

"Thanks, Dad."

An hour later they were pulling into the driveway. Darkness was making way to a glorious sunrise, but all Sam wanted to do was close his eyes, even as he saw his family pouring out the front door into the driveway. He got out of the SUV and for five minutes was enveloped in hugs from his mother.

"Thank God for Skylar," Kate said. "She's opening the diner and taking care of everything there. I haven't had a bit of sleep in days."

"I don't think any of us has," Donald said.

"Before you all head to bed while the rest of the population goes to work, I have some news," Ethan said. He was dressed in his police uniform and had been heading to the cruiser when they arrived.

"What's that?" Sam asked.

"I didn't want to tell you this while there was so much tension surrounding Sam, Summer. But I got a call from the police chief in Montgomery. They caught the man who'd murdered the woman there. He was a local business owner and had no connection at all to the Providence killings. You can rest knowing the serial killer in Providence wasn't following you."

A wave of relief consumed Sam. "That's good news."

Ethan's face grew serious. "Unfortunately, they still haven't found the man they're looking for in Providence. He may have moved on. They're still checking similar crimes in the neighboring states to see if there are any similarities. But at least for now, you're safe."

"Thank you so much, Ethan. For everything," Summer said.

"I don't know about you two, but I'm getting some sleep," Donald said. "And I'm taking my wife with me."

A few minutes later, Sam followed Summer up the stairs to her room over the garage. Once inside, he said, "I was so worried about you."

"Me?" Summer asked. "You were the one in danger. Not me."

"Any time you're not with me I worry."

"Hmm, you're forgetting a promise you made to me, Sam," she said, wrapping her arms around his neck.

"I am? What's that?"

Her mouth dropped open, and he saw the hurt in her eyes. "Sam McKinnon! How quickly you forget!"

He laughed. "I didn't forget anything about you. I love you, and everything about you, Summer Bigelow."

She purred against his lips as she kissed him. "I like it when you say that. I love you too, Sam."

Then she sighed as if she were carrying the weight of something on her mind.

"What?"

"I don't know what I'm to do without you when it's time for me to leave here."

"Why do you have to leave?"

She shrugged. "Fire season only goes until the fall. Once I'm not needed here ... well, I can't go back to Providence."

"Exactly," he said.

Sam didn't know exactly when it had happened, or even how, but he had fallen in love with Summer. And at this point, the idea of not being with her every single day for the rest of his life just wasn't an option. All he knew was that he loved her and that he wanted to spend the rest of his life with her.

"You said you wanted me to come home to you, and I did," he said.

"Yes, you did," she said smiling.

"Home is where we are together. Whether it's here or somewhere else, I want you to be my home, Summer. I don't want to live my life without you."

"What are you saying?"

"I don't care if they never find that killer in Providence. Well, that's not exactly true. I want them to find him. It just won't make a difference between you and me. Because I never want you to be anywhere but with me."

"But … you're not staying in Rudolph. Are you? Where would we go? What would I do?"

"Exactly what you're doing now. Maybe eventually I'll stop going out in the field and try for a superintendent's position with an Interagency Fire Crew."

"That'll keep you safe," she said, the smile on her face growing bigger.

"Until then, it'll be you and me together. Where I go, you go. Where you go, I go. All I know is that I don't want to be without you. I want you in my arms and in my bed every night."

"Or every morning. Starting now."

"I like the sound of that," he said, his body already getting hard and wanting her.

"I love you, Sam," Summer said, smiling as tears rolled down her cheeks. "I always have, and I always will."

"I love you, too," Sam replied, brushing her tears away with his thumbs. "I've loved you from the moment you came into my life. And I will love you for as long as I live!"

They made love as the morning filled the room with sunshine. With every kiss, and every caress, they made a promise to always face the uncertainty of life and love together. And when they fell asleep, safe in each other's arms, they knew it was just the beginning of a beautiful lifetime together filled with love.

~The End~

WILD DAKOTA HEART
Dakota Hearts Series Book Four

Chapter One

Ten years of doing right didn't erase one moment of stupid in the course of a man's life. Ethan McKinnon knew that more than anyone. There were some things you couldn't change no matter how much you wanted a do-over. No matter how much *you* had changed.

Eight years of military service, most of them as a Navy SEAL and the past year as a police officer hadn't prepared him for what he had to do in the next few minutes.

Facing Maddie Newton.

The sounds of his cruiser's wheels on the pavement drowned out whatever thoughts cycled throughout his mind during the few hundred yards between seeing the red compact car plowed into the tree. He didn't have to radio in the license plate to know who the driver was, making this stop all the more difficult.

Pulling the mic from the radio attached to his duty belt, Ethan called into the station.

"Dispatch, this is W17. I'm at the scene of a one car accident on Buena Vista Road. Vehicle is a red sedan." He paused to read the license plate and transmit it to the dispatcher. "I'll need a tow truck. Checking for injuries now and will radio back if an ambulance is needed."

"Copy that," the dispatcher said.

Ethan pushed the door open and stood for a second with his heart lodged in his throat, choking him. On pure adrenaline, he quickly moved his legs forward until he was standing just outside the driver's side of the car.

He'd seen Maddie from afar while he was driving in town and then down at the shelter just after the ice storm hit months ago. But he'd never ventured this close to her.

The last time he'd seen Madelyn Newton, she'd been crying. She'd walked right up to him with half the town of Rudolph standing around them, her eyes lifeless and her body fragile with emotion. Then she'd slapped him across the face, telling him she never wanted to see him again. A few hours later, Ethan boarded a plane heading to Fort Benning, Georgia so he could start the basic training that launched his career as a Navy SEAL.

That was nearly ten years ago. Ethan had been back in Rudolph for nearly a year, and he'd done everything possible to remain invisible to Maddie. *Until now.*

Peering in through the window, he found Maddie slightly slumped over the deployed airbag, looking down at the red on her fingers. His mind focused on the red spot on the left side of her temple.

Blood.

Instantly, all his specialized training kicked in. His senses came alive, and he quickly scanned the immediate area. The smell of antifreeze hung heavy in the air around him, and steam rose slowly from beneath the hood of the car. But to Ethan's relief, there was no smoke, and he didn't smell gasoline.

As if just realizing Ethan was standing there, Maddie lifted her face and glanced up at him with a bewildered expression. Ethan opened the door and saw the red spot was now a streak trailing down the side of her face. Panic hit him hard in the center of his chest. He'd dealt with all types of emergency situations in his life, first as a Navy SEAL and now as a police officer. But this was Denny's kid sister! And she was bleeding.

"Maddie? Don't move. Just let me know if you're hurt."

She said nothing. Her eyes were void of the lifelessness he'd seen the last time they'd been this close. He'd braced himself for hatred. Maybe even another slap across the face. But Maddie just looked at him as if she were trying to piece the course of events that brought them there together.

"You just plowed your car into a tree. Your airbag was deployed. Do you feel any pain in your chest?"

She shook her head weakly.

"You hit your head during impact," he said. "Do you understand what I'm saying to you, Maddie? Do you know who I am?"

Lisa Mondello

♥ ♥ ♥

Of all the cops in the great state of South Dakota, how in the hell had she gotten stuck with Ethan McKinnon? Maddie slowly glanced up at the familiar face of the officer as his features came clearly into focus, trying her best to keep her emotions at bay. Her head throbbed where it had hit the window, cracking the glass. The adrenaline rush from swerving on the road, hitting the tree, and feeling the impact of the airbag against her chest had left her winded and a bit frazzled.

Ethan pulled the door open wider. "Maddie, do you know where you are? Can you tell me if you're hurt?"

Ethan McKinnon was standing inches away from her asking her if she was okay. If she knew who he was. How could she possibly forget the man who was responsible for bringing her such heartache years ago? Heartache that never seemed to go away despite the years that had passed since.

"Go away."

"I see we have recognition. That's good. Are you hurt anywhere else but your head?"

"I said—"

"I heard you the first time. I need to make sure you don't need an ambulance. So please cooperate."

There were words running through her mind that were not fit for good company, and yet as much as she wanted to say them to Ethan, she held them back.

"I'm fine. Now leave me alone."

"Can you stand?"

She unclipped her seat belt and let it slide back into place against the door. He extended his hand to help her out. She took it in hers momentarily forgetting all the reasons she didn't want to be near Ethan McKinnon. When she was standing outside the car, she pulled her hand away and leaned against the car, glancing to the front to see the damage.

"It's dented," she said with a heavy sigh.

"It's a little more than dented. Maybe even totaled. I had dispatch call George to come pick it up. If it's fixable, George can do it."

Ethan stood very close to her by the car—enough so their shoulders touched, and she could feel the heat of his body. It was strange. This was the hottest time of the year in Rudolph with mid-summer temperatures making the sun feel infinitely hotter than it was. But Maddie felt a rush of cold run through her body.

"Your body is in shock," he said, guiding her so she was leaning against the car for support. "Can you tell me what happened?"

"A mule deer and her fawn ran in front of the car. I tried to avoid them, but I might have hit one."

"I'll check the car for signs of that later. Can you tell me what day it is?"

"Tuesday."

"Who is the president of the United States?"

"What is this, a game show? I know who the president of the United States is and what year it is. I even know who you are."

"That much I figured out when you told me to go away."

"But you're still here anyway."

"Lucky for you I was driving by. This road doesn't get a whole lot of traffic these days since the bridge got washed out." Ethan sighed slowly. "You have two choices, go to the clinic by ambulance or be driven there. Take your pick. If it were up to me, I'd call an ambulance."

"No, thank you."

"You could go to the hospital if you'd prefer. Your head needs to be looked at."

"I'm not going to the hospital, and I'm not going in an ambulance."

"Then, being driven to the clinic it is. Stay here just for a minute while I look at the scene and radio into the station."

Before she could protest further, Ethan was gone. Maddie closed her eyes and tried to ignore the throbbing in her head and the ache in her shoulder caused by the seat belt. Her heart was pounding, and she shivered despite the sunshine beating down on her. The feel of a blanket being wrapped around her shoulders had her opening her eyes again. Ethan was careful in his movement, making sure she was completely covered.

"If you think you're going to throw up, I'll help you walk over to one of the bushes."

She pulled the blanket tighter, relishing the warmth. "I'm not going to throw up."

"It's not uncommon when you're in shock. If you need anything from the car, I'll grab it now."

She turned back to look inside. "Just my purse."

"Where do you keep your registration?"

"In the glove compartment."

"I'm going to retrieve that for you along with your purse. Is that okay?"

"My, you're being so polite."

Ethan shrugged. "It's protocol."

After walking around the car, he opened the passenger side door and retrieved her purse from the floor. Then he opened her glove compartment and rifled through some papers until he found her registration.

"Protocol? It's not like you haven't known me most of my life."

As Ethan handed her the purse, Maddie turned to the sound of a large truck coming down the road toward them, steadying herself against the car with her hand.

"What's this?"

"The tow truck. Are you dizzy?"

"Just a little."

"Let me bring you up to the cruiser."

Ethan held out his arm for her to take. Instead of doing so, she glared at him. "I'm fine."

"I'd prefer you not fall on your face on the way to the car. If you want to be stubborn and walk yourself, then be my guest. But I'm walking alongside you to make sure you don't fall."

She yanked the blanket around her body and started walking up the small incline toward the shoulder of the road. Black tire marks stretched across the hot tar from her skidding when she'd swerved to avoid the deer. She could only imagine what Ethan had thought when he'd come upon her car plowed into that tree.

No matter what had gone down, no matter how strained their relationship was, Ethan would always look out for her. He and Denny always had when she was a kid. Despite their shenanigans, they never once put her in harm's way. Denny would have liked that Ethan was still this way.

She pushed the thoughts of Denny and childhood memories aside. She didn't want to think about Ethan this way. She didn't want to be near the man after what he'd done. Because of him, her beloved brother had paid with his life while Ethan came out a hero.

Maybe she was being childish, but time didn't heal all wounds, and even after ten years, hers were still very raw.

All these years while Ethan was gone it was easier to hang on to the bitterness of losing Denny and the part

Ethan had played in his death. As Ethan eased her into the back seat of the cruiser, she laughed bitterly at the irony that he was here for her during her accident when he'd left Denny to die alone.

"What's wrong?"

"Nothing.

The tow truck pulled up alongside the cruiser. Ethan walked over to the truck as the driver rolled down the window and leaned over to talk to Ethan. Then the driver climbed out of the truck and walked with Ethan down the slight embankment to look at her car.

Damn Ethan for still being so handsome. The teenager that Maddie was couldn't help but be starry-eyed over her big brother's best friend. She'd been a fool for him with the kind of crush that was fuel for made-for-TV-movies and teen magazines.

Years of being in the military and working out hard had changed his body, giving Ethan muscles that were clearly visible beneath his short-sleeved police shirt. He'd never been a scrawny kid like a lot of high school boys. But now ... He stood tall and very sure of his every move, something Maddie had always been drawn to.

The tow truck shifted gears suddenly, startling Maddie out of thoughts of Ethan. She was thankful for the diversion.

Ethan smiled at her as he walked back to the cruiser. She turned her head away.

"George will take care of this. I had a chance to quickly look at the car. I didn't see any sign you hit the deer. There was no fur or blood on anything I could see. You more likely hit a rock or log when the car went off the road."

She breathed a sigh of relief. She hated the idea of an injured animal out in the wilderness, vulnerable to prey.

"There is some serious damage though. You have a dent in your hood, and your radiator is caved in. There's probably more underneath that I couldn't see. George will have to tow it back to the garage to get a full assessment. But your insurance company might total the car."

"What? It can't be that bad."

"George will let you know."

"The garage is clear across the other side of town. How am I going to get home from there?"

"Your parents—"

"My parents went to Rapid City to visit my aunt. She's in the hospital."

"I hope it's nothing serious."

"No, just minor surgery. But they won't be back until late."

"That's no problem."

"For you."

"After Hawk checks that bump on your head at the clinic, I can drive you home."

"You?"

"Sure. My shift is ending soon. I can do my paperwork on the accident while I wait for you."

"That won't be necessary."

"I could call an ambulance."

"Don't be ridiculous. I don't need an ambulance."

"Then we'll stop by the clinic. Hawk is probably still there." He leaned closer to Maddie. "Just stay in the car for a minute while I take some pictures."

"Pictures? What for?"

"The insurance company."

"It's that bad?"

He stood next to her and just looked at her face, directly in her eyes.

She held up her hand to push him away. "What are you doing?"

"I'm a first responder. All police officers are. I just want to make sure you're not in shock."

"Are you always this thorough?"

"Yes. Even when dealing with difficult people."

"I'm difficult just because I don't want you staring at me?"

"Look, you just plowed your car into a tree. You might think you're fine. And you may be. But I have to check."

"I'm not going to spend a few hours in the ER waiting to be checked. Your brother can check me at the clinic. But I'm not going to the hospital." His brother, Hawk

McKinnon as he was known to most people, was the local doctor with a clinic in the center of town.

Frowning, Maddie settled herself against the plush seat. She reached to her side and grabbed the strap of the seat belt and secured it.

The door on the driver's side opened. Ethan slipped into the cruiser, grabbing his keys from his pocket. It had been years since they'd both been in any car together.

As he started the car, his eyes met hers. "You buckled in?"

Maddie glanced out the window. "Yes."

And panic suddenly hit her hard with the thought that for the first time since Denny died, she was inescapably stuck with the man who'd caused his death.

Chapter Two

"You're going to feel this for a couple of days," Hawk said as he looked intently at her temple.

"I don't have to miss work, do I?"

Hawk chuckled. "I'd say I'd write a note to stay out of work for a few days, but I know you won't need one."

She smiled warmly. "Your father has a great work ethic. I don't want to disappoint him. But deep down, I know he's a softy and will probably be upset when he finds out about the accident tomorrow."

"Tonight. Ethan still lives at home."

"Really? I thought by now he'd have set himself up in some bachelor pad somewhere."

Hawk grinned at the mocking tone of her voice. "Actually, he was all ready to put in an offer on a house near the river. But then the ice and rain storms last spring caused all that damage at the Nolan place."

Surprised, she pulled back and looked at Hawk. "Ethan was going to buy the Nolan farmhouse?"

"Yeah, that's the one."

"That house had been abandoned for years. It needed a lot of work, didn't it?"

"Yeah, that's why Ethan wanted it. He said he needed something to get his hands into. But after that was destroyed in the flood, he turned his attention to the Wounded Veterans Center. That's keeping him busy these days."

"That's ... amazing. I didn't know Ethan was handy that way."

Hawk placed some ointment on her wound, making her skin sting. She winced with the pain.

"That will stop in a minute," he said as he placed a small bandage on her head. "You won't need to wear this in the shower. In fact, it's better if you don't. You'll want to make sure it stays clean. But for tonight, keep the bandage on just to give it time to scab over."

Maddie touched the spot on her head where the gauzy bandage protruded. "Will this leave a scar?"

"No, it should heal over fine. You really should have gone to the hospital by ambulance. With head injuries, you can never be too careful." Hawk discarded his latex gloves and the medical waste in the pail and then turned to her.

"Well, it worked out well. You were here."

"Yeah, but this is a small clinic set up for minor situations so the people in town don't have to travel all the way to the city every time they have the flu or need a shot. If this were more serious, I would have had to transport you anyway."

"I'll remember that next time. But hopefully there won't be a next time."

Hawk started writing notes in her chart. "You live alone now, don't you?"

"Yes, I have a condo over at the Wingate."

Hawk thought a minute. "I don't like the idea of you being alone tonight. Head injuries can be a little tricky. You seem okay, and your initial shock from the accident seems to have subsided. But sometimes even the smallest bump on the head can become something more. You might want to consider staying at your parents' house tonight just so that someone can wake you up periodically to make sure you're okay."

"Is that really necessary?"

"It's up to you. Is there a problem with staying at your parents tonight?"

"Yes ... well, no. I can stay in my old room, but my parents aren't home. My aunt had surgery today, so they're staying at her house in Rapid City."

Hawk nodded. "Then perhaps they can call you periodically through the night to check on you."

"Soon as I get home I'll call them."

"I want you to follow-up with me in a few days even if you feel better."

Maddie agreed to come back for a follow-up visit and climbed off the examining table. Ethan was waiting for her in the waiting room when she emerged from the exam room. Nancy, the clinic's receptionist, was laughing hard at something Ethan had said. But they both stopped and looked up as she approached.

When Ethan saw her, he tapped his hand on the counter lightly and asked, "Did you get a clean bill of health?"

Maddie didn't say anything and Hawk, who came into the waiting room behind her, didn't elaborate.

"Are you driving her home?" Hawk asked.

Ethan nodded. "I'm off-duty now."

"Good. I need to head home so I can help Regis scout some volunteers to do work this weekend at the Wounded Veterans Center. Now that the foundation has been repaired, we can start working on the inside." Hawk's face brightened as he turned to Maddie. "Hey, what are you doing this weekend?"

"I don't think I have any plans."

"A lot of volunteers are coming out to help," Ethan added. "Mom is catering for the day so everyone will be well fed. It should be a lot of fun. You and your parents should come over. That is if your aunt is on her feet again by then."

"We'll see." Turning to Hawk, she said, "Thanks for everything. Goodnight, Nancy." She waved at the receptionist as she headed for the door.

"Night, honey! I hope you feel better," Nancy said.

Maddie walked down the clinic's ramp to the small parking lot. The McKinnons had always been a big presence in Rudolph. Early on it was MW Oil that had given work to a lot of people during hard times. And then Kate McKinnon, Ethan's mother, had opened a diner when

Hawk was just a baby and Wade was a toddler. Maddie's gaze was drawn to the building across the street. The little diner was a focal point of town, sitting at the crossroads of the two main streets in and out of Rudolph. It held memories for most everyone who had grown up with her. The lights were still on, and cars were still scattered in the parking lot.

Suddenly her mind wandered to a hot summer day much like today. She was much younger then, and the McKinnon boys were out for mischief and wanted to rile their mother up. They'd loaded the back of a truck with laundry baskets filled with water balloons and called everyone down to the diner for a water balloon fight that had everyone laughing and cooling off in the hot sun. Maddie had never laughed so hard in all her life. She'd worn a pair of cut-off jeans and a bikini top just to make herself look older like Poppy and Kelly.

And so Ethan would notice.

She smiled with the memory, but felt the bittersweet tug in her heart thinking about how it was one of the few times when Denny had not only let her tag along with him and Ethan, but he'd purposely drove to the house to pick her up so she could join in the fun. Kate McKinnon was rip-roaring mad at them for the mess they made of the parking lot that day. But she still laughed along with them while they lined up so she could take a picture, all of them dripping wet and holding spent balloons in their hands.

♥ ♥ ♥

She was lost somewhere, Ethan thought as he took in the wistful expression on Maddie's face. She stared across the street as if she were looking at something from the Ghost of Christmas Past. Something tugging at her, and she couldn't break free.

"Are you hungry?" he asked.

She blinked hard and then shook her head, pulling her attention back to the clinic parking lot. "Where's the cruiser?"

"I swapped vehicles at the station while you were in with Hawk. The SUV is mine."

"If you don't mind, I just want to go home."

They drove most of the way to the condo in silence. It had been a long day for him, and by the vacant expression on Maddie's face, he knew she was upset.

Now that the adrenaline rush of seeing her bleeding had worn off, Ethan had a chance to really look at her. She'd always been a pretty girl, and it always puzzled him why men weren't falling at her feet. Truth was, he'd been watching her, and he knew she wasn't dating anyone. It helped that his mother knew just about everyone in town, including Maddie's parents.

Maddie's brown hair was streaked with golden strands throughout, something she'd never done before. And she smelled nice. Her perfume was light and citrusy. Nothing heavy. She'd always liked lotions and cologne when she was younger. When Ethan had teased Denny for smelling like a department store make-up counter, Denny had always complained, saying it gave him a headache just to walk into Maddie's room because she had all that "stuff" lined up on her dresser.

"I've been back in Rudolph for almost a year, and I barely see you," Ethan said.

Silence.

"You know, you can't avoid me forever," Ethan said, taking his eyes off the road for a second to see her reaction.

"Wanna bet?"

Ethan smiled. At least he got that much out of her. *Progress.*

"So, you *have* been avoiding me."

With his help, Ethan thought. Only Maddie didn't know that. And maybe his brother, Sam, was right. They couldn't dance around a ghost forever. Some things had to be faced head on.

"I don't want it to take another car accident for me to see you again. Besides, Rudolph is a small town, and we know all the same people."

She continued to look out the window.

Ethan put his directional on to pull into the parking lot of the Wingate Condominium complex where Maddie lived.

"Which one is it?" he asked.

"Number eleven."

He found the parking space marked number eleven and parked the SUV. Before he could undo his seatbelt and get out of the car, Maddie turned to him and placed her hand on his arm.

"Thank you for bringing me home. But you don't have to see me inside."

"Why not?"

"It's not necessary." She drew in a slow breath and looked out the window toward her condo. "Thing is, the last time I saw you … well, I shouldn't have let my emotions get the best of me. I shouldn't have … behaved the way I did."

"You were upset," Ethan said. "You had every right to be."

"But I meant what I said about not wanting to see you again."

Her admission was like a blow to the gut. "What?"

"It's too difficult seeing you. Everything about you reminds me of Denny and what happened. I've never been able to reconcile what happened out in the Badlands that day. And … I don't know that I'll ever forgive you for what you did."

It was hard to swallow the lump of truth she was feeding him, but Ethan listened. It was a long time coming, and he'd bet a week's pay this was harder for Maddie to say than for him to hear.

"I don't expect you to forget what happened or think I have forgotten Denny."

Her expression turned cool. "Haven't you? As soon as the funeral was over, you headed to the airport to play the hero. You spent eight years in the military being the hero. Every time I went anywhere in town all I heard was Ethan got an accommodation for this or Ethan just finished BUDS training or ... It was like you had a damned publicity department singing your praises. Everyone forgot what really happened out there with Denny. All they saw was 'Saint Ethan, the Hero.' Look at you, even now you're playing the hero cop, coming to my rescue. No wonder everyone has forgotten."

She drew in a deep breath as if she were searching for courage or getting ready for a battle she'd waited ten years to fight. Ethan wasn't sure which, but he remained silent and would take whatever beating she gave him.

"But I remember, Ethan. I remember seeing my parents grieve for years until all the life in them drained away. They're only now back to doing things like normal people do. For years I don't think I even heard them laugh. They didn't spend eight years forgetting and living life on the edge, playing super hero."

"Is that what you think I did?"

"I know that's what you did. You always took everything to the edge. If Denny dreamed up a prank, you took it one step further. But one thing I know for sure is that you didn't grieve for Denny." She pointed out the window. "Out there, doing whatever it was you were doing, it was easy to forget that a kid like Dennison

Newton died because of your prank. But here … it was with me every day."

Maddie pushed the car door open with more force than needed and climbed outside to the parking lot. Ethan did the same.

"Don't follow me, Ethan. I'm not Denny's little kid sister anymore. I'm not going to follow in your shadow, and I don't want you following me."

With both of the car doors ajar, Ethan sat in the driver's seat and watched Maddie rush to the door of her condo. The only thing he could hear was the sudden rush of blood storming through his veins and his heart hammering in his chest.

He'd done this to her. No one else. People said time healed all wounds. But Maddie's wounds were as fresh as the day he'd stood in her living room and told Denny's family that Denny was dead. He'd stayed away because he thought it would be easier for all of them. And now he knew for sure that he'd been wrong. And he had no idea how to even begin to make it right.

Chapter Three

He pulled into the parking lot of MW Oil, the company his family had founded and where his father still worked. Maddie had accused him of playing the hero. Well, hero wasn't a word he'd ever used when describing himself. None of the Navy SEALs on the team he'd had the privilege of working with did. But it still surprised him when others used that word associated with him. Especially in his home town of Rudolph where he left for the Navy over ten years ago as anything but a hero.

The normally warm summer weather had settled into a cool day thanks to the cloudy sky that covered the sun. The light rain shower that had caught him off guard earlier had stopped a few minutes ago, but the strong smell of moisture and wet earth still hung heavy in the air. As he pulled into a parking space and stepped out of his SUV, Ethan could still see steam rising from the ground, caused by the rain hitting the hot pavement.

He stepped out of the car and sat on the curb under a shady tree with his legs stretched out drinking the cup of hot coffee he'd picked up at the diner before coming over. He'd been to MW Oil at least a hundred times in his lifetime. He'd never been nervous about walking inside.

But then, Maddie Newton wasn't sitting behind a desk just inside that door.

Ethan had spent most of the night walking the floor until his father finally came downstairs. Unlike when he was a teenager, getting caught for sneaking into the house after a night of fun, Don McKinnon didn't yell. He was concerned. But he didn't ask any questions beyond how his day was before getting a glass of water and urging him to go to bed. Even when Ethan finally crawled under the cool sheets in his room, sleep eluded him, and he was paying for it today.

He couldn't get the words Maddie had said to him the other night out of his mind. She meant what she'd said at Denny's funeral. She never wanted to see him again. That was her choice and for years Ethan had respected that.

But no more.

During the long hours of the night, he realized that Maddie was right. Not about him forgetting Denny. Ethan couldn't possibly forget their friendship, or how Denny died. But he had escaped his grief in the military. Being in the military and then becoming a Navy SEAL had taken all his focus. He didn't have time to dwell on what he couldn't change, and he didn't have a constant reminder of how he'd failed. He focused on not failing for the sake of his SEAL team and the special ops they'd done.

But Maddie was left here to grieve every day. The only difference between her and her parents was that they'd finally found a way to live again. After seeing

Maddie yesterday, it was clear to Ethan that she hadn't. But he was going to change that. Even if it killed him.

♥ ♥ ♥

"I was wondering if I could have an extra hour or so off for lunch," Maddie said, standing in Don McKinnon's office while he signed papers that needed to be mailed today. "My car is fixed. George is closing the garage early today to go to his nephew's Bar Mitzvah, and I want to pick it up before he leaves. I hope that won't be a problem, Mr. McKinnon."

Don McKinnon sighed as he leaned back in his leather chair, shaking his head. "I've told you since the day you started working at MW Oil that you don't have to call me Mr. McKinnon. You're making me feel ancient."

Maddie smile sheepishly. "Old habits die hard. My whole life you've always been Mr. McKinnon. I guess it's going to take more than a few months to get used to it. But I will try my best to work on it."

"Why don't you take the rest of the afternoon off?"

She raised an eyebrow. "No, I just need to pick up my car."

"You didn't even take a day off after you had the accident. It's a nice day. Maybe you and Ethan can find something fun to do. He's been brooding for the last few days."

"Ethan?"

Don glanced up and handed her a stack of papers. She gave him a new set to sign. "I know there's some bad blood between you because of what happened to your brother," he said, signing and shuffling the next round of papers she handed him.

Maddie shrunk a little where she stood.

Don stopped writing and looked up. "I'm sorry. I know it's sometimes hard to talk about a loved one, even when they've been gone a long time."

Tears filled her eyes, but she knew Don was referring to his eldest son, Wade, who was presumed lost at sea during a tsunami that hit the Asian island he'd been working on several years ago.

"It's okay."

"Take the afternoon off. You deserve it."

A few minutes later, Maddie walked down the hallway, slipping her purse high on her shoulder. As practical as her little car was, she was happy to finally be getting it back after the few days without it. George had given her a sweet deal on repairing the radiator and body damage. And he'd turned the work around in a matter of days, which meant she could drive again and not rely on being driven.

Denny had taught her how to drive when she was only fifteen, right before she'd begged her mother for legitimate lessons. And Denny had died before Maddie had received her license. She never got the pleasure of thrusting her new paper license in her brother's face and hearing him rib her about how the roads will never be safe again now that she was driving. Yet every time she backed out of the driveway or out of a parking spot, she remembered how Denny told her to sit her arm at the back of her seat as she backed out, making sure the area was clear before she put her foot on the gas.

As she pushed through the front door of the building, Maddie thought of the irony. She hadn't allowed herself to visit those memories in years, and yet, so many of those good times seem to flood her mind lately. Denny's warm smile. Denny and Ethan laughing out in the yard. Camping trips with her family. She remembered everything.

As the sunshine hit her face, she froze on the top step of the walkway and stared out into the parking lot.

Ethan was leaning against his SUV holding a Styrofoam cup in his hand, smiling at her in a way that melted her heart. She cringed with embarrassment just thinking about the way she used to hang on his every move when she was a kid.

When she reached the parking lot, she said, "If I didn't know any better, I'd say you were stalking me."

"So call the police," Ethan said smiling wider.

"Very funny. What part of 'I don't want to see you' didn't you get?"

"This is official police business."

She glanced at Ethan, trying not to hold his gaze. She narrowed her eyes, just enough to attempt to discern the situation happening in front of her.

"You need to look these over and sign them," Ethan said, breaking her out of her trance. There were papers in his hands. When she peered closer, she saw the official police station seal on the top.

"What's this?"

"The report I wrote up about the accident. I want to make sure I didn't miss any details that will be problematic with your insurance company. The way people are getting denied for claims around here, you can never be too careful."

"When do you need this back?"

"I need to file it today."

"I need to pick up my car at George's before he closes."

"I'll drive you."

She shook her head. "Look, I appreciate all your help the other night, but that won't be necessary. My mother is coming to pick me up."

"No, she's not."

"What do you mean? What did you do?"

"I called her and told her I had police business with you, so I offered to pick you up myself."

"What is it with you? You're like a mosquito that I can't swat away."

Ethan placed his hand over his heart in mock distress. "That hurt."

"Get over it."

"I prefer to think of myself as determined."

"I prefer not to think of you at all," she said, rummaging through her purse for her cell phone. She found it and quickly dialed her home phone number, then listened.

"She's not home."

"Who?"

"Your mother. Since I told her I'd pick you up, she said she was going to head out to Rapid City again to do some shopping for your aunt who just got out of the hospital."

Her mouth gaped open. "You're too much."

"It's a ride, Maddie. No big deal."

"You expect me to believe that?"

"I don't really care if you believe it. That's what it is. Do you want a ride to the garage or do we look over the paperwork here in the parking lot and you call a cab. Your choice."

"I never like any of your choices."

She stared at the paperwork in Ethan's hand and remembered the feel of his hand taking hers as she climbed out of her wrecked car a few days ago. He had callouses and cuts from working hard, which surprised her at the time, but now made sense given what Hawk had told her about Ethan wanting to fix up that old Nolan farmhouse.

She grabbed the paperwork from Ethan's hand. "I'll read them while you drive."

"You get car sick when you read in the car."

She stopped walking and glanced at him. He remembered. "So?"

"So I don't want you to throw up on me."

"I'll roll down the window."

Ethan smiled the most amazing way that had her heart hammering in her chest like it used to do when she was a teenager. She hated it. She didn't want to remember those days with Ethan and Denny. She didn't want to like anything about Ethan. She just wanted to forget.

Ethan's SUV was parked in a visitor's parking space near the front of the building. It was only then that it dawned on her that he wasn't wearing his police uniform. Instead he wore a dark gray T-shirt and jeans.

"Official police business?"

Ethan shrugged, but his unabashed expression was unapologetic. "It's my day off."

She grunted with frustration and yanked the passenger side door open. To her relief, he gunned the engine and pulled out of the parking lot without saying another word. She took that opportunity to bury her head in the paperwork he'd handed her. But although the words were right in front of her, Maddie found she couldn't concentrate on them enough to read what they said.

She just wanted to pick up her car and go home. She didn't care about her car insurance company taking care of the repair costs. She'd pay George herself and forget about the insurance reimbursement. She blinked as she looked at the papers until a stinging sensation started to burn the corners of her eyes.

"Do you need a pen to sign it?"

"Ah, no. I have one. This looks fine."

Maddie's hands trembled as she rummaged through her purse in search of a pen. Frustrated with finding nothing, she pulled the zipper closed.

"Check the glove compartment."

"I'll wait."

She kept her eyes on the moving scenery out the window as they drove down the familiar road. Ethan had his window open and was resting his arm on the door. His short crop hair was barely touched by the wind flying through the window. Strands of her hair whipped in her face.

"Is this bothering you?" Ethan asked.

There was a whole lot bothering her. She just shook her head.

"You used to laugh a lot."

Pulling the hair away from her face, she said, "What?"

"That's what I always remembered the most about you when I was away. You used to find amusement in the oddest things, and you laughed like you didn't care if anyone else got what you were laughing about."

"You thought about me?"

He glanced at her quickly. "Of course. I missed Rudolph and everyone back home. You used to twirl your hair between your fingers when we sat in your front yard.

You never sat Indian style. You always sat on the grass with both legs either stretched out in front of you or to your side. And you sipped your soda. I could drink three cans of soda before you even finished one."

She always burped when she drank soda too fast. If Ethan wasn't around, she didn't care. But she was too self-conscious to do it when she was with him.

Maddie looked out the window at the scenery disappearing as they passed, then back at Ethan. With his eyes focused on the road ahead, she could see his strong profile clearly. Her eyes traced along his broad-set jaw, catching the curves of long sloping nose and lips. Heat crawled up her face.

He'd thought of her. Somehow that had never crossed her mind.

"So?"

"So nothing. I just noticed. You haven't laughed once since I've seen you."

His expression was wistful, as if her emotional state bothered him. But Maddie found it hard to believe that Ethan would even care about how she'd been feeling today or any other day.

"Maybe it's the company."

"Ouch. You don't hold back at all. You never used to be this mean to me."

She chuckled at his reaction and fought to quickly hide it. But the wide smile that split his face told her she'd been caught.

"There. Isn't that better?"

"Better than what?"

"I don't know. Just better. That's the first time I've seen you smile since ... I don't know when."

Maddie rolled her eyes. "I was in a car accident, Ethan. What was there to smile about?"

"George was able to fix your car."

"Okay, you've got me there. But despite what you think, life's not a bunch of laughs all the time."

His expression grew grim. "You don't have to tell me that. I see enough of it all the time."

She turned her attention to him but remained silent.

"When I became a police officer here in Rudolph, I never thought I'd be going on a domestic violence call to a house where the guy involved is someone I played in Little League with."

"When did you play Little League?"

"The year my dad coached."

"You're talking about Pete and Janice Avery?" When Ethan shrugged uncomfortably, she added, "It's okay, you don't have to say anything else. I know Janice."

"This storm has been rough on a lot of people. When the roof caved in on the manufacturing plant where Pete worked, everyone thought insurance was going to cover it and they'd be back to work by now."

"I know. It shocked a lot of people when the owners decided to take the insurance money and relocate the operation to another state. No plant. No jobs. No money."

"Money problems are causing lots of arguments these days. But thanks to Regis, at least the Wounded Veterans Center will have what it needs to rebuild."

"Regis is Hawk's fiancé, right?"

"Did you meet her at the clinic?"

Maddie shook her head. "Regis and Hawk came in to MW Oil to give the news of their engagement to your father. They look like a nice couple."

"Yeah, Hawk's real happy. And Regis is a peach. Sometimes I think she gets a little overwhelmed with all of us McKinnons crowding around her. But she fits in with us fine."

When Ethan pulled into the parking lot of George's Auto, Maddie saw her car sitting out front. Ethan pulled his SUV into the parking space next to her car.

"Looks as good as new. Well, at least as good as it did." She put the papers Ethan had given her on the seat next to him. "I found my pen. These are all signed."

"Thank you." As she got out of the car, he added, "You're going to be at the Wounded Veterans Center tomorrow, aren't you?"

She peered into the car at Ethan, torn. "I ... don't know."

"You wouldn't be doing it for me. It's for Ian. Regis, too. She's worked real hard to get all the funding together so we could finally move forward. There are going to be a lot of people there. Sort of a like an old-fashioned barn raising. Except, we're not raising a barn. We'll mostly be painting and building some walls and—"

She put up her hand to stop him. "I get it." Standing in the sun on the hot tar outside of a gas station was weighing her down. Or maybe it was just Ethan's relentlessness.

"I'll think about it."

Wide smile. Damn him. She didn't remember him being *that* handsome when he smiled. And she'd forgotten about that dimple on his cheek that only showed itself when he was really happy.

"Then maybe I'll see you tomorrow."

"Maybe." She turned and walked to George's office without turning back. She didn't hear the purr of the SUV's engine firing up or the sound of tires on the pavement. That could only mean one thing.

Maddie refused to turn around to see Ethan watching her walk away.

Chapter Four

For the better part of the morning, Ethan and the rest of the crew continued to haul all of the supplies needed to work on the Wounded Veterans Center that day. Looking at the work needed and the supplies, there were already more volunteers than Ian and Regis had hoped would show up. That left Regis, and Logan's fiancé, Poppy searching for more brushes and rollers for painting. A lot of people who showed up brought their own tools. Ian was acting as foreman for the project, and if all went well, they'd get a lot of work done before the day was through.

The delivery of materials the center had been waiting for arrived mid-morning. Ethan, along with his brothers, Logan and Hawk, and several other volunteers, worked to bring in all the materials they needed. He was already sweltering from the heat of the sun by late morning, so he pulled off his shirt and used it to wipe the moisture off his face.

That's when he saw a white minivan pull into the dirt parking lot. His heart pounded in his chest. Ethan had a feeling all along that Denny's parents would show up to help because Maddie's mother had talked to his mother at the diner earlier in the week. But seeing Maddie climb out of the back of the minivan was a surprise Ethan had hoped for, but didn't think he'd realize.

"You made it," Hawk said, holding the bundle of fresh two by four boards snugly on his shoulder.

Dave Newton walked up to them, keeping in step with his wife, Julie. Maddie trailed behind the two of them and looked less than thrilled to be there. But she *did* come. Ethan chose to take that as a good sign.

"It looks like the whole town showed up," Dave said.

"Just about," Ethan replied. "We even got extra carpenters coming in from Fort Pierre. If we're lucky, we'll get most of the painting finished in the upper level so we can start working on the construction of the recreation room and the kitchen downstairs where the flood really caused some damage."

Maddie's mother frowned. "I see most of you McKinnons. Where's Sam?"

"Fire season is in full swing," Ethan said. "Being a Hotshot, Sam is pretty much on call all the time. Right now, he's working in the Black Hills doing some prescribed burns."

Julie shook her head. "I don't know how your mother sleeps at night." Then she smiled, extending her hands. "Well, where are the paint brushes? I got my old clothes on, and I'm ready to get started."

Logan called out to her. "Follow me. Poppy and Regis have all the paint and supplies ready inside."

Dave propped his fists on his hips and laughed. "Looks like I showed up at the right time. All the heavy lifting is done."

Hawk laughed, still holding the two by four boards on his shoulder. "There's still plenty of that to go around inside. Why don't you come with me?"

Maddie didn't even look at him. She started to follow her father until Ethan caught her arm with his hand.

"Hold on a sec."

She turned and lifted her eyes to him, and suddenly he couldn't find the words he wanted to say.

"I'm glad you decided to come today," he finally said.

She held his gaze for a lingering moment. The warmth of her skin beneath his fingers reminded him that he was still holding her back. He let go of her arm. But instead of saying anything, she turned on her heels, leaving Ethan to watch her walk away with that fiery determination he'd never realized she had until now.

He watched until she reached the open door of the Wounded Veterans Center and wondered how he never noticed the slight sway of her hips as she moved, or the way the sun kissed her high cheekbones when she was fired up.

He and Denny had given Maddie plenty to get fired up about when she was younger. But the Maddie Newton he'd known had grown up to become an exquisite woman. That same temper that he and Denny used to laugh about was still there, but now there was an elegance about the woman that replaced the kid he used to tease.

She had always been a pretty girl. But the fact that Ethan was seeing Maddie Newton as a woman, and not Denny's kid sister, suddenly made Ethan uncomfortable. He had no business thinking about Maddie in that way. If Denny were here today, seeing Ethan's reaction to Maddie just walking away, Ethan would be down on the ground with his face buried in the dirt. And he wouldn't blame Denny one bit for doing it to him.

♥ ♥ ♥

They spent at least three hours inside the un-air-conditioned building putting up trim, painting walls and trim in the upstairs rooms, and hauling debris outside to the dumpster. Despite not wanting to come, Maddie found herself having a good time. It'd been a long time since she held a paint brush in her hand. Granted, this wasn't the kind of paint brush she used to love using. But it was still nice to see a blank wall and transform it into something beautiful.

There were people at the Wounded Veterans Center that she hadn't seen in years and working together made each task go that much faster because of the good conversation. But inevitably someone would mention Denny or she'd see Ethan across the room or down the hall, and all Maddie wanted to do was hide.

Lisa Mondello

Grabbing a paint can, some rollers and a tray, she found a small office that no one had worked in yet and decided to tackle it by herself. She'd made pretty good time, getting three-quarters of the room painted before Ian came up behind her.

"This is looking real good," he said. "Ethan tells me you were quite the artist when you were younger. Is that true?"

Ian's words caught Maddie off guard.

"It's just primer. It's hard not to look better than it was. What did Ethan tell you?"

"That you were a talented artist and could probably help us out."

"Help you with what?"

"Regis and I were thinking that it might be nice to have a mural on the wall of the recreation room. I'd love for you to take a look at it. The walls are still being constructed downstairs, and we still need to do some work down there, adding the kitchen and the bathrooms, so we probably wouldn't need you to start painting until September."

Maddie dropped the paint roller into the tray. "I really haven't done much painting in years. I'm not sure that I'm the right person for something like this."

"It doesn't have to be anything fancy. We're pretty much open to any ideas you have. Why don't you come take a look to get a feel for the space?"

She hated the idea of feeling cornered, and wouldn't you know, Ethan was behind it all. But the fact that he remembered her love of art at all gave her mixed feelings. She followed Ian to the stairs and watched as he slowly took each step down until they got to the bottom hallway. She had heard from Kate McKinnon that Ian had survived a bombing in Afghanistan and lost his leg. He was still getting used to walking with a prosthetic limb.

After all he'd gone through in his military service, the Wounded Veterans Center was important to Ian. Because of that, Maddie felt compelled to at least give him some ideas of what he could do.

As Ian mentioned, the recreation room, which was to house an open space for families to get together, have meetings, and to have the occasional special occasion, was still being constructed. Insulation had been put between the studs in the wall, and some of the Sheetrock had been hung. Plumbing pipes were exposed as was newly run electrical wire. Looking around, Maddie decided that Ian's September timeline might be too soon.

Ethan was standing at the far end of the room with his father, Hawk, Logan and a few other people Maddie didn't know. On the floor were two by fours arranged in parallel lines. At the top, there were more two by fours loosely placed on the floor, and the crew was getting ready to nail. Her father was standing inside an area that was already framed in, nailing the studs into place.

"I was thinking it might be nice to have a mural on the wall near the windows."

Maddie looked around, thinking as she rolled a thin strand of her hair between her thumb and fingers, trying to imagine what the finished room would look like. "I don't think you want a mural on that wall. I would just paint the walls by the windows white so you don't compete with the beautiful view from these magnificent windows."

Regis came up behind them. "See? That's exactly what I told him."

Ethan was watching her. He tried to hide it. But every time Maddie looked in that direction, their eyes connected before he quickly turned away. Realizing what she'd been doing with her hair, she combed her fingers through her hair, then tied it back, securing it with a clip she kept in her pocket.

"If you are going to do a mural, I would do it on this back wall," Maddie said, walking over the long, inside wall. But I don't think you need to fill it completely. Just add something to give it interest."

Regis smiled. "I like that idea. What about you, Ian?"

Before Ian could say anything, Maddie added, "But I don't think I should be the one to do it."

Ian looked at her, puzzled. "Why not?"

"I told you, I haven't done any artwork in a very long time. I wouldn't even know where to begin."

Ethan walked over to them. "Then why not start here?"

Maddie glared at him. "Because I'm not."

She then realized she'd raised her voice. Everyone in the large room seemed to stop what they were doing and look at her. Her eyes connected with Ethan's father. Terrific. *All I need is to make a fool of myself in front of my boss.*

She forced a smile she didn't feel and said, "You know the high school has been struggling with art funding. You could use something like this to bring attention to the importance of art by bringing in some of the high school students to do it."

Ian sighed, crossing his arms over his chest as he thought. "I still like the idea of you doing the artwork. Maybe you could direct the kids using your vision."

Maddie sighed, suddenly uncomfortable with all eyes on her. Turning her attention to something other than herself, she pointed to the old pipes strewn about in a pile on the floor. "What's all this?"

Don wiped his hands on a rag as he walked towards them. Her father walked behind him. "Those are old pipes the plumbers pulled out of the walls. Normally they haul all that away but they left it for the center. They'll fetch a good price down at the scrapyard."

"Looks like that heap of motorcycle parts in those boxes in our garage," her father said.

Ethan's eyes widened. "Do you mean Denny's bike?"

"If you can call it that. It's just a bunch of metal pieces."

417

"We used to go down to the junkyard all the time. Every time he saw a motorcycle part, he took it."

"And left it in my garage. He was always tinkering with something. I even found some of it in his room." Dave shrugged, a flash of pain crossing his face. "Can't seem to bring myself to bring it down to the scrapyard, even after all this time. You know how it was. For months before Denny died, all he did was talk about building a motorcycle and bringing it to Sturgis. I was never one for motorcycles myself. But something in me always wanted to see that motorcycle completed."

Ethan wiped the sweat off his face with a towel. "Denny definitely had a passion for motorcycles. Much more than I did."

"You're welcome to try your hand at putting it together yourself."

"Me?"

"Dad," Maddie warned. How could her father even think of letting Ethan touch Denny's things? "Why would you want to bring up all of that now?"

Maddie hadn't heard her mother come into the room with some of the other people who'd been painting upstairs.

"If I remember correctly, you had done some drawings of that motorcycle, too," Julie said, a hint of pride in her tone.

Ethan looked at her with surprise. "Denny never mentioned that to me."

"Maybe he didn't think they were any good."

"I doubt that. He kept them, so he must have been proud of them," Dave said. "Like I said, all those motorcycle parts, including the sketches are still sitting in boxes in the garage. If you want to stop by on your day off and take a look at it, you're welcome to see what you can do with it, Ethan."

Julie added brightly, "Yes, and you should stay for dinner. There was a time you were a regular fixture in the Newton kitchen. I miss that. It'll be nice for the four of us to catch up."

Maddie made a face that earned her a disapproving look from her mother. Okay, so maybe she *was* being a bit childish. But the last thing she needed was to sit at the dinner table and reminisce with Ethan McKinnon. She couldn't believe her parents were being so easy-going with the man responsible for the death of their son. How could they just put all that aside and pretend it never happened?

"Are we done here?" she asked.

Dave glanced at Julie, and she shrugged.

"You all did great today," Ian said. "Thank you for coming to help. You don't know how much this means to us."

Dave shook Ian's hand. Then Ethan's. "Glad we could do it. It was good seeing everyone, too." Dave turned to Ethan and said quietly, "Don't be a stranger. Make sure you stop by the house soon."

"I will," Ethan promised.

Chapter Five

When Maddie was a teenager, she'd been consumed with finding out absolutely every move Ethan McKinnon made. Just having him stop by the house to see Denny was enough to make her day. On the rare occasion he got to her parents' house before Denny got home from work, Ethan would hang out in the front yard. He always brought over an extra soda for Denny, but since Denny wasn't there, Maddie would sit and drink it while Ethan would talk. And she'd hang on his every word until Denny drove into the driveway and told her to scram.

He'd reminded her of those days when he'd driven her to George's to pick up her car. It had been years since she'd even allowed herself to think about them. Everything about Ethan McKinnon was larger than life to Maddie back then. It was a lifetime ago and yet … it felt so close.

She pulled into the driveway of her parents' house. But instead of going inside to say hello, she saw that the garage door was open. She knew who was there. Ethan's SUV was parked next to her mom's sedan in the turnaround under the shady sunset maple tree they used to climb as kids. In a few months, that tree would be brilliant with orange and red leaves as if it were on fire.

She walked towards the garage, shielding her eyes from the blinding sun until she stepped inside. Her eyes adjusted quickly to the change of light. Ethan was crouched over the three big boxes that housed all the used motorcycle parts Denny had collected the last year of his life. Ethan had taken most of the parts out and spread them all over the garage floor.

The aching in her gut grew the closer she got to Ethan. Why had her father mentioned this to him?

"So what's the prognosis?" she asked.

Ethan looked up at her, his face serious with concentration from focusing on each part and its purpose.

"I was wondering if you'd show up today."

"I don't know why. I always come here for Sunday dinner."

"You knew I'd be here."

She lifted her chin. "Why would that stop me?"

A slow smile played on his lips. "I don't know. Maybe it's the fact that you keep telling me you never want to see me again."

"I belong here. You don't."

"I was invited." He reached back and picked up a soda can from the floor. The outside was wet with condensation. "This is for you."

She glanced at the floor by his feet. An empty soda can was laying on its side.

"That's yours."

"You know I always bring an extra."

She took the can from his hand. "For Denny. But Denny's not here anymore, which you seem to keep forgetting."

Irritation rose up in her, but before she could give into it, Ethan stopped her with a strong look as he slowly stood up, wiping his wet hand on the front of his jeans. "The extra soda was always for you."

"Oh."

"You know, you and me have something very real and important in common. We both know what it's like to lose a brother."

As fast as her anger came, it evaporated. "It's not the same thing. You didn't lose Wade the same way."

"That's beside the point," Ethan said. "The point is, you don't understand what truly happened that day."

"Would it make a difference?" she said. "Or change anything that has happened since?"

His expression was thoughtful. "Probably not. But I do know this. Denny had passion for his ideas." He picked up a piece of greasy metal that looked like an engine part.

"It's just heaps of metal," she said. "It means nothing."

"That's where you're wrong. It was Denny's dream."

She gave him an incredulous look. "He was a just a teenager. All teenagers have stupid dreams like that. You sure as hell did."

"Yeah, I did. I wanted to drive in the Indy 500, but that never happened. I became a SEAL instead."

She huffed. "Please spare me."

"Your parents kept the bike parts for a reason, Maddie. Didn't you ever wonder why? They must have known Denny had a passion for building bikes. It wasn't just kid stuff. He really liked it. If given enough time, he might have even made it his life. He wanted to take that bike to Sturgis."

She laughed and paced a few steps. "Sure. That was right up his alley all right. Sturgis is nothing but a party town and an excuse to behave badly. You two did that pretty well all the time."

Ethan shrugged. "Well, I can't argue that Sturgis has the reputation for being a wild time."

"I'll say."

"But it's also where all the best bikes are showcased every year. People come all over to show their creations, show what they can do. That's what Denny wanted. He had ideas. He was an artist."

She looked at him, trying to remember the sketches Denny had made when he was a kid. "Denny always loved motorcycles," she whispered.

"He didn't have a chance to realize his dream."

She gave Ethan a hard look.

"Because of you."

He did nothing to mask the hurt that crossed his face with her harsh accusation. "You're not always going to hate me, are you? You liked me once. I know you did."

"I was young."

"We used to talk … and laugh. You used to stand by the garage and watch me and Denny. I always thought you had a little bit of a crush on me."

Her cheeks flamed. "I was stupid. Young girls sometimes do stupid things. I'm not stupid anymore."

♥ ♥ ♥

She was still so angry at him. He deserved it, of course. He'd deserve her anger for the rest of his life. But holding on to this anger was destroying her. How could she ever live her life and let someone into love her if she were so angry?

And the thought of another man loving her was something that had Ethan's stomach burning with envy. In his mind, Maddie had always been Denny's little sister. But not anymore. Maddie was a beautiful woman with a lot of love inside her, and right now that love was being swallowed up by grief she couldn't let go of. He'd already spent far too much time over the last few days thinking about how beautiful a woman Maddie was.

"No, you're not. Not about that," he admitted.

She lifted an eyebrow in challenge.

"Why aren't you with someone?" he asked, not really wanting to know details of a love life she may have had in the years he'd been away. But his curiosity was too strong to hold back.

"What?"

"A guy. I have been home for a year, and I've never once seen you with another man. Not around town. Not anywhere. I've never even heard of you dating anyone."

"That's my business and my choice."

"I don't buy that."

"Who cares?"

He sighed heavily and tossed a piece of tailpipe into the cardboard box, making a loud clank. "Aren't you tired yet?"

"Of what?"

"Of this hatred for me that you carry around with you. Your back is breaking from it."

Her back straightened as if to prove him wrong. "I beg your pardon? You're a fine one for talking to me about—"

"You play a good game. You pretend that you have it all together and that you're living your life. You tell me you're happy that your parents have started living again. When's your turn? You used to be artistic."

"So?"

"Nice answer," he said, shaking his head.

"What do you want from me?"

"Help me fix this bike up. Help me put it together and make it what Denny wanted."

"You're nuts."

"I thought we'd established that a long time ago."

She smiled despite not wanting to. And Ethan could tell she was fighting hard not to enjoy the little banter back and forth. If she really hated him, really hated being with him, she would never have come out to the garage. And for sure, she wouldn't still be standing here.

"I can't believe you're even asking me to do something like this."

He picked up a folder tucked in one of the boxes with the pieces of metal motorcycle parts. He opened up the folder, pulled out a few sketches and thrust a few of them at her. "You did these."

"It was Denny's work."

He pulled the rough sketches apart and quickly looked at them, handing one back to her. "This one is Denny's. He was always good at drawing, but certainly no artist. That was your specialty. This one is definitely yours." He handed her the detailed picture of what the finished motorcycle would look like.

Maddie looked at the picture, and he saw her shoulders sag.

"I don't need to be an expert in art to know that these drawings were done by two different people. And I'd seen enough of your work to know you had a real talent. Denny always said so."

Her head snapped up. "When did you ever see my work?"

"Denny showed me. He was real proud of what you could do. Envious even. He told me no one could touch what you did."

Tears filled her eyes. "He said that?"

Ethan nodded.

She cleared her throat; Maddie handed the sketch back to him. "Things change."

"Yeah, they do. But not everything has to."

"I didn't realize he showed you my work. I thought …"

"You didn't end up going to school for art either. Don't bother denying it. My dad told me you went for business, and that's why he hired you. You're good at what you do. He really likes you. But that's not your passion. You gave that up."

She cleared her throat. "I can't do it, Ethan."

"Denny wanted to build the bike. He wanted you to do this artwork on it. I can get this bike together somehow. I know I can." He handed her the sketch she'd made of the final bike again. "But I can't do that. Only you can. And when it's done, we can take it to Sturgis and show it off, just like Denny dreamed of doing himself."

Tears filled Maddie's eyes as she looked at the sketch, and then back at him. She looked at him for a long time. "Denny is gone. No good deed is going to change the past."

She dropped the sketch on the ground and walked out of the garage.

♥ ♥ ♥

He'd spent three of his days off working on the motorcycle, trying to piece together metal pieces and decide whether a carburetor was worth using or tossing for a new one. Maddie hadn't been out to her parents' house since that Sunday he'd asked her to help him build the bike. Ethan wanted the motorcycle to be as authentic to what Denny had visualized, using the parts he'd hand-picked. But he was short of more than a few major items.

The frame was good. Whatever was missing from the boxes could be found at the local junk yard or ordered at the auto center. Unlike when they were younger and couldn't afford anything, they had to make do with what funds they had. But Ethan had what he needed to do it right. When it had become clear that Maddie didn't want to help him work on the motorcycle, Ethan moved all the boxes to the garage at his parents' house. He could work on the bike at all hours of the day if he wanted to there.

"You've got a lot of work ahead of you," Logan said, walking into the garage one evening. In his hand was the impact wrench Ethan had asked his brother to bring over.

He chuckled at the look his twin brother gave him. "You can say that again."

"Need any help?"

"Yeah, but she's not willing."

The one thing about growing up in a close family was that you didn't have to do a whole lot of explaining about the meaning of your words.

"Everyone grieves different, Ethan. You were still stationed overseas when Kelly died. But when she did, I wanted to shut myself in the barn and never come out. If I hadn't had Keith and the farm to think about, I'd probably still be in there. And even then it took Poppy coming back into my life to make me feel alive again."

Ethan had seen just how much of a wreck Logan had been when Ethan finally came home. He'd never seen his brother in such rough shape. He'd worked hard to re-establish their relationship while forging a bond with the nearly five-year-old nephew Ethan had just met. Now, little Keith and Uncle Ethan were buds.

Logan glanced up at the ceiling. The room above the garage was a small apartment that used to belong to their brother, Wade. "When we heard the news about Wade, I didn't think Mom would ever get out of bed again. But then she found out about Keith and when he was born it was like Mom was reborn too. Maddie just needs to find that thing that helps her feel reborn."

"It's been ten years, Logan. She doesn't want to have anything to do with me. In her mind, I killed her brother."

"Does she know the truth?"

"Denny's dead. What difference will it make if she knows all the details of how he died? I don't want to do that to her."

Logan sat on his father's workbench and placed the impact wrench next to him. "The truth is everything. It sets you free. I should know. It took years for me to finally get things back on track in my life, and that's only because Kelly finally told me the truth about tricking me into marrying her. I just thank God I have this second chance with Poppy. She's everything to me."

Ethan shook his head and sighed. "It's different with us. Denny was Maddie's brother. It's not like there was ever anything between me and Maddie like there was with you and Poppy."

"Are you sure about that?"

Ethan looked at his brother. "She was Denny's kid sister."

Logan stood up. "You're never going to know if she's ready to hear the truth until you tell her." Logan started to walk out of the garage, but he stopped and turned back. "Oh, and in case you haven't noticed, Maddie's not a kid anymore."

That was just it. He had noticed. From the curves of her slender body, to the way she put her hand on her cheek when she was thinking, to the slow smile that played on her lips. He'd even heard her laughing that day at the Wounded Veterans Center. She didn't know he was watching her or that every time she talked, he could pick her voice out of the crowd.

He'd noticed too much. And he liked it.

Chapter Six

He was still in his police uniform when he stepped into the house. Her parents had invited him for dinner and insisted she come, with a warning to be polite. This was Denny's childhood friend after all.

Yeah, and he was the one responsible for the death of your son. Why was it that she was the only one who remembered that?

Maddie set the dining room table as Ethan greeted her parents in the hallway.

"You look very handsome and official in that uniform," her mother said.

Ethan seemed to blush. Maddie rolled her eyes and dropped a fork on a napkin by the plates she'd just set down.

"Dinner smells wonderful," Ethan said.

"I'll be serving it in just a few minutes. Why don't you sit down? Dave will be downstairs in a few minutes. He's upstairs going through some old pictures he wanted to show you."

Her mother walked into the kitchen and left her alone with Ethan.

"How are you?" he asked.

"Couldn't be better," she said dryly.

Ethan chuckled. "Don't hurt yourself with your enthusiasm."

She glared at him.

Her mother came into the dining room with a platter of roast beef and scalloped potatoes, handing it to Ethan. "Can you put that in the center of the table? I need to get the serving spoons and salad."

Ethan did as he was asked just as her father came into the dining room. He held a stack of pictures in his hand, but placed them on the buffet before seating himself at the head of the table.

A few minutes later, the food was served, and they fell into quiet conversation about general stuff that Maddie found safe to talk about.

"Don insists I call him by his first name."

"Well, he's your boss now," Julie said. "If he asked you to call him Don, then it's not a problem."

She made a face. "Yeah, but it still feels weird. He's been Mr. McKinnon to me my whole life."

"What do you think, Ethan?" Dave asked. "Now that you're a police officer in the town you grew up in, you must have to go on calls occasionally with people you knew. How do you deal with that?"

"Protocol," Maddie said.

She lifted her gaze from her plate to Ethan, who was sitting across from her. Amusement played in his dark eyes.

Her mother looked confused. "Protocol?"

Ethan put his fork down and wiped his lips with his napkin before speaking. "It would be weird going up to Mr. Stein and calling him Rufus."

"Mr. Stein. Wasn't he your English teacher in high school?" Julie asked.

"Yeah, and he's like a hundred years old by now. I didn't know his first name was Rufus."

Ethan shrugged. "It's easier to just be polite and use formalities."

Her father chuckled. "That's quite a change for you. I'd forgotten just how wild you and Denny were in your younger days."

"We weren't that wild."

Her parents both sat back in the chair and laughed harder.

Her mother said, "Didn't you blow up your mother's kitchen once?"

Ethan's eyes grew wide. "That one wasn't me. That was Sam and Ian."

"Well, there were plenty of other experiments that ended in broken bones and destruction. And I have the evidence to prove it."

Ethan made a face. "Oh, no."

"Remember this one?" Her father handed Ethan a picture he'd pulled from the pile he'd retrieved from the buffet.

Her mother shook her head and chuckled, taking his empty plate and stacking it on top of hers. "You can't escape your past, Ethan. Not here. We were too much a part of your shenanigans."

Ethan stared at the picture, his expression wistful before he chuckled. "Denny thought he could float down from the roof."

"He was determined to do it. He used my best sheets to prove it," her mother said. "That trip to the ER was interesting, trying to explain how he broke both of his legs."

"But even with that he was trying to convince the doctor that he would have jumped to get a better view over the trees. Remember that, Julie?"

Her mother nodded. "I thought they were going to commit him right then and there."

"We used to go up on the roof all the time," Ethan said. "Denny loved it up there."

"Why?" Maddie asked.

"He said it helped him think, dream. He was a big dreamer. He always had all these ideas," Ethan said.

"I thought you were the one with all the wild ideas."

"No, Denny had them. I was just stupid enough to follow along most of the time."

Her father looked down at a picture, and his eyes grew sad. "He did have ideas. That's for sure. I don't know why he insisted on trying to drive The Mammoth that day."

"He was upset," Ethan said quietly.

Her mother got up from the table. "Because you were leaving?"

"Partly. I suppose that had something to do with it. We were always joined at the hip back then. But Denny, for all his wild ideas, was a pretty complicated guy."

Maddie shifted uncomfortably in her seat and then got up from the table. "I'm done eating, Ma. I'll take the dishes."

She grabbed the dishes from mother's hands and walked into the kitchen. Dropping the dishes into the sink, she turned around and felt the swell of tears in her eyes. No one knew how much Denny suffered from depression more than she did.

She heard laughter from the other room and wanted to just run. Did they even understand how difficult it was for Denny when he heard Ethan was leaving for the Navy? She'd never seen her brother so lost. And Ethan just left him to play the hero. Always the hero.

Wiping her face of moisture, she pasted a smile on her face, grabbed the double chocolate cake her mother had made earlier from the counter and brought it into the dining room.

"I hope you have room for cake, Ethan."

He patted his stomach. "Always for your cake, Mrs. Newton."

Maddie made a face at her mother. "See? Old habits die hard. He can't even call you by your first name."

"He doesn't do it here out of protocol. We have no protocol in this house," her mother argued.

"Even when he was so young, Denny loved bikes." Her father handed Ethan another picture.

"I remember that bike. We bent the frame after making a jump out back on that big tree stump. I think I was the one who had the hospital visit that day." Ethan lifted his arm to reveal a scar on his elbow. "Twelve stitches."

"The only time I saw Denny truly inspired was when he was talking about that motorcycle. He worked for hours on those sketches and brought so many greasy parts into the garage." Her father laughed, but it was bittersweet.

"The motorcycle rally in Sturgis is a few weeks away, isn't it?" her father asked.

"Yeah, but the building of the motorcycle is slow going. I don't know if I have enough time to do it justice, especially without the artwork Denny wanted on the bike."

"I'd love seeing Denny's unfinished business completed."

"That's only going to happen if Maddie helps me," he said, looking directly at her from across the table.

"What?"

"I can't finish the bike with just metal parts. It needs the artwork you and Denny designed. Otherwise, it's just a shell. There isn't anyone who I'd trust to do it right but you."

"Oh, honey, that would be great!" her mother said. "You still have all those drawings you did—"

"I'll think about it." She abruptly got up from the table and made her apologies. "I'm really tired, Ma. Do you mind if I don't help with dishes? I have to get up early for work tomorrow."

She kissed both her parents and headed for the door.

"I'll walk you out," Ethan said.

A few minutes later, Maddie walked down the driveway with Ethan by her side.

"I wanted to thank you," she finally said when she reached her car.

He raised an eyebrow. "Why?"

"It's just," she said, pushing a lock of her hair behind her ear. "I've never been able to make my parents laugh like that. It's been a long time since I've seen them that happy. At first, I didn't agree with my father's suggestion to finish the motorcycle that Denny started. But ... I think it will do some good. It'll give them closure."

"Having everyone around the table like that ... everything seemed like the old days, when Denny was still with us. You even managed a few laughs yourself."

She shook her head. "Don't make this more than it is. We've probably done that hundreds of times when we were kids. Just all of us at the table. It didn't matter if we were having grilled cheese and tomato soup or a full course dinner like tonight," she said. Maddie stopped speaking for a moment and took in a gulp of air. "Seeing them laugh like that was ... amazing really. I really miss it."

"Me, too."

"For that reason, I'll do it. I'll work on the artwork for the motorcycle."

If Ethan had expected Maddie would put up more of a fight, he didn't show it.

"That's great."

"On one condition."

"What's that?"

"I'm not going to Sturgis. You'll have to do that alone."

"Why?

"I saw my father's face at the dinner table. He wants to see this thing through, and he's really happy that you're the one doing it. So I want to give him closure on that. I'll paint the fuel tank cap like Denny wanted me to. I'll even help you put it together. But you can take the bike to Sturgis and be wild with all the other motorcyclists."

"Don't you want to see his bike compete with all the other bikes? People will be looking at your artwork, too. Your creation."

"This bike is your creation, Ethan. Not mine and … it's not even Denny's. Not really. He had a bunch of metal pieces and a few little sketches that didn't look like much of anything. You're the one who is making this."

"With your sketches."

She shrugged. "I only want to do this so my father can finally move on completely."

"What about you?"

"What about me?"

"Nothing."

"No, finish what you were going to say."

He hesitated a moment. This wasn't the time. "The old fuel tank cover Denny had in the box is shot. I can't use it. There's a motorcycle junkyard in Rapid City. It most likely will have what I need. I went there years ago with Denny. I'm sure this is the place where he got most of his pieces. But after looking at everything in those boxes, I'm missing a few pieces, including a big enough fuel tank cap."

"Can't we order the right one?"

Ethan made a comical face that had her laughing. He'd missed that sound.

"It might not be delivered in time for you to work on it. Besides, this bike was about rebuilding something from nothing. Making something old new again."

"Like you wanted to do with the Nolan house?"

He looked at her with interest. "Who've you been talking to?"

"Hawk told me you were going to buy the old Nolan farmhouse before the flood destroyed the house."

"He did, huh?" Ethan sighed, clearly disappointed the flood had caused him to lose his opportunity to do what he'd planned there. "It would have been a beautiful place."

Maddie leaned back against her car. "Why do you need me to go with you for this?"

"Because you're the one who has the design. Only you know how to execute it. You need to pick it out. Would Picasso allow someone else to pick out his canvas?"

She sputtered. "So now you're comparing me to Picasso?"

He leaned in closer to her. She could feel the heat of his body and the scent of the coffee he'd just had with his dessert.

"I want you to be a part of this. Will you go?"

She sighed. "Pick me up at my place on Saturday."

She got into her car and could still feel the energy of standing so close to Ethan. Before she'd arrived at her parents' house tonight, she thought she'd never make it through dinner for fear of how she'd feel.

She'd felt so much anger toward Ethan for so long that it was hard to imagine anything else. Now she was realizing her biggest fear.

She was still very much in love with Ethan McKinnon.

Chapter Seven

They'd spent the afternoon searching the junkyard for the right fuel tank cap until they'd found the perfect one that would be easy to clean up so Maddie could paint it. She hadn't been paying attention to where they were going until one sign caught her eye. Maddie tilted her head, and then twisted in her seat as she looked back at the sign. "Where are we going, Ethan?"

"Taking a little detour," Ethan replied, not looking at her.

"Isn't this the way ... You're not taking me up to the trail where Denny's truck crashed?"

Ethan said nothing.

Panic filled her. "No, Ethan. I don't want to go there."

"I have to tell you something," he said. Ethan's fingers tightened on the steering wheel. "It's really important. There are things you don't know about what happened the day Denny died."

"Don't do this to me. I don't want to see the place where my brother died!"

"Why not?" he said, taking his eyes off the road for just a second.

"Because it was awful."

"Yes, it was. I know because I was there. But you weren't. You don't know what went down that day. For ten years you've been blaming me as if I held a gun to Denny's head."

"It was your idea!"

Ethan turned off the main road to a dirt road. He gunned the engine.

"Who the hell gave you a badge? You drive like a maniac!"

"I'm not the one who plowed into a tree."

"I was trying to avoid hitting a deer."

The tree-lined dirt road they were driving on was filled with ruts that caused the SUV to bounce up and down. Maddie held onto the door and her seat as Ethan drove. They drove until the road opened to a clearing that led to huge rock formations that were weathered smooth from years of erosion. Maddie had never been here, but she knew plenty about it. Lots of the kids from school would come out here with their 4-wheel drive vehicles and take turns driving down the rock wall. Some even talked about trying to drive down The Mammoth, the rock formation where Denny had died.

Maddie wanted no part of it. Most of the rocks were steep, but still safe enough to drive down safely if you were careful. But Denny had to push it further. He had to drive The Mammoth just to prove something to Ethan. And it killed him.

"I don't want to do this Ethan. I'm not crazy like you and Denny were. I don't need to live my life on the edge."

He stopped the SUV on the top of the rock formation and got out. Walking over to the passenger side door, he yanked the door open and extended his hand.

"I don't expect you to do any driving. But I do expect you to at least live. That's only going to happen if you get past this."

She sat still in the seat, seething with anger.

"Just come with me for a minute. I want to show you something. I promise I'll take you home right after."

"I hate you," she said, pushing his hand away, getting out of the car and slamming the door.

"Tell me something I don't already know. You made that more than clear at Denny's funeral and every day since. You wear your anger for me like it's some accessory. I get that you have every reason to be angry with me. Even hate me. For a while after Denny died, I had enough anger and hatred for both of us. But I learned to channel that anger. Look what it's still doing to you."

Old anger resurfaced with a fierceness she couldn't control. She'd felt it the day they'd buried Denny. She'd walked right up to Ethan after the service and slapped him across the face, screaming that she never wanted to see him again. She'd caused a scene that day, and people talked about it for weeks. But what stuck with her was the way Ethan stood and just took it from her. Stone cold and emotionless.

Then he left. It would be years before she saw him again from a distance standing outside of the diner in town.

Ethan took her by the hand and led her toward the edge of the cliff. Rain and erosion had smoothed out most of the rocks, making it possible to drive down the side of the rock slowly and reach the bottom.

"Denny and I used to come here a lot. We got used to taking turns driving his truck down this rock trail." He pointed to a rock formation with a gradual decline. "Denny and I mastered that slope the first day we were here. It got so easy that we didn't even get nervous when we couldn't see the bottom of the rocks below.

"Why the hell did you take him here that day? One last hurrah before you left for the Navy? You knew how depressed he was."

"Yes, I did. That's just the point. I didn't want him to come here. I came with him because I was scared for him to come here alone."

"You expect me to believe that?" She took in a breath of air to keep her anger from becoming a sob. "I was fine before you came back, Ethan. Why couldn't you have just stayed in the military?"

He swung around and looked at her straight on. "Better yet, why didn't I just die there?"

His words left her cold. "I didn't say that."

"You wanted me dead."

Tears stung her eyes. "I never wanted you dead, Ethan. Why would I want that? I didn't want either of you dead. But the two of you had this death wish anyway. And when he died you just left him here alone. He died alone, Ethan."

"He did. He was alive when I left to get help, and by the time I got back, he was gone. But he wanted to die that day, Maddie. That's what I'm trying to tell you."

She was sure her heart stopped beating. "What?"

Tears filled Ethan's eyes, and his expression was shattered. She'd never seen Ethan cry, not even at Denny's funeral. But then she was too wrapped up in her own fragile emotions to remember.

"Look out there," he said, his voice low against the whistle of the wind blowing past them. "Denny used to look out there at the view and say this was the closest to heaven he was ever going to get here on earth."

Ethan took a few steps closer to the edge of the cliff.

"I came here with him that day because he was talking crazy. It only got worse the closer it got to the time I was supposed to leave for boot camp. He kept telling me I was going to be someone. I was going to be a hero. People were going to respect me. But he couldn't be that way. He always built me up to be more than I was." He looked back at Maddie, and she saw the tears rolling down Ethan's cheeks. "He believed in me when I didn't believe in myself. I never thought I'd be any of that. Not back then. I was just as lost as he was. Or so I thought."

He swiped his face with his hand. "You remember what we were like. My father used to say me and Denny were two bullets just waiting for the right gun. But it was more than being wild at heart for Denny. He … wanted to die, Maddie."

She couldn't talk. All her emotions were lodged in her throat, choking her. Her brother *wanted* to die? She knew he was depressed. But he always put on a brave face for her. Could it be that he'd confided his darkest feelings to Ethan?

"I don't believe you," she finally said. "Denny never would have done that."

Ethan cleared his throat and pointed to the steepest decline on the rock formation they were standing on. "He told me he was going to try driving down The Mammoth. I didn't want him to. He'd been drinking. He had this wild look in his eyes, and it terrified me. So I stayed in the truck and told him to just give me the keys. But he wouldn't."

"You weren't driving? They told my parents you jumped out of the truck before it went over. They found Denny on the passenger side."

"He didn't have his seat belt on. I took mine off just as he started down the incline. I was afraid the brakes were going to lock. But as soon as I jumped out of the truck, he hit the gas. He disappeared over the side. I couldn't see him. By the time I got to my feet, I heard the crash."

Ethan's whole body looked depleted. His shoulders shook, and Maddie knew he was sobbing.

Consumed with emotion, Ethan bent down and snatched a handful of rocks from the ground and starting throwing them out into the direction where Denny's truck plunged off the cliff with all his strength.

"You stupid idiot!" he yelled at the top of his lungs. "I was your friend, Denny! You didn't have to do this! I wouldn't have left you if I thought you'd go through with it!"

She couldn't hold back the tears. "Why didn't you tell my parents this?"

Ethan turned to look at her, unashamed of the outburst that had left him raw. "How could I tell your parents something like this? What parent wants to think their kid wanted to die? It's horrible."

She started to sob. "But you left anyway, Ethan. All these years you were gone. You never came back. I hated you for it."

She walked over to him, and she started beating Ethan against the chest with her fists. But he grabbed her hands and held her back as she sobbed. "You left him to die alone, and then you never came back."

Ethan pulled Maddie close to his chest, feeling her tiny body quaking against his. Every bit of him was raw and aching, but not from the lashing Maddie tried to give him. It was because he finally had some clarity that eight years as a Navy SEAL had never given him.

"You don't hate me because I left Denny alone, Maddie. You hate me because I left you alone. I'm sorry.

I'm so sorry I did that to you. I couldn't save Denny. But I should have been there for you."

Her sobs grew louder and mingled in with his own.

She pulled away from Ethan and wiped her face. "After all this time, why are you telling me this now?"

"Because I see the way Denny's death is still eating you up inside. You're existing. You're not living, Maddie. You're just as angry with Denny as you were with me. Maybe it was easier to hate me than hate him for what he did. I don't know."

"His death didn't seem to hold you back at all. And you have all the military accommodations to prove it."

He shook his head, trying to make her understand what had been driving him all these years since Denny died. "Denny believed in me. Don't you see, I thought if I didn't achieve all those things Denny thought I could be that it would somehow mean his death was meaningless. It drove me every single day to be the man he saw through his eyes."

Her tears returned anew. "How could Denny want to die? Didn't he know how special he was? How much he was loved?"

Ethan shook his head. "He was in a lot of pain. I never knew just how much until that day."

"Why did you let me believe all these years it was your fault, Ethan? That wasn't your burden to carry."

"He was my friend."

Her bottom lip trembled. With a shake of her head, she said, "Take me home."

Ethan pulled her closer and walked with her back to the SUV. When she climbed inside, he said, "I'm sorry, Maddie."

"I am, too."

Chapter Eight

The ride home brought silence. Maddie held the fuel tank cap in her lap and kept her eyes glued to the scenery out the window, watching their surroundings accelerate alongside the SUV's movements. The sun was already sinking low, just touching the tree line. In a few minutes, it would be dark, and she wouldn't have to hide her face by turning away.

Ethan had tried to save Denny. All these years, why had no one told her? Of course, he would try to save Denny. Not because he was a hero. Because he loved Denny. They were like brothers.

It had never occurred to her that Ethan had been suffering over Denny's death as much as her family had. He'd stayed away to spare her and to make himself into the man Denny insisted he could be. And Ethan had achieved all those goals and more by earning his place as a Navy SEAL and then becoming a police officer.

She'd been so wrong about Ethan. And for what?

As the car rolled up in front of her condo, she placed the fuel tank cap on the seat and released her seat belt.

"Do you mind taking this into the house? It's a little heavy," she said.

Ethan nodded.

Maddie rummaged through her purse for her house key as they walked to the front door of her condo. The key slipped easily into the lock and the door opened. A cool rush of air, from keeping her air conditioning on during the day, bathed her face as she stepped inside.

Maddie led Ethan through the hallway to the kitchen.

"You can put the fuel tank cap on the kitchen table for now. That's probably where I'll work on it."

Ethan carefully placed the metal piece on the table and awkwardly turned around. She moved in close to him.

"Maddie, I …" he started to say, but she stopped him by placing her finger over his lips.

She looked up into his eyes feeling a swell of emotion so strong it consumed her. Ethan held her gaze, giving her strength to take her feelings one step more. Lifting up on her toes, she brushed her lips against his and waited. She felt his hesitation, felt the heat of his body against the cool air inside the room and wanted his heat. She wanted it like it was a drug she had to have to survive.

After only brief hesitation, Maddie felt Ethan surrender to the kiss. In one quick movement, his arm was around her waist, pulling her against the rock hard wall of his chest. His mouth devoured hers, teasing her lips with his tongue until she opened up to him and let him taste her.

Reaching up, she placed her hand behind his head, pulling him closer with an urgency she'd never felt before. He followed her lead. His hands roamed her body, caressing her back and shoulder. Then his fingers were in her hair as he deepened their kiss. And Maddie wanted more. So much more.

But before she knew what was happening, Ethan abruptly pulled away and took a wide step back. Her mouth still moist and swollen from their kiss, she looked at him, confused by his sudden retreat.

"What's wrong?"

He shook his head as if to shake something clear of himself. "I'm sorry."

"For what?"

"For this. For kissing you."

She smiled shyly. "In case you didn't notice, I was the one that started it. I was kissing you. And then you kissed me back."

"But …"

"But what?"

"I can't do this to you."

"Do what?"

"You're my best friend's kid sister. What happened today out at the cliffs; that's enough to send anyone over the edge. I'm not going to treat you this way."

A chill raced through her, and Maddie longed for the warmth of Ethan's arms. It had been years since she'd dreamed of being in them, having him hold her and kiss her the way he had just seconds ago. And now he was telling her it was a mistake.

Crossing her arms over her chest, she said, "I don't understand."

"I can't … I won't do that to you, Maddie. You're vulnerable right now. Only a bastard would take advantage of that. You deserve more."

As Ethan turned to leave, Maddie thought she'd die. All the times she'd dreamed of kissing Ethan, she never thought it would turn out like this, with him leaving her standing there alone. It was eerily reminiscent of the day he left the Navy.

He reached the door, but before he could leave, she stopped him.

"You're a hypocrite, Ethan."

He stopped with his hand on the doorknob.

"You told me I had some feelings to get over so I could move on and have a full life. You need to open your eyes to a few things."

He gave her a sidelong glance. "What's that?"

"How about the fact that I'm a woman, not a kid?"

Ethan stared at her from down the hallway. All the heat she'd felt moments ago was there in his eyes. "I know," he said, his voice low. "That's why I'm leaving."

The walk back to his SUV left Ethan empty. He'd just kissed Denny's kid sister.

Except …

Maddie didn't feel like Denny's kid sister when she'd been in his arms. And he wasn't thinking of Denny when her body was pressed against the length of his. Every bit of her was woman, soft, sexy and desirable. And all Ethan knew was he wanted her. All of her.

He climbed into the SUV and looked back at her condo door, pulling in a deep breath to steady himself. His quickened pulse was like a timpani in his ear, pulsing through him at rapid speed.

He'd wanted Maddie. And what startled him more was it wasn't the first time.

He thrust the key in the ignition with more force than needed and fired up the SUV's engine. It was still early enough that he could do some work on the motorcycle when he got home. But something told him he'd only sit and stare at metal parts all night.

He pulled out of the parking space and drove to the entrance of the Wingate Condominium complex. Hitting the directional for a left turn that would take him home, Ethan glanced in the opposite direction. The Nolan property was to the right.

He recalled the day he'd walked the property and saw the farmhouse in disrepair. The Realtor had long since left, but Ethan walked down to the river's edge and sat on a boulder for at least an hour, listening to the frigid water of January breaking through chunks of ice and snow to make it down river. He remembered thinking about Logan's farm being just a half mile further down that same stream and how nice it would be to build a life someday with someone special.

The ice storm and floods had destroyed his vision for rebuilding the property. But there was still something that drew him there. Clarity. Contentment. He'd felt those that day even though he felt frozen by the time he went back to his SUV and headed home.

The tick, tick, tick of the blinker pulled him from his thoughts. He turned the wheel and headed in the opposite direction of home, toward the Nolan property.

♥ ♥ ♥

Ethan hadn't seen Maddie in a few days. He'd called her house but got no answer. He'd driven by MW Oil and seen her car in the parking lot. He'd even asked his father how she was doing. But she hadn't shown up at the house to help him with the motorcycle.

He wanted to kick himself from one end of the garage to the other. He'd kissed her. The way she felt in his arms had been so wonderful. And he knew without a doubt that if he hadn't left Maddie right at that moment, he would have made love to her.

Frustrated, he put too much force behind tightening a bolt on the motorcycle. His hand slipped and brushed up against a sharp piece of metal that was protruding too far out.

"Damn!"

Ethan looked down at the blood and grease on his hand.

"Now you've done it."

Deep in his thoughts, he hadn't heard footsteps or even a car pulling into the driveway. But Maddie stood just outside the garage door, peering in with a wide smile that took his breath away.

"Did you break it?" she asked.

He looked down at his hand and moved his fingers. "No, but I have a gash. I'm getting blood all over the floor."

"I was talking about the motorcycle. It'd be a shame if you did, especially after all the work I've done on the fuel tank cap."

"Gee, thanks." He stood up and walked over to her until they were both standing outside the garage. In her hands, she held two soda bottles. Both were unopened.

"What's that?"

"One's for you," she said, handing one of the bottles to him and then unscrewing the top of hers. Looking at his hand she said. "You need to wash that out first."

She placed her thumb over the mouth of soda bottle and shook it. For a second, it caught Ethan off guard. But then he saw her mischievous grin, and he started laughing.

"What do you think you're going to do?"

"You need to cool off."

She released her thumb from the mouth of the bottle just a little to allow a stream of soda pop to spray and directed the spray at Ethan. He quickly did the same and started spraying her. The two of them laughed as they chased each other around the front lawn, spraying until there was no soda left. Then Ethan ran over to the hose on the side of the house and turned it on full blast. The surprised look on Maddie's face when she rounded the corner and he blasted her with water was priceless.

"No fair!" she screamed, laughing. "You have the advantage. I don't have a hose."

"You started it." That alone was enough of a surprise for Ethan. She ran to the faucet and quickly turned the water off. The hose slowly drained of water until it was just a trickle. Ethan used the remaining water to clean out the cut on his hand.

Still chuckling, and drenched to the bone, Maddie came over to him and pulled his hand towards her to inspect it. The feel of her hands on his left him light-headed.

She glanced up at him and smiled. "You'll live."

"Yeah."

Her hair was soaking wet, and the white T-shirt she wore clung to her skin. And every bit of him wanted her as much as he had the other day when he'd kissed her in the kitchen.

"You haven't been around."

"I've been busy. I finished the artwork on the fuel tank cap."

"You did? But you left the sketches here. How did you do it?"

"I was inspired by something else. Something more beautiful. I think you'll like it."

"Great. Where is it so I can see it?"

"It's still at my condo. It needed to dry a little more before I put the final coat on it. Now I need to dry off. Thanks for the shower."

"You're welcome."

She turned and started walking down the driveway to where her car was parked. "Stop by later."

"You're leaving already?"

"I need to take another shower to get all this sticky soda off me."

He watched her walk away and heard her musical laugh, and he was suddenly a teenager again. His heart swelled with emotion that bubbled up in his throat and threatened to choke him. The Maddie he'd always known and loved was back.

And with that thought, his heart stopped. Loved? Well, sure, he loved her. Ethan had known Maddie since she was just a little girl, and he used to visit Denny at the house after school. But the love he felt now was different. And he did love her. What else could this be?

Ethan had done so many wild things in his life. He'd been on black op missions that still made him nervous to think about. He and Denny had done countless pranks throughout their childhood that had left him trembling with fear along with the excitement.

But none of that compared to this feeling. This love he felt for Maddie terrified him to the core.

Chapter Nine

As far as bad ideas went, going over to Maddie's condo was as bad as it got. He hadn't been able to shake off the feelings he'd had earlier when they playfully ran around the front yard like kids. That kind of playfulness was something he'd forgotten about. He'd been so absorbed with becoming the man Denny thought he was that he'd forgotten.

He walked up to the door, anticipation coursing through him like one of the freight trains he and Denny stupidly decided to jump on when they were thirteen. By the time they'd been able to jump off, they were already in Wyoming, and they had to call their parents to pick them up. That long ride home felt like the walk to Maddie's door.

He'd known her practically his whole life and yet … it felt like he was meeting her for the first time.

He rang the doorbell. After a few seconds, she opened the door. Her hair was tied up in the back of her head in a clip. She'd put on a light coating of lipstick that made her skin glow. She'd changed out of her wet shorts into a fresh pair of cutoff jeans and a coral tank top.

"Come in. I'm making dinner."

"I can come back."

She turned and gave him a look. "Don't be silly. I was expecting you."

He walked behind her, taking in the sway of her hips and the lightness of her step that was almost like a skip. She did that when she was happy. He'd forgotten.

"The fuel tank cap is on the coffee table in the living room. I'll meet you there in a second. I just want to turn off the stove so dinner doesn't burn."

It wasn't the first time Ethan had been to Maddie's condo. But last time he'd only gotten as far as the kitchen where he'd kissed her. The living room was decorated much like he'd expected it would be. Light, minimal and homey. There were pictures of her family on the fireplace mantel. The one of her and Denny in high school had Ethan walking right to the fireplace to take a closer look. He picked up the picture and studied it.

Maddie came into the room. "That one was taken about a month before Denny died. Dad just gave it to me the other night. I think that one is my favorite."

"It's beautiful."

Her mouth seemed to tremble as she spoke. "There's one of you and Denny, too."

She walked to the fireplace, pulled a smaller frame out from the crowded mantel and handed it to him. Tears stung his eyes as Ethan looked at the picture of his best friend with his arm wrapped around his shoulder.

"He loved you," she said. "I had a hard time admitting that for a long time. You know, I really hated you taking me to the cliffs. But I'm glad you told me what really happened. I wasn't fair to you." She placed her hands on her cheeks as they flamed with color. "The way I treated you at the funeral. I hit you. I'm so ashamed of the way I behaved."

He put the picture back in its place. "You were grieving. People grieve different," he said, recalling the words Logan had said to him in the garage.

"I … just never once thought that you were grieving as deeply for him as I was. I should have known. That kind of grief never really goes away."

"It's okay."

She sniffed back a few tears and then smiled. "Come see?"

Maddie led him to the table near the window where she'd worked on the fuel tank cap. Ethan knew she'd put everything into her artwork. But he didn't expect to see the amazing picture she'd created. Instead of painting the picture that she'd originally done in the sketch, she'd surprised him.

"You changed it."

Maddie shrugged. "You said Denny thought the cliffs were the closest thing to heaven he'd ever seen. I admit I cried a lot of tears while painting this, thinking of what he saw when he looked out at that view. But I think he would have liked this better. Don't you think?"

"He would have been blown away by what you created. I know I am."

Ethan crouched down to get a closer look at all the detail Maddie had put into the project. She'd put every bit of her heart and soul into this project.

"Ethan?"

He stood up with the sound of her voice. "Thank you for pushing me. I feel ... so light, like this huge weight has been lifted from me."

He smiled. "I'm glad." He bent his head to kiss her on the cheek, but she turned at the last minute and their lips met, igniting a fire so strong deep inside him, he thought he'd explode.

Maddie leaned into the kiss, holding nothing back, much as she had done when creating her masterpiece. She wrapped her arms around him, and he could have easily pulled himself away. But he didn't want to. Something about being in Maddie's arms felt like coming home.

She pulled away just long enough to gaze into his eyes.

"You are so beautiful."

Her smile was so radiant, it took his breath away.

"I thought you'd never notice."

"You weren't paying attention. I always noticed everything about you."

"Like?"

"You have a scar on your eyebrow from when you fell and hit your head on the coffee table."

Her hand went to her head. She ran her fingers over the spot he was talking about. "How did you know that? You didn't even know Denny then."

"Denny told me he pushed you because you were taking too long jumping off the couch. He felt guilty."

"I don't want to talk about Denny right now."

"You don't?"

"I want to talk about you."

"What about me?"

She gazed up at him, running her hands slowly up his chest and over his shoulders until she laced her fingers at the base of his neck.

"Do I really have to spell this out? Because I will."

"We don't have to talk at all."

She smiled, reaching up on her toes and kissing him softly. "I like that idea. I like it a lot."

She stepped back and reached out her arm to take his hand, and his body kicked into overdrive. In all his life, he'd never wanted anything as much as he wanted Maddie right now.

♥ ♥ ♥

Maddie's heart pounded in her chest as Ethan followed her upstairs to her bedroom. She'd dreamed of making love to Ethan a thousand times in her youth. That dream had faded, never to be replaced with anyone else who came close to how she felt about Ethan.

She stopped by the bed and turned to him. If she lived to be a hundred, she'd never forget seeing that smoldering flame burning in his eyes. The fire he felt for her.

She slowly lifted her arms and waited. Not missing a beat, Ethan grasped her shirt from the bottom and pulled it over her head, leaving her wearing her bra. She reached back and unclasped it, watching his face as her breasts spilled out of the fabric, and her bra fell to the floor. She heard his sharp intake of breath along with the pounding of her pulse in her ear. Still, she held his gaze and went the final step, unzipping her cutoff jeans and dropping them to the floor, showing him she wasn't wearing any underwear.

He smiled with the discovery.

"I'm afraid you're overdressed for the occasion."

"Something I'm going to rectify right now."

Ethan quickly rid himself of his clothes and joined her on the bed. Their hot bodies melted together and moved in rhythm, stroking, tasting, caressing, loving each other like there'd be no tomorrow.

And when he finally entered her, Maddie cried out with a pleasure she'd never known. In all her dreams, she never imagined how amazing and loved she'd feel being in Ethan's arms. And when she couldn't take it anymore, he slowed his rhythm, waiting for her to catch her breath again.

He rolled her over so that she was laying on top of him. She moved her hips and began her own rhythmic dance of pleasure, watching his face with every move. His hands were all over her body, caressing her breasts, playing with her nipples, sending wave after wave of pleasure through her body until she could take no more.

Arching her back, he used his fingers to send her over the edge, bringing on an orgasm so strong that she thought she'd split in two. She was only vaguely aware of what was happening when moments later she felt the tension in Ethan's body grow stronger and he, too, joined her.

They silently laid in each other arms for a long time. Maddie wasn't sure exactly how long. But the room gradually began to grow darker and the shadows from the summer moon created lines on the walls around them. Then they made love again, giving in to a wild hunger they'd denied for so long.

"You don't really have to go so soon, do you?" Maddie said, resting her chin on Ethan's chest. He didn't want to leave her arms. His choice would be to stay in bed all day and make love until hunger for the dinner Maddie had left on the stove pulled them downstairs.

"I have to work and then finish putting the motorcycle together."

"Want me to help?"

He smiled down at her. "You'll be too much of a distraction."

She chuckled sleepily. "I see. My competition was never my brother. It was this motorcycle."

"Not even in the same ballpark. I'd much rather stay here with you. But ..." He climbed out of bed and searched the floor for his clothes.

"I know. I'll leave you alone. You're not hiding anything else from me, are you?"

"Now that you've seen me naked, it's hard to hide anything."

She laughed.

"I want to finish the motorcycle and bring it by your parents' house."

"The Sturgis rally is starting in a few days."

He sighed. "I'm not going."

She sat up in bed, unabashedly exposing her naked breasts to him. "Why?"

"I've changed my mind. It just doesn't feel right going alone." He pulled on his jeans and zipped them quickly. "But the motorcycle will be finished, and your parents can do whatever it is that they want to do with it. Hopefully, it will be enough to help give them closure about Denny's death."

Maddie pulled the sheet up to cover herself. "Are you ever going to tell them what you told me?"

"I don't know. Maybe someday. I just don't see how it will help. Like you, I think they already knew Denny was on the edge. They don't need me to tell them the details."

He got dressed quickly and gave Maddie a kiss before leaving. As he drove back to the house, his head felt heavy with thoughts and turmoil. Denny was gone. He couldn't think about what his friend would feel about Ethan and Maddie. Life had to go on.

In his heart he believed that. It was what had driven him for so many years while he served in the military. But something had changed, and he couldn't quite figure out what was holding him back. He thought that telling Maddie the truth about what happened the day Denny died would be liberating for both of them. And for Maddie, it seemed it had.

They'd shared the most amazing night together. He wouldn't change it for anything in the world. He just couldn't shake the aching feeling of dread that settled deep in his gut as he drove back home that when this motorcycle was finally finished, it would all end. Maddie wouldn't see him as a hero like Denny had. She'd see that he was just a flawed man who loved her. And he was terrified that it wasn't enough.

Chapter Ten

"It looks good," Kate McKinnon said, standing just inside the garage.

"I didn't hear you come in."

"I didn't think you did. You were so engrossed on your task."

Ethan looked up as his mother came closer. She was dressed for work. In her hand was a folder, the same one he'd seen her take to work every morning since he was a kid, and most likely contained orders for the next week's inventory, details she'd pored over before going to sleep every night.

"You did a beautiful job putting that motorcycle together."

He smiled at the compliment.

"So when are you leaving for Sturgis?"

"I'm not going."

She looked at him surprised. "What? I thought that's what you were working so hard for."

"It doesn't seem right. I'm going to bring the bike over to the Newtons' later. Maddie is going to meet me there so she can see it. But I'm just going to take it for a spin first."

"You didn't come home last night."

Ethan lifted his eyes to his mother. "Let's not go there."

Kate smiled and then shrugged. "A mother notices."

He leaned back on the bench next to where he was working. "You ever wonder why you married Dad?"

She gave him a strange look. "That's an odd question for a man who just said he didn't want to go there."

"No, really, tell me."

She placed her free hand on her hips. "You already know why."

"His money, right?"

She made a disgusted face. "Please. That's why I opened a diner in town. No, I loved his confidence and determination. It made me want more and push for more. You have a lot of that in you, you know," she said, stopping for a moment to sigh. "There was something about your father that I couldn't forget."

"Like what?"

She gave him an odd look. "I don't know exactly. Some things you just can't define. They just are. There starts to be a point when you can't imagine yourself with anyone else."

"Yeah?"

She sighed. "So I married him. All things considered, I think it worked out pretty well, don't you?"

His mother bent over and took a closer look at the motorcycle. "Maddie's artwork is exquisite."

Exquisite. He remembered thinking that was exactly what Maddie had grown up to become. An exquisite woman. She had a love so strong it was hard to ignore.

Kate placed a hand onto his shoulder. "You grew up with a strong woman as your mother. I'll never understand how my boys became so stupid when it comes to women."

He chuckled. "Thanks a lot."

"You're welcome. You know what you have to do. So go do it. I don't want to have to give you the boot."

Ethan looked at his mother. "I may have ruined a good friendship."

"Or … laid the foundation for a good marriage. It's all in the way you look at it, dear." She smiled, then added, "I have to get to the diner. I think I've left Skylar on her own long enough."

"What would you do without Skylar," he teased, mimicking the words Kate McKinnon said on a daily basis regarding the woman who helped her at the diner.

"Don't be fresh. Skylar is like the daughter I never had. She's a breath of fresh air after dealing with all you McKinnon men."

As she walked away, his mother added, "Remember what I said. Life is just too short not to grasp every bit of happiness you can get."

♥ ♥ ♥

It was a good thing Maddie had stopped by the diner on the way to her parents' house. Kate McKinnon was always pleasant to Maddie, but today Ethan's mom took it upon herself to pull her aside when she'd ordered a cup of coffee to go. After their brief conversation, Maddie knew exactly where to find Ethan.

The drive out to the Nolan farm wasn't all that far. Maddie knew that Logan's place was a few miles down from the Nolan farm, but his property didn't sustain nearly as much damage as the Nolan property did in the ice storms over the winter. As she drove, the road showed signs of new repair. The flooding was heavier at this end of town, but the views of the river were spectacular, especially at sunset. Maddie was sure this was the reason why Ethan had wanted to buy the Nolan property so badly.

She pulled into what was once the driveway. Then she saw it. Ethan had parked the motorcycle right next to what was left of the concrete foundation. Debris was still scattered all over the yard from the river depositing everything it took with it wherever it landed. There was a large boulder right on the river's edge, and that's where she spotted Ethan.

She parked the car, and a few minutes later she was dodging rocks and pieces of plywood and insulation that had been pulled from the house when the river claimed it. Ethan sat on the rock, looking out at the water and banks on the other side, unaware of her approach.

"I didn't realize the house was completely washed away," she said, startling Ethan. He quickly turned to the sound of Maddie's voice.

She smiled at him, cocking her head to one side as she walked down the slight embankment towards him. "Something told me I'd find you here."

"Yeah, there's something about this place that always felt like ..."

"Gives you peace?"

He shrugged. "Helps me think. The world doesn't seem so crazy here."

"Is this the closest to heaven that you feel?"

He looked at her for a lingering moment.

"When I'm with you I feel that way."

She couldn't help but smile. When Ethan had left her condo the other morning, she'd actually thought he was having reservations about making love with her. How he could think that what they'd shared was anything but right was beyond her thinking.

"The For Sale sign is still out front."

"The house is gone, but it's still a great place to make a home."

"Then you should do it."

Ethan shook his head. "Maybe I'll work on a house someday. But right now ..."

"What?"

"This could be a great home for someone," he said, looking around the property. He jumped off the boulder and walked over to her. "I had big plans to fix what had been broken. But this is unfixable."

"Some things are. You can't go back and make everything right. But you can start over, make it brand-new."

"It's not the same."

"It's never going to be the same."

"Are we talking about the house?"

She shrugged, then took his hand. "Ethan, you didn't kill Denny. His illness did. I shouldn't have blamed you for it all those years. But you shouldn't blame yourself or think that you need to live up to his expectations of you. There's no reason you shouldn't be happy living *your* life. Whatever it is *you* choose. I made that mistake myself. No more."

He took in a deep breath and looked around. "A house isn't a home unless you have someone to share it with, Maddie."

"Is that a proposal?"

He chuckled. "You don't exactly move slow, do you?"

"I've waited to live my dream for a long time. I can wait longer if I have to. I just know I want to be with you."

"I don't want to cause you any more pain, Maddie. I don't want every time you look at me to be a reminder of what happened to Denny."

"When I look at you, Ethan, I see you. I always have. You said yourself that you can't change the past. As much as I want Denny back in our lives, it wouldn't change what I felt for you then … or what I feel for you now. So let's start brand new. Let's build this home from scratch and make new memories for us."

Ethan's heart hammered in his chest. He was almost afraid of hoping for something that she didn't mean. It amazed him how much clarity he'd had in the last few weeks. And the one thing he knew for sure was that he couldn't live without Maddie Newton.

She came impossibly close to him. He could smell the fresh scent of the soap she'd used from her morning shower. Her hair shone in the afternoon sun, and her eyes sparkled with amusement as she looked up at him.

She reached up and brushed her fingers against his cheek. He leaned into her touch wanting so much more than the simple connection. He wanted to kiss her and hold her in his arms. He wanted that every day of his life and couldn't believe it had taken them this long to see it.

"You know I love you," she whispered. "I've always loved you, Ethan."

He scooped her up in his arms and held her tight against his body. Bending his head, he claimed her mouth with his, kissing her fiercely with every bit of emotion he had in his soul.

He recalled the words his mother used when talking about his father. *There starts to be a point when you can't imagine yourself with anyone else.*

"I love you," he whispered against her ear. "I don't know how I'll live another moment if you're not with me, Maddie."

"You know, I've always heard that the right woman could tame a wild man's heart."

He laughed and spun her around. "Well, you certainly did that to me. Marry me, Maddie. I never want to know what it's like to not have you with me."

"I guess we're going to have to finish the Wounded Veterans Center real soon," she said, looking at him directly.

"Why?"

"Because there are a lot of McKinnon weddings lined up waiting to happen there."

"Does that mean I can take your answer as being yes?"

"You bet," she said, wrapping her arms around him. "On one condition."

"What's that?"

"We go to Sturgis."

Confused, he said, "I thought you wanted nothing to do with Sturgis?"

"I didn't. But that motorcycle is too beautiful not to show off. Look at it, it's incredible. We have to go show it off. We'll just drive up there and ride down Main Street once, just to say we did it."

"Denny would have liked that."

She kissed him. "I think he would have liked us being together, too. But let's not do it for him. Let's do it for us."

Minutes later they climbed on the motorcycle and headed up the highway toward Sturgis. Maddie sat on the back of the bike with her arms wrapped around Ethan. Along the way, other motorcyclists passed them and stared. But Maddie didn't stare back. She knew she had the best of the bunch.

~The End~

HIS DAKOTA BRIDE
Dakota Hearts Series Book Five

Chapter One

The McKinnon clan didn't need a reason to get together and celebrate, but this Labor Day weekend they were going to get one. Homecomings were always a good cause for a party. But this was one homecoming no one was expecting.

He parked his car under a shady tree along the driveway, making note of the fact that there was a pick-up truck parked next to the garage in the spot where he used to park his old sixty-seven mustang. He recognized the truck, although the last time he'd seen Logan McKinnon driving it, the truck had been in better condition.

He paused at the corner of the house and heard laughter filtering through the air. The boisterous laughing he always heard when his brothers were all together. The giggles and shouts of young children he'd yet to meet. It called to him as strong as the smell of food being cooked over an open flame that tickled his senses. But a hunger of another kind was stronger. The voices he heard had been missing from his life for too long. But he listened closely until the female voice that had haunted him grew louder.

"I need to finish up in the kitchen. Hawk, can you give me a minute and then come carry a few things out to the table? No, Kate you put your feet up. You're always serving everyone at the diner. Let me do this."

The screen door on the back deck opened and then shut. With his heart pounding, he walked to the front door so he could have the precious few moments alone with her before the rest of the family converged on him. He needed those few moments.

His old key still fit the lock on the front door. Turning the knob slowly, he pushed the door open quietly and stepped into the foyer. He glanced into the living room, taking in every detail and exchanging what was different with what he'd committed to memory long ago. The familiar smell of the house magnified the realization that he had finally made it. *He was home.*

He didn't want to scare her. He could only imagine her reaction when she saw him. So he slipped through the living room and into the kitchen through the dining room so he wouldn't startle her. And when he finally saw her, he thought his legs would crumble beneath him.

Skylar Barnett. If there truly was just one great love in the universe for every person, Skylar was surely his.

She buzzed around the kitchen, almost dancing on the balls of her feet as she moved. He used to say she looked like a ballerina, dancing as she walked in the sand. She'd told him it was only because he made her happy.

"I heard the front door. Did I lock the screen door on you by accident again, Hawk?" Skylar asked, licking her fingers of the dressing she'd just stirred in the bowl. "This potato salad has to get into the ice bowl on the table or it will spoil in this heat."

She turned in the opposite direction towards the refrigerator, opened it, and then pulled out a bottle. "Oh, and I forgot the Italian dressing for the salad. Would you mind bringing that with you, too?"

She still hadn't lifted her gaze to him. And he didn't rush to get her attention. He enjoyed just watching her move. He'd always loved the way she moved as she rushed from one side of the kitchen to the next.

Picking up the bowl of potato salad from the counter, she turned to him, her smile as bright as the blazing sun outside, and said, "Those barbecue ribs your dad has on the grill smell so good, it's making me ..."

Their eyes met for the first time in over five years and she gasped. He should have done something to prevent the bowl of food in her hand from slipping through her grip and crashing to the floor. The bowl shattered, and the potato salad splattered on the tile floor and the cabinet Skylar was standing near. She barely noticed the remnants of the mess at her feet.

"I'm not Hawk," he said, never taking his eyes off hers.

Her mouth dropped open as tears welled up in her eyes. "Wade?"

He barely heard the words escape her lips, but he felt them just as strong as he had the last time they'd been together. The memory of what it tasted like to kiss her, and that small intake of breath she made before her lips touched his.

"Is it really you?"

Her voice was a whisper and surged him forward. He took a slow step toward her as she took in seeing him for the first time in years. Her hand came up to touch his face but stopped short before making contact.

He leaned closer, giving her access to reach him without overwhelming her. When she still didn't touch him, he took her small hand in his and pressed it against his cheek.

"Flesh and blood, sweetheart."

He'd had years to dream about this day. He'd waited until the time was right, agonized over the best way, and played this moment in his mind a thousand times. And yet, nothing prepared him for what it would be like to touch Skylar again.

Tears streamed down her cheeks. She did nothing to wipe them clean.

"Wha ... where have you been?" A sob escaped her lips before she could finish.

"We have plenty of time for that. I just want to hold you now for a minute." And then he slipped his arms around her waist and pulled her close against his chest. The heat of her body penetrated the thin fabric of his shirt, bringing back memories of their burning lovemaking on a hot evening.

Her sob against his neck tugged at his gut. "I've missed you so much. How can this be happening?"

"It's happening. It's real. I'm never leaving you again."

"What the hell took you so long? When they couldn't find you after the tsunami, I called everyone we knew in the Peace Corp. They said there was no trace of you at all. Then your father used whatever connections he had and called every hospital in the region."

"I wasn't in the hospital."

"I heard lots of stories where people had amnesia because of head injuries. They didn't know who they were. I can't imagine what that was like."

He pulled back just a little to look at her face. The last thing he wanted to do now was lie to her. "That's not what happened. I didn't have amnesia."

"Then ... where were you? Why didn't you follow me here like you said you would?"

"It wasn't safe."

"Of course it wasn't safe. There was a tsunami, for God's sake! That small village we stayed at was washed away by the tide. And all this time I thought you were washed away with it. You know we lost six people from our group that day."

"I know."

"You know." She touched his face and searched his eyes for answers. "Wade, what happened to you? Where have you been?"

"Do you remember me telling you that I was involved in something dangerous?"

"Of course. That was the reason you wanted me to leave the island so quickly. You told me not to tell a soul until you came back and that you'd explain everything then. Oh, my God, are you telling me you were in prison? Couldn't the State Department have helped you get word to us?"

She hugged him tight.

"There was no way I could get word to you. Not at first."

"At first. What does that mean? Why couldn't you have gotten word to me? For God's sake, why didn't you get word to your parents?"

"You have to believe me that I wanted to. But it was impossible."

"I don't understand, Wade. What happened to you? Where have you been all this time?"

"Watching you."

Her mouth dropped open. "Watching? For how long?"

"Ever since you came to South Dakota. I know about Jay, Skylar."

The screen door creaked. Skylar abruptly pulled away from Wade, leaving him cold. Her eyes widened with confusion and anger as she stared at him. She turned her gaze toward the doorway, placing a hand on her chest. "I … ah … dropped the bowl."

Wade turned to see which McKinnon Skylar was talking to, and his heart filled with emotion beyond capacity when he recognized his best friend and brother Hawk standing there. Hawk didn't look at Skylar or the mess on the floor around her feet that she'd just confessed to making. Instead, his brother had the same confused expression Skylar had greeted him with.

"Wade?"

The next moments were a blur filled with lots of tears and hugs and jumping up and down as Hawk pulled Wade outside into the yard and announced his return to the family. Each of the McKinnons ran to greet him. The moment that was most difficult was seeing his mother and how much the news of his death had worn her down. She still had the twinkle in her eyes, but the years had taken a toll.

"My boy is home," Kate said through sobs, pulling him into an embrace. "I have all my boys again."

His father wrapped his arms around both Kate and Wade and gave them a long hug. "Now I believe in miracles," he said.

They made quick introduction of all the new people in the McKinnon family. Although Wade had been watching closely to make sure his family had been safe, he knew none of the details that changed the dynamics of his family.

He quickly learned that Hawk, the closest in age to him, was now engaged to Regis, a beautiful woman who'd traveled the world with her father while he was in the military. His family as well as Hawk had won her over, and now Regis was determined to dig some roots for the first time in her life here in Rudolph.

Wade had known for some time that Logan had lost his wife, Kelly, nearly two years ago and that in the time he'd been gone, they'd had a son who was now five years old. But he was equally pleased to see that Logan's old flame, Poppy Ericksen, had healed Logan's broken heart. A wedding was already being planned for the end of the year.

Wade didn't think he'd ever seen Ethan, Logan's twin, in love before. But after a stellar military career as a Navy SEAL where he dealt with the tragic death of his best friend, Denny, he'd managed to capture the heart of Denny's younger sister, Maddie. Whatever ghosts had been haunting his brother all these years were now gone.

But the biggest surprise of all had been Sam, who'd always had a passion for women and for fighting fires. He'd met his match with Summer Bigelow, a dispatcher who'd moved to South Dakota from Providence. He soon learned that the two of them had taken up residence in his old room above the garage.

As he moved through the crowd of family, Wade stopped in front of Logan and peered down at the young boy who had wrapped himself around Logan's leg.

"I know who this little man is," Wade said. "But does he know who I am?"

Little Keith half hid himself from view. "Daddy says you're Uncle Wade," he said in a small voice.

Wade laughed as he crouched down. "That's right." He held out his hand to shake Keith's. Keith glanced up at Logan who gave him the okay. Keith reached out and gave Wade a hard shake of his hand.

Wade tried to act surprised by Keith's grip. "Wow, he's a McKinnon all right."

"And who's this little guy in Auntie Poppy's arms?" The little boy buried his face in Poppy's neck, hiding from his view. Wade already knew the little boy's name. He'd done his homework before deciding to finally come home.

Hawk tried to pull the boy from Poppy's arms, but the little guy wouldn't budge. Then Hawk turned to Wade and said, "This is Alex. Skylar's son."

Looking around, it suddenly dawned on Wade that he hadn't seen Skylar in a while.

"Where did Skylar go?"

"I don't know," Poppy said. "Alex didn't want to leave, so I said I'd take him for the night. Then she ran out."

His stomach sank. "Wait, she just left? Where did she go?"

His mother's eyes probed his face. She must have sensed the unrest in him from his reaction. She said to Poppy, "Why don't you bring the boys to the table for something to eat. I'm sure they're hungry after all this excitement."

Poppy lowered Alex to the ground and took both Alex and Keith by the hand. "Sounds like a good idea. Let's go see if Grandpa saved the hamburgers from burning. If not, we'll skip lunch and eat some watermelon first."

Both of the boys yelled, "Yeah!" Then they pulled from her grip and ran to the other side of the yard where the picnic table was set up.

Kate waited until the boys were fully out of earshot. "What's going on, Wade?"

He watched the two boys laughing as they climbed onto the picnic table, sitting next to each other. "They could be brothers."

Hawk took a deep breath and placed a hand on Wade's shoulder. "Close. They're cousins."

Kate's eyes widened with surprise. "What?"

Wade stared at Hawk's face to see if he was serious, to confirm what he'd long suspected, but didn't know as fact.

Hawk nodded. "Alex is your son, Wade."

Chapter Two

Skylar sat on the edge of the bed she'd shared while married to a man she never should have married. Her heart pounded so strong and fast that she thought her chest would burst open.

Wade was alive. He was *here.*

The day she'd heard Wade had been lost during the tsunami, she thought her world had shattered. It had taken so long to feel steady on her feet again. Seeing Wade again, learning he'd always had the power to come back to her felt as if she'd been hit with a tidal wave herself.

I've been watching you. Ever since she'd come to South Dakota, Wade had been watching her every move. He'd known that she was pregnant. He had to know it was his baby. He had watched while she'd married another man. And he'd said nothing. Done nothing to let her know that he was alive.

Skylar buried her face in her hands, not wanting to think about those dark days surrounding the aftermath of the tsunami. The phone call from her former colleague telling her that the island had practically been wiped off the map and the loss of life was catastrophic seemed like it was yesterday.

She looked around her bedroom and tried to breathe steady. She couldn't cry. She couldn't connect all the pieces of the last five years and make them fit into anything that made sense. She'd loved a man and lost him. She'd married another man and divorced him. Both had been devastating. And none of it ever had to happen. How many women could look back at their life and say that their heartache was completely avoidable?

Jay hadn't taken anything with him but his clothes when he'd left. He wanted nothing in the divorce. He'd insisted there was nothing left in Rudolph for him anyway, and nothing worth taking.

Sadly, Skylar had taken that to mean Alex, too. Jay had done nothing to fight for Alex. Not even to set up a visitation schedule. Not to discuss his birthday, or Christmas, or talk about his first day of kindergarten. Alex was the reason she'd married Jay in the first place. She'd wanted him to have a father. But he'd just checked out of their lives.

And so had Wade. But the difference between Jay and Wade was that Skylar never did love Jay. She had tried. But somehow the marriage she had pieced together out of necessity never ended up being a marriage of love. She didn't blame Jay for leaving or for being bitter.

Anger simmered inside of Skylar, bubbling up her throat until she thought it would choke her. Feeling the movement in her lap, she looked down and realized her hands were trembling.

What had just happened? One moment she was scooping potato salad into a ceramic bowl, getting ready to enjoy a late afternoon barbecue with her favorite people. The next moment she'd been transformed back to a time when life had promise, and she'd looked forward to a future with a man she'd fallen helplessly in love with the moment she'd looked into his blue eyes.

She tightened her fist in her lap and then opened her fingers, shaking out the pain she'd caused. And then panic struck her hard in the chest. She'd left Alex at the barbecue with Poppy. Alex would be well cared for. He always was when he was with a McKinnon. After all, they were family even if they didn't know it. From the moment Alex had been born, Kate McKinnon had referred to Alex and Keith as Irish twins, born just a few months apart and always inseparable. She'd said the two boys always reminded her of her twins, Logan and Ethan, the youngest of the McKinnon boys.

Her little boy! He had no idea Wade was his real daddy. How could she tell him the truth when he was still mourning the loss of the father he'd always known?

The phone rang, sending a shrill through the quiet room and shocking Skylar's already fragile senses. It took a second to register what to do. Taking a deep breath, she pulled herself up from the bed and walked to the phone on the nightstand. She barely had the phone to her ear when she heard Kate's voice.

"Skylar? Honey, are you okay?"

Okay? No, she wasn't okay. She didn't know what she was, but she definitely wasn't okay.

"I can't talk, Kate."

"I'm sending Hawk over there to check on you. You looked like you were ready to faint before you ran out."

"Please don't. Tell Hawk I'm fine."

"He's already on his way."

There was a short pause that left Skylar empty. There'd never been uncomfortable feelings between her and Kate. But all that may very well change today when she learned the truth about Alex.

"I don't know what's going on, Skylar. Or what went on. There's plenty of time to sort out all those things. But it's going to be okay. My Wade is home again. He'll make it okay."

She wished she could believe that. But so much had happened between the last time she'd seen Wade McKinnon and now. The short time they'd shared together seemed like a lifetime ago. She'd had a child, been married and then divorced. How could anything be okay after all that?

♥ ♥ ♥

Hawk had come and gone from Skylar's house. The address was something Wade had committed to memory a long time ago. All part of making sure both Skylar and Alex were safe, he'd told himself at the time. But as he drove the distance from his parents' house to Skylar's across town, he realized he'd really been waiting for this moment when he could finally come back into her life again.

Alex was snug in bed at Logan and Poppy's house. There was no chance someone would walk in while Wade talked to Skylar. He only hoped she'd open the door and let him get that far.

Wade parked his car behind Skylar's in the driveway and got out, easing the car door closed. After taking the few short strides to the front door, he looked through the window into the kitchen. The light over the sink was on, but the rest of the house was dark. He tried the doorknob and found that the door wasn't locked.

Wade let go a guttural grunt of frustration. "Why not invite the whole damned world in?" he muttered.

Deciding Skylar probably wouldn't have answered the door if he had knocked, he eased himself through the door and slowly stepped into the kitchen. He got three steps into the kitchen when he caught the fast moving shadow on the wall. He ducked just in time to avoid being hit by the object that was aimed at his head. Instead, the airborne shoe slammed against the wall behind him and fell to the floor.

"Skylar, it's me," he said. "It's Wade."

"Get out!"

This time he saw the small vase coming at him. As he ducked, the vase flew past him and crashed against the door. It fell to the floor, breaking into several pieces, much as the bowl of potato salad had earlier.

"I hate you!"

Skylar stepped into the kitchen and turned on the light. She'd never been one to hold her emotion back. Now her face was red with rage. Her eyes were blazing, just the way he'd remembered them. But any chance of a homecoming filled with kisses and the hot lovemaking they used to share instantly evaporated. Still, the unbridled passion in her that he'd always been drawn to was still there.

His lips lifted to a slight grin. "No, you don't. You love me, Sky. You'll always love me."

She pointed a finger at him. "I used to love you. For five years, I didn't even feel like I was living because I loved you so much losing you nearly killed me. Nearly. *Now* I hate you. Get out!"

"Sky."

"Don't you dare even try to get on my good side. Five years, Wade. You *watched* me? You couldn't call? You couldn't send me a note? Hell, I would have settled for a homing pigeon. Something! Anything!"

His stomach burned. "You were married."

Her eyes flared again, but Wade still caught the slight sag in her shoulders. "Don't you dare put this on me. I didn't just run out and get married. I thought you were dead! For four years, I tried to have a marriage where you didn't creep into my mind every time Jay touched me. It's your fault. You destroyed me, and then you destroyed my marriage. All because you selfishly faked your death. Why, Wade? Why did you do that to me? For God's sake, why did you do that to your family?"

"It was too dangerous."

"You keep saying that. But what does that mean? Kate. My God, I can only imagine what she's thinking right now. Do you know she was like a mother to me all this time? I lied to her because you said it was too dangerous. And I believed you. For who, Wade? Who was it dangerous for?"

"All of you." He watched the rise and fall of her chest. "Are you going to throw anything else at me, or can we sit down and talk?"

"I'm not making any promises. And I don't want to sit down. I'm too angry! I've been sitting here in the dark, playing the last five years of my life over in my mind trying to make some sense out of how I could have lived this life and still have you standing here in front of me now. It doesn't make sense, Wade. Help me make sense out of it!"

"I never worked for the Peace Corp," he confessed.

She shook her head. "Of course you did. I was there, remember? We worked together. We were part of the same team."

"I worked for the government. If I could have told you that I was alive, I would have, Skylar."

"I don't believe you. Your brother was a Navy SEAL for eight years. He couldn't tell your parents a lot about what he was doing, but he could at least have gotten word to them if he had to. He wouldn't have let them believe he was dead for five years!"

"If something had gone wrong on any one of Ethan's missions, it may have been different."

"What were you? What are you?"

Wade drew in a deep breath, not sure how much Hawk had managed to tell Skylar before he'd gotten here.

"The Peace Corp is a United States Government Agency. That's why it was easy for me to use it as a cover. But there are some military operations that ... step outside of the boundaries. There've been military personnel working alongside the Peace Corp in delicate regions all over the world for many years. That's what I was doing."

"You told me you were no longer in the military."

"I was officially discharged from the Navy. But not from duty."

She looked at him like he was crazy. "What does that mean? Were you a spy?"

"I worked for a branch of the CIA."

"You were undercover?"

"Yes."

Her bottom lip quivered. "Then what the hell was I? A cover, too?"

His heart melted. He took a step closer to her, wanting to touch her as he had in the kitchen of his parents' home earlier. But she quickly took a step back and folded her arms across her chest.

"You were and have always been the love of my life, Skylar."

Chapter Three

Skylar gave Wade a hard look of disbelief. She couldn't believe what was happening.

"The love of your life?"

"Always."

She clenched a fist and laughed bitterly. "If that were true, then why did you sit back and watch me marry someone else? You said you've been watching since I came to South Dakota. If you'd loved me even half as much as I loved you, if anything we'd shared on that South Pacific island meant anything to you, then you never would have sat back knowing another man was making love to me if you could have stopped it."

He jaw tightened, and she knew she'd hit a nerve, and yet, Skylar didn't care.

"Would it be easier for you to understand if I did have amnesia and couldn't remember who I was until now?"

"Yes."

"It'd be a lie."

"Then lie to me! At least there'd be an explanation I could wrap my mind around. This … I can't."

"What do you want me to say? I'll say it. Just tell me."

She shook her head. Unshed tears hung heavy in her eyes. "I want a truth I can understand."

"I can't give it to you."

Feeling betrayed, she folded her arms across her chest.

"The less you know about what I do, what I did, the better."

"Why were we in danger? At least tell me that."

"Can we sit and talk about this? We used to talk all the time."

And make love. They used to talk and argue and make love. Skylar remembered every moment of it. She'd played it in her mind over and over during her marriage to Jay. Lying awake in bed, she'd listen to Jay's breathing and hug the edge of the bed so he wouldn't cuddle with her. Then she'd lose herself in the memories of dancing naked in her small cabana with her body pressed against Wade's as the breeze from the ocean billowed the curtains and refreshed them after a luxurious night of lovemaking.

Sky looked at the chair pushed against the table as a tear trickled down her cheek. She pulled the chair out, letting the legs scrape against her floor, then eased herself into the seat. Wade sat down in a chair on the opposite side of the table.

With his hands folded on the table in front of him, he said, "The decisions I made were some of the toughest decisions I've ever had to make. But you have to believe me when I say I did it because I love you."

"What happened?"

"The moment I met you, I decided I was done working for the agency. Every moment we shared was real, Sky. Every plan we made to come back to South Dakota and start a family ... I meant all of it. But then I learned through one of my sources that the cover for one of our agents, Adam Calhoun, was blown. In the process, a lot of sensitive information was leaked into the hands of the wrong people."

"Who?"

"It doesn't matter who. What matters is that these are the kind of people who will do anything to take down anyone who crosses them. Calhoun was captured and tortured. He had a wife and a young daughter who lived with his mother and his brothers because he traveled so much. No one was sure how much information he revealed, if any, while he was imprisoned. But they got enough information out of him to warrant keeping him alive in order to get more information."

"That's horrible."

"What little information about the agency that leaked out was just the tip. When these people take someone out, they take out their whole family. They have people all over the world who do their work for them. Anyway, by the time the agency got word of the leak, it was too late. A team was sent to Chicago to protect Calhoun's family, but his two younger brothers and his mother were found dead in their home. They made it look like a burglary. But it was a hit. His wife and daughter disappeared. No one knows if they were killed or if they managed to escape."

He leaned forward, putting his elbows on the table.

"These people don't care how many they kill if they can somehow profit through money or information. If Calhoun had leaked information about me while he'd been tortured, then you and my whole family would have been killed in order to get to me."

"I still don't understand."

"We had no way of knowing how many agents still in the field were at risk. We were all told to disappear until information filtered through our sources. That's when we started making plans to leave the island and come to South Dakota. But about a week before we were supposed to leave, some information surfaced with my name attached to it. It could have only come from Calhoun. Very few people knew the details of some of the missions I'd worked on. But I'd worked with Calhoun on this particular mission, so it was clear Calhoun had been broken and given up information about me.

"I had to get you off the island and somewhere safe. I was trying to figure out a way to protect you all in Rudolph when the tsunami hit the island. Mother Nature provided the perfect cover. If I were dead, there'd be no reason for them to come after you or any of my family. So I disappeared. I figured I'd lay low and wait for all the details to emerge. And it worked. Everyone bought my death."

"Yeah, it worked a little too good, Wade. The only problem is, you never came back."

"By the time it was safe for me to come home, I'd learned you'd married Jay."

Anger surged through her as she pushed back from the table and walked to the sink. There were no dishes to wash. No busy work she could do that could deter her from memories that converged on her. She fisted the kitchen towel she always kept folded on the counter for cleaning up quick spills and swung around to look at Wade directly.

"One call could have changed that. I would have waited. You gave me nothing to wait for!"

"Weren't you just listening to me? Calhoun's family was murdered. In all likelihood his wife and daughter were taken hostage or killed. No one knows. I needed to make sure you were safe. Everyone needed to believe I was dead."

"Well, you did good, Wade," she said, "we all bought it. And we all moved on without you. Isn't that the way it's supposed to work? Life goes on? Or did you think everything would just be suspended in time?"

"It was for me."

Skylar squeezed the dish towel she held in her hand. "Well, it wasn't for me. It was hell."

"Sky, listen to me."

"Why?"

He got up from the table and took a step toward her. She put her hands up to stop him. Despite the years that lay empty between them, Skylar remembered with too much familiarity how easy it was for Wade to break her down.

"Don't touch me," she said.

He put his hands up in surrender. "Sky, we loved each other once. I know you still do. I know I do. We just have to find our way back to each other. We can do that now."

She shook her head again, ringing the kitchen towel in her hand so tight her fingers hurt. "I meant what I said, Wade. I used to love you more than anything in the world. So much I thought I died with you. But the truth is, so much has changed since we were together. I'm not the girl you fell in love with in the Peace Corp. That girl believed all those promises you made about our future together. Remember those? That girl is never coming back."

His smile became wider. "Hey, I came back."

She stumbled on the word. "You waited too long to come for me. That girl doesn't exist anymore thanks to grief and a bad marriage."

"Then we'll find her."

"Do you know what I was doing here when I left your parents' house? I was sitting here alone for the longest time, trying to figure out what I've done for myself over the last five years that has been for me. Truly for me. And I couldn't think of one thing. I came to South Dakota because you wanted me here. I stayed here because Hawk convinced me it was the right thing to do. I married Jay because he asked and I thought, why not give Alex a father."

"I'm his father."

"Yeah? That's news to him. He thinks Jay is his father. Are you going to be the one to tell that little boy he's wrong?"

"What are you saying?"

"I'm saying that Alex and I are leaving Rudolph."

"What?"

"Not right away. I can't do that to Kate. She needs to find someone to replace me. And Alex won't be happy leaving his best buddy. But I think it's time. There's too much here that is a reminder of ... of things I don't want to remember."

"You can't leave now, Sky. I just got back."

"Well, I am. I'll probably go back to Massachusetts for a while. My college roommate, Cara, still lives in Boston."

"Boston is a long way from Rudolph. What about Alex?"

"What about him?"

"I have a right to see my son and get to know him. He has a right to know me."

"Biologically, yes, he's your son. Jay isn't considered Alex's father legally because we were married after Alex was born. But to Alex, Jay is his father. He doesn't know anything else. It's already been hard on him since Jay left.

I'm not going to confuse him more by telling him anything different. At least not right away."

The look on Wade's face was heartbreaking. She couldn't have hurt him more if she'd stabbed him in the heart.

"It's a lie."

"No bigger lie than the one you left me with. All this time you were alive, Wade. Every day I thought of you when I looked at Alex. Every day I kept the love I felt for you hidden from everyone because I was scared. I didn't know why I should be scared because you never told me until right now. I thought I'd lost you forever. And all that time you were alive. I know you believe you were protecting us. But I don't know if I can forgive you for what you put me through. I know I can't live here pretending anymore. That's why I have to leave."

Chapter Four

Don McKinnon was sitting on the front porch, looking up at the stars when Wade arrived home. Wade remembered the familiar scene from when he was a teenager. His father was still smoking cigarettes back then, despite Kate McKinnon's constant lectures about good health. But he'd given up that habit long ago. Now he just sat in the quiet and enjoyed the night sky.

Wade parked his car next to the garage where Logan's truck had been earlier. Then he got out and slowly walked to the porch and joined his father.

"I didn't expect you back so soon."

Wade didn't respond. He was still reeling from his talk with Skylar.

"It's not the homecoming you thought it would be, is it, son?"

"No," Wade admitted, looking up at the garage. "It's hard to see how replaceable I've been in everyone's life."

His father gave him a hard look. "Don't you twist this, Wade. Do you have any idea how long it took for any of us to even venture inside that room over the garage? The only reason why your mother agreed to clean it out a few months ago was because Summer needed protection, and Sam and Ethan were right here. You want your old room back? That's easy enough to rectify. Sam and Summer will move into the house tomorrow."

"It's not the room, Dad. I don't care if Sam and Summer stay there."

"Yeah? Well, the other stuff is not going to be so easy to fix." His father looked at the dark windows over the garage where he knew Sam and Summer were sleeping, then back at Wade.

"Hawk filled us in about how he found out about Skylar. I'm surprised she was able to keep it secret for so long. Poor thing has been terrified of a ghost for years. No wonder she ran off earlier."

"I told her everything."

"Yeah? You mind filling your old man in on the details? Because to be quite honest, I'm having a hard time processing everything."

Wade spent the next few minutes explaining in detail what he'd never been able to tell the family before. His father listened without interruption.

"The agency raided the compound where Calhoun was being held captive. The threat was eliminated."

Wade didn't have to elaborate any further for his father to understand his meaning. There was no one left to come after him.

"Skylar didn't move on with her life because she didn't love you, Wade. She moved on because you gave her no other option."

"I was ready to come back sooner. But I couldn't while she was still married to him."

"Him. You can't even say his name. That's not her fault. It wasn't his. Jay isn't a bad man. If you'd known him under different circumstances, you would have liked him. I did."

Even knowing his father was right, it irritated Wade to hear talk about Skylar's ex.

"We all did the best we could," his father said. "Life and death happened while you were gone. Babies were born and people we loved died."

A sense of sadness filled Wade, understanding fully who his dad was talking about. "I wanted to come home for Kelly's funeral. I know Logan and Kelly didn't have the best of marriages, but I know he must have been a wreck when she died."

"He was for a long time. That grandson of mine helped a lot. Keith kept Logan going. Then Poppy came back and things just fit into place."

Wade couldn't help but smile. "I don't think I've ever seen Logan that happy."

"Poppy is a ray of sunshine in that boy's life, for sure. But when Keith was born, he helped us all move forward after we got the news you were missing. All that time we had another grandchild right here. But Skylar never said a word, even though she's so close to your mother."

"It wasn't safe. She didn't know what was going on when she left, but she knew there was danger. I told her not to tell anyone."

"Come on, Wade. This is family. Not some Top Secret CIA file."

"Hawk told me he knew."

His father shrugged slowly. "Hawk always did have a special bond with both Keith and Alex. Now I know why."

"I saw them together at the picnic earlier. My son would rather be with him than me."

"Things changed, Wade. They changed plenty while you were gone. If you want to change it back, you have to be the one to do it. It's not going to come easy." Don was quiet a moment. "There are some things I can't wrap my mind around myself. Ethan was a Navy SEAL. He tried to explain about it to me earlier when you were at Skylar's. All that secrecy with family makes no sense to me."

"If I could have gotten word to you, I would have."

"In the beginning. I can understand that. But after a while you must have known it was safe to come home."

"Skylar had gotten married."

Don's anger rose. "What about your mother? Me? I thank God I'm able to sit with you now. You don't know what it was like for us when we got that call that you were missing and then presumed dead."

"I know."

"Do you?"

"You have every right to be angry. I just couldn't come home. You have to trust me that I couldn't."

"I guess that will have to be enough. Just tell me one last thing."

"What's that?"

"Are you home for good?"

"Yes. I'm not going anywhere."

But from what Skylar told him tonight, she was. Getting her to change her mind and stay was going to be a lot harder than he thought.

♥ ♥ ♥

"What are you doing here? You don't have to be here this morning," Kate said. "I already called Rachel to come in for you."

"There's no need. I need to work, Kate. I have to find normal again." She quickly got to work filling containers with supplies needed for the morning breakfast rush. The smell of freshly baked muffins and cookies Kate had already made hung heavy in the restaurant. Skylar pulled plates off the shelf so she could quickly transfer the goodies from the cooling racks to the display cases in the diner.

Kate placed a hand on her shoulder to slow her down. "You look like you didn't sleep at all last night."

"That's because I didn't."

Skylar stopped what she was doing and turned to Kate. All the questions were there. Skylar knew she'd have to give Kate answers to them. But not now.

Kate finally gave her a wide smile. "It's a big day. The boys are starting school today."

Tears filled Skylar's eyes. "I know. I'm having Poppy and Logan bring Alex here so we can all drive together to afternoon Kindergarten."

Kate laughed. "Good. I brought my camera. Did you lay out Alex's clothes for him? I used to do that with all the boys. Unfortunately, they'd always decide on their own at the last minute that their choice was better than mine, and I'd end up with pictures of them wearing camouflage shirts or clashing plaids."

Skylar chuckled as she put a plate of muffins into the display case to keep them fresh. Kate always had a way of making her smile. "I think I've seen pictures."

"I have about three or four of them on the mantel in the living room."

"I completely forgot about his clothes for the first day of school. I'll call Poppy and see if she can stop by my house and get Alex ready there."

Their daily ritual of getting ready for the morning breakfast run kept Skylar from having to face Kate directly. She hated it. She'd never been uncomfortable with Kate McKinnon in all the time she'd known her. But when Skylar finally lifted her gaze from the gray silverware tray, she saw that Kate's smile was hesitant.

"I'm sure Wade would like to go with you."

She nodded slowly. "I know."

"And we should probably spend some time talking about more than just the first day of school, too."

"I know that, too. Just … not yet. I'm still trying to process everything."

Kate took her hand and squeezed it the way Skylar's mother used to do whenever they'd argued and called a truce. "Okay."

The rest of the morning, Skylar busied herself with work. She was relieved when the first customers started pouring in through the front door of the restaurant. Routine was what she needed. It had gotten her through the pain of her divorce. It would get her through this next phase of her life, however painful it might be.

She'd just gotten finished taking two more orders when she walked into the kitchen and saw Hawk and Wade sitting at the little table in the back of the kitchen where the McKinnon family would come and share a meal during the day while Kate was working. Alex and Keith had sat in those seats hundreds of times over the last few years, waiting while Kate would dote on her boys and cook them a meal while still working at the restaurant. It felt strangely odd and yet familiar to see the two older McKinnon men sitting where she'd always seen the boys.

Wade glanced up at her as she placed the new orders on the clip above the food station, then pressed a button to signal a new order. Their eyes connected for a brief moment until she dragged herself back to working on a food order that was ready to be served.

♥ ♥ ♥

She was dancing on her toes as she moved around the kitchen. Wade watched Skylar move from one station to the next, picking up a tray of food and then disappearing into the dining room. Only then did he turn his attention back to Hawk, just as his mother walked over with the coffee pot. She poured two cups of coffee for the boys.

Touching Wade's cheek, she smiled and asked, "Pancakes or eggs?"

"Just coffee, Mom. Thanks."

Kate gave him a stern look that made Hawk laugh. "You know the rules. I'm making you breakfast."

Although the diner had several cooks working the kitchen, Kate McKinnon had always insisted on making meals for her family herself. This morning was no different. Although he had no appetite, he knew it was important to her to mother him for a while.

"And you thought you were going to get away with that?" Hawk asked, laughing harder.

"At least some things never change." Wade took a sip of coffee and watched the kitchen door. When it opened, he was disappointed to see another waitress walking through the door.

"How did you know?" he asked Hawk.

"About Skylar or about Alex?"

"Both."

"I came home for the memorial service. Sam had just given me the cross you'd given me to hold for you. I put it on the chain with the medallion I found on that camping trip. Skylar saw it."

"It's a cross. There's nothing spectacular about it. There's probably thousands of them just like it."

"Yeah, I know. And if that was all, then I don't think I would have made the connection. But I thought it was strange for someone so new to town to come to a memorial service for a man she'd never met. Everyone waiting in line to get inside knew you or the family, and yet she didn't know anyone. Not one single person. The room at the funeral hall was packed to overflowing, so a lot of people spent a long time outside in the sun waiting to get in. I don't know, it just felt strange to me. Why would she wait like that? And then I thought, maybe she had known you. So I went over to talk to her."

The kitchen door opened again, and Wade could see into the dining room for a split second. Skylar was leaned over the counter talking to a little girl who was all dressed up. He smiled, remembering how Skylar used to be with the kids back on Samoa while in the Peace Corp. She loved working with the children. That hadn't changed.

He blinked as the kitchen door swung shut, bringing his thoughts back to the diner. Hawk seemed oblivious to the fact that Wade's mind had wandered, and just continued his story.

"Anyway, it was so hot that day, and Skylar nearly passed out in line waiting to get in. Being a doctor, someone came to get me so I could make sure she was okay. She told me she thought she was pregnant, so I got her a cup of water from the bubbler inside and helped her to a shady spot under a tree. When I bent down to hand the cup to her, the cross and medallion fell forward and she saw it. She just stared at it for the longest time and cried. The pieces just seemed to fall in place from there."

"Why didn't she tell the family?" He looked at his mother, who was laughing about something, clearly feeling in her element as she prepared their meal. "She's so close to Mom. I'm surprised she didn't at least tell her about Alex."

"Skylar was terrified, Wade. She begged me not to tell anyone. Whatever you told her before she left Samoa was enough to keep her quiet. She was going to leave town. I convinced her to stay as long as I promised to keep her secret. And let me tell you, it was hard keeping something like that from Mom and Dad. But I'd convinced her that South Dakota was as safe as anywhere else in the world as long as no one knew her secret. She never told me what happened to make her so frightened."

"And you never asked?"

"No. I just wanted her to stay, for Mom and Dad's sake. For Alex's sake. You know how Mom is. She treated

Alex just like she treated Keith when they were together. She even let Alex call her Grammie because she knew Skylar was alone, and Alex and Keith were practically joined at the hip once they could walk."

"I imagine Jay wasn't too happy about that."

"He wasn't too happy about a lot of things. That's why they divorced."

"Such as?"

Hawk shook his head. "That's not my place to tell. You need to ask Skylar about that. I've already said too much."

Wade thought about it for a minute. "She's never going to forgive me. She won't even talk to me."

Hawk made a face. "I've never known you to give up on anything. Why start now? She just needs time to get her equilibrium back. Having you come back from the dead was a shock to everyone."

Kate brought over two plates full of food and placed them in front of her boys.

"Thanks, Mom," Wade said.

"Anything for you, sweetheart." Kate bent down and kissed Wade on the cheek before she went back to work.

Hawk rolled his eyes and gave Wade a disgusted look.

Wade chuckled as he picked up his fork. "What? I've always been the favorite."

He only wished Skylar still saw him that way.

Chapter Five

There was no avoiding the inevitable. It may have been nearly six years, but Skylar knew Wade well enough to know he'd sit in that back room all day if it meant he'd get five minutes with her.

It's how he had gotten her to go out with him on their first date. He'd sat under a tree outside the small school she'd been working at for five hours. She'd seen him through the window all day, and when she'd left for the day, curiosity got the better of her.

Wade had watched her walk over to him the whole way. When she finally reached his shady spot under the tree, she asked him if he was lost. He just smiled up at her and said, "Not anymore."

She'd spent the last eighteen hours pushing memories of the two of them aside, only to turn every corner and be flooded with more memories. She hadn't thought of that day in years. Seeing him sitting at the table in the back of the kitchen, playing with a salt and pepper shaker like she'd seen the boys do countless times, it's all she could think about.

Taking the bull by the horns, she walked over to Wade to get the inevitable over with. She grabbed two glasses from the shelf and poured milk into them. As she walked up to the table, Wade looked up at her with surprise.

"I get it," he said before she could utter a word. "You don't want to see me. But what about Alex?"

She placed the two glasses of milk on the table in front of him. He gently placed his hand over hers before she could turn away.

"You don't have to serve me."

"It's not for you. The boys usually have breakfast or lunch here every day and then go play in the back room with the babysitter."

His face brightened. "They do?"

She nodded. "But today is a big day. Alex and Keith have their first day of kindergarten. They will be here any minute. We're going to take pictures of them in the back room and then bring them to school."

"School. Wow. Already?"

"They're five years old. It's time. Anyway, Kate arranged for extra coverage here at the diner, so I'm going to drive over to the school with Poppy and Logan to see both of them off."

His face brightened. "I'll come with you."

She inhaled deeply. "Fine."

Skylar was dying. How could she be this close to Wade and not have everyone in this diner see exactly what she was feeling. She couldn't be this close to him.

Turning on her heels, she walked to the back room where the kids played with a babysitter while Skylar worked. When Logan's late wife was sick, he used to bring Keith here to be near Kate. Once Kelly passed away, Logan continued to bring Keith over to play with Alex to help him get over the loss of his mother.

Wade followed her to the back room. When Skylar and Wade were finally alone, she turned to him.

"I know you were expecting something different from me. But if I've learned anything at all, it's that what's done can't be undone. I'm standing here feeling guilty for something I have no reason to feel guilty about. I didn't do anything wrong by marrying Jay. I shouldn't feel this way, Wade."

"How's that?"

"Like I betrayed you. But I didn't. You left me. And no matter what we shared in the past, these last five years happened and will always stand between us. You can't erase them just because Jay is no longer a part of my life."

"What does that mean?"

"It means that I'd like you to have a relationship with Alex. I think it's important. At least while I'm still here in South Dakota."

"Well, gee, thanks. He's only my son."

She gazed up at him, hoping he'd understand. "But he doesn't know that. You can't just come back here and think you can push Jay out of his life for good. He's a little boy. He won't understand. It was hard enough for him the first time."

He looked stricken. "So what am I supposed to be? Another uncle?"

She heard the bell ring, signaling the food for one of her orders was ready to be served. "I don't know. Maybe. I haven't thought that far ahead."

Color filled Wade's face. He ran his hand over his face and looked up at the ceiling.

"He's not always going to be a little boy, Wade. Someday he'll learn the truth. Can't we just try it this way for now? Just until I get my bearings again? Until we can figure it all out?"

"I can't believe this."

"Well, that makes two of us. There are a lot of things I still can't believe myself."

"Look, I have a lot to do today. Alex is going to play with Keith over at Logan's house after school. The boys have always loved playing together. Logan and Hawk have always treated Alex the way they treat Keith."

His eyes widened in surprise. "Of course they would. Alex is family."

She took a deep breath. "That's probably the easiest way to introduce you into Alex's life. He's comfortable at Logan's. If you want to see him this afternoon, he'll be there. Would that be okay?"

"I guess it will have to be, won't it?"

Skylar started to leave, but he caught her by the arm.

"What about you and me? Have you thought at all about us?"

She eased her arm out of his grip, feeling the weight of tears stinging her eyes. "Wade, you and I stopped being 'us' a long time ago. There is no us anymore."

"She hates me," Wade said. He'd been sitting at the kitchen table, looking at a photo album of pictures of him and his brothers when they were kids. Kate sat across the table with a new photo album open. She had photos of Alex and Keith spread out on the table in front of her. Some were new pictures she'd taken today and she'd had his father print up. Some were from yesterday's Labor Day barbecue.

Kate shook her head. "What you did to her ... What she went through was terrible. I was there for it all, Wade. She was shattered. Even when she said she was marrying Jay, it just didn't feel right. I always knew Alex wasn't Jay's son."

"Do we have to talk about him?"

Kate glanced up from the picture she was pasting to the photo album. "He wasn't a bad man, Wade. And he wasn't mean to Alex. He did treat him different, though. There was never that bond that is so strong between Logan and Keith. And Skylar? Well ..."

Kate sighed, shaking her head as she picked up another picture, scrutinizing it before deciding on a different one. Wade could tell his mother was struggling with something.

"Just say it."

"It was a very difficult time for all of us. I knew Skylar and I were connected through grief. I knew there was someone who broke her heart. She never spoke of it. I just knew. And as we grew closer, I actually hated that man for breaking her heart. She's such a sweet girl." She looked up at him from the pictures and smiled ironically. "Can you believe that? I actually hated him. And all that time it was you."

He deserved his mother's honesty no matter how much it hurt. He'd done all that and more to Skylar. And to his family.

"She's hates me," he said again.

Kate chuckled, then rolled her eyes at the sky. "She's angry,, I'll give you that. And I can't say that I blame her. Part of me wants to put you over my knee like I did when you a boy."

Wade grinned and gave his mother a sidelong glance. "When did you ever put me over your knee?"

"Well, I may not have done it, but you gave me plenty of reasons to want to on a daily basis. And if I wasn't so thrilled to have you home, I'd do it now. You have no idea what it did to us when we thought we'd lost you."

"I'm sorry."

She shook her head. "They're words, Wade. I know you said you have your reasons. I'm sure they were good reasons at the time. I also know I'll probably never understand them as being valid enough for the broken hearts you left here. But if you say you had no choice, then I'll eventually get over it. With Skylar ... you're going to have to work harder there, son."

He looked down at the pictures of him and his brothers in the photo album. When he looked at his face, he saw Alex. *His* son.

"She's leaving."

"She told me."

"I ... don't want her to leave."

"Neither do I, but it's her choice."

"I just met my son. If she leaves, I'll never have a chance to be a father to him. I'll never have another chance with her."

"Then give her a reason to stay."

He hesitated a moment. "I don't know how."

Kate's shoulders sagged as she rolled her eyes. "Sure you do. You got her to fall in love with you once. Just help her remember why."

Chapter Six

"What are you doing here?" Skylar asked.

Wade walked over from the back of the parking lot and leaned his body against her car. "This is the end of the first week of school. It's a big deal. I thought we'd celebrate with some ice cream down at the dairy."

She looked at him skeptically. "You're plying Alex with ice cream?"

"No, I'm plying you with ice cream. I know how much you love maple walnut."

"How would you know? There was never any good ice cream places on that island we stayed on."

"I remember. You said that many times, when you had a craving it was for maple walnut ice cream like you used to get in Vermont. You said it every time you tried to make pineapple papaya ice cream."

She made a disgusted face. "I can't believe you remember that."

"I remember everything." He looked at her for a long moment until the school bell rang, signaling the end of the school day. Within seconds, the doors to the elementary school opened and kids filed outside, walking toward the buses.

"I don't know. I have a lot to do when I get home, Wade."

"I'm surprised you don't work at the school. You were always good with the little ones in Samoa. You used to talk about wanting to get your teaching degree when you got back to the States."

"I couldn't. Alex was too little," she said. "I wanted to spend as much time as possible with him."

Skylar saw Poppy's car pull into the parking lot. There were no free parking spaces now that most of the parents picking up their kids were here. The five buses that would transport the remainder of the school population home were blocking the small parking lot entrance. Poppy parked on the grass, got out of the car and walked over to them.

"We're going to be seeing a lot of each other," she said, watching the faces of all the kids coming out of the school just as Skylar was doing.

"Maybe we should set up a schedule and take turns picking the boys up," Skylar suggested.

"Sure. It might be easier. I can pick them up and drop Alex off at the diner if you're still there. Otherwise, I'll let the kids play and you can pick him up at Logan's when you're ready. There's no need for you to rush."

Skylar wanted to mention that she may not be living in Rudolph for very long, but decided against it. She hadn't even spoken to Cara yet. She had no firm plans. When she had them, she would let everyone know, just as she promised Kate she would do when they'd spoken earlier in the week.

The boys took that moment to come rushing over to them. The backpacks on their backs bounced up and down as they ran. In their hands were pictures they'd colored in class.

"This is for you, Mommy!" Alex said, handing her the picture.

"Thank you, sweetie. It's beautiful. We'll have to put it on the refrigerator when we get home." She turned the picture so Wade could see it. His eyes were immediately drawn to the name Alex had written on the paper. Even though she'd wanted to give Alex Wade's surname, she'd used her maiden name of Barnett on his birth certificate, just to be safe.

"I'm impressed boys," Wade said.

Keith handed his picture to Poppy, who inspected the picture and said, "I think we have a couple of artists here."

Keith smiled at the compliment and then asked, "Can Alex come over today?"

"Not today, Keith. Your dad wanted to take a ride to Rapid City. We'll probably have dinner there."

That seemed to satisfy Keith. He waved to Alex as Poppy led him by the hand to where she'd parked the car. "See you both on Monday!"

Wade waved and then turned to Skylar.

"So? What do you say?" She appreciated that he didn't mention ice cream out loud while Alex was in earshot, giving her the opportunity to shoot down the idea.

"I don't know. I have a lot of packing to do tonight."

His bright expression collapsed. "Already? I thought you said you were staying in Rudolph for a while."

"I am. But there are a lot of things in the house that I've accumulated over the years. I want to sort it all out and get rid of it before we make the move."

"Where are we going?" Alex asked.

"Home," Skylar said, brushing her hand over his head, messing up his hair. Alex giggled in response.

"How about dinner then? I can stop by the market and get something to grill. This way you can work without having to worry about fixing dinner. I can even pick up a half gallon of your favorite i-c-e c-r-e-a-m."

She grunted. "You do know how to get to me."

The smile on Wade's face told her he knew it, too.

He was wearing her down. But Skylar knew the work she had ahead of her, and she was already wiped out from a week of being on an emotional roller coaster.

And it would give Wade more time to spend with Alex. It didn't have to be the two of them. The McKinnon men had always been strong male figures for Alex in his young life. But none of them was his father. That was Wade's role.

"Make sure you pick up a half gallon of mint chocolate chip, too. That's Alex's favorite."

"Is it?"

"Yeah!" Alex said, finally understanding the conversation.

"And don't get vegetables. I have plenty in the garden that I have to use up."

"You still tend a garden?"

"It's not nearly as big as the one we had on Samoa. But you know how it is. Old habits die hard."

"Okay. I'll meet you both at the house in a little while."

She watched Wade as he turned away. His shoulders were still as strong and wide as she'd remembered in her dreams. She'd forgotten just how wide a gait he had when he walked until she saw him pulling the keys to his car out of his denim pocket and rushing across the parking lot.

She looked down at Alex, who was now pulling at her arm.

"Come on, Mom!"

"Okay, okay."

For the past five years, she'd relied on memory when looking at Alex, or the precious pictures Kate had shared with her. But the resemblance between father and son was even more striking than the resemblance everyone always saw between Alex and Keith. One day her little boy would grow up to be a mirror image of Wade.

She led Alex to her car and helped him strap himself into the booster seat in the back, all the while thinking of Wade. That's all she ever seemed to do these days.

A half hour later, she was freshening up while Alex chattered on about how he couldn't sit next to Keith in class because the teacher said they talk too much.

"Then don't talk to him when you're in class, and maybe she'll let you sit next to Keith," she said.

Alex pondered the thought for a moment. "But he's my best friend."

Skylar laughed and proceeded to put colored lip-gloss on. Then she turned her face to the left and then to the right as she inspected herself in the mirror.

When she looked back at Alex, she saw the frown on his face.

"What?"

"You look funny."

"Thank you."

"What's that stuff on your lips?"

The doorbell rang and her pulse quickened. What was she doing? She couldn't remember the last time she'd put makeup on for a man. What did it matter what she looked like tonight?

Glancing at herself in the mirror, she realized it did. She'd put on a fresh pair of blue jeans and a crisp white shirt that she only wore when she wanted to look nice. Most all of her other shirts had stains on them from working in the yard or just doing activities with a young boy who didn't think twice about getting messy.

The doorbell rang again.

"Mom? Someone's at the door."

"It's probably your ... Uncle Wade. Why don't you let him in?"

Alex ran out of the bathroom quickly. Even without his sneakers on, he sounded like a stampede of elephants running down the hall to the door.

Placing a hand over her heart, Skylar took a deep breath. The anger that had sustained her earlier in the week, making her charge like a workhorse through a field, had eased. She needed to give Wade a chance to build a relationship with Alex before she left Rudolph. She only hoped that she wasn't setting their son up for another heartbreak.

She walked out of the bathroom and strode into the kitchen with more confidence than she felt inside. Her nerves were frazzled, but she kept her hands tucked into the pockets of her jeans to help steady them.

Alex was standing on a chair at the kitchen table helping Wade take items out of the shopping bags he'd just brought.

"What's all this?" she asked.

"We have ice cream!" Alex said, his eyes bright with excitement. "Uncle Wade brought chocolate sauce and whipped cream, too."

She chuckled and glanced at Wade. "You scored some major points there."

"With which one of you?"

"Both."

He looked at her for a lingering moment, noticing the wardrobe change she'd made and perhaps even the small extra step she took in applying some makeup, something she normally didn't do. She knew Wade too well to imagine the thoughts running through his mind.

He lifted his eyebrows with a smile. "You look nice."

"She put red stuff on her lips," Alex added without looking up from the bag he was emptying.

"It's called lip-gloss." She gave a little shrug, slightly embarrassed by how obvious her transformation had been. "It's supposed to protect the lips from the sun."

Wade's gaze dropped to her lips, and he gave her a slight grin. "Very nice."

Heat filled her cheeks. "Alex, why don't you show Uncle Wade where the grill is outside? I'll make a salad."

Within minutes, she was standing at the counter with an assortment of washed vegetables in front of her. The kitchen window was open. An early September breeze made her white linen curtains billow. As she cut vegetables on the bamboo cutting board, she heard the chatter of a deep male voice and a high-pitched young boy's voice as they got to know each other.

For a moment, Skylar's world seemed to be suspended. It was almost as if she were living the fairy tale she'd dreamed of so long ago. And yet, reality slapped her in the face when she looked around the kitchen and realized where she was.

Buying this house had been Jay's idea. He'd wanted to give her a home as a way to tempt her into marrying him. But when he'd left, he'd wanted nothing of it or from it.

She pushed thoughts of her ex-husband aside as she cut the carrots and red bell peppers she was putting in the salad. That was her past, and she wanted to keep it there. She didn't want it to intrude on her evening. She could allow herself at least one evening with Wade and her son, and cherish what could have been with them if things had been different.

They sat down to dinner, and Alex regaled both of them with the wonders of being in kindergarten and how hard it was. Little Susan Weston didn't like to share the blocks and kept throwing them at Keith. Alex felt the need to defend his friend. But that resulted with the teacher shutting down the block station, which in Alex's opinion, was utterly unfair.

He seemed to get over that travesty quickly while they were making hot fudge sundaes with mint chocolate chip ice cream, and instead announced how cool it was that he and Keith would have recess every single day. As Alex sat in front of the television, eating his ice cream and watching his favorite DVD, the house was finally quiet.

Skylar took that time to finish cleaning up the dishes and let the boys have more one-on-one time. But as she turned on the faucet and filled the sink with hot, soapy water, Wade came up behind her. She felt the heat of his body first, coming in close, but not touching her.

"He's amazing," Wade said. She could hear the pride in his voice. "He could only have become this amazing because of you."

It was something so simple, and yet Wade's validation for the job she'd done with their son meant the world to her.

She turned off the water and turned around. Wade was impossibly close to her, making all her senses come alive. She had no willpower with him. She never did.

Clearing her throat, she moved around him to the table where the ice cream cartons were still open. She closed them and used a paper towel to clean the drippings on the outside of the box. Then she put them away in the freezer.

"You're more beautiful than I remember, Sky."

"Please don't do this."

"Do what?"

She needed distance. But after all this time, she didn't want to run. Not like she had the other day.

"You stand there as if no time has passed. As if you understand what I'm feeling."

Chapter Seven

"I do. I have been going through hell without you, Sky."

And she didn't know the half of it.

"You have no idea what my life has been like."

"Then tell me. I want you to share that with me."

Skylar quickly glanced through the doorway into the living room. Alex was sitting on the floor with the bowl of ice cream in his lap. He was totally engrossed in the movie he was watching.

With her voice lowered, she said, "You don't know the half of it, Wade. Jay isn't a monster. I'm the monster. I should have never married him."

"Then why did you?" He hadn't meant his voice to sound so accusing, but from the range of emotions that crossed Skylar's face he realized it had.

Looking wounded, she said, "I wanted to have a family. I was *having* a family. All by myself. But I didn't want Alex to grow up without a father."

"Why Jay? You had the whole McKinnon clan to step in and be a father to Alex."

Her eyes blazed. "Don't turn this into something it wasn't. You were dead, Wade. Dead. You know, no passing GO. No collecting two hundred dollars. Game over for us. I realized pretty quickly that it didn't matter who I married. No one was ever going to be you. So why not Jay?" She lowered her voice to a whisper. "I thought he'd be okay with Alex not being his son. I think it surprised even him that he wasn't. He wanted more children. But deep down I knew it was because he wanted a child of his own."

She turned her back to him, picked up the few pieces of silverware left on the table and dropped them into the soapy water in the sink.

"Anyway, he didn't want to be in South Dakota anymore, so he got a job in Casper. He didn't tell me about the new job until he'd accepted it because he knew I wouldn't want to go to Wyoming."

"But he did."

"It was away from here. He did the every-weekend-visit thing for a while. But the drive was tiring. Pretty soon every weekend stretched to every other weekend and then once a month."

Hearing her talk about a man who'd shared her bed was killing Wade. But he hung on every word Skylar said, hungry to understand why they'd drifted so far apart. If he had any chance at all of winning Skylar over again, he had to know what was haunting her now.

"The hard truth of it is that I was relieved when Jay would leave. It was easier to be away from each other than to be together. I didn't have to pretend when he was gone. That's when I realized how unfair I was being to him."

Her heavy sigh should have made him feel bad, but Wade couldn't help but think the reasons Skylar couldn't make her marriage work was because she was still in love with him. That gave him hope, even if Skylar wouldn't.

"He wasn't a bad man. It was all me. I failed our marriage. Anyway, he's engaged to someone else now. I hear she's a nice girl, and my ex-mother-in-law loves her." Skylar laughed, shaking her head.

"What's so funny? She didn't like you?"

"Not at all. Right from the beginning, she'd made up her mind about me. And she was right. I can't really blame her for that."

"You're being too hard on yourself."

"No, I'm not."

Skylar laughed. He realized it was the first time since he'd been home that he'd heard a real laugh from her that wasn't filled with cynicism.

"She's always referred to me as 'the other woman' in his life." Her face changed and the humor that he'd seen moments ago evaporated. "I didn't have a problem with the way she treated me. But she never warmed up to Alex. Kate has always been more of a grandmother to Alex than Jeannine was. It wasn't just the distance. Who knows, maybe she knew it wasn't going to last, and she didn't want to get attached. In any case, she hasn't seen Alex since he was a baby. Alex only remembers them through pictures."

"Did you ever tell Alex about me?"

"No."

"You just pretended I never existed?"

"Jay asked about you once, and I told him. But that was near the end of our marriage. He told me never to talk about it again. Let's face it, there are a whole lot of McKinnons in Rudolph. It's kind of hard to ignore them. I think that's why he wanted to get away from here so badly."

Music from the show that Alex had been watching grew louder, signaling the end of the program.

"I should get him ready for bed and then start my packing.

"Surely you don't need to do any packing tonight. What's the rush?"

"I have to. I just do."

They walked into the living room and found Alex propped up against the sofa. The half empty bowl of ice cream was now soupy and still sitting in his lap, although his hands were barely holding it in place. His head was drooped over, and he was fast asleep.

"The poor guy is wiped out," Wade said, smiling down at him.

"If I get him changed into pajamas now it'll just wake him up, and he'll be up half the night."

"I'll carry him to bed."

Skylar picked up the bowl of ice cream from Alex's lap and rushed to the kitchen. Wade lightly brushed his hand over Alex's head. The boy didn't rouse at all.

Scooping him up in his arms, he carried Alex down the hall to his bedroom. Skylar moved ahead of him, pulling the blanket back so Wade could set him down."

Once he was under the covers, Skylar bent down and kissed his cheek. They quietly left the room and closed the door.

"Thank you," she said as they walked down the hallway. "And thank you for dinner. I think he had a good time."

"I had a good time. But then I always had a good time when I was with you."

She drew in a slow breath. "Yeah, well."

"I should probably go, too, then."

Leaving now was the last thing he wanted to do. But the day had been good. He didn't want to push it too far and ruin what had been wonderful. So he followed Skylar as she walked him to the door. Still, there was one thing he had to know before he left.

"Can I ask you something?"

Her delicate eyebrows drew together. "Sure?"

"Was it hard letting him go?"

Her lips tilted on one side of her mouth. "You mean, Jay?"

He nodded.

She clearly struggled with her answer as she shifted in place. "The truth? No. Admitting that was harder than going through it. He got the job in Wyoming. He wanted me and Alex to go with him. I didn't want to go. It was that simple."

"Was it Wyoming or him?"

She closed her eyes for a brief moment as if she were hiding from ghosts again.

"I hear Wyoming is a beautiful place to live," she said. "But it didn't have what I wanted. It was never going to have what I wanted."

Relief washed through Wade.

"Thank you for that."

"You're welcome."

Wade felt infinitely better as he stepped outside onto the porch. As he looked up at the sky, he said, "Would you look at that moon."

Curious, Skylar followed him out to the porch. The front yard was lit up from a near perfect full moon hanging high in the sky. And Skylar was truly breathtaking under the moonlit sky. But then, her beauty had always taken his breath away.

Skylar looked up at the sky, amazed at the brilliance of the moon. "Wow."

"I love looking up at the stars here in South Dakota. I missed that while I was away. But this moon is drowning out any stars we may have been able to see tonight."

A small ache formed in the center of her chest.

"What are you thinking?" he asked.

"Nothing."

"It's not nothing. Tell me."

She shrugged as memories invaded her mind. "Do you remember when we were on the island and we'd sit out on that old lawn chair with the broken pieces that kept coming unwoven?"

"The one I eventually fell backside first through?"

She laughed, recalling the never-ending quest they'd had to always repair it. "Yeah, that's the one."

"I remember that well. I remember getting stuck with my behind on the cold ground and trying to pull myself out with my legs and arms. But the chair just kept breaking."

Tears filled her eyes as she laughed. "I can't believe that chair held the two of us for so long and then the one time you sat in it alone, it broke."

His rich laugh stirred a longing deep in her belly that was familiar and yet terrified her.

When their laughter calmed, she took a cleansing breath. "You used to say there was nothing like a Dakota sky."

He looked at her directly. His face was so handsome and sure. She'd always loved that confidence in him. She wished she had even an ounce of that now.

"I've been all over this world, and I can honestly say there isn't," he said. "There's nothing like you either, Sky. There's still no one else I'd rather be with."

He reached for her, and to her surprise, she didn't pull away. The memory of the first time Wade had brushed his lips against her after a long midnight walk on the beach consumed her. His arms had enveloped her, yet she could have slipped away from him at any time.

She'd been nervous then. And now Skylar thought about how foolish she'd been to feel that way. Wade McKinnon was the most intoxicating man she'd ever met, and she'd never had anything to fear with him. Especially when she was in his arms.

She reached up, touched his face and traced his lips with her fingers. He kissed each fingertip as she moved them across his mouth. And when her hand settled on his cheek, he bent his head and brought his mouth over hers.

She'd wanted this for so long it was hard to believe it was really happening. She was in Wade McKinnon's arms again.

Skylar abruptly pulled away from him. "This shouldn't happen," she said, out of breath from their kiss. She turned her face away from him with all the strength she had. "Alex is in the house."

"And we're outside on the porch. He can't see us. Besides, lots of married couples kiss in front of their kids. They make love when their children are asleep in the next bedroom. It's not scandalous."

"We're not married."

"We were planning to get married. Just say the word, and we can pick up where we left off, Sky. I'm ready."

"I'm not. Don't make this complicated, Wade. This is already confusing enough for me."

"I want you, Sky. Not just to make love with you. Although I very much want that, I know it's probably too soon. I just want you next to me when we sleep. I want to feel your warm skin. Leaving you the other night nearly killed me." He bent his head and nuzzled her neck, brushing his lips lightly against her skin.

"Please stop. You and I know from experience it won't end there."

He smiled devilishly. "Would that be such a bad thing?"

"Yes."

"Why? We've made love before. Many times. We made a baby. We're wonderful together. You can't deny that."

He'd leaned over and whispered the last words against her ear, tickling her senses, making her light-headed as if she'd been drugged by him. He'd always had that way with her. Damn him!

"Wade, please stop."

Instead of pouting as Jay used to do when she'd refused him, Wade simply leaned against the porch rail and draped his arm on her shoulder.

"In my mind, we've made love a thousand times," she confessed. "But that's where it has to stay. I can't allow myself to go there again, Wade."

"Why not? I can see it every time you look at me. You still love me."

Moisture filled her eyes. "Yeah, I do. That's the sad thing. I wish I had gotten over you."

"Then I don't understand why you're holding back."

"Wade, we can't just pick up where we left off."

She cleared her throat and slipped her hands into the pockets of her denim jeans to keep from reaching out and touching him.

"Why not?"

"You don't want to hear this."

"If it gets us to the place we need to be, then yeah, I do. It's okay. You're safe with me. You can tell me anything."

Skylar shook her head. Thinking these thoughts in her mind was horrible enough. Confessing them seemed so much worse.

"Just say it."

Skylar swallowed to rid herself of the lump in her throat. "I wasn't the wife I should have been. Not in the way it mattered anyway. Every time Jay wanted me, I ..."

She felt his body tense, but he didn't turn away. She almost wished he would.

"It wasn't like with us. When I had sex with Jay, it was just that. Just sex."

Wade shifted uncomfortably as she knew he would.

Lisa Mondello

"Forget it," she said, waving a hand as if that would wipe a slate board clean of all the things she'd just said. "This is what I mean. Too much has gone on."

Before Skylar could go into the house, Wade caught her arm.

"Don't go yet. I want to know. I want to understand this."

The night had turned cooler, and the breeze floating across her skin caused raised goosebumps on her arms.

She took a deep breath and blurted out the very thing that had been haunting her for so long. "I thought of you. Not all the time. Alex kept me busy. My work at the diner, too. But you'd creep into my mind at the most odd times. Sometimes ... during the most intimate of times."

She looked at his face and saw his jaw tighten, telling her he understood her meaning.

"I thought that if I kept my fantasy to myself, it wouldn't matter. But Jay must have known. How could he not have known? I gave him the shell of who I was."

Wade dragged his fingers through his short-cropped hair.

With a heavy sigh, he said, "It doesn't have to be a fantasy anymore. I'm right here."

"That's the problem. I don't know how to separate the two anymore. It wasn't fair to Jay for me to be thinking of you when I was in his arms. I don't want to be in your arms and remember what it was like with Jay."

"It won't be that way with us."

She took a step back toward the kitchen door and just stared at him. Every feature of his face had haunted her for years.

"Are you sure about that? Everything about my time in South Dakota is filled with all these memories that didn't include you. I can't piece what we had together overseas to fit my life here. How can I be with you and not have Jay intrude on what should have always been just us. Look at what it's like with Alex. Jay never wanted to be his daddy but he's still here in Alex's life even if he's not physically here."

"Don't we owe it to ourselves to try?"

"What we had was beautiful. It was special. So much so that it ruined my marriage to Jay. I don't want the ghost of my life with Jay to turn what we had ugly like that. And I'm so afraid it will. There are too many things I can't wipe from my mind. That's why I have to leave. You belong here, Wade. Not me."

She turned and ran into the house before he could reach for her again. She knew that Wade would. And when he did, he'd win her over. At least for tonight.

Chapter Eight

They'd spent the week trying to be "normal." But it quickly became apparent to Skylar that normal was never going to be a part of her life again. At least not while she was in Rudolph.

She'd finally gotten up the nerve to call her college roommate, Cara, and to her surprise, she learned that Cara had gotten married over Labor Day weekend. Although happy for her friend, Skylar couldn't deny the twinge of jealousy she'd felt when she'd learned that the man Cara had married was an old friend who'd reappeared in her life after seventeen years apart. She listened to her friend talk about their romantic and "odd" reunion that Cara's mother had orchestrated. But in the end, Cara realized her mother had been right, and Devin Michaels was the only man that Cara had ever loved.

Skylar understood exactly what Cara was saying.

She was happy for her friend. But now the idea of staying in Boston for a while would need to be revisited. At least for a little while.

She and Wade had fallen into a routine of seeing each other at the diner when Wade would eat meals there and then on the days when Skylar would pick up Alex and Keith from school. Skylar found that she looked forward to seeing Wade, even though she didn't like feeling that way. She tried to keep their time together all about Alex. But she couldn't deny that Wade, in his charming way, was getting under her skin.

And when she was alone at night in her bed, she'd think of him again until memories of her time living there with Jay would intrude on her mind, and she'd force thoughts of Wade into the past.

The next Friday, Wade wasn't at the school when she picked the boys up. She tried to squash her disappointment as she looked around the parking lot. But when Alex and Keith got out of school, and it was clear Wade wasn't coming, she piled the boys into her car and drove over to Logan's ranch. She was surprised to see Wade's car sitting in the driveway.

After parking the car, she climbed out of the driver's seat and opened the back door so the boys could get out. Logan came out of the house with an armful of camping supplies in his arms. Wade suddenly appeared from Logan's barn carrying several fishing poles and a tackle box.

"What's going on?" she asked.

"We're going on an overnight fishing trip," Wade said.

"Where?"

"We're going camping?" Keith asked, running over to Logan.

"Sure are. Right here in the back of the ranch. There's a nice level spot near the river. I finally had a chance to clean out all the debris from the storm. We'll have ourselves a nice campfire and roast marshmallows."

"And make S'mores?" Alex asked.

"He's got your sweet tooth," Wade commented. "Is it okay with you if he camps out with us?"

Alex glanced up at her with pleading eyes.

"Of course. It sounds like fun. But I don't have any of your clothes."

Logan dropped the camping gear he'd been carrying into the back of his truck. "He's the same size as Keith, so he can wear his clothes. I have extra sleeping bags. He'll be fine."

Feeling a little disappointed that she wasn't going to share in the fun activities planned, she said, "I guess I'll spend the night packing and cleaning."

"He's going to be fine," Wade said.

"Oh, I know." She looked at Wade for a long moment and then added, "Well, have fun."

The boys were already climbing onto the back of the truck with excitement. She gave Alex a quick kiss and then waved to the boys as she climbed into her car and drove home. Alone.

♥ ♥ ♥

The only thing to make this overnight complete would be to have Skylar and Poppy join them. But Wade wasn't about to complain. He had some real time with his son, and he'd hoped that their time together would be the start of a real father and son relationship that had been missing in Alex's life.

They drove the truck out to the back of the property and found the perfect camping spot that Logan had cleared. It was far enough away from the water that they wouldn't worry about the boys playing, but close enough that they didn't have to walk far to go fishing. It was already too late in the season to swim.

They unpacked the camping gear, fishing poles and tackle box. But seeing that they were still missing one sleeping bag, Logan drove back to the house to retrieve it while Wade set up the tent. The boys were supposed to help him, but like all young boys, they soon tired of the details of constructing a tent and decided to go in search of worms so they could fish.

He'd just hammered the last stake into the ground that would hold the tent in place when the air around him became eerily quiet. The sound of little boy laughter had faded while he'd set up the tent, and yet he hadn't noticed until just then.

"Alex? Keith?"

It had only been a few seconds. But with little boys, that's all it took. He glanced around the camp. The fishing poles were gone. The tackle box was open and new lures he'd bought to try out were gone.

"You two weren't supposed to go to the river without us," Wade called out as he hastily walked down the short trail toward the water's edge. He shook his head as he saw the two boys on the trail ahead of him, running toward the large boulder Logan had said was the best spot for them to stand while fishing. Alex climbed up the boulder first, holding his fishing pole in one hand. Keith followed.

Wade couldn't help but smile at the unbridled determination both boys had for this adventure. It reminded him of Hawk and himself when they were kids.

"Don't go to the edge of the rock, boys," Wade called out, keeping his voice steady so as not to startle them. "I don't want to have to rescue you two if you fall in the water."

Keith laughed, giving him a look that reminded him of his late sister-in-law, Kelly. Alex took an unsteady step back as he struggled with the fishing pole, making Wade's heart jump in his chest.

"We'll be careful," Alex said, looking up at Wade with a wide smile. Wade saw the stick under Alex's foot before he stepped on it. The stick rolled under Alex's sneaker and made his already unsteady step more unstable, causing him to fall backward.

"Alex!" Wade yelled. But it was too late. Alex tumbled off the boulder onto the hard ground below. The fishing pole was still in his hand when Wade reached him.

Terrified, Keith slowly climbed down from the rock to see if his best buddy was okay.

Alex was momentarily quiet as if the shock of the fall was still stunning him. Wade pulled the fishing pole out of Alex's grip and looked him all over to inspect him. Blood was already pouring down the front of Alex's face, covering his cheek and staining his shirt.

Keith started crying before Alex did, and when Alex saw the blood, he wailed. Wade scooped Alex up in his arms and started running.

"Stay with me, Keith," he called out, looking over his shoulder to make sure his nephew was with him.

Relief filled Wade when he heard Logan running down the trail before he actually saw him.

"Get the truck," Wade yelled to Logan.

The drive to the clinic was a blur. Keith stayed behind with Poppy as Logan drove Wade and Alex to Hawk's clinic. His mother and Skylar were waiting at the clinic when they arrived. When Alex saw Skylar, his wails increased. Wade didn't want to upset Alex any more than he already was, so he stayed in the waiting room while Hawk examined the gash on Alex's head. Skylar stayed with him to keep him calm while the wound was being stitched.

Wade sat in the chair, looking at the blood on his shirt, knowing it was his child's blood and feeling guilty and helpless that he'd done nothing to stop Alex from getting hurt.

"Knock it off," his mother said, settling into the chair next to him. "Why are you beating yourself up about this? You and your brothers have had a million scrapes like this. Hell, Hawk was getting to the point where he knew how to stitch himself up. It's no wonder he became a doctor."

"I should have been watching him closer. I didn't even know they went down to the river."

"Kids do things in the blink of an eye," Kate said, chastising him for his reaction, not his actions. "You said yourself he was standing on the rock with Keith when you got there. He fell right before your eyes. So you tell me what you could have done to prevent it?"

"I don't know. I keep thinking if I hadn't noticed they were gone, he might have fallen into the water and drowned."

"And a meteor can strike us all tomorrow."

He looked at his mother, wondering what she was talking about.

"It's the same thing. Don't look at me like I'm an old, crazy woman. I raised five boys to adulthood. Stuff happens. Boys get into messes. They get scrapes and stitches and broken bones. Lord knows you all had enough of those. If you let yourself think back to how many emergency room visits I had to bring one of you to, then you'll understand that this won't be the last time either of those little boys gets into trouble. This is just the first of many. It's called life."

♥ ♥ ♥

Silence had a way of healing. And sometimes, it had a way of hurting. Skylar looked at Wade while he drove her car back to the house. He'd left his car at Logan's, but Skylar was glad that Wade offered to drive her home so she could sit in the back seat with Alex, who was still clinging to her after getting five stitches in his forehead. Hawk had been quite animated as he stitched up the wound, easing some of the trauma of it all for Alex.

For Skylar, it was a different story. Looking at the worried lines on Wade's face in the rearview mirror as he drove, Skylar knew it was the same for Wade. It always is when it's *your* child. And Alex was Wade's son.

She hadn't been fair to Wade. But life hadn't been fair to any of them. She thought back to the conversation she'd had on the phone with her friend Cara. The one thing she'd taken away from that phone call was that Cara was happy. She'd heard it in the bubbly way Cara spoke. It dawned on Skylar that it had been a long time since she'd ever even considered that notion.

When they got to the house, Alex was so emotionally exhausted that he didn't even argue with Skylar when she got him ready for bed and tucked him in. She went to the kitchen to grab him the glass of water he'd asked for, and by the time she returned, Alex was fast asleep.

Wade was sitting on the sofa with his head in his hands. She was tired. Too tired to keep fighting battles she was creating. Walking up to him, she put her hand on his head and pulled him close to her so his head was nuzzled against her stomach.

"It's not your fault."

He lifted his head to look at her face. "Yeah? He never needed five stitches when you were watching him."

She chuckled. "He gave himself a black eye on the coffee table right in front of me. For a week I felt like I'd been the one to give it to him. He's had plenty of falls and scrapes. There'll be more. Are you going to blame yourself for all of them?"

Wade leaned back on the sofa. "I guess not. It's just, I spent all this time trying to protect the two of you. The one time I had him alone, he nearly loses an eye."

Her mouth dropped open. "Quit being so dramatic! The stitches aren't anywhere near his eye."

"They could have been."

Disgusted, she grunted.

"I should call Logan. He said he'd pick me up here."

She took a deep breath.

"He already called. I told him not to come."

"What?"

"You ... don't have to leave."

Skylar could see Wade spark to life right in front of her. She quickly put up a hand to halt him from moving closer and taking her invitation the wrong way.

"Before you go getting excited about the offer, I'm talking about this couch, not my bed. It's been a trying day, and I can see how wiped out you are. There's no need having Logan come out here and then having you drive all the way back to your house. So just stay here."

His disappointment clouded his expression. She couldn't help but laugh. She shook her head, and under her breath, she said, "You'll never change."

"Not where you're concerned. You ruined me, Sky. I haven't been with another woman since the last time we were together in Samoa."

His blue eyes were beautiful as he gazed up at her. She remembered them so well. The sincerity of his words made them hard to ignore. She shifted uncomfortably where she stood, unable to squash the flash of guilt that she felt.

"Don't. This was my choice. Even after I learned you got married, I didn't want to be with another woman. No one was you."

"You had all the choices, didn't you?"

"Not all. If I could have stopped Jay from touching you these last few years, I would have. It damn near killed me thinking about that."

Chapter Nine

Wade watched Skylar as she turned away from him. But not before he saw her bottom lip tremble with emotion. Wade wondered what was haunting Skylar the most. Was it the failed marriage, or the fact that it hadn't been him loving her as she'd confessed she'd wanted?

Before she could leave the room, he asked, "Did you ever love him?"

Wade told himself plenty of times he wasn't going to ask Skylar that question. Ever. It wasn't fair to her, and she didn't have to tell him. But the need to know the truth was so strong, he couldn't stop himself.

"Sadly, no. That's the worst of it." She laughed at the look he gave her. "Don't look so relieved."

"I never claimed to be perfect, Skylar. But I can't help the way I feel."

"There was so much I wanted to say to you. I would find myself standing in that kitchen wondering about what you'd think about Alex. He'd reach a milestone, and I'd ask Kate about you. All that time she never knew. At night I'd sleep on the corner of the bed and cry. I was wearing another man's ring and yet I was crying for you.

"They say it takes two for a marriage to fall apart, but it was my fault. All mine. I didn't let Jay be a father to

Alex, and he always felt it. Something in me was always holding back. I never should have married him." She said the last part quietly. "You ruined me, too."

The urge to touch Skylar overwhelmed him beyond what he'd imagined was possible. She was still standing across the room. But Wade could almost smell the scent of the citrus lotion she used to put on right before bed. He wanted to lean into her to see if it was still part of her nightly ritual.

But they'd already been through enough today. The fact that she was even willing to let him stay the night was a war he didn't think he'd win just days ago.

She took a deep breath and lifted her chin. "If you need another blanket, there are more in the linen closet in the bathroom. Fresh towels, too, if you want to take a shower. You used to always take a shower before bed," she said quietly.

"That's right."

"Well, goodnight, Wade."

"Sleep well."

He dragged his gaze away from Skylar as she left the room and headed down the hallway, but only because watching her leave would have pushed the longing he felt to have her in his arms deeper into his gut. It was already so strong it threatened to level him. He waited for the sound of her bedroom door to shut before he turned back to look in the direction she'd just walked, wishing he was on the other side of that closed door with her.

He pulled himself up from the sofa that would be his bed for the night and walked to the bathroom. Once inside, he closed and locked the door, but didn't feel the lock connect. He played with the button again and pressed on the door to see if the mechanism wasn't connecting with the metal plate against the doorjamb. When the lock failed again, he abandoned the door. Although he'd love it if Skylar joined him in the shower, the likelihood of her doing so with Alex sleeping just a few feet down the hall was zero.

Pulling the linen closet door open, he found the towels stacked neatly inside. He grabbed a fresh white towel from the top of the pile and closed the linen closet door, tossing the dry towel over the shower curtain rod to keep it dry while he showered. He was inside the shower and just soaping his body under the hot spray when he heard the door creak as it opened. A few seconds later he saw the shower curtain billow from the cool rush of air that came in with the opening of the bathroom door.

"Alex, sweetie, you have to wait," Skylar whispered. "No, you can't go in there yet."

The toilet seat dropped with a thud and Wade immediately got the image of a little boy struggling to do right, but who was too sleepy to be coordinated.

"Alex?" The whisper was a little louder, and this time Wade couldn't help but laugh.

He turned off the water and pulled the towel from the shower curtain rod. He quickly dried what he could and wrapped the towel around his waist. Then he pushed the shower curtain open. Skylar stood in the doorway, flustered by the site of him. Alex barely turned to notice Wade standing there.

"Why don't I give you a little privacy, Big Guy?" Wade said, walking toward the bathroom door where Skylar was standing. "You may want to grab me another towel so I don't drip all over your hardwood floors."

Skylar disappeared for a second into the bathroom. "There you go, sweetie," she said before he heard the linen closet door open and then close. When she came out of the bathroom, she handed him a dry towel which he immediately put on the floor under his feet.

"I'm sorry," she said. "The lock on the bathroom door is broken. Alex had a habit of locking himself in there a few years ago, and after a few times of jimmying it open, it finally broke. I never got it fixed."

"That's okay."

"It's a really big deal he's not wetting the bed anymore like he did after Jay left. We've been working on that for a long time."

She looked down at the towel wrapped around his waist. Her eyes slowly made a trail from the towel, up his broad chest and to his face. The smoldering light he'd seen in her eyes earlier ignited to a full flame.

"My clothes are still in the bathroom," he said.

"I'm so sorry, Wade. Half the time, I think he's still asleep when he does this." The flustered look on Skylar's face was truly adorable and he couldn't help but smile.

"I did the same thing when I was a kid."

"I know. Kate told me. She said you didn't grow out of it until you were in junior high school. The sleep walking part."

His cheeks flamed. "How much did she tell you about me?"

"A lot. Probably every embarrassing thing imaginable. You know your mother. Let me get him back to bed before he really wakes up. He'll be up all night if he does."

Still wrapped in the towel, Wade watched Skylar take Alex by the hand and lead him to the bedroom. He took those few moments to return to the bathroom, finish drying off, and get dressed.

The shirt he'd worn on the camping trip was covered with bloodstains. Logan had been the one to pack up all their gear while he'd been at the clinic with Skylar getting Alex's head stitched. He decided not to wear the shirt to bed and walked into the living room wearing just his jeans. He was surprised to find Skylar waiting for him.

"You might be more comfortable sleeping in these," she said. In her hands, she held a pair of gray sweatpants.

He stared at the clothes and tried to relax his tightened jaw. "I'm fine."

Skylar cocked her head to one side. "These are yours."

"Mine?"

"Well, the sweatpants are anyway. When I left Samoa, I took one of your T-shirts and a pair of your sweatpants so I could sleep with them. For the longest time they had your scent. It was comforting. Especially after we got word of the tsunami. Don't worry, I've washed them a few times since I stole them from you."

He shook his head as he took the sweats in his hand and unfolded them to see. "I thought …"

"You thought they were Jay's. Shame on you. Do you really think I would do something like that to you?"

He shrugged. "It's been a long time."

"The T-shirt is long gone. I wore it out until it was pulling apart everywhere, and I eventually threw it away. I got this shirt from a fund-raiser Regis did for the Wounded Veterans Center your cousin Ian is working on with Ethan. It should fit you."

"This will be fine."

She walked to the hallway leading to the bedrooms and then turned back.

"Just for the record, I didn't keep any of Jay's clothes." She looked directly at him when she spoke. They were simple words, but they filled an empty spot that had been aching inside Wade since he'd arrived back in Rudolph.

He'd seen that look on her face before. Five years ago it had been an invitation. She wasn't wearing a bra under the over-sized T-shirt she wore now. She'd managed to put on a pair of fleece shorts that were barely visible beneath the hem of her shirt.

Everything in him was alive, on fire and wanting nothing but to be gloriously naked with Skylar. But he didn't want to misstep or misread the signs after how far he'd come.

Then she lifted her hand to him, and his heart slammed against his chest.

"There was a time I didn't have to do this," she said with a coy grin.

"If that time is now, just say the word. You'll never have to do it again."

The smile that played on her lips faltered. "He usually sleeps through the night after getting up like this. But we should still … be quiet."

She turned and walked to the bedroom slowly. Wade followed her as if he were in a dream. If he was, he never wanted to wake up from it.

Shutting the door behind him, he turned just in time to watch Skylar slip out of her T-shirt. She looked around the room. At the bed. At him. And then she covered her bare breasts by crossing an arm over her chest.

He walked over to her slowly, looking into her eyes and then slowly letting his gaze make a trail down her body as he ran his fingers gently down her arm. He pulled her arm away from her chest and basked in the beauty before him.

"They changed when I was pregnant. And then I nursed for a while." She drew in a heavy sigh and looked up at him.

"They've always been beautiful. You are so beautiful."

Tears welled up in her eyes. But then as she looked at the bed, she bit her bottom lip.

"There are no ghosts in here with us, Sky." He tipped her chin up with his fingers until she looked at him. "But if it makes you feel better, we can keep the lights on and make love on a blanket on the floor."

She chuckled. "I wouldn't mind looking at you."

Slowly he lowered his head until his mouth connected with hers. Wade thought that nothing could ever be better than the kiss they'd shared on the porch the other night. But he was wrong. With Skylar in his arms, feeling her moist mouth pressed against his, he was about to self-combust.

As he ran his hand slowly across her bare back, Wade felt Skylar's sharp intake of breath against his mouth. Her skin was warm and smooth, the way he remembered it to be.

He made a trail of kisses from her face, down her neck and then to her chest. His hand grazed her breast, and he felt her nipple harden beneath his touch. His mouth came down over her other nipple, and he gently sucked it, teasing it with his tongue and reveling in the taste of her until he heard her soft moan.

Her body stiffened, and he stopped abruptly to see what had caused her reaction.

♥ ♥ ♥

Skylar had forgotten the kind of passion Wade McKinnon could bring out in her. It wasn't until she was hearing her own moan of pleasure that she realized if she could hear it, so could Alex.

"I need to be quiet," she whispered, chuckling softly. "Let's get the comforter on the floor."

They made a soft spot on the floor out of the blankets and pillows from the bed. After ridding themselves of their clothes, they quickly crawled on top of the blankets. Skylar loved the feel of Wade's hard body pressing against the softness of her skin. It had been too long.

She wanted to feel every touch, every kiss and know that it was really Wade loving her. Her hands roamed his body as if they had a mind of their own. Each touch, each taste ignited a flame so strong she wanted to scream. She kept herself mindful that they weren't alone in the house.

And when Wade finally entered her, and she felt the completeness of a long journey that had been off course for far too long, she cried. This was the way it should always have been. Just her and Wade. No ghosts or pretense or lies.

His hands cupped her bottom and pulled her closer to him, making him go deeper with every thrust of his hips.

She felt the building of tension inside her, rising higher to a point she could no longer control until her orgasm ripped through her in waves of ecstasy.

Wade stifled her cries with a kiss so passionate she barely felt herself floating back to reality. And then his body became stiff, and his thrusts became more pronounced. He closed his eyes as his orgasm took hold. She watched the joy play on his face and couldn't help but reach up and touch his face. When he opened his eyes, she saw they were filled with tears. And her heart burst with love for the first time in years.

Chapter Ten

"You can't stay in here," she whispered against his cheek. She wanted Wade to stay. She didn't want to let go of him. Ever. But tonight wasn't like those long nights of lovemaking they'd shared in Samoa.

His eyes were closed as he lay half next to her, half on top of her. "Are you already sick of me?"

"Alex can't find you here."

"I'll stay on the floor. You can get into the bed in the morning."

"No. He always comes into my room in the morning and crawls into my bed if he gets up before me. He'll see you. What am I supposed to say if he sees a naked man next to me in bed?"

"But we're not in bed."

"Wade, I'm serious."

"So let him come in here. My brothers used to pig pile onto my parents' bed when we were his age."

She sighed softly. "Wade, he won't understand. It's too soon."

Wade opened one eye and looked down at her. "You really want me to leave?"

"I'm not talking want here. There's a big difference."

He groaned his displeasure, but then gave her a half grin that told her he understood.

"Our first night together, and I'm already in the dog house?"

"I don't have a dog."

"Would you like one?"

She chuckled. "Don't ever mention the word dog to Alex, or I'll never hear the end of it."

"A boy needs a dog."

"Forget it. I'm busy enough as it is. Help me get these blankets back on the bed."

Together they quickly made the bed. Skylar pulled on her T-shirt and shorts and watched as Wade pulled on the sweatpants she'd stolen from him over five years ago before she'd headed to the airport to come back to the United States.

"I can't believe you're sending me to the sofa."

"Don't pout."

"I'm going to be thinking incredibly sinful thoughts of you all night. You do know that, right?"

"You can fill me in with the details in the morning."

She kissed him goodnight and let her lips linger on his. And when she climbed into the bed she thought would always haunt her, she felt only one thing. *Happiness.*

"Alex?"

Wade opened his eyes and tried to focus on the room around him. The image of a little boy sitting on the coffee table started to come into view. Alex didn't seem to be concerned with the stitches that had caused him so much trauma the day before. Instead, he just stared at Wade quizzically.

"Good morning," Wade said.

Alex frowned. "Did you sleep over?"

"Alex? Come get breakfast," Skylar called out from the kitchen.

"Seems so," Wade said, slowly pulling himself up to a sitting position.

"You slept on the couch?"

Wade glanced at Skylar, who rolled her eyes as she stood in the doorway. "I'm making scrambled eggs, honey. Your favorite."

Alex didn't pay any attention to his mother. He just sat, swinging his legs back and forth under the coffee table as he waited for an answer.

"Ah, there wasn't a bed for me to sleep in. So I slept on the sofa." Wade glanced again at Skylar, whose face was growing more crimson by the moment.

"Yes, there was," Alex countered.

"Really? Where?"

"Enough, Alex," Skylar said. "The eggs are almost done."

Alex didn't even look at Skylar. "Next time you can sleep in my room. I have another bed under my bed. Keith sleeps on it all the time when we have sleepovers. But you can't sleep there when Keith sleeps over cuz you're too big, and there won't be room for both of you."

Wade couldn't help but smile at the simple purity of Alex's offer.

"Thanks for the invitation. I'll remember that next time."

Alex nodded, then hopped off the coffee table and ran into the kitchen. Wade could hear the low chuckle Skylar tried to stifle as Alex climbed into a kitchen chair.

"Hurry up and eat your breakfast. Uncle Keith is going to be here to pick you up soon."

Since the overnight fishing trip was cancelled due to Alex's fall, Hawk had promised Alex an afternoon of fun riding the four-wheeler with his best buddy over at Uncle Logan's house. Although it was the perfect activity for Wade, Alex didn't ask him to go. Rather than push, Wade decided to stay back at the house and give Alex a break.

Once Hawk drove away with Alex, Wade walked barefooted into the house and stopped short when he saw Skylar putting photo albums in a cardboard box she had set up on the coffee table.

He stared at the box and then her face. "What are you doing?"

She glanced at Wade but continued putting the items she'd pulled off the bookcase into the box. "I told you. We're moving."

The disappointment that pulled at the handsome features of Wade's face was almost heartbreaking. *Almost.*

"I thought things were going good between us," he said. "I thought they were changing."

"They are changing. That's why we're moving across town."

"What?"

Skylar looked around the house she'd lived in for the past four years. "I woke up this morning and decided that I've never really liked this house. It's only big enough for a small family, and I want to have a big family. McKinnons have big families. So that's what I want."

Wade looked into her eyes for a moment, searching. Abandoning the box, she reached for him and wrapped her arms around his neck, kissing him firmly on the lips.

When they parted, she said, "It's going to take some time, Wade. I don't know how long. But I do know one thing. You make me happy, and I don't want to live another day without you. I think we've waited long enough to start the life we dreamed of having together when we were in Samoa."

Relief washed over his face. "I couldn't agree more."

Her heartbeat quickened as she thought about her fears. "I can't say that I'm not scared that everything that has happened over the last five years won't somehow build a wedge between us. All I know is that I'm willing to fight for you. For our love."

"It's worth fighting for."

"Yes, it is."

He pulled her closer, crushing her against the length of his body and making her feel so complete.

"Oh, and I was thinking that maybe instead of calling you Uncle Wade, we could come up with something else. I think it might be too confusing for Alex to call you Dad. How do you feel about being called Papa?"

Moisture filled Wade's eyes. "You were doing a lot of thinking last night after I left you. How'd you come up with that?"

"I had a friend who used to call her father Papa. I never really thought much about it until this morning when Alex was scrutinizing you as you slept on the sofa." She chuckled. "I can't believe he offered to let you sleep on the trundle bed in his room."

Wade laughed softly, nuzzling her neck as he kissed it. Then, with his fingers buried in her hair, he whispered against her ear, "We're going to have to work on the sleeping arrangements. But I'm willing to take it slow."

"Good, because he's going to need that." She placed both of her hands on his face and kissed his lips. "We'll get there, Wade. I never thought we would. But we will."

"You don't hate me anymore?"

"No. I'm not happy about how things happened. I wish they hadn't. But I can't change any of it. All I know is that I have always loved you, Wade McKinnon. Always. Even when I was throwing my shoes at you."

"You're not going to do that again, are you?"

She touched Wade's face and brushed her fingers across the light stubble of his morning beard as he smiled down at her. "No. As long as you promise to never leave me again."

"That's a promise that I will fight until the end of time to keep."

"I'm holding you to that."

Wade took Skylar by the hand. "You know, I just realized something."

"What's that?"

"We have the whole day to be naked together without anyone barging in on us."

She smiled as she started to unbutton her shorts. "You're just figuring that out? Why do you think I called Hawk to take Alex for the afternoon?"

Wade turned back slightly to look at her as he pulled his T-shirt off. "You wicked woman."

She pulled his shirt off the rest of the way and tossed it to the floor. "You love it."

"I love you. I always have."

As they collapsed on the bed, naked and laughing, Skylar knew it would always be that way.

~The End~

ABOUT THE AUTHOR

NEW YORK TIMES and USA TODAY Bestselling
Author, Lisa Mondello, has held many jobs in her life but
being a published authors is the last job she'll ever have.
She's not retiring! She blames the creation of the personal
computer for her leap into writing novels. Otherwise, she'd
still be penning stories with paper and pen. Her first book,
All I Want for Christmas is You won Best First Book in
the Golden Quill. Her books have finaled in the HOLT
Medallion, and the Colorado Award of Excellence
contests. In 2011 she re-released her award winning book
All I Want for Christmas is You along with a re-issue of
her romantic comedy, The Marriage Contract, with a
contemporary romance called The Knight and Maggie's
Baby. In 2012 she reissued the first 3 books of her popular
Western Romance Series TEXAS HEARTS including Her
Heart for the Asking, His Heart for the Trusting and The
More I See. Writing as LA Mondello, her romantic
suspense, MATERIAL WITNESS, book 1 of her Heroes
of Providence series made the USA TODAY Bestsellers
List. You can find more information about Lisa Mondello
at lisamondello.blogspot.com.

Made in the USA
Columbia, SC
12 December 2021

51150973R00350